THE SUMMER I FOUND YOU

THE SUMMER I FOUND YOU

A Novel

JENNIFER O'BRIEN

Books should be disposed of and recycled according to local requirements. All paper materials used are FSC compliant.

Published in the United States by Alcove Press, an imprint of The Quick Brown Fox & Company LLC.

Alcove Press and its logo are trademarks of The Quick Brown Fox & Company LLC.

Library of Congress Catalog-in-Publication data available upon request.

ISBN (hardcover): 979-8-89242-256-7
ISBN (paperback): 979-8-89242-279-6
ISBN (ebook): 979-8-89242-257-4

Cover design by KE Birch

Printed in the United States.

www.alcovepress.com

Alcove Press
34 West 27th St., 10th Floor
New York, NY 10001

First Edition: April 2026

The authorized representative in the EU for product safety and compliance is eucomply OÜPärnu mnt 139b-14, 11317 Tallinn, Estonia, hello@eucompliancepartner.com, +33757690241

10 9 8 7 6 5 4 3 2 1

To my mother, the wind beneath my creative wings.
The one who gifted me art supplies on every occasion, hoping
I would see my worth, and taught me to DIY before
it was even a thing.

To my father, my humble hero. Whose blind leap of faith
led him to Hollywood in the 1950s and inspired this story.
Whose grit to return home and raise a family meant more
to him than any Oscar-nominated movie.

CHAPTER ONE

July 1

Dahlia Newberry glanced out her car window and watched as her past faded into the Connecticut coastline. As she drove, she leaned her face into the familiar breeze of the Long Island Sound. Rich blue lagoons flanked both sides of the sandy road, and the remnants of low tide hung in the air. A white heron gracefully disappeared into the wetlands.

She smiled wistfully, inhaling every last particle of North Fork air. This was a moment she'd anticipated for fifteen years but never had the guts to leap blindly into until now. After Aunt Lil's passing, another day of pretending would feel like another death, this time her own.

Dahlia firmly gripped the steering wheel as if it would anchor her to the decision. The truth was, she didn't need an anchor this time; she had never been more certain of anything. No longer could she embrace a life that had never belonged to her. She didn't care about most of the things she was leaving behind in Greenwich, yet her white farmhouse overlooking the tranquil stream tugged at her heart. It wasn't because it was big and newly renovated; it was because Aunt Lil took her last breath in that house. Despite all the nonsense with Spence through the years, there were memories that took root. It was a good house, despite how hard it had been after Lil moved in with her, with them. Seeing someone slowly wilt away before your eyes was like watching a beautiful garden be starved of water.

She drove through a puddle and heard Lil's labored last words move through her mind like a fast-moving storm. "Promise me you'll spend the summer at my house, Dahlia. It's crucial."

What was so important, Dahlia wondered, besides selling the house? She inhaled deeply, trying her best to override the heaviness in her chest. Thinking about Lil and the last three months without her still made her heart ache. It was that fresh and raw.

Harry lifted his head and let out a long moan.

"We'll be to Lil's soon. Then you can run free," Dahlia said into the rearview mirror. There would be an unlimited amount of seagull chasing, which he loved. The heat? Now that was another story, but at least he would have the bay in his backyard, something he didn't have at their Connecticut house. And once they moved south after the summer, the heat would only be that much worse. But there'd be other things to love in Charleston, she justified, glancing back at him. "You'll be happy there, I promise, boy."

He let out a piercing bark, which made Dahlia laugh. "You like that, huh?" Her voice dropped as she realized it would just be them this time. No Lil to nudge him off the couch, make his sweet potato chips, or take him for long walks on the beach. This visit was going to be different, there was no doubt about that. But was she ready for that? Deep down, she knew she was a loner, but being *lonely* was entirely different. She had enough loneliness to last a lifetime.

"We need some music," Dahlia mumbled. It was way too quiet and her thoughts had the potential to run away on her like a stampede of mustangs. She turned the sticky radio knob, a testament to the car's age. The changing of the stations felt like her brain, staticky and cluttered. When "Every Day Is a Winding Road" echoed through the dusty stereo panel, her stomach swooped, not knowing if it wanted to fly or fall.

She couldn't help but think about that last trip to Lil's and Gran's when she was thirteen and still full of wonder, before everything changed.

"Dahl girl, put that teenybopper magazine down. You'll get carsick again," her father said, scanning the radio in his tropical shirt, ready for the vacation ahead. He turned his head so she could see his ear and the graying scruff that peppered his square jawline. "And don't be so boy-crazy. There's more to life than the opposite sex. Like getting a good education."

"Okay, Professor Pete," Dahlia playfully snickered, laying her *Teen Beat* down on her suitcase covered in Backstreet Boys stickers.

"Cheeky girl. Stealing my line." Dahlia's mother, Rose, laughed, grabbing her hand over the seat. Her face sparkled in the sunlight. The blush highlighted her high cheekbones and porcelain skin. Dahlia smiled, pushing up her sunglasses, hoping someday she'd be that pretty. "Oh, turn this up, hon, I love Sheryl Crow," her mother sweetly demanded as she belted the lyrics to her father. He responded with his famous air guitar move. Dahlia watched them with both embarrassment and awe, giggling discreetly at their silly banter.

Now, her eyes began to burn as she weaved around the trademark Long Island puddles. Already, this trip was rekindling old memories, but maybe that's exactly what she needed. Enough time had passed since her parents' deaths that she could compartmentalize her grief. She'd survived a quarter of a century without them, though it didn't stop her from imagining what life would look like if they hadn't gone to dinner that night. She knew that as quickly as the tide rolled in, it would move back out again. Dahlia was good at navigating the murky waters of debilitating pain and loss. It was her superpower. She knew if she could get through losing her parents the way she had so young, followed by Gran, Pop, and now Lil, she could get through anything, including her divorce from Spence.

Harry stood with his front paws on the center console and licked her cheek. With that simple gesture, she knew she wasn't alone. No, it wasn't the same as being with a person, but often Dahlia enjoyed the company of animals more than people. Animals love you just as you are, rarely stray, and are fiercely loyal, unlike husbands. Although her marriage was anything but conventional, Dahlia tried. She tried for fifteen long years, but a person can only take so many betrayals and words that cut like a freshly sharpened blade.

One thing was for sure, though: Dahlia had played enough of her adult life like Monica from *Friends*. Now she wanted to feel like Rachel, spontaneous and free. She hoped the happy-go-lucky girl from her youth was still in there. Goosebumps ran across her chest as if she glimpsed a whisper of her adventure ahead. Her intuition was in overdrive. Her circumstances were about to change; she could feel it in the wind.

Dahlia sipped her iced coffee from the ferry, which was now watered-down muck. Every house, every business, every road, and every beach she passed reminded her of the summer visits with Gran and Lil after her parents died. They'd do their weekly shop after church, and they'd bicker over something or someone—usually produce. While Lil was the flower expert, Gran considered herself the Produce Queen. No one stood a chance in an argument with her over peaches or pineapples. Aunt Lil tried a few times but was met with a pushiness that could only come from a grandmother's well-earned life experience.

As she was about to take another sip, her cell rang. It was her cousin Kara, who was more like a sister, given that Dahlia was sent to live with Aunt Cathy, her dad's sister, shortly after her parents died. Kara and Dahlia were raised together after that. Despite being the same age, Kara was the hipper of the pair. Dahlia often thought Kara was a twenty-something trapped in a thirty-something body. And Kara embraced that theory with all she had.

She pulled into the grocery store parking lot and answered it on the last ring. "Hey, Cuz."

"You made it? How was the ferry ride over?" Kara asked with a distinctively perky tone. "I figured you would have called with an update by now."

Dahlia knew Kara worried about her. "I'm sorry," she said, looking for a spot. "It was fine. Ugh, where did all these people come from?"

"Did you take Betty?" Kara asked.

"Of course. Why?" Dahlia pulled the old hatchback Saab into a parking spot.

"Because I can hear her," Kara said with wit.

"Oh, stop. No, you can't." Dahlia's eyebrows furrowed. "Can you?" She immediately turned the car off. "You know how much this car means to me," Dahlia said, glancing over at the empty back seat beside Harry, where the indentations in the leather made her smile. "How could I not bring her? Hoping she'll make it to Charleston too."

"Now that's where I draw the line. Why wouldn't you take the new car?"

"Because it's his," Dahlia said flatly, inviting no further discussion.

"What if you break down?" Kara asked. "You have absolutely no one there besides Lil's handyman."

"Betty won't break down. She's reliable and trustworthy, unlike *some* people I know." Dahlia was reminded that she still hadn't heard back from Hank, the handyman. She stared into the parking lot, making a mental note to text him again after the quick shop. As she snapped out of her daze, her eyes locked on a tall guy in a leather jacket mounting his motorcycle.

"Still there?"

"Ah . . . yeah." She caught a glimpse of herself in the rearview mirror and pulled back in horror. She tried to fix her tangled honey locks, tucking a loose wave behind her ear and wiping the morning residue of mascara from her eyes. She didn't feel her best, but after Lil died, she'd found herself coasting. Yet another reason she needed this summer in Southold.

"So I was thinking . . ." Kara began.

"About?" Dahlia put in her earbuds and kissed Harry on his pink-speckled nose as her eyes trailed the mystery man exiting onto the main road. "Be good," Dahlia whispered, but she didn't know if that was meant for Harry or a reminder to herself.

"You should make this your hot girl summer," blurted Kara. "Date a little, maybe get laid."

Dahlia coughed. "Are you crazy? I could be kidnapped." She passed an older white-haired man pushing his grocery cart and nodded, hoping he couldn't hear their conversation.

"You watch too much *Dateline* and listen to too many true-crime podcasts," Kara snickered.

"And you watch too much reality TV. The only action my bed will see is sleep."

Kara audibly yawned.

Dahlia laughed as she pushed through the thick crowd of people whispering and grinning about something she wasn't privy to.

"You need to get your mojo back! This quiet, good-girl thing is boring me. How on earth am I supposed to live vicariously through your single life if you don't embrace it? Come on, Dahlia. This mama of three needs some excitement!"

Dahlia heard her phone vibrate and looked at the screen. It was Hank the handyman, thank God. "Can I call you back? This is important."

"I suppose. Don't forget to call me as soon as—"

And with that, Dahlia accepted the other call. "Hello, Hank?"

"Hi, Dahlia, this is Jean, Hank's wife. I have some unfortunate news." She got eerily quiet. "Hank's had a heart attack. He's still in the hospital. I'm sorry no one called you sooner."

"Oh my God," Dahlia muttered, pausing mid-aisle, her heart racing. "Please don't be sorry. I'm sorry. Don't give the house another thought. I'll figure something out."

"He went to Lil's last week. He took the sheets off the furniture and turned on the water. A few appliances weren't working, so he ordered some parts. When they come in, I'll reach out."

"Thank you. I'll be praying for him," Dahlia said, feeling her neck stiffen.

"Thank you, dear."

Dahlia hung up as she leaned against the canned vegetables. Poor Hank. What was she going to do? She shook her head in disbelief. She hoped it wasn't the refrigerator that was broken. She needed a fridge. That was a nonnegotiable.

What was she going to do without a handyperson? Lil's house had been vacant for two years; it was going to need a lot of work. Dahlia fanned her face with the store circular, hoping her cheeks would stop burning. The smell of deli meat turned her stomach, a reminder of another uncertain time in her life. She needed to get to the house as soon as possible.

She ran through the store, throwing in just the necessities, and bolted onto the line.

Kara was right—Dahlia didn't know anyone here anymore. She could feel beads of sweat lace the crease of her cleavage. She didn't know the first thing about fixing up houses; being without a handyperson was like having a boat with no captain.

"Hello." Dahlia gave a weak smile to the grocery clerk.

The teen girl texted feverishly, snapping a bubble.

Dahlia loaded the groceries onto the belt. "Oh, I have bags."

The girl looked up. "Okay." And then she returned to typing.

Dahlia tapped her foot. "I'm sorry, but I have a dog in the car. Could we move this along?"

"Oh, sure. I'm sorry. I'm just excited. That stud from *Hamptons House* just came in."

Dahlia shrugged. "*Hamptons House*?"

"The reality show? It's filmed out here—well, in the Hamptons. Every summer, a group of young, creative singles—who also happen to be gorgeous—fix up an old house for the summer and live there while they do it." She finally started to scan. "He was so nice. Noah, I mean. Taller than I imagined. And what a smile, it could melt an iceberg." Another snap of the gum, and Dahlia involuntarily recoiled.

"Cool," Dahlia said, realizing Noah was probably the guy on the motorcycle. But she needed to focus, despite her momentary lapse in the parking lot. No men this summer, under any circumstance. Dahlia knew the plan and was determined to stick to it. She would fix Lil's house and get it ready to sell before she took the gallery job in Charleston. And she'd try to find some peace and quiet in the process—it was the only way to find out if the old Dahlia was still in there.

After paying, she caught a glimpse of the community wall by the exit. Dahlia knew this wall had been Lil's favorite place to scout for furniture and local happenings. Being the small town it was, this was the hub of action, where people connected on everything from animals to tools and help wanted. She slung the grocery bag over her shoulder and walked past, knowing if a miracle didn't land in her lap by tomorrow she'd be back to scour the classifieds for a replacement handyman.

CHAPTER TWO

"Almost there, Harry." Dahlia looked down at the empty water bottle on her seat. "As soon as we get there, we'll get you a big bowl of ice-cold water."

He leaned his whole body out of the opening as if he would leap at any moment.

"And don't you think about jumping when we turn down her street. You hear me?'

Harry yelped with excitement.

"I mean it, Harry," Dahlia said, trying not to smile at the sweet and eager face in the rearview mirror.

The pebbles crunched beneath her tires. A sure sign she had reached the Prescott Family Compound—or what was left of it anyway. Through the years, whenever finances got tight, they'd sold a parcel of land or a house here and there. The only things that now remained of this compound were Aunt Lil's house and the stories. She braked in front of the brick pillars and admired the perfectly groomed boxwoods, courtesy of their neighbor Bruce. There was no longer a need to rush. Her smile grew, and her posture relaxed. The breeze that grazed her neck and slipped under her hair felt invigorating. It was the gentle nudge she needed to slow things down after that unexpected call. But there was still a small part of her that was nervous. This wasn't just a house; it was Lil's house, and Dahlia's grandparents' before that, and their parents' before that. She realized she'd never been alone here for more than a few hours. This time, it was just her.

She gulped hard and looked up at the rusted, crooked sign that read Meadow Lane. Squaring her shoulders, she drove through the stately opening.

The first cedar shake house on the property was built in the late 1800s and faced the bay. It was the grandest and her favorite architecturally. It had arched dormers on the third floor and an expansive wraparound porch. Her great-great-uncle had lived there with his family after they came over from England. It remained in the family until it was sold to a city family before Dahlia was born. Although she'd never been inside, she knew, like many old houses, it was where secrets were kept. The tennis court still looked pristine, as if not a single ball ever bounced on the surface. There was a thickness in her throat and a quiver in her belly as she continued to drive. The 1970s split-level to her left still didn't belong among the backdrop of the more mature Nantucket-style homes, but Dahlia never lost sight of why her grandparents sold it. "We had to pay for Rose's extended education somehow," her Gran would say of Dahlia's mother as they passed it.

Dahlia finally made it to Lil's house. She pulled into the long driveway with expansive views of the steely blue Peconic Bay and parked. Her heart raced as she looked up at the regal New England facade. It was beautiful, just as she remembered. Well, minus the few shingles missing and shutters hanging on by a screw. And the landscaping, geez, it was neglected. She leaned her head out the window to get a closer look. The blue hydrangeas that ran the perimeter, which were once Instagrammable, were now stalky and wild.

"We definitely have some cleanup to do. What do you think, boy?"

There was silence.

She looked to the back of the car, but Harry was nowhere in sight. Dahlia threw the car in park, flung open the door, and marched down the front lawn. "Harry!" She whistled through her fingers, prompting him to come back. "We literally just got here," she muttered in defeat.

Just then, she spotted him next door. "They aren't home!" she shouted across the lawn as if Harry could understand why his favorite people weren't outside, ready to greet him. Bruce had been in touch with Lil before she died, letting her know they'd be in Italy for the summer, but Dahlia still hoped she'd see them before she left to thank them properly. Bruce and Garrett were a lovely couple who lived right next door and had been like surrogate sons to Lil. If it hadn't been for them finding Lil after she fell down the stairs, she might have been there for days without food or water. Breaking her ankle was the catalyst for her move to Greenwich with Dahlia. As much as Lil didn't want to leave her house on the bay, she didn't have a choice after that.

The sandy shore called to Dahlia as Harry strolled back in defeat. She made her slow descent to the beach as he trailed behind her, doing his best detective work. The grass was dry, sparse, and tall in places. She needed to get someone to cut it—it was probably loaded with ticks. She winced at the thought, making sure to stay on the path.

Dahlia was hyperaware that the poppy seed–sized arachnid could wreak havoc on one's health and mental well-being. Lil's undiagnosed Lyme disease hadn't helped her memory or her ability to fight the cancer, especially toward the end. The ovarian cancer had metastasized rather quickly to her bones.

Dahlia stood facing the water, her feet sinking into the cool, wet sand. A gust blew, fanning her body as she stared at the catamaran in the distance. Its size, sleek navy bottom, and cream USA sails were commanding. Exactly like Spence's dad's boat. It took her back to the day she told him the news that would change the direction of her life forever.

"So, what did you want to tell me?" Spence dropped the anchor. "That you adore me and can't wait to visit me at BC? You're going to love Boston, Dahl. The football games, the parties, the city," he said with his pretty-boy smile.

"I know." Dahlia rolled her eyes. "My parents both went there, and I lived there, remember?" Did he ever actually listen?

"Then what is it?" He reached for her trembling hand. "We'll be fine, babe. It's not that far from RISD. Plenty of people have long-distance relationships and make it work."

"That's not what I'm worried about." Dahlia was woozy; she began to wane. This was a bad idea. She held back the urge to puke up her egg sandwich. "I'm pregnant," she blurted, holding her stomach.

Spence froze; he looked like a deer in the headlights. "Are you sure?"

"Very." She nodded.

"It's mine, right? I mean, I'm only here on weekends, and we used a condom."

What an asshole. She'd only ever been with him. Her eyes locked with his in disgust. Who'd made him so suspicious? So cynical?

He shook his head. "I'm sorry, of course it's mine. My father's going to kill me." He paced the deck, chewing his lip. Dahlia watched his forehead wrinkle, a telltale sign he wasn't in control anymore. "You start college in two months, and so do I. Okay, we'll take care of it before you go. It will be fine."

She drew in her breath. "I don't know what I want to do yet," Dahlia said, looking at the birds that circled overhead. It felt like the moment in a movie right before something bad happened. That couldn't be a good sign.

"You can't just throw your whole life away. And I'm certainly not. For a moment that lasted all of five minutes in the back of my Rover?"

The seagull's cry woke her from her memory, and with that, she walked back up to Lil's house. She blew out a cathartic breath. It was time to let go of Spence, the bitterness, and the role that never suited her from the beginning.

Dahlia grabbed her purse and Lil's box from the back seat and walked onto the front porch. "Come on, boy. Let's get that bowl of . . . *ahh*!" She screeched as she lunged forward, her foot going right through the decking. "Seriously?" she huffed, unable to move her foot, feeling the broken shards of wood stab her ankle. Sweat pooled on her upper lip, and she had never been so glad to be neighborless at the moment. The idea of someone seeing this blunder sent a rush of heat to her face. She grunted, carefully pulling her tennis shoe from the large, gaping hole. *Lil*, she thought, *if you're up there, please send a handyman ASAP*. Was she going to be able to handle this project alone? That was quickly becoming the question of the day.

Thank goodness the flower pot was exactly where Lil had said it would be. Dahlia didn't need any more mishaps. She tiptoed to it, trying to avoid putting too much pressure on one spot. With one hand and one foot, she leaned over and pulled the soiled key from underneath as if she were playing a game of Twister.

The stately colonial blue door stared at her as she brushed the hair from her eyes, trying to regain her composure. Dahlia was numb, her heart heavy. Her hand wouldn't move. She was frozen, imagining a different reality, one where she was here with Lil this summer. Without warning, another gust carried through the porch, this time wrapping her like a blanket. She tipped her head back and closed her eyes, feeling Lil with her in spirit.

Dahlia slipped the key in and turned the knob. slowly pushing the door open. Harry snuck in as it gave a loud creak, grazing her leg. "Glad you could make it," she said, shutting the door behind him. It smelled like must and mothballs. She stood there, feeling her shoulders finally relax, feeling the house's presence. It was a pleasing aroma for Dahlia's old soul. It reminded her of the best summers in this house by the bay with Gran, Pop, and Lil. "Don't go too far, Harry."

The air was stagnant—she needed to open a few windows. She laid her purse and Lil's box on the long Windsor bench. Gazing at the long entry and original molding dating back to 1865, she smiled. "I'm finally home, right where you wanted me, Lil." This was the only house that had ever felt like a home after her parents' deaths. Every summer after 2001 had been like a homecoming of sorts. After the car accident that changed her life, she needed home like flowers needed sun and fish needed water.

But when she entered the family room, she gasped, clutching her fist to her chest. The room looked like it had been ransacked. The linen curtains were ripped and mangled, suspended by mere threads. The picture frames that held generations of memories were broken and scattered across the floor, the moldings mangled, and the slipcovers and rug were covered in soot. Her heart sank like a brick to the ocean floor. Who could have done this, and why? And were they still in the house?

"Harry," she called again. Her body shuddered. She didn't know who to call or what to do. She'd never felt so unsafe and alone in this house before. She needed a baseball bat . . . or a knife. Her heart raced like a greyhound as she rushed to the kitchen.

She heard Harry's footsteps overhead.

"Okay, stay there, bud, while I figure out what to do." Dahlia exhaled through her fear. No one was home next door. Hank couldn't help, and most of Lil's friends were gone. Maybe a few of Lil's students were still around, but Dahlia didn't remember many of them. Her thoughts were ablaze as she shuffled through the drawer. Then she looked down and saw a tiny flour paw print on the counter's edge.

It wasn't a burglar. It was an animal. Was that any better? She quietly backed away as if any movement might prompt an attack. Her eyes bulged as she perused the place. "Rabies, Harry. Please stay put," she whispered as she opened the basement door and grabbed the largest fishing net she could find. Thank God Lil had kept Pop's nets.

She heard thuds from above. "Mother Machree, he's up there with it. Of course he is." She slithered against the hallway wall that led to the staircase and barreled around the corner. A squirrel hurled toward her, and Harry flew down after it. All she could do was scream as loud as her air would flow. It was a scene out of *Christmas Vacation*, only Dahlia wasn't on the couch holding her stomach in laughter. Nothing about this encounter was funny.

It was too quiet. Harry sniffed around the kitchen, and Dahlia bravely peeked out from behind the hallway wall. With the net in hand, she paced the family room. Her chest tingled; she never felt this kind of rush before. She bravely pulled back the curtains, ready to catch the bugger.

The squirrel leaped past Dahlia's face, grazing her cheek with its furry tail, and flew into the entry, all while she screamed and squealed in disgust. Dahlia thrashed the net wildly, sending Lil's box crashing to the floor. Dahlia spotted Harry as he brazenly headed toward the action. "Oh no, you don't." She grabbed him by the collar, his nose covered in white powder. "This is for your own good," she said, locking him in the bathroom.

She slowly backed up toward the door and made a *psst*, *psst* sound, hoping to lure the furry creature. And sure enough, it came barreling toward her. She swiftly opened the back door just in time for it to exit through the hole in the screen porch. Her limp body leaned against the wall and slid down in relief, hoping and praying he didn't bring friends. "What a welcome, Lil."

After letting Harry out, Dahlia checked the old faithful cream fridge that Lil and Gran had for the last thirty years. Sure enough, her bad luck ensued. Not only was it tepid inside but it smelled of decay and mold. With a pinched expression she pulled back, shutting it immediately. This was now the third luckless event of the day. There were droppings in every crevice and urine caked onto every surface. She wondered where to even start, but then she spotted Lil's teacup collection, still intact. With a shaky hand, Dahlia held up a tiny pink, cream, and green rosebud cup. She had no idea where they would end up in the move, but she was glad they were safe for now.

Dahlia swept and sifted, still in shock, grabbing garbage bags from the pantry. On the floor, among the wreckage of her family's story, was her grandparents' wedding picture encased in broken glass. She carefully lifted it from the rubble, noticing how well dressed they were in the photo, her grandmother in a two-piece light suit with a hat and her grandfather in a navy one. Their embrace was tender but choreographed, as if they had gone to the justice of the peace, and this was the only record of it. They were a good-looking couple, even by today's standards. Gran with her petite features, loose curls, and slender physique and Pop with his slicked-back dark hair and chiseled jawline. Her nose tingled as she turned it over. It read, *Lizzie and Leon 1950*. She placed it back on the weathered green nineteenth-century hutch, along with the other family relics, feeling her chin tremble.

She'd laugh about this someday, she hoped. Just not today. She squatted to inspect the chimney and noticed sticks were covering the brick landing. She bravely poked her head inside the opening as if she hadn't just experienced the most terrifying animal encounter ever. The flue was open, which was strange. She knew they'd closed it when they left. That squirrel was probably making a nest for her babies in there. Dahlia was grateful she'd made it out unharmed, despite the mayhem she'd caused, especially if there was a young family waiting for her.

The soot-stained cream carpet would have to wait, along with the curtains and chewed moldings. She knelt on the dirty, wide-planked floor and slowly placed Lil's belongings back in the box. There were old books, art books, flower books, art projects, her watch, flip phone, glasses, seed packets, and multiple bags filled with pictures. Dahlia paused. Did she even belong here without Lil? Was this all a big mistake? A lonesome book caught her eye, tucked under the buffalo-check wingback in the adjoining room. She dragged it out and smiled wide at the cover that read *Simple Abundance*. She knew this book all too well. It must have fallen out of the box during Squirrelgate. When she got to her feet and once again scanned the disaster site, she felt her arms go limp. She had an empty tank, and it wasn't even noon. The book would have to wait, along with everything else. She made a mental note to take it to look at it later, maybe for the sunset glass of wine.

"Right now, I need a shower." She looked at Harry, still covered in flour. "And it looks like you do too."

CHAPTER THREE

The sun was setting, casting a warm glow over the landscape and even the broken bulkhead. Everywhere she looked, there was more time, money, and work. There was a tightness in her chest, one she suspected wouldn't leave anytime soon. The screens that once lent a fluid view of the rolling lawn down to the bay were torn and missing and now served as an escape hatch for critters. She took a long, earned sip of her rosé as she sat in Lil's worn wicker chair, followed by another and another, desperately trying to release the angst in her body.

Her palm grazed the pretty botanical cover of *Simple Abundance.* It had been one of Lil's treasures, especially at the end, always beside her bed. There was a pink ribbon marking a page. Dahlia opened it and immediately did a double take. It read *April 7,* which was the day Lil died. Tears rushed to her eyes like a tide during a storm. The words were blurry, but she read them anyway. *Come Alive with Color . . . with color, for the price of paint, people can express their own style and individuality. But, as with style, a gift for color has to be developed by experiment. If you don't dare, you are doomed by dullness.—Shirley Conran*

Dahlia pulled the old, musty book close to her chest. Who was this for? She couldn't help but think the words were meant for her. She wiped her wet eyes and laughed quietly. "Why am I not surprised you're sending me messages from the grave? You always saw the beauty in the simple things." She shook her head and sat in silence. She wished she could be more like Lil, living a life full of color. God knew she'd experienced enough black and white to last a lifetime. She sank deeper into the chair and whispered, "But to seek it, you must walk toward it with confidence and courage. And I'm not confident about anything anymore, especially who I'm supposed to be in this next chapter."

Dahlia finished her wine, trying to look past the wild prairie of a backyard. She'd had enough of this day. She forced her tired body up from the chair. As she stood, a letter fell from the book to the floor. The envelope read *To Dahlia*, and *IMPORTANT,* in large, thicker letters.

She swiftly opened it, sliding her finger through the top recklessly, and noticed Lil's beautiful cursive writing. Her heart felt burdensome as she read it to herself.

Dear Dahlia,

I'm sitting here overlooking your stream and snow-covered garden. Even under the thick blanket of white, I can still see your beautiful blooms. I can hardly believe this is my ending, but it is. Don't feel sorry for me; I've had a good life filled with flowers, art, and laughter, thanks to you. You are the best niece and friend a woman could ask for. Thank you for taking such good care of me. I leave this life as a rich woman.

But before I go, please do a few things for me. You've sacrificed so much of yourself, putting others' needs before your own. This summer is your turn to find some simple abundance. Please humor me with the list below and follow it, especially number thirteen.

Your Southold Summer Bucket List

1. *Make my famous lavender scones.*
2. *Bike into town and shop at the farmer's market.*
3. *Read a book on my back porch with a nice glass of wine.*
4. *Take a walk in the rain.*
5. *Do something just for fun.*
6. *Swim in the sea as much as you can.*
7. *Listen to music and dance.*
8. *Sleep with the windows open.*
9. *Find someone to play poker with. And be fair.*

Dahlia laughed through the ache. That might be hard, seeing as she was unbeatable. She leaned forward, eager to read more.

10. *Watch the sunrise and sunset as much as you can.*
11. *Bring my garden back to life.*
12. *Find a home for my paintings in the barn.*
    Last but not least, the most important . . .
13. *I have a safe-deposit box at the bank in town. You need to find the key. It's somewhere at the house and holds a secret that shall set you free. I realize that sounds a bit dramatic, but you deserve the truth. Don't leave or sell the house without finding it. Promise me. It's vital. I can't stress this enough. Check all my favorite places. I'm sorry I can't remember where it is. My memory hasn't been the same since my first diagnosis.*

I love you with all my heart and soul,

Lil

Truth? Secret?

And now Dahlia had to find a key before she could leave? Her eyes blinked rapidly, trying to process this new information and the uncertain task. What on earth could be so important? And why wouldn't Lil have told Dahlia when she was alive? Her mind swirled, hoping to find a landing spot. Something that would offer an explanation. What kind of family secret would set her free?

Suddenly, Dahlia felt angry. Her breaths became labored and loud. Dahlia didn't like secrets. It reminded her of the time she overheard Gran whisper to Lil in the pantry the summer after her parents died. She'd only been thirteen, but some memories stay with you forever. "We can't keep her. She needs to be with people her own age. She and Kara are already close. Plus, Peter's sister wants her. It's for the best, Lil." Dahlia was crushed. She'd assumed she would live with them come fall and go to school in Southold. That was what she wanted more than anything in the world. But like most things in life, you don't always get what you want.

Things just got way more complicated, and her summer plans to "find herself" hit a significant snafu. Where would she even start with this new revelation? She needed to talk to Kara.

She let Harry out to do his business; this time, he didn't wander. Perhaps he, too, sensed Dahlia's uncertainty. "Come on, boy." Dahlia looked down at her shadow. With every step up the stairs, he was right by her side. He understood her when few people did.

"How could anyone give you up? You are the best dog. Well, aside from your roaming."

There was a ruff, followed by a giant leap onto the bed. Dahlia followed suit with a slow climb and FaceTimed her cousin.

"Kara," Dahlia said, feeling her voice break, holding back her tears.

"Are you okay? You don't look good." Kara's nose crinkled.

"Thanks." She exhaled. "I just really needed to talk to you. Is this a bad time?"

"No, it's fine. The boys are watching a movie with Tony. What's up?" Kara said, her bun bouncing as she walked through her house.

"Where do I start?" Dahlia shook her head.

She told her about Hank having a heart attack, being left without a handyperson, the hole in the porch, the squirrel invasion, and the fridge and stove not working.

"And that's not even the worst part. Lil left me a letter, Kara. It started as a summer bucket list with everything I need to do for myself."

"Which is awesome. Go, Lil."

"Yeah, well, she went on to say there's a ginormous family secret and that it will set me free. That I need to find a safe-deposit key and open this box before I go, but she forgot where she put it. How am I going to get all of this done before I leave for South Carolina at the end of the summer?"

"Okay, wow. Let's unpack this. I've known Lil my entire life; she didn't keep secrets."

Kara was right. Lil had never been the mysterious type. So then what on earth did this all mean? "I know, that's why I'm so rattled, Kara. But honestly, I'm a little annoyed she didn't tell me what it was before she died." Dahlia shook her head. "How could she leave me with all of this to figure out without her?"

"She obviously wanted you to see whatever is in that box. You have to believe that whatever's in there is that important. And maybe she couldn't find it before she left for your house. I'm sure there's a logical explanation. She loved you so much; the last thing she'd want to do is hurt you."

"Thank you. You're right—I'm just overwhelmed. Harry's a good listener but not great at small talk." Dahlia laughed for the first time in hours.

Harry cocked his head.

"Listen, tomorrow is a new day. You'll head into town and ask around. Go to the hardware store first. There's got to be someone who's retired that would love to help you." Kara took a much-needed swig of air. "Plus, everyone loved Lil, so that shouldn't be hard. Maybe even an art student from the high school?"

"That's a good idea. I'll also go back to the grocery store and check the community board. I didn't have the bandwidth for it today."

"Lil's favorite," Kara said with a warm smile.

"I know. Oh, speaking of the store—I must have just missed him, but apparently, this guy from *Hamptons House* came in."

Kara squealed. "*Who?* And why are you just telling me this now? Oh my God. They're all so hot," she rambled, yanking her long brown hair from the bun.

"I think his name was Noah." Dahlia shrugged, spotting a large crack in the wall over the door. The work was never going to end.

"What?" Kara screamed. "He's my favorite—very mysterious. He got double-crossed last year in a big way by his best friend. Poor guy. Have you googled him yet?"

"No!" Dahlia said, noticing a light go on next door. "That's weird." Dahlia peeled herself from the sticky sheets.

"What's weird?"

"The guys next door are away for the summer, but a light just went on." Dahlia peeked out the window. No one was supposed to be there. Bruce and Garrett would have told her, wouldn't they? "Maybe someone's breaking in?" Dahlia could feel her eyes widen.

"No, it's Southold. The safest small town in America. It's probably just someone checking on the house. Or maybe a timer on a light."

"You're probably right." Dahlia hesitated. "Kara, thank you."

"For what?"

"For listening?"

"Always. Now, get some rest. I'll check in tomorrow—and Dahl?"

"Yeah?"

"You're Dahlia Fucking Newberry, and don't you forget that. You had Daisy on your own and raised her without any help from Spence or his family, at least until—"

"Ugh, don't remind me." Dahlia wanted to say marrying Spence was the biggest mistake of her life, but then Daisy wouldn't have had two loving parents all those years. Him coming back when Daisy was five and begging Dahlia to marry him as a new graduate about to take over his father's business was unexpected, to say the least. But when Spence wanted something, he was very persuasive. Plus, Dahlia was tired, and any partnership sounded like music to her ears. Yes, she had Lil and Gran, but Dahlia had had to move closer to campus once she started taking classes. Being a single mom while trying to accumulate one hundred and twenty credits *and* working wasn't for the faint of heart.

"Remember how strong and resilient you are. You're a badass."

Dahlia lifted her chin and straightened her posture. She did do that, didn't she? And she stood up to his family when they wanted to pay for her pregnancy to go away. That was by far the toughest thing for her to get past once she became part of the Newberry family. "True, but—"

"No buts about it. And you just landed your dream gallery job. I'll leave you with that little morsel of truth. Night, love you."

"You too."

Dahlia hung up feeling taller, braver, and stronger, remembering her early days as a young, single mother and how each day brought its own unique challenges. And how determined she was to build a loving home for Daisy despite the insurmountable roadblocks.

I am Dahlia Fucking Newberry. She looked into Lil's mirror in her simple tank top and sleeping shorts. *I get things done, and I figure shit out.* "Everything is figureoutable," she whispered, looking closer at her summer freckles and aging forehead. Well, maybe not everything. If she was going to embrace this new season, she'd have to up her beauty game. She waggled her eyebrows a few times and added wrinkle cream to her mental list.

Then, against her better judgment, she searched "Noah *Hamptons House*."

She scrolled through the countless profile images. He was definitely the same man she'd seen on the motorcycle. And he was everywhere.

Then shirtless ones popped up. Oh, boy. His wavy hair tousled to the side, sparse mustache, and chiseled abs made her mouth moist and her insides tingle.

"That's enough of that." Abruptly, she closed the tab. She didn't need to be thinking about boys right now. That's what got her into trouble in the first place. A new email from the gallery sat in her inbox. She inhaled through her nose and out through her mouth and opened it.

Dahlia,

I know you spoke briefly with HR, but I wanted to congratulate you personally on securing the Chief Curator position at the Whitmore Gallery. The pool of candidates was impressive, but your six years at MoMA, along with your positive team attitude and references, won us over. I know we'd originally given you an early September start date, but our new exhibits start in September and run through November. Because it's imperative that you are here early, your start date is August 5. Please confirm.

Best,

Christine Smyth

Dahlia grinned. It felt good to be wanted and needed. All those years of sacrifice, taking the graveyard shift at the ambulance dispatch to get her degree, and earning her MFA while Daisy was in middle school.

But soon her grin soured. They wanted her to start in *one month.* How in the world would she pull all of this off in a month? And without help?

Not only did she have a house to fix, but now she needed to find a key that held a secret that could change everything. She rested her head on the pillow. Tomorrow would be better; it had to be.

CHAPTER FOUR

July 2

Dahlia couldn't remember the last time she slept in. The cool top sheet clung to her legs. The birds' sweet chorus played outside her window, and she could hear the sailboat masts echo in the distance. The breeze billowed through the open windows. It was exactly what she needed after yesterday's unexpected revelations.

She fought every urge to move from this spot and greet the day. Remaining in Lil's bed just a few minutes longer meant she didn't have to cross anything off her now lengthy to-do list just yet. There was such peace here. Dahlia was beginning to understand why Lil had fought so hard to stay here, even when she no longer had her independence.

A few more minutes, then Dahlia would grab coffee. She'd have it on the sleeping porch and watch the sailboats. She'd always wanted to do that.

BANG! BANG! BANG! SCREEEEEECH!

Dahlia hurled forward, ripping the eye mask from her face. "What the hell?" She tossed the covers aside. Who had the audacity to run a saw at 7:57 in the morning on a Saturday—on a holiday weekend, no less?

Her feet hit the cold floor, and so did Harry's, looking for action. She could feel her cheeks grow warmer with each nanosecond that passed. Harry bolted down the old, narrow staircase first, followed by Dahlia.

Out the back door, she followed the sound, which appeared to be coming from the barn. No one was supposed to be using it but her this summer.

Dahlia charged into the barn. She didn't know what she'd find, and she didn't care. After yesterday, she wasn't in the mood to play nice. She stumbled through the door only to be met with a haze of dust particles that burned her eyes and made her cough.

"It's eight o'clock in the morning!" she yelled over the noise. She could barely hear herself over the table saw. "Stop it!" The screech suddenly stopped. Her ears rang as she watched the man slowly remove his goggles and the handkerchief over his mouth.

Oh, God—it was him. Noah Sterling from Hamptons House. He was so much taller up close. She stood motionless, staring at the man who was now petting her dog. She glared at Harry. *Traitor.*

Seconds felt like long minutes. She was braless, standing before Noah Sterling in nothing but a tank top and undershorts, her nipples like headlights on a foggy night. She tried to cover herself with her hands and, despite knowing exactly who he was, blurted, "Who the hell are you? And why are you in my barn?"

He straightened his posture, his broad chest straining the buttons on his flannel. A puzzled look flashed across his dirty face. "Me?" he asked. "What are *you* doing in *my* barn?"

Dahlia shook her head. "This is my Aunt Lil's barn." And now it was hers. "No one is supposed to use it but myself, Bruce, and Garrett—and they're away for the summer. You're trespassing on her property." Her armpits started to sweat, and other parts too.

He cackled with a condescending tone, and it hit her last nerve.

She covered her breasts tighter. "Is something funny to you?"

"No. But it's not trespassing when you have a signed document from the owner."

"What?" Her posture shifted. How could he possibly have a note from Lil? "Um, I don't know what you think you have, but my aunt passed away a few months ago, and there's no way she could have signed anything."

He lifted his T-shirt to wipe his mouth, showing the contours of his chiseled stomach. Her breath hitched. "Well, she did." He handed her a paper he'd tucked beside some tools on a shelf, like he knew he'd need it someday soon. He had a goofy grin on his face and sawdust in his 'stache. His hands were sweaty and dirty, yet her stomach took flight when his hand grazed hers.

Dahlia opened it and read it to herself, going right to the crux of the letter. *I hereby give permission to Noah Sterling, who is residing at 8 Meadow Lane, Southold, NY, to use and share my barn with my niece, Dahlia Newberry. He may enter and use at his convenience until my house at 6 Meadow Lane is sold.* Sure enough, the signature was Lil's. At that moment, she felt betrayed. Twice in the last twenty-four hours, Dahlia was hoodwinked by a woman whom she'd thought she knew better than herself. How could she have given him permission to be here when she knew the only thing Dahlia wanted was to be alone? She leaned back onto the workbench, speechless, feeling the paper crinkle in her grip.

"Bruce is my uncle. He said I could crash here this summer while they were in Italy. During the winter, he reached out to Lil to see if it would be okay if I used the barn to build furniture. And she mailed him this note." He paused, taking a sip of water. "My guess is she figured you'd give me a hard time."

"Well, she was right." Dahlia wanted peace and quiet, not this kind of noise all summer long outside her window. What was Lil thinking? "But it's my house now, so my rules," she said with a firm nod.

"What?" He set his water jug down.

"You're going to find another barn to borrow." Dahlia looked away.

"Another barn?" He moved closer, and she could smell his sweat. "Like it's that easy?"

Adrenaline rushed through her body. "I don't care what you do." She didn't care how hot he was, either. "But you're not sharing my barn."

"You can't be serious."

"Dead serious." And with that, she stomped her barely dressed self out of the barn.

"I know women like you," he called after her. "You want to give a guy a hard time just for breathing."

She marched back; she could feel her face getting hot. The audacity of him. She already couldn't stand this man. "Listen, bucko. I know plenty of guys like you too."

"Oh, do you now?" He folded his arms and leaned against the doorjamb.

"Yes, entitled and ego-driven. You may have everyone fooled, but not me." Dahlia waved her hand toward her dog in a come-here motion. "Harry, come!"

Harry didn't budge, just sat there happily on the cool barn floor.

Noah smirked. "I think he wants to stay with me. Maybe until you cool down."

"Ugh!" Dahlia tossed her long hair as if such a move came naturally to her and headed back to the house.

The man was infuriating. He had to go. Dahlia felt deceived by Lil; first the letter, and now this? Kara was going to need to be resuscitated after this little update.

* * *

After Dahlia collected herself from the morning face-off, she called Kara. She filled her in on her new neighbor and the argument that still had her frazzled. To say Kara was in shock was an understatement. She implored Dahlia to give him a chance, at least for her sake, and was suddenly all too eager to come for an impromptu visit. After ending the call where Dahlia essentially softened, ever so slightly, she went in search of the mysterious and elusive key. Like it would be that easy. The first stop on this puzzling mission was the home office. Dahlia yanked the drawers open in Lil's library desk and riffled through her papers. Something as small as a safe-deposit box key could be anywhere, but this was the likeliest of places.

She poked around the hunter-green built-ins her pop painted back in the eighties when it paired well with mauve. She flipped through a random biography of Hollywood actor Charles Halston, called *Rags to Riches*, and shook a ratty paperback beside it, as if Lil were the type of person who would hide something important in a book. She sat on the floor, the scattered papers around her, and hugged her legs. All she wanted to do was cry. Maybe if she gave in to it, it wouldn't feel so overwhelming. She tucked her head into her knees, about to succumb to her grief and frustration, when there was a knock at the front door.

Maybe it was Jean with the appliance parts. Perhaps she had good news and found someone to help. Dahlia rose from the dusty floor and wiped the dirt from her shorts.

Harry was already at the door when she opened it.

"Hello," said a rugged voice attached to a cleaned-up version of the man from earlier.

Dahlia bravely faced him head-on despite the belly swoop that made her want to sink her teeth into her lip.

"Listen, I'm sorry about this morning," Noah said, putting his hands in his pockets. "I shouldn't have been causing such a commotion that early. I couldn't sleep, and I thought, well . . . Anyway, it was a bad idea. I take full responsibility."

"Okay." She stepped into the doorway with folded arms. So, he could admit when he was wrong. She felt a slow smile building, but she couldn't show her hand just yet. Harry parked himself right next to the man as if telling her to hear him out.

"And I'm sorry for what I said. I'm a little jaded right now."

She wanted to correct him and say "grumpy" because "jaded" sounded way too polite, but she just stood there, waiting for him to finish.

"I shouldn't have taken that out on you. I honestly don't know why I was so triggered." His cheeks began to flush. Noah Sterling from *Hamptons House* was feeling uncomfortable. And that could be the victory right there. As if he sensed Dahlia's awareness, he blurted, "The last thing I'm looking for is . . . you know." He pointed to her and then himself.

"Well, that's a relief," she said with enthusiasm, trying to hide a tinge of inexplicable disappointment. "You don't have to worry. I'm not either."

He nodded. "Say, if I promise never to build that early again, if you'll reconsider letting me share the barn for the summer?" He raised his brows in a playful plea. "I mean, I know technically it's yours."

"Damn straight." Dahlia exhaled, trying not to connect with his Pacific blue eyes. She had no plan of losing herself in them, but they were stunning and utterly hypnotizing.

Noah leaned closer. "Listen, I see you've got some things that need fixing." He pointed to the hole in the decking. "I can help. I did construction all through college and . . ." He paused as if he were trying to find the right words. "I also renovate houses in the Hamptons. Maybe we can barter help with the house in exchange for barn time."

Dahlia stood frozen in place as she bit the inside of her cheek, something she did when she was nervous or confused. On one hand, she could use the help, but on the other hand, Noah was a very *leading man* kind of sexy, and Dahlia was human, after all.

"I'm sorry too. I was a hard-ass this morning. But in all fairness, yesterday was the absolute worst day. I came here this summer looking for tranquility, a bit of peace, and as you can see, it's been the exact opposite." She points to the hole in the porch. "I'm not sure a carpenter next door aligns with that." However, the house needed fixing, and Dahlia had no other potential hopefuls in mind.

"I need to build." He held up his hands, and even they were cute. Manly, rough, and big, with nice nail beds.

Dahlia drew in a breath, imagining what they would feel like against her skin. A smile pulled at her cheeks, but when she looked up, she was met with an even bigger smile, this one laced with mirth. "Sorry, you were saying?" Her face felt as hot as a tamale.

"Ahh." Noah was at a loss for words too, it seemed. "Oh, yeah, just that it's the only thing that's grounding me right now. And keeping me from going completely bonkers." As quickly as his bright smile came, it faded like the sun.

Dahlia was quiet, unsure of what to make of his abrupt shift. He could actually be worse off than she was. Suddenly, she felt terrible for the hunk standing at her doorstep and carefully weighed her words. "If I agree to this—and I'm not saying I will—I would pay you for any work you do on the house."

"I don't need your money. I've got enough."

Must be nice to get paid the big bucks to be on TV. She wondered why he wasn't filming. Something must have happened. Perhaps it had to do with what Kara mentioned yesterday, about his best friend double-crossing him.

"Look, think about it. I'll be gone until tomorrow evening." He stepped back. "I'm headed to Southampton to meet some friends. How about you sleep on it?"

"Sure. Sounds fair."

"I'm Noah, by the way." He reached for her hand.

"I'm Dahlia." His touch sent racing tingles up her spine and trailed right up into her lifeless heart.

"Tomorrow, then." He gave a warm nod, leaving a trace of hope floating through the air.

"I'm not making any promises," Dahlia said with a playful shrug.

"But you're not saying no," he said, walking backward to his motorcycle while putting on his aviators.

She was so screwed.

CHAPTER FIVE

July 3

Dahlia's body glided through the cold water. After another sleepless night of unanswered questions and sticking to the bed sheets, she welcomed the chill. With each stroke, her mind sought answers. Being a Pisces and a water sign, she often found herself drawn to water when she needed to think. Should she let Noah help her? She'd said no distractions, and he was definitely a distraction. Yet Lil's secret was the biggest distraction of all. Dahlia expelled the bay water as she returned to the surface, turning onto her back to do the backstroke. What could it possibly be about? Maybe there had been a murder, and someone buried the body in the backyard. The tiny hairs rose as she lifted her arm. Kara was right—she was watching too much *Dateline*. Maybe she would give that a rest, at least for the summer.

Dahlia reached the buoy. She clung to it as her body lifted with the current. The neighboring island was so close she could practically touch it. She remembered all the ferry trips she'd taken with

Gran, Pop, and Lil. How they would walk on, grab lunch at the Dory, and watch the yachts pull into the harbor while they shared an apple pie from the deli. The good old days when the gang was all together. Dahlia was caught like a fish in a net between the memories of yesterday and the new reality of being alone at Lil's.

The sun was already intense, and she squinted to see the shoreline. Her favorite Greek revival home was now visible from the water; it had once belonged to a famous seventies rock star. The lawn looked regal against the steely blue water. Dahlia began to drift away, feeling her body release. She could hear Pop's words echo in her mind with a lingering French accent: "Feel the rhythm, Dahlia. Let her carry you."

Her grandfather Leon had been a cliff diver and a French Olympic hopeful in his youth, but his winning attribute was his patience. They'd spent countless hours in this bay together, swimming, fishing, and talking. Being here was cathartic. He would remind her, "There's always a silver lining somewhere. You just have to keep your heart open to find it."

She headed back, varying her strokes, and wondered about that silver lining. What if there wasn't one? What if opening Pandora's box would only bring more pain? What if the secret was about her parents and that night? Or maybe it was about Dahlia herself. Suddenly, her heart felt weighted. She began to tread water, making herself think of something happy. Lil's garden in its glory days. She could see her Rosanna roses with salmon-pink petals as they canopied over the gate. She could almost smell their fruity flavor drift over the bay. There was lavender, echinacea, and daisies as far as the eye could see. The anxiety eased, and she felt steady enough to finish her swim.

The minute her feet hit the sand, Dahlia felt the day had a renewed purpose. She flung off her swimsuit and ran back up to the house in nothing but a towel, meeting Harry halfway. There was something about being naked that made her feel young and free. She eyed the outside shower and wondered if it still worked. There was only one way to find out. The heavy wood door opened with a squeak. She closed her eyes in prayer and turned the knob. The steady spray hitting the weathered wall was music to her ears. Upon second glance, it was a bit dirty but not too bad. Dahlia let the water run, hoping it would get hot while she grabbed some toiletries.

Upon returning to the small unit, she threw the towel over the rusted fish-shaped hook that was a permanent fixture on the wall. After checking the temperature, she planted herself right under the aged copper spout. She soaked in every bit of warmth her chilled body would allow. The water rushed over her hair, down her back, and over her chest. The brine from the bay just thirty feet away infiltrated the tight space. She buried her face in the water, letting it cascade down her bare form. It felt healing, precisely what she needed before she got her hands dirty in Lil's garden.

Hands. The word lodged in her brain and anchored there. Which led to Noah, of course. Soon enough, her imagination began to wander. The image of his gorgeous, Greek-like hands caressing her naked skin played in her mind. Her body flooded with warmth and tingles that traveled south. Then she imagined her fingers tracing the well-defined lines of his abs and his delicious V of tight muscles just above his length. *No, no, this can't happen. I have work to do, and men are a big fat mistake right now.* With that, Dahlia flipped the water to cold, hoping it would douse the unyielding heat in her core and the remnants of her body's betrayal.

A short while later, after she was dry and dressed, Dahlia found herself standing at the entrance of Lil's garden with a shovel and clippers in hand. The thorny roses overhead were wild, and the weeds were taller than the blooms. She wiped the sweat from her forehead. This job was going to be bigger than a day's worth of work, of that she was certain. Harry tilted his head and barked as if he was now aware of the magnitude of bucket list item number eleven.

Dahlia stepped up into the first large raised bed. "This looks like a good place to start. I'll need to dig some of the perennials up if the rest have any chance of surviving," she mumbled.

Harry barked louder.

"No, not you, Harry. No digging."

The soil at Lil's had a distinct smell; it was an earthy sea medley. A breeze carried from the water, drying her moist body as she pulled large clumps. Motorboats quickly sabotaged the peaceful summer mood, and the heat was almost too much to bear. She ran to the shed to grab the wheelbarrow. Each time she wiped her forehead, she could feel the soil stain her face. She fixed her hat and went back to work.

With a hand on her hip, Dahlia scanned the garden. The roses would need too much work, and the dahlias hadn't started to bloom but were close. It was a true miracle that they'd even come up this year considering the tubers were never dug up and stored last summer. The violets were crowding the zinnias, so she started there while Harry rolled in the dirt. The violets were thick, but Dahlia kept jabbing, trying her best to lift the roots. The humidity weighed the air, and she knew once the afternoon hit, it would be unbearable. Just as she was about to call it a day, she hit something hard and hollow.

That was odd. She hit it again, only to hear her phone ring inside the shed. Yanking off her gloves, she rushed to look. It was her girl. She swiftly accepted the FaceTime. "Daisy!"

"Hi, Mom."

"You're a sight for sore eyes. Gah, I miss you, baby girl," Dahlia said, walking toward the house, taking in her bright appearance. "What time is it there?" Aside from last summer, Daisy was typically with Dahlia for her summer visits to Southold. But ever since arriving at the College of Charleston, Daisy had wanted this summer abroad in France. Dahlia swore that when she became her mother, she would never hold her back from seeking adventure. She wanted things for her daughter that she'd never had the chance to experience herself. Like the many vacations Spence had promised but was always too busy for.

"Just after six."

"I'll never get used to this time difference. And when I do, you'll be home," Dahlia said with a wistful tone, missing her something fierce. "Are you okay? I haven't heard from you in a few days."

"Everything is good. The weather's been great, and we've hit the beach almost every day." Daisy let out a contented sigh. "More importantly, how are you? I see you've been gardening?"

"It's that obvious, huh?" Dahlia said, wiping her face with a wet towel. "I'm . . . good." Dahlia debated for a split second whether to share the particulars of the critter invasion, how empty the house felt, and the letter, but decided to keep it light. Worrying Daisy was not something she needed to do. "Enough about me. You look pretty; where are you going?" And she did in her floral dress, blonde hair tucked behind her ear, and glossy lips.

"To dinner. Come on, Mom. Give me something, so I know you're okay. How about tonight? Any plans? Fireworks in town, maybe?" Daisy asked with a broad, hopeful smile.

"Of course I'm okay. I'm back in Southold, my favorite place on earth, remember?"

"But you're also alone," Daisy said, furrowing her brows in concern like she was the mother this time.

"I'm good, Dais, really. There's nothing to worry about here." Dahlia leaned against the counter as if it would ease her longing heart. At that moment, she wished she could travel back in time to a summer when everyone was still together. "And as for tonight, I'm not quite sure. I'll probably cozy up with a book on the porch."

"That sounds . . . eventful."

"It is to me. When you get to be my age, you'll think so too."

"Mom, you're thirty-eight. Stop acting like a Golden Girl."

"God, we loved that show, didn't we?" Dahlia gazed inward. "Anyway, now it's time for me to worry—who are you going out with? The girls from school?" She pulled the lemonade from the cooler. She needed to get more ice if there was any chance of the food not spoiling.

"No, with Pop's first cousin's daughter."

"Oh. You found a relative of his? That was fast. Does she live in La Rochelle?"

"Yeah, I went to the village hall and found a registry. Her name is Eloise Laurent. I didn't want to tell you unless I was fairly certain."

"You know his last name is very common," Dahlia said, not wanting her to get her hopes up. Finding her grandfather's lineage had been proven to be an arduous task in the past, but Daisy was determined. When she heard about the exchange program to her grandfather's hometown during orientation, she was immediately sold on the idea. Ever since the family-tree assignment during middle school, she was obsessed with putting the pieces of the past together.

"Yes, she confirmed some particulars, like his parents' names, military rank, oh, and his birthmark. That can't be a coincidence. I have a good feeling about her, Mom. She's bringing pictures too."

"Fair enough. Please have one of your sorority sisters go with you."

"Don't worry so much," said Daisy. "I'm twenty. We're just going to a cute café up the block." Daisy turned the phone to face the water.

"Oh, that view! It's just as Pop described." Dahlia heard the motorcycle pull in next door and froze. He was back. She was a little nervous about facing him again. She didn't know what her body would do next.

"Mom, try to have some fun this summer. If nothing else, do it for me."

First Kara, now Daisy. If it were only that easy to let go. As much as Dahlia wanted that too, she didn't know the first thing about how to do it. Again, more of a Monica than a Rachel. "I'll try, how's that?"

"I'll take it. Okay, gotta run, Mom. Love you."

"Love you—" The call ended as Dahlia whispered, "Too."

Dahlia leaned her elbows on the butcher block counter and wondered for a brief moment what her life would have looked like if she had done what Spence wanted. Some may have made a different choice than she had with a full college scholarship ahead, and Dahlia would have wholeheartedly respected that decision. But after her parents died, she'd felt anchorless, but something inside her shifted when she found out she was pregnant. What would Dahlia's life even look like without Daisy? She was her entire world. Her heart felt sliced open by the thought. Immediately, she shook the inconceivable image from her mind. She couldn't go there. Plus, there were more pressing matters that needed her attention.

"Okay, Lil, where should I look next? Give me a sign." She held up her hands. Why couldn't Lil have left all this alone? And why did she tell Noah he could use the barn? Dahlia exhaled. "You're still not off the hook with me," she said, looking up at the cracked wainscotting ceiling as if Lil could hear her.

Dahlia eyed the pantry door, remembering how Lil hid candy in tin cans for her and then Daisy when she was little. Of course. The key had to be in there.

After scouring every inch of the pantry to no avail and mending Lil's damaged curtains, Dahlia was in bed by nine, just as she'd hoped. She couldn't wait to go to sleep and was glad to be tired enough to finally do that. The daylight was almost extinct, and the moon was beginning to shine through the upstairs windows and porch. The slight waft of air was enough to make sleeping possible. She loosened the flat sheet and finally relaxed after a hard day's work, but her mind had other ideas.

She heard a groan from the hardwood floors.

"I know, bud, it's a little hot tonight." She added "bring a fan up from the basement" to her mental to-do list. How did Lil sleep up here without air conditioning? Dahlia hated to admit it, but she missed her central air conditioning in Connecticut. As much as she liked the windows open, the humidity was beginning to creep its way into her Long Island summer and cramp her style.

The back of her palm rested on her forehead. She lay there, her body tired, her mind still awake. She wasn't usually the type to wonder about someone she had just met, yet Noah Sterling had stolen her thoughts like a thief in the night. She tossed left, then right, tangling herself in the sheets. Dahlia knew it was more than just her attraction to her neighbor. It was also that she'd only ever been with Spence and one other person before.

His name was Tristan, and he was what Lil liked to call a stallion: jet black hair, green eyes, and a way with the ladies. He was newly assigned to the graveyard shift at the ambulance company. Daisy was three and spending two weeks with Gran and Lil while she worked. It was a few dates, then one drunken night before Daisy came home. It fizzled fast once he realized she had a daughter. After that, Dahlia hadn't seen much point in dating. But Noah was another story, and she was curious.

"Curiosity killed the cat." She couldn't help but hear Gran's words ring in her ears. But this was different.

Dahlia thought about him standing on her porch and how his facial hair outlined his mouth ever so perfectly. She'd never seen a cupid's bow so perfect and lips so pink on a man. Her heart raced. She couldn't help but think about what happened to her body when his hand touched hers in the barn and then again on the porch.

What was she doing? He couldn't be much older than Daisy! And he was clearly not looking to date, which was good. Her mind darted to all the scenarios. Something awful must have happened to him, but what? She looked at her phone on the nightstand, tempted to google him again and find out the tea once and for all. But instead, she just stared at the willow branches shadowing the ceiling. She wasn't that kind of person, and she didn't care. Dahlia pressed her eyes shut, trying to convince herself of that.

"Oh, for Pete's sake. This is ridiculous," she said, throwing on her cardigan just as the fireworks started. And with that, Harry began to howl and bark.

Dahlia was now fully awake. She poured a glass of water and headed out the back door. A hint of night-blooming jasmine drifted through the night air. Dahlia would know that intoxicatingly sweet scent anywhere. She and Lil had planted it beside the porch the summer after her parents died. It was her mother's favorite scent. Her mind rushed to the memory. "That way, when we're out here at night, we can feel her with us," Lil had said with tears in her eyes.

Everywhere she looked and everything she smelled was a subtle reminder of why she loved this place as much as she did. Harry led the way to Lil's barn. There was a familiar scent in her studio too. It was fresh cedar and must with a hint of WD-40. Dahlia inhaled the aroma as if it would take her back to the days when her pop would work on his ride-on mower and she'd poke through Lil's stuff.

She had only passed through a few times since she arrived. This time, there was no table saw or sander going. Dahlia could hear her feet on the worn wood below; it was that silent. Lil's botanicals covered the walls in bright hues that felt like childhood: bubblegum, sunshine, and sherbet. Her smile grew as she continued to wander. There were dried flowers that still hung from the rafters above and coffee cans that lined her shelves. What on earth, Lil? There wasn't enough candy in the world to fill all these.

There were bins and bins of paintings. She pulled one out. It was an impressionist-style painting of lilacs in a clear vase. The purples were vivid against a robin's egg blue background. Lil had been a talented artist. One who could have had gallery shows and made an income selling her art. It made zero sense why these paintings were in a dingy barn, hidden away. "These are too good. Right, Har?" She looked around. "Harry?"

The fireworks *bang* startled her again. It sounded like gunfire right in her backyard. Then came Harry's howling, right on cue. She followed the sound to Bruce and Garrett's house and noticed a fire going in the pit. She hid behind the side of the barn like a sleuth.

Noah was there, sitting alone, having a beer. Well, not alone. He was canoodling with her dog, face to face, trying to calm him. "It's okay, boy, I've got you," he said while resting his head on his. It made her feel something else altogether this time; if there was a way to Dahlia's heart, it was through her dog.

Noah cleared his throat, which made her wonder if he was upset. Her eyes narrowed, and an odd sensation of guilt rippled through her belly. Maybe she'd been too hard on him yesterday. Perhaps he genuinely needed to build and use his hands to stay sane. What was he even doing at home on a holiday weekend? He should be in the Hamptons having fun. That's what most people his age did, after all. So far, she hadn't googled him, but she knew she was older, or maybe she just felt older because she had a twenty-year-old daughter.

Dahlia's nurturing instincts kicked in, and she walked over.

"Hey," she said, covering her braless chest with her sweater. This was becoming a habit, one she needed to break immediately if there was any hope of them having a working relationship.

"Oh, hey." He got up. "I was wondering if you'd come by. To get your dog, I mean." He let out a playful chuckle, one that made Dahlia want to inch closer.

Every part of her wanted to scream yes, yes, yes, but the words were stuck on her tongue.

"Want a cold beer? The view is amazing." His tone was enticing. "You can see the Shelter Island fireworks from the cove," he said, pointing above the water.

"How could I say no to that?" She took a seat in the empty Adirondack chair next to him. "I see Harry's made himself comfortable." She laughed.

"He came right over," Noah said, handing her the bottle. "Smart little dude. A little skittish, though."

"Yeah, he has a love-hate relationship with bangs and booms or any disturbance for that matter." She took a sip of the craft beer and looked at the label. "Hmm, that's good."

"Yeah, it's from the brewery on Shelter Island."

"Nice, I'll have to check it out." Dahlia pressed the bottle to her lips and took another sip. "Sorry he wandered over. He's a roamer but always comes home, so I never worry. I think that's why he got returned to the shelter so many times." Dahlia got quiet. She didn't know Harry's entire story, but he was very badly neglected and malnourished when he arrived at the shelter the first time.

"Lucky you found him, then," he said.

"I think it's the opposite. I was lucky he found me," she mumbled, looking at Harry with a tender smile.

"I love dogs. I had a black lab for sixteen years." He cleared his throat again. "Nemo."

Babies, dogs, and grandparents. You can always tell a person's heart by how they treat any of the three. That's what Lil would say, anyway.

Noah gave him a good scratch. "So, Harry, huh? Solid name."

"Yeah, it's after Harry Styles—you know, the singer? Dais . . . I mean, I adore him." He didn't need to know she had an adult daughter. Right now, she just wanted to be Dahlia. "So, how was your night away?"

"Eh, it was okay. Same shit, different day," he said, making a fist.

"Oh." She raised her eyebrows. *Someone did a number on him*, she thought.

"The garden is looking better. You got to it today?"

"Thanks. How did you—"

"I passed it on my way in."

"Right. The irrigation system was on this past month, thank goodness. Otherwise, the plants would be all wilted by now." Dahlia shook her head. "I have to thank Hank."

"Hank?"

"My aunt's handyman." She paused. "He had a heart attack recently and will be laid up for the next few months. In case you were wondering why the house is in disarray."

"I wasn't. I just noticed the house needs some work." He took a long sip of his beer. "Oh, and I was the one who turned on the irrigation system."

"You did?" Her insides tickled. One small act from a stranger, and she was giddy inside. She supposed Harry wasn't the only one who'd been neglected. "Thank you. You have no idea how much that means to me." Her eyes pooled with tears, and she looked away, trying to hide her oscillating emotions. She wiped her nose with her sleeve and laughed. "Sorry, it's been a rough few days." And she missed Lil terribly. "If you can believe it, we were greeted by a squirrel inside the house when we first arrived."

"No way." His words lingered in astonishment.

"Yes, way, and she terrorized the place." Her neck stiffened. "To top it off, the appliances aren't working, and so many things need fixing."

"See? You need me," he said with a smooth grin.

Her cheeks were warm. Maybe she did.

"You probably have a hole in your chimney cap; that's how the critter got in."

"You think? I did notice the flue was open." Dahlia took a sip. It was one more thing that needed fixing.

"Pretty sure. My stepdad owns a construction company. I am a wealth of random house facts." He got up and threw another log onto the fire. "Plus, the last few years of fixing up houses have made me somewhat of an expert," he said, avoiding any mention of a reality television show. Dahlia so wanted to ask more, like how he'd gotten into it, how long he'd been doing it, and if he was still filming—just to be sure. But she didn't. She was too preoccupied by the Fire God who was making her body feel things she hadn't in a very long time.

"Listen, I need to make furniture this summer. If I don't, well, let's say it won't be fun living next door to me." He frowned.

"Well, we wouldn't want that." Dahlia tried to be playful.

"My sister Gretchen is opening a new restaurant on Shelter Island, and she needs my help building the bar, tables, and banquettes. The permits have been a bitch, and it's held everything up. She needs to open by mid-July if she hopes to make any money back before the season ends," he said, running his fingers through his thick chestnut locks.

She tried to look away but couldn't. "How wonderful and terrifying to be under that kind of time crunch." She wouldn't know anything about it.

"Yes, but I'll still have plenty of time to help you."

"You think? I wouldn't want to . . ."

"I know," he said with a relaxed smile. It was one that oozed confidence, and Dahlia was in for whatever that meant. Noah had a presence that felt safe and secure, which was a stark contrast to Spence.

She nodded. "Okay, then."

"Really? Okay?" He jumped up and hugged her just as the fireworks resumed.

Stunned, Dahlia took in his scent. It was clean and woodsy, like fresh laundry and pine. She could feel her heart beating against his flannel shirt despite the blasts going off around them.

"You're not going to regret it." He pulled back, and his eyes met hers.

She lost her air. "Right. I'm sure I won't." She looked away before she did something stupid, like stay for another beer. "I'd better get home. It's getting late."

"So soon?" He shrugged, disappointment laced through his voice.

"Thanks for the beverage." She gave him an easy nod while inside wanting to die. Who says beverage? "Come on, Harry."

"I'll come by tomorrow," he called after her.

Dahlia gave a thumbs-up and kept walking. She stepped inside the house and shut the door, letting out a long breath. She'd forgotten how nice it was to have company. The armor she'd built around her heart after her parents died was slowly loosening.

What on earth had she agreed to?

CHAPTER SIX

July 4

"We'll miss you today. FaceTime me later. I want an update on McHandy," said Kara, prepping her cheese platter for her annual July Fourth extravaganza.

"Don't get your hopes up," Dahlia said, leaning her elbows on the kitchen table. Her hair still smelled like smoke from Noah's fire pit. Even though she'd showered when she came home after she called Kara, the smell lingered. "If it's anything like last night, it will be very PG, maybe even G."

"Let's hope not. You might wilt if you don't get some action soon."

Dahlia spit out her coffee. "Kara!"

"I'm only stating the facts. We both know it's been a while. My guess is it's been a few years with Spence, at least," Kara said, holding up the salami she was slicing. "You've gotta get back out there, girl. You're allowed to have a summer fling if you want to. You've earned that right, living in that lifeless marriage all those years."

Dahlia pursed her lips, not wanting to show her amusement even though she almost died when Kara held up the length of meat. She didn't need any further encouragement—plus, she was right. Dahlia did need to get laid—it had been almost two years, to be exact. What happened two summers ago was the final straw, although it had been over longer before that. After the first six months of marriage, Spence treated Dahlia like an inconvenience he had to manage. Which likely came from her confronting him about the actual reason he'd come back and proposed. Apparently, the keys to his father's financial kingdom warranted a little pretending. He was so callous about it too: "What's the big deal? Do you know how many women would die to be in your place? Be more grateful, would you?" Her hopes of being a real family began to wilt, while he put on a show, something he was well-versed in. Only behind closed doors came a loathing she could feel deep in her bones. Most likely because she didn't put him on a pedestal like everyone else. At the end of the day, intimacy came with feeling safe and loved, which was something he promised but never could deliver. Plus, who needed a man to be pleased? They both knew there were plenty of other ways that didn't include the opposite sex or possible heartbreak.

"Would you look at the time?" Dahlia glared at her watch. "I have to run."

"Think about what I said."

"Bye." Dahlia let out a sarcastic chuckle. Kara was right. Dahlia was a grown woman who could make her own decisions. But what she needed to do was focus on finding that key and getting this place in tip-top shape, as Lil would have wanted. Dahlia traced the ring embedded deep into the wood surface made by Lil's teacup. She could still hear Gran's words so clearly. "Use a saucer, Lil; you're going to stain the table."

Dahlia looked at her list of *Things That Need to Be Fixed* and felt her neck stiffen. The pen lodged in between her fingers suddenly was heavy. She needed to respond to the gallery about the moved-up start date by tomorrow. What was she going to do? She wasn't sure she could get everything done in a month. Dahlia looked around the kitchen at all the small projects she knew would add up. She looked up at the wainscotting that needed to be caulked and the chipped windows that needed to be painted if she wanted a quick sale.

Dahlia sat back in Lil's vintage bentwood chair and gazed through the pitted screen. The bay looked peaceful and still, quiet for a Long Island Fourth of July. The bottom of the café curtain curled with each warm waft of air that blew through. She played with her D necklace, zipping the monogram back and forth to steady her racing mind. She added *appliance parts* to the list and wondered how Hank was.

Just as she reached for her phone to text Jean, she heard a knock on the back door. With that, Harry flew past her, leaving a wake of black fur that hung motionless in the air. Harry leaped onto the back door, his nails hitting the glass, and whined with excitement.

"It's me, Noah. I hope this isn't a bad time."

"Uh, yeah. Gimme a second," she yelled, bolting to the bathroom mirror. She wiped the smudge of mascara from her lid and checked her breath. It would have to do. She opened the porch door. "Hey."

"Sorry, are you busy? Hi, boy," he said, giving Harry a good scratch. He was in a simple white T-shirt, faded jeans, and old Timberlands. The jeans hugged low on his hips, showing a glimpse of his Calvin Kleins, and one cuff was unknowingly tucked into his boot.

She held the air in her lungs as if it would somehow mute this unbridled sensation flooding her insides.

"I can come back." He slowly looked her up and down. "I didn't wake you, did I? Cute shirt."

"Thanks." Did she look like she just woke up? Dahlia felt the intensity of his stare go right through her like a laser beam. Her hands were damp, and her heart pulsed under her Jason Mraz pink tie-dye shirt. "No, it's okay. Come on in." Dahlia waved her hand toward the kitchen.

"Oh, wow, it's like a time capsule in here," Noah said eagerly. "Smells like it too."

"Yeah, I suppose it does." Was that a diss? Maybe she needed to get some candles and spray some air freshener. She'd gotten used to the signature smell that reminded her of them.

"These recessed cabinets look original." He ran his strong hand across the surface. A close-up confirmation that his nail beds were indeed attractive. What was it about a man and manly hands? Dahlia's gulp felt audible. "Just look at the craftsmanship on these. They don't make stuff like this anymore." Noah turned to her with a charming grin, as if he knew old house talk would weaken her knees.

Why did he have to look at her like that? A sex-deprived girl could only take so much. Dahlia walked to the coffee pot, feeling her face blush. "Yeah, I think a great-great-uncle made them back in the 1930s."

"And the wainscotting on the ceiling *and* the walls! I bet the farm sink is original too," he said eagerly as he inspected it.

Dahlia nodded as she topped off her coffee.

"Is that a butler's pantry? May I?"

"Sure, be my guest." She remembered how she would find Lil there now and then, sitting on a stool by the window, writing away. To this day, Dahlia didn't have a clue what she was writing or to whom.

"Very cool. Whoever built this pantry was a real tradesman," Noah said, knocking on the Palladian Blue cupboard door. "This is oak. What old ships were made of."

Wasn't he just a medley of surprises? "You don't say."

Noah nodded. "I grew up in an old farmhouse just outside Denver. I loved the creaks and the strange sounds it would make. Uncle Bruce gutted their place and removed all the old charm." He motioned next door. "There are no squeaks left. It's sad."

He sounded like an old soul. And a match for Dahlia's love of history and the past. "That's a shame. There was so much history there. Did you know a famous playwright once lived in that house for a summer? And it was said that Einstein once spent the weekend there." Dahlia grinned with satisfaction, feeling empowered by her catalog of random facts that Spence had never seemed to appreciate.

"You're kidding!" Noah's voice was eager. "I had no idea. I'm also a huge history buff. Uncle Bruce never mentioned it. That blows my mind," he said. "I'm living in a house where Albert Einstein played for a weekend. Very cool."

Dahlia smiled at the simple yet intriguing man standing before her. On the one hand, his eagerness was youthful and untainted, yet his sensibility was mature and comforting. She almost forgot that he was a reality TV star. To her, he was just the guy next door who would hopefully help her put her house back together.

She picked at the chipped Formica in the built-in nook, stealing a lingering glance.

"You know, I could replace that with soapstone or marble," Noah said. "The rock quarry should have a scrap that fits. It's a small area and would go nicely with the butcher block."

"It would." Dahlia felt her face light up.

"Okay, so let's see that refrigerator of yours," he said, wiggling it from the wall. The veins on his arms bulged, and she could see the tail of some creature sticking out from under his sleeve—a tattoo.

Lordy. Kara would unalive herself with this view. "The stove too. It turns on but then off right away. Should I text Hank's wife to see if the parts are in?"

"Nah, I'll look first and see what we can do. I mean, it's not that old, so it should just be a few adjustments," Noah said.

Why was this exciting to her? Oh yeah, because Spence barely knew how to use a hammer. Dahlia watched Noah yank back the beastly appliance. Now, the veins on his neck bulged, and his face grew beet red. His sleeve crept up with each movement, revealing more of a scaly tail. Dahlia leaned against the counter, feeling like maybe she should get some popcorn.

"And it looks like you have mice too," said Noah, waking her from her morning fantasy and back to reality. "Do you have a dustbuster or vacuum?"

"Yeah, sure." Dahlia grabbed the dustbuster from the closet, feeling like she was under some spell where her anxiety was suddenly masked by longing or even desire. "Here you go."

"Thanks."

Dahlia watched him disappear behind the fridge.

"I can grab some traps at the store once we figure out what parts we need," he said, peeking his head out.

"You have cobwebs in your hair." Dahlia giggled. "Here, let me."

Dahlia's hands trembled as she inhaled the notes of peppermint still lingering in his damp hair. It had been an eternity since she was this close to a guy, let alone an attractive one. "There," she said, pulling the last bit of white from his dark, messy hair.

His eyes met hers in a long, tender pause. "Thanks."

Her body flooded with warmth. "No problem. It's the least I could do." She shrugged, looking over his rugged but chiseled face. Tiny freckles peppered the side of his nose, and his eyelashes curled on the ends. How was he even cuter this close up?

"Anyway." Noah smiled. "Got a stronger vacuum by chance? I can clean up the coils back here. It might help."

"Sure."

Just then, her phone buzzed on the counter, and he grabbed it as if by instinct. "Here, sorry."

It was Spence. *The papers are in. I signed. They need your Hancock.*

Dahlia swallowed hard. He'd done it; he'd signed the papers. She leaned against the counter, stunned. As soon as she signed the papers, she would be free. Free of the lonely charade, free of the lies and control, and the guilt of wanting more. She hadn't thought this day would ever come—for many reasons. The main one being he had hid Lil's deed after she died. His last-ditch attempt at keeping her beholden to him. He had to know she would eventually find it in one of three places: his personal safe (with Daisy's birthday as the code), his false-bottom sock drawer she wasn't supposed to know about, or behind the Cezanne painting he inherited from his grandmother. The irony that he'd taped it to the back of a floral still life that Lil had gazed at for hours in her final days was bewildering but somehow fitting. Still, to this day, Dahlia didn't know exactly why he'd done it; he clearly didn't want her. But she guessed he didn't want anyone else to either. An insecure man needs control to survive, and Spence had it in spades. She shifted her position.

"I've got it from here if you need a minute."

She should take care of this. "Are you sure?" He nodded. "Oh, let me grab that vacuum; I almost forgot." Dahlia ran into the hallway and opened the linen closet, feeling hopeful for the first time in over a decade. She smiled wistfully. Good things were on the way, she could feel it.

"Here you go. I'll be outside working in the garden if you need me." Dahlia walked toward the back door and paused, turning on her toes. "Oh, and feel free to help yourself to coffee. It's on the counter, and milk is in the cooler."

"Sounds good."

Dahlia grabbed her coffee and old sneakers, then popped a squat on the stoop and laced them up. It was here she'd learned to shuck corn, peel potatoes, and split beans from Gran's vegetable garden many moons ago. She heard Gran's words echo through her ears as she leaned her face into the sun: "Don't rush, Dahlia. Be sure to get all those hairs. Haste makes waste, you know."

Dahlia blew out a cleansing breath. No more pretending. The life she'd committed to for Daisy was done. Finished, finito. Her shoulders dropped as she watched a white butterfly frolic above the lavender. No more doing what was best for everyone else. This was *her* time.

Dahlia made long strides across the yard. For the first time in forever, she was grounded to the earth beneath her feet. She walked the path in between the plant beds, feeling the maple leaves dance overhead. The last thing she wanted to do was to see Spence or drag this out, especially after every other horrible thing he'd said and done over the years.

She found a shady spot and finally texted back Spence. *That's good news. Can you email them to me?* Once he did that, she could have them printed so she could look them over with a fine-tooth comb. Being a visual person, she needed a physical copy in hand. Perhaps it would feel more real that way too. Also, to be certain that it was everything they agreed to. If there was one thing she learned over the last fifteen years, it was that Spence couldn't be trusted. Often, she'd thought about leaving sooner, especially when he got mean. Oddly enough, it was never when Daisy or anyone else was around. At times, Dahlia thought she was going crazy. To everyone else, Spence was this great guy. But she knew better. She also knew Spence would have managed to get sole custody somehow, if Daisy had still been underage when Dahlia left.

She paced, waiting for the three bubbles, only there weren't any. "Shit," she whispered, knowing full well how easily distracted he could get and that it could now be hours before she heard from him again.

The screen door snapped closed. "I'm heading into town. Need anything else? I won't be long," Noah said, shielding his eyes from the sun.

"Light bulbs and wood spackle?" Dahlia called back. "I can grab some cash from inside or Venmo you."

"Nah, don't worry about it." He waved and kept walking.

A few hours later, Dahlia was still in the garden. She'd gotten through most of the raised flower beds. Now she just needed to split some of the perennials, including the violets she'd never gotten back to the day before, and trim back some of the stalky bushes. The scents weaved together like a symphony, creating a sweet, intoxicating aroma, one that reminded her of the childhood before her parents died. She leaned her face back and inhaled the new beginning like it was the very first time.

The cosmos looked wild, growing between the slats of the wooden bench. Her smile grew, and she felt her nose prickle. She laid her soiled gloves on the bench and took a load off, feeling her tacky skin stick to the weathered wood. She should power wash this bench too. Lil would like that. She looked up at the vibrant cloudless sky, then landed on the house's weathered cedar shake siding that once upon a time looked bright and new. Her list was getting longer by the hour, but all she wanted to do was sit and smell the roses. She used to spend hours in this garden as a kid, daydreaming and even taking naps now and then on Gran's old quilt. Dahlia never found tranquility like this anywhere else and could never explain how or why this small slice of heaven could make her feel so weightless, like anything was possible. And now that she remembered, she would never again forget how it felt to be home.

Dahlia closed her eyes and floated away with the breeze. She was taking root in the present when a cold, wet something grazed her thigh. Without opening her eyes, she said, "Harry, is that you?"

He nudged her, dropping a tennis ball at her feet. Dahlia had missed their morning stroll on the beach with Noah's impromptu visit and felt guilty. She leaned forward and felt for the ball to play fetch, but it rolled away.

Harry reached his paw under the bench too. Dahlia laughed. "I got it, bud." With that, she knelt and reached far under the bush, hitting her head as she pulled back up. She noticed an etching on the wood border of the garden bed. It read *RIO* inside a heart shape and looked like someone had carved it with a Swiss Army knife. It was weird; Dahlia knew Lil had never traveled abroad. What did it mean? And who could have carved it? It didn't seem like something her aunt would do. But then again, what did she know about what Lil would do?

"I'm back with the goods," Noah said, strolling toward her, holding a brown bag. "Sorry, I ran into a few friends in town."

"No worries," she said, getting up from the ground, still clutching the ball. "Harry, go get it, boy." She hurled the ball toward the bay.

"Wow, you've got a great arm," Noah said, stepping back.

"Thanks, I was the pitcher of my high school softball team." She could feel her face flush. Dahlia wasn't one to talk about herself. But something about Noah made it all too easy. When you've been in a relationship where you have to stay small to survive, you get used to being invisible.

"You've got dimples." He slowly walked closer with a wide, toothy grin.

Dahlia could feel his energy even though he was still a few feet away. Butterflies danced in her belly. If she didn't know better, she would think he was flirting. "Yup. Just like my mom," she said softly, feeling a tug at her heart.

"So what else do you have to do out here? Want some help?" he asked, setting the bag on the bench.

"Don't you have things to do?" Dahlia asked, eyeing his eagerness that felt youthful. Why was he being so nice?

"Nah. I have to finish a piece I'm bringing to Shelter Island tomorrow and fix your fridge. But I can help here."

"And look at the oven?" Dahlia playfully smiled.

He grinned back. "Of course. Happy to."

Dahlia sensed he wanted company too. "Okay then. You can help dig. Can you grab the pointed shovel in the shed?"

"Your wish is my command," he said, bowing to her. He was funny too—bonus points.

Dahlia explained how much to dig up and how to split the roots. "I couldn't get these up the other day. I kept hitting something." She pointed to the half-wilted violets.

"Got it." He met her hazel eyes.

He had to stop looking at her like that; otherwise, she might have to have a hot girl summer after all. "I'll work on the Montauk daisies over here." She walked to the other raised bed, hearing the pebbles crunch under her sneakers.

"So, want to come by later for a burger? I mean, it is the Fourth," he said, flinging dirt.

She could feel her pulse quicken as she watched him step onto the shovel in his old Timberlands and take command of the earth. Biting her lip, she considered her options. If she went, what would it mean? If she didn't, she could keep going with the list.

"Maybe," she blurted, covering her eyes from the sun.

He wiped the beads of sweat from his forehead. "Okay, I can live with maybe." Noah stabbed the ground again, and this time, she heard a sharp, hollow sound.

"That's it. That's what I hit yesterday." She dropped her shovel and headed over to him. "What is it?"

Just as she got there, he pulled it up. It was an old, rusted coffee can.

Could this be where Lil's key was hidden? "Is there anything inside?"

"Nah, it's empty. Whatever was in there is gone." He shrugged his broad shoulders, flipping the can around. "Wait, there's something written on the bottom."

"May I look?" Before he could answer, she pulled it from his grip. Dahlia wiped the remaining soil from the base. It read "18" in worn black paint. "That's strange. Why would Lil bury an empty coffee can with a random number painted on the bottom?"

Did the number eighteen mean anything to Lil? Dahlia held the rusty, dirty vessel in her hands, memories unfolding like a flower in bloom with no clear answers or resolution in sight. What was Lil trying to tell her?

CHAPTER SEVEN

"This should do it," Noah said, his head in the oven, as he aligned the vent cover on the oven fan. "Can you hand me the screwdriver?"

There was silence. Dahlia was too busy staring at his dirty jeans and how they framed his fit and firm butt perfectly.

"Dimples, you there?" He felt the floor, where he thought he left it.

"Ah, yeah, sorry," Dahlia reached for it on the other side and slipped it into his grip. That was a close call. Harry's panting by the door pretty much summed up how she was feeling inside. However, it wasn't just an attraction. It was a feeling of being helped and looked after. And perhaps she'd needed that more than she realized, especially lately.

"You shouldn't have any more problems with it."

"I don't know how to thank you, Noah." Not only was she grateful, but she was impressed too. Was there anything he couldn't fix? Dahlia couldn't wait to find out. Sure, he was handy, but he also helped her clean. That took his sex appeal to a whole other level. Maybe Lil knew what she was doing after all.

"I do." He poked his head back out with a grin full of mirth. Not only were his jeans dirty, but his face was too. "Come over, let me cook for you."

Why was he being so nice? Did he need a pet project? And really, who in their right mind could resist such an offer? Plus, after all he had done, she couldn't be rude. So three hours later, she found her feet moving across the damp grass that joined the properties with an apple pie she had bought in town. It wasn't as good as the one from Shelter Island that she, Pop, Gran, and Lil would get, but it was a close second. Harry caught up quickly once she neared his back door. Chasing bunnies wasn't more exciting than hamburgers, apparently.

Dahlia lightly knocked on the light aqua door, which was flanked by two large containers of vibrant blue hydrangeas on either side. She took in the aesthetic of the small porch. The modern bench, which hung from the ceiling, was the only piece of furniture aside from the planters. Bruce and Garrett seemed to be more traditional than Lil. If she had to pinpoint their style from the conversations over the years and the minimalist elements of the porch, it would be transitional. They preferred new and tidy, and I'm sure would be appalled by the current state of Lil's. Her head fell back in relief that they were still in Italy. Then she knocked again. This time a little louder. Nothing. It was at this time that she realized Harry was missing, so she wandered to the back.

"Harry, Harry," she whispered in a clipped tone as she followed the path to the back, lined with hostas, daisies, and various hues of echinacea. Her pastel chiffon strapless dress billowed in the breeze, hitting some of the colorful stems as she strolled. Dahlia's smile grew, knowing Daisy would be happy she left the house tonight. But this wasn't for Daisy, it was for her. She has gotten a taste of what it was like to feel something besides despondency, and she wasn't going to squander it by staying home for no good reason.

She ducked under the willow on the other side of the path and lifted her head. She covered her smile, which only grew wider by the second. A person needed preparation for such a sight. Lit string lights framed the small patio, a small vase of flowers and votives anchored the sleek teak table, and two wine glasses finished it off. She cocked an eyebrow at the glasses that made this feel like a date, but she knew it wasn't. It was simply a neighborly get-together. Plus, Noah made it clear from the beginning that he needed a friend, nothing more.

Harry reappeared just as she turned toward the back door. All she could do was shake her head and say, "Stay. I'll only be a minute." Dahlia wanted to set the pie inside so it wouldn't spoil in the heat. Although it had cooled off, the salt air hung motionless, as did the gnats. She swatted a few and stepped up the new mahogany steps. A few more knocks, still no one answered. The door was ajar, so she pushed it open. The blast of air conditioning felt good against her tepid skin. She was still suffering at Lil's with only fans. She really did need to get those units up from the basement. "Noah, it's me, Dahlia."

Still no answer. At this point, she felt like an intruder, so she tiptoed in and set the pie on the sleek white marble surface with veins of brown and gray. That's when she heard singing and the lyrics to "Born in the USA" coming down the hallway. Peeking around the corner, she saw that the bathroom door was ajar. Then the shower abruptly stopped, and her posture straightened, not wanting to make another sound. She remembered Noah telling her Barry and Garrett had removed all the squeaks and creaks when they remodeled, but with her luck, she'd find that one spot. She closed her eyes, pursed her lips, and took one small step away. A shrilling creak came from the floorboards below, and then, "Dimples, is that you?".

"Yup, it's me. Just brought you a pie." Dying inside, she peeked through her fingers. "I'll wait outside." She felt hot and combustible.

Just the mere thought of his naked body on the other side of the door made her pulse gallop.

'No, wait," he said, moving his highly contoured bare form past the open door. That little glimpse was enough to make an unknown sound, something between a groan and a squeal, spill from her lips. With cheeks that felt like an inferno, she debated what to do. She could wait for him outside and cool down. Or she could be a big girl and stay. She knew he didn't want anything romantic, but at the same time, Dahlia no longer felt in control. But maybe that was precisely the point.

She inhaled deeply, leaning against the counter, and said, "I'll be in the kitchen."

Prepared dishes lined the surface. There was corn salad, white bean salad, burrata, and oysters on the half shell. Bottles of rosé and white wine sat next to the elaborate espresso machine, along with an assortment of buns. When did he have time to do all this? A lightness spread over her chest that this was for her.

"There you are." He came out in a towel tucked at his hip, with wet, messy hair. Beads of water dripped from long lashes and every single burly surface. The desire to lick the single bead that trailed down his corded neck was intense. She watched it disappear down his chest and into his sparse area of hair circling his navel. Who was she? What was happening to her?

Harry's bark outside the back door woke her from her lust-filled haze, and she tried to recover. "Yup, here I am." Suddenly, her arms and legs felt awkward, and she didn't know what to do or say next. Words were trapped in her mouth. He scanned the counter, his hand holding his towel up. "I wasn't sure what you liked, so there are a few choices."

"Did you make all this?" Dahlia asked shakily, feeling the heat from his body. He was that close. She looked down and saw that the towel had tented. A possible sign she wasn't alone in these layered feelings. Perhaps he wanted to be more than just friends after all.

"No, my sister had someone drop it off from her restaurant. I have burgers too, as promised." He reached for an oyster with a free hand and slurped it down. All she could think was the word *aphrodisiac.* He did the same for another, then held out one for her. "You've gotta try these, they came from the bay this morning." Their eyes connected in an innocent but seductive way, and that was all she needed to let him feed her. Her lips grazed his finger, and her body zinged like a pinball machine. That small gesture felt so intimate, more so than any moment with Spence. The briny taste flooded her mouth, along with lemon, thyme, and white wine.

"Wow. That's delicious." She covered her mouth as she chewed. "Wait. Isn't her restaurant on the island? That's a hike."

"Yeah, but she's testing new recipes this week and has a ton of food. The caveat is that she wants our honest opinion." He took a tortilla chip from a bowl. "These are handmade too. There's guac in the fridge."

"Cool." She said, hoping he wouldn't feed her again. Although she wanted more, she needed to get her head back on straight. And cool her body down.

After a delicious dinner al fresco and the best burger and conversation she'd had in a long time, they decided to go for a walk on the beach. They cleaned up quickly, putting the food back into the containers and loaded the dishwasher. In just a few short days, this stranger felt more like a partner than the one she had had for the last fifteen years.

They walked the narrow path that connected the two houses down to the water. Noah picked a flower from the many that were growing wild and gently tucked it behind her ear. The sounds were as bright as crickets, and cicadas filled the quiet air. The bay lapping the shore echoed over the beach grass. Notes of jasmine and crustations mingled in the air. Noah led the way, letting her know if there was something for her to watch out for. He hopped to the sand first, holding his hand out for her. Her eyes met his, and she wondered why he was single or seemed to be anyway. She didn't know him all that well, but from what she saw and felt, he was a nurturer who genuinely cared about people.

Noah stopped briefly to cuff his jeans up so he could walk the waterline, and then he did something she never expected. He reached for her hand and slipped his fingers inside hers. Dahlia's heart somersaulted. There were so many firsts she missed being a young mother with an almost nonexistent dating life. This simple gesture felt like the sun, the moon, and the stars rolled into one.

They strolled hand in hand as the sun set behind the row of houses. It was painted in short strokes of bubblegum pink, magenta, and blue, a palette she'd rarely seen at Lil's. They continued their conversation about music and movies from dinner. They both agreed that classic artists like Billy Joel, Sting, and The Boss were the OGs and that movies like *Jerry Maguire* and *Good Will Hunting* would always be relatable. To her amazement, he also knew about *The Notebook*, *How to Lose a Guy in 10 Days,* and *Twilight*. However, the biggest surprise was that he also watched *Dateline*. Then it started to feel more personal when the why behind her summer visit piqued his curiosity.

She started with Lil and how, after her fall, Lil came to live with her in Connecticut. The closeness of their relationship and Gran and Pop came up too. Noah mentioned the history he knew from his uncles about the property and her family that settled there. He was genuinely interested, which tickled something deep inside her. There was no mention of Spence. She didn't know what tonight was, but she wasn't going to ruin it with stories of exes.

There was talk of Lil passing in April, which led her here to sell her house, as well as a highlight reel of the last few days.

"That, in a nutshell, is why I'm here for the summer." Her feet sank into the cold sand.

"Let me get this straight. You need to find a key that could unlock a secret, fix this house, and sell it all while you're here?"

"Yup." She left out the part about moving to Charleston. There was no reason to share. Plus, this was the first real choice that felt like hers since she married Spence. Aside from it scaring the hell out of her, in a good way, it also made her feel like she was finally steering her own ship.

"Yikes. I can see why you've been a bit stressed. And you really have no one here." He kicked the sand. "No one but me, of course."

God, he was charming. She could feel her cheeks ache from an entire night of smiling.

"There it is, that dimple," he said, walking backward. "It's adorable.

The heat traveled to her ears, leaving her unsure what to make of this foreign feeling. On the one hand, she had so much to accomplish, but on the other, she wanted to slow the pace and savor everything. For the first time, she didn't feel left; she felt found. There was still no mention of her old life or his, what they left behind, or what was on the horizon. She and Noah were in a bubble, one of their choosing. Dahlia paused, looking out onto the water and the neighboring island, fading with the setting sun. She wondered if he was holding back and, if so, why. Dahlia hadn't looked him up online again after that first night. She wanted things to unravel with time. And if he wanted her to know, he would tell her.

"You look cold."

"I'm okay." Her insides were warm, but her skin was covered in goosebumps.

"Here, take my flannel. I insist." He said, lifting it from his white T-shirt.

They stopped, and he wrapped it around her petite shoulders; his hand grazed the nape of her neck. Their eyes locked. In his blue orbs, she saw comfort, a sense of ease. Her heart raced like a sprinter about to cross the finish line. A second seemed like an eternity. She felt seen for the first time in her life. This was crazy. She barely knew him, yet there was a kinship here. It was one she could feel but couldn't explain. Not yet anyway.

CHAPTER EIGHT

July 5

The next day, Dahlia biked into town, and the wind carried her into another world. One where she felt things with all of her senses again and wanted to lean into them daringly. Her body was airy as she pedaled past some of her favorite old houses, replaying the events of last night. The aroma of fresh-cut grass and sun-ripened honeysuckles filled the air, and the weekday sounds of landscapers occupied the airwaves. Dahlia forgot how much she loved this place. She lifted her hands from the handlebars and let this new mood carry her. Maybe Kara was right—a summer fling with her handy hunk was just what she needed.

Dahlia's hip buzzed, waking her from her tempting thoughts. It was probably Spence. He always had the worst timing. She stopped her bike along the shoulder and pulled the phone from her side purse. It was Daisy. Her face brightened as she read her text. *Eloise canceled, wasn't feeling well. We rescheduled it for next Sunday. KYP.*

"That's a bummer," Dahlia mumbled, then typed back, *K, love you. Be safe.*

LY2.

Dahlia leaned her face into the warm sun like she was leaning into hope. Her body felt expansive and free. Bit by bit, Monica was disappearing, and Rachel was slowly taking her place. It was apparent her feelings were evolving. But into what? Dahlia still didn't know, and she was okay with that.

She parked her bike outside the five-and-dime, in between the planter and a display of American flags. Dahlia pulled the oil-making list from her pocket and grabbed the sack inside the bike basket, excited to try some of Lil's essential-oil recipes. The bells chimed as she opened the door, along with a waft of cold. She stood there, feeling unhurried. It was a familiar summer sound and smell. As much as the outside world had changed, Southold remained stuck in time. And Dahlia was happy to time travel, even if it was for a short stint.

The list included mason jars with lids, cheesecloth, coconut oil, and vitamin E capsules. She slowly walked the aisles, dropping what she needed into her bag. Lil had some 100-proof vodka, but she'd get witch hazel, just in case. She retrieved a jar from the old metal shelf; it reminded her of the can she and Noah found yesterday. The significance of the number eighteen remained a mystery. She shook her head and tossed it in, along with a few more. Dahlia noticed two girls in their twenties trying on sunglasses at the end of the aisle. The short blonde lifted her chin and asked, "How do I look, darling?" with a Zsa Zsa Gabor accent.

The taller one with a slicked-back pony spun the rack and said, "Marvelous! Hey, you think we'll see Noah Sterling at the vineyard? Page Six said he was spending the summer out here."

"I don't think so. I heard he's still in hiding, grieving Josie."

Dahlia stumbled into the display stand. Josie? And what exactly was he grieving? She still didn't have specifics. After regaining her footing, she walked closer, pretending to look at the vitamins. She gripped the closest plastic container; her eyes focused on the nutritional information while she eavesdropped. She was wildly aware that just last night, she'd wanted him to be the one to tell her about his life, but in that moment, that small detail seemed insignificant.

"She did a number on him, and with that best friend of his. What a total douche. Poor Noah. She was the love of his life."

Dahlia felt her body shrink at the sound of those words. She couldn't compete with the love of his life.

"Yeah, he deserves so much better, but she is gorgeous and a TikTok star with millions of followers, so I'm sure it won't be long before he takes her back. I mean, he always does," the blonde said.

Dahlia's stomach dropped to her feet, and her throat was bone dry. This changed things. There was no reason to feel rocked—no promises had been made beyond house support—yet Dahlia couldn't help but feel duped. Like she was in a bar having the time of her life, and suddenly someone turned on the lights and said, "It's over, folks; go home."

She rushed to pay and rode back to Meadow Lane.

* * *

With Noah gone all day helping his sister with the restaurant, Dahlia took a break from gardening to explore her creativity. Or, as Lil would advise from her bucket list, a "hobby." There was still plenty to do around the house, and the list was growing by the hour, but she needed a break. The anxiety might swallow her whole if she couldn't connect with nature. Plus, she felt connected to the flowers in ways she never had before. She wanted to claim the unspoiled feeling for as long as possible while contemplating this new Noah intel.

It would seem he was emotionally unavailable. And the bit of happiness she felt when she was around him was still in the infancy stage. She could easily let it fly away and be fine. But did she want to? Being alone was something she was used to, even when she'd been married to Spence. Just because she was good at it didn't mean she didn't deserve more.

Dahlia's thoughts continued to meander. *It's good that I know what I'm dealing with*, she thought. The cards were now on the table. She couldn't conceive of competing with someone like Josie, the TikTok star. She gave herself a once-over: Her bare legs were covered in soil and scrapes. She could feel her stale skin and her humid hair curling at the base of her neck. Dahlia had a girl-next-door charm, and many told her she looked like Allie from *The Notebook*, but she couldn't see it.

With the phone in hand, she was tempted to look Josie up. She wanted to know exactly what she was up against. But the majestic English-looking flower beds captured her attention and interrupted her quandary; with that, she set the phone back down again. She needed to focus on the house and herself—things she could control.

Dahlia clipped the blooms exactly where Lil had shown her to, a quarter inch above the leaf, smelling the aromas as she went along. There was a pang of guilt in her chest for not driving out in the spring to prune. But how could she have? She was grieving Lil.

She hummed Miley Cyrus's song "Flowers" as she filled the copper bowl with cuttings she would use for the enfleurage and cut more for a bouquet. It would be nice to have fresh flowers in the house again, and she certainly didn't need a man to buy her any when she had all this outside her door. She looked out over the blanket of colors that reminded her of the inside of a candy shop. Her eyes welled with happy tears.

Dahlia could still hear Lil's sweet voice the day before she died. "Remember, the garden first when you get to my house." She finally understood why Lil had loved gardening as much as she did and how the flowers kept her company.

After dusting off her mucky hands, she grabbed her camera and wandered through the beds. She ran her palms along the blood-orange poppy petals. She would miss this. The reality was setting in, and it was hard to believe she wouldn't be here next year to enjoy it. It was the middle of the day, and the sun was intense. Dandelion fur drifted through the tepid air. The lonesome mourning dove above offered her another element of peace. She took a few botanical photos and then captured a ladybug on an alyssum stem. The strong fragrance grounded her in the moment. She didn't know what she'd do with all the pictures yet, but she wanted to document everything. That much she knew.

The kitchen was muggy when she entered through the back door. With flowers in hand, she filled Gran's blue and white chinoiserie vase with water. Leon had bought it for Lizzie for their fifth wedding anniversary. Gran wasn't the type for lavish gifts; she liked purposeful gifts with style. Whenever she pulled it out from the hutch, never fail, she would retell the story over and over again to anyone who would listen. "When I arrived home, he was there, waiting for me in the kitchen with this vase, a dozen long-stem roses, and chocolates. The card read, *I missed you, mon amour.*"

Dahlia placed the vase on the counter and filled it with blooms. Then she stood back in awe, letting everything else fade away. Her grandparents' love story was something else, like something out of a movie or a good book—the kind of love that happens once in a million. They were lucky to have found that kind of love. Dahlia, on the other hand, not so much. And poor Lil was luckless when it came to men.

"Well, that's enough of that," she mumbled, wiping her moist eyes. It was good to feel something again besides anger and grief. Dahlia reached for the supplies she bought earlier from the store and headed back to the barn.

Harry greeted her halfway, shaking his wet body onto hers. "What is the world? You're covered in sand. Have you been swimming?" Harry panted happily. "Ugh, I need to keep a better eye on you. Come." She marched them into the barn and grabbed the towel from the rusted nail. "This will have to do until I put you in the shower." Dahlia swaddled his head with the towel, making him look like the wolf in Little Red Riding Hood, and laughed.

Dahlia reached for one of Lil's coffee cans from the shelf and filled it with water outside. Why had Lil buried an empty coffee can? Did the aluminum have some miraculous growing property or ward off root rot? God knew some of these plants were decades old, and Dahlia was surprised she wasn't greeted by fungus and aphids. These questions burrowed in her brain. Lil always had such interesting anecdotes. Who knew why, and at this point, it was the least of her concerns.

The water spilled as she walked, staining the wood floor Lil had painted by hand decades ago in a harlequin diamond pattern. "Shoot," she murmured as she set the can on the potting bench. Grabbing the towel from Harry's head, she started wiping, noticing a chunk of wood missing from the corner of one of the floorboards. She ran her index finger over the groove. The chipped piece was lighter than the rest. It wasn't time-worn and looked out of place. She stood and bounced on the wood to see if it was loose. Sure enough, it was. Dahlia ran into her pop's work area for a nail, tempted to open the sliding door and peek at what Noah was working on. "Focus," she said to herself. Pop's rusted-green toolbox was still in the same place. It lay on the shelf under his workbench next to the bucket of random nuts and bolts.

Dahlia held it at eye level, remembering all the times he carried it, saying, "Anything worth doing is worth doing well," in his raspy French accent.

Harry barked.

"Aren't you bossy? I'm getting it." She grabbed a few long finishing nails and a hammer.

Dahlia pounded in the nail so hard she split the wood right up the middle. "Shit," she mumbled, realizing she had just ruined Lil's beautiful paint job. Noah wouldn't have done that, she was convinced. He didn't seem like the impulsive type or the kind of person to rush through things. She was mad that she couldn't handle something as simple as nailing a floorboard. At some point, she'd have to come back to fill the crack and repaint the area, but she didn't have the bandwidth for it now.

Harry just stared at her, panting. "Oh, right, water." She chuckled, finally setting the water back on the floor. Harry lapped it up, and Dahlia watched in reflection. The idea that she could need Noah for more than just house maintenance made her uneasy. Needing people meant the potential of losing them. But first things first, she needed to know exactly what she was getting herself into and who her competition was. Dahlia nuzzled her face into Harry's and breathed in his wet dog flavor. "Maybe we should take a peek at *Hamptons House*."

Harry barked.

Dahlia knew the answers were right at her fingertips; all she had to do was search, but she didn't have the nerve. So she did what any painfully curious person would do, and she stayed busy making essential oils. When she was done, Dahlia took a picture of the mason jars tied with cheesecloth that lined the potting bench. They read *Lavender*, *Gardenia*, *Night Jasmine,* and *Heritage Rose*.

But try as she might, her mind was elsewhere. She would bet money that whatever happened on the show last season was why Noah wasn't filming this year.

* * *

It was hours later. Dahlia sat on the sleeping porch attached to Lil's bedroom with Harry, admiring the bubblegum sky. The air felt cooler than usual as she sipped her chamomile tea. She snapped a photo of the colorful horizon, sank further into the chair, and let out a lengthy sigh. She still had to email the gallery back; she'd taken enough time as it was. The to-dos ran directionless through her mind, like a sailboat without a rudder. What was her priority at this point? She had to find that key, but would she in time? All she really knew was that she couldn't let this job slip through my fingers. And Noah . . . she bit the inside of her cheek. What was the deal with his ex, and was she really that beautiful?

Dahlia couldn't fight her curiosity any longer and searched, "Josie, *Hamptons House*."

She gasped so loudly she was sure the beach walkers below could hear her. Every picture was more stunning than the next. She was curvy but thin with great boobs, dark hair, and angelic features. The girl looked like she never had a pimple, bad hair day, or period bloat. Even without makeup, she was beautiful.

"Ugh!" she yelled in frustration as she slammed the phone onto the side table. The girl next door couldn't compete with that. She was an average divorced mom who still bought her clothes at Old Navy and had no idea who she wanted to be when she grew up. She looked again; this time, Josie was in black leather, looking a bit like a vampire goddess. Dahlia decided she couldn't be much older than Daisy. Another swipe, and this time, it was a picture of both Josie and Noah. They looked happy. They looked perfect together.

Heat rushed through her body, and suddenly, she was angry. Dahlia wondered why a girl like that would ever cheat on a guy like Noah. Although she didn't know him well, she knew enough to know he was one of the good ones.

Her fingers feverishly typed away. "Noah Sterling's age." The air in her body went still; he'd be turning twenty-eight on July 19th. She was *ten years* older than he was. She'd suspected a slight age gap, but this much was mind-blowing. "Oh God, I'm a cougar, Harry." He lifted his head and just sighed. This could never work—gorgeous ex, and now a decade in between them. She had zero chance, not even for a one-night stand. Suddenly, she didn't want to take a romantic leap. She needed to protect her heart, just as she had done most of her life. It was much easier that way. The moon created a sparkly path across the peaceful ripples. What was she so afraid of? That Spence might be right, that she was unlovable? Undesirable? He still hadn't texted back, but Dahlia remained hopeful that he'd do the right thing and send the papers.

Dahlia finally stopped procrastinating and opened her computer to email the Whitmore Gallery. It was the only way forward, so she typed.

Thank you for this opportunity, Christine. I'll be there ready to start on August 5. And with that, she hit send on the next chapter of her life, hearing the paper plane take flight. There was no turning back now. With the start date solidified, she would have to stick to the plan; there was no other choice. Dahlia knew that whatever happened this summer at Lil's was now just a stepping stone toward her next season.

CHAPTER NINE

July 6

Dahlia rolled the white primer onto the bathroom ceiling. Even with the small window open, the odor was strong and noxious. With each motion forward and backward, the yellow stain slowly disappeared. Cold speckles hit her long lashes from above. She couldn't believe it had taken this long to repaint. She chuckled silently, remembering the day fifteen years earlier when Daisy filled the upstairs sink to wash her American Girl dolls.

"Daisy, come on, we're late. Your dad is waiting at the church," Dahlia said, sweating through her white lace dress. She couldn't believe she'd said yes to a church . . . and yes to Spence. But how could she not, after Daisy had made a birthday wish for Spence and Dahlia to get married after he showed up out of the blue? Daisy was so happy, and Dahlia couldn't dash her hopes of having a "real" family. Plus, he was very convincing. He said he'd changed, that he thought about them every day and wanted to be the dad and husband they deserved. More than anything, Dahlia wanted a partnership; she was tired of being alone.

"Mommy, Kaya's not ready," Daisy shouted from the top of the stairs in her sweet little voice.

"Then get her ready and quickly." What if he thinks she's a no-show? Is that a bad thing? Dahlia sat on the Windsor bench and anxiously rubbed the arm. What was she doing? They didn't work then, and what was to say they'd work now? But she had to try for Daisy.

"Coming," said Daisy, running down the stairs with her two dolls tucked under her arm.

"Carefully, we don't need any accidents today," Dahlia said, getting up. "Daisy, you look so pretty and very wet."

"It's okay, Mommy. Don't sweat the small stuff, remember?" Daisy said with her lisp.

"How could I forget? Pop used to say that all the time. Did you turn the water off?" Dahlia asked, holding her hand.

"Of course, silly pants," Daisy said in midskip.

"Okay then, let's go get married, Daisy girl."

What an omen that was. Nothing like a monsoon inside your house on your wedding day to bring you impending doom. She should have known that the dream would be better than the reality. And it most certainly was. It turned out that she and Daisy were mere pawns in his becoming the token family man in a well-crafted plot to take over the family's wealth management business. Once Dahlia found out he'd lied, he treated her like the help. He was indifferent, emotionless, and cold. He was the same person he'd always been. She was told she was ungrateful many times and that any woman would die to be in her position. Who would have thought she'd feel more alone being married?

The old, rusted ladder wiggled as she climbed down. Every stain on the metal marked a project that still seemed relevant.

Dahlia pushed it into the hallway, hearing the plastic feet skid across the floor. Her phone vibrated in her pocket; it was a text from Kara.

Is McHandy over yet?

Dahlia rolled her eyes and typed. *He's working on the porch. Just finished the refrigerator.*

When am I going to get to meet him? How about a quick Face-Time? Kara asked.

God no. Not today. Not any day.

You're crushing my dreams.

Lol. I doubt that. FYI, we're making good progress. And we'll need to continue since I'm now the chief curator at the swankiest gallery in Charleston. Dahlia felt an enormous sense of relief wash over her, knowing she wouldn't have to run any more ridiculous errands or report to her a-hole boss ever again. Now she could focus on the job ahead and find a place to live in Charleston. She wondered if the cute apartment with the great kitchen and period details in the French Quarter was still available from her search before she left.

I'll settle for a pic. Kara's text interrupted Dahlia's panic.

You're incorrigible. Not happening.

Dahlia put her phone away, feeling a rush of anxiety swell through her veins. As soon as she picked the brush back up, she was greeted by loud music outside. "What the . . . ?" she mumbled.

With each step, the song became louder. The lyrics to "Dancing in the Dark" echoed through the window screens. She peeked out the back door. And there it was, Noah karate chopping the air. He also kicked, swayed, and twerked his fine hips to good ol' Bruce. Wow, he really likes him. It was another affirmation of the "old soul" that lived inside him. She could feel the heaviness lift, and all she wanted to do was join the fun-loving guy bobbing around the sawdust dance floor to her dad's favorite song. Her smile extended ear to ear until he spotted her.

"Come join me?" He playfully summoned her with his finger from the back porch.

Lordy. "I'm good," Dahlia yelled back, watching his hips move effortlessly with the rhythm. Her mouth was moist, and her chest fluttered. She couldn't look away.

"Dancing is good for the soul." He continued kicking and punching the air in his dingy baseball hat and a graphic tee while singing into a hammer.

Dahlia smiled, feeling her face blush. She held up the brush covered in white paint, hoping he would stop asking. Not because she didn't want to, but because, deep down, she did. She wanted to feel his body next to hers and dirty dance with him into the sunset. At that moment, she wanted nothing more than to be Baby and him, Johnny.

She filled the cup next to the sink with cold tap water and gulped it as if she had been stranded in the desert for days. The gallery job was the right decision. The only decision.

"Got some for me?" Noah asked, bopping his gorgeous, dirty body through the back door.

"Oh, sure." Her voice pitched embarrassingly high when he grabbed her arm and twirled her. He smelled like rugged goodness, like a cowboy at the end of a long, hard-earned day. Then he pressed her body into his and swayed. She had two choices: go with it or fight it. After taking a beat, she realized he wasn't going to take no for an answer anyway. At least she'd be able to cross something off her summer bucket list.

His eyes were mesmerizing this close, like an ocean you could get lost in. His hold was firm but soft, like in a leading man kind of way. When his stare lingered a little longer, her body began buzzing with a joy unlike she'd ever felt. Then he dipped her, and she let out a sudden squeal.

"And that's why they pay me the big bucks." He laughed, setting her back on her feet.

"Water, right?" She cleared her throat, still reeling from what that was, and poured him a glass.

"Thanks." After three large swigs, it was gone. "How's that working?" He pointed to the cream-colored refrigerator that now had a consistent low hum.

"Great. It's nice not having to pull things from a wet and leaky cooler. And to be able to cook if I want to. Not that I need to make this house any hotter." Did she just say that out loud? She did.

"I'm almost done with the screens. Then I can get up to check out that chimney cap." Noah wiped his 'stache with the back of his hand.

Dahlia gulped; this time, she was sure it was audible. "Are you sure? That's pretty high." Nothing could happen to him. She needed him. And . . . perhaps she wanted him too, despite what she found online.

"Yup, we've got a couple of ladders that will reach the roof." He paused, putting the glass in the sink. "I was thinking. I've got to return to the island tonight to drop off the banquettes. Want to join me?"

She pushed the hair off her face. "I don't know, I have a lot to do here. That long list of mine isn't going to take care of itself."

"Oh, come on. You need a break. There's a great little brewery in town, where I got the beers the other night, and you can meet my sister," he said, heading for the back door.

His *sister*?

"I'll pick you up at, say, four." He smiled confidently.

Who was she kidding? She was no match for his perfectly sculpted jawline, 'stache that made her core feel things it shouldn't, and gorgeous get-lost-for-days eyes. "I guess I can spare a few hours on one condition."

He raised one brow.

"You let me help you with the screens."

"Deal." And with that, he shook her hand, sending tingles up her spine.

* * *

Dahlia heard the pebbles crunch from inside the entryway. It was exactly four.

He was on time, and she was impressed.

Dahlia hadn't been on a first date, if you could call it that, in . . . seventeen years. It felt strange to go on a date now but oddly comfortable. Although she had only known Noah for a few days, it felt like a lifetime.

Right after Noah left, she made an emergency FaceTime call to Kara. Kara was driving, so she pulled over until they found the right outfit. One that said, "Hey, look at me," without trying too hard. After all, this wasn't a date; it was a last-minute afternoon brewery trip. Which also screamed casual. It was decided that the short, strappy cream-colored floral dress would be best. Kara tried to convince her to pair it with her slip-on Birkenstocks, but gold flip-flops felt more fitting with the dress.

She pulled up Noah in her contacts, which she'd added the other day. *I'll be right out*, Dahlia typed with raw fingertips. All that pinching and pulling of rough metal to get the screens tight enough was hard work. But she was happy to help. It felt like they were a team to some degree, and that the possibilities of their working relationship were endless.

"Harry, you be good while I am gone." She lowered his bowl of kibble and sliced chicken. "Who has it better than you?"

He just moaned.

Dahlia slid a fireplace screen found in the basement in front of the fireplace opening and anchored it with a basket of wood. The last thing she wanted was more squirrel guests.

She took one last look at herself in the mirror. Her lips were a matte pink that felt like summer, and her hair curled in big, flowy waves. Her lashes were painted with a thin layer of mascara, and a light dusting of bronzer highlighted the high cheekbones she inherited from her mother. She always wanted to feel as pretty as her mother, and in this moment, she did. She tucked a blonde curl behind her left ear and let out a lengthy sigh. All she had to do was be herself and have a good time. If it were only that easy.

Dahlia closed the thick door behind her and walked toward the old, rusted mustard truck, feeling a bounce in her step. Noah had already gotten out like a gentleman and was leaning against it. He had on navy cargo shorts, a white shirt that complemented his tan, and his Timberland boots. His hair was wet and slicked back, and there was something in his hand. Upon further inspection, it was a single Montauk daisy.

"You look . . ." Noah was at a loss for words as he closed the gap between them. "Incredible." He held out his hand for her to twirl, and she obliged.

She was on a cloud with cartoon hearts in her eyes.

"Oh, I almost forgot. This is for you."

"For me, wow." She took the stem from his grip casually, as if it were no big deal, when inside she was a gooey mess. He was thoughtful, and little by little, all the reasons why she shouldn't give this a chance were fading away. And more and more, this was starting to feel like a date. "You clean up nice too," Dahlia said, noticing he'd shaven some of his scruff. "I'm glad you kept the 'stache."

His eyes sparkled. "You like it?"

"I do." She smiled. He reminded her of a young Magnum P. I., another classic show she'd watched with Gran and Lil.

Noah opened the passenger side door for her.

"Thanks," she said, climbing into the truck, feeling her dress stick to the taped pleather seat. Chivalry wasn't dead after all.

He hopped in and closed the door. "So, you ready for a great night?"

"Yes," she said with enthusiasm, meeting his assuring glance. A thousand butterflies released inside her. She was warming up to this idea of a no-strings-attached summer fling, but that's all it could be, as much as she liked him. She had plans, and no boy would stand in her way. Not this time.

CHAPTER TEN

Dahlia glanced at Noah as he casually hung his left arm over the peeling steering wheel, his elbow permanently fixed to the window frame. The cool breeze caressed Dahlia's hot summer skin. She leaned her head against the door, feeling content. For so long, Dahlia had tried to anticipate Spence's moods. Surviving her marriage had meant being hypervigilant at all times, which left zero room for inner peace. The worst was when he drank. He knew how to hit below the belt. Things no woman wants to hear, like "I was never attracted to you, get a personality." And the cherry on the sundae was "You'd have nothing if it weren't for me." But now she was never more ready to welcome a new season and a new sense of self in her life.

"You smell really nice. Like . . . gardenia and coriander," Noah said softly.

"Well, thank you." She laughed, feeling utterly weightless. "I'm impressed. Are you daylighting as a perfumier or something?"

"No, I just have a good nose," he said, driving down tree-lined Main Street.

"You certainly do. Full of surprises," she muttered.

"I'm excited you said yes." He glanced her way.

"Me too."

He cleared his throat. "I have to say I was a little nervous to ask."

"Why?" she asked playfully, in shock by his confession. How could *she* make *him* nervous? He was the one on a reality show and who'd dated a supermodel vixen who defied all laws of science.

"Well, you seem to have your shit together." He smiled.

Dahlia coughed. If he only knew. "You think?"

"And look at you. You're beautiful. Way too pretty for this mountain man." He pointed to himself.

"Not so." She laughed.

Then he added. "In a girl next door kind of way."

"Oh." Her voice sank with disappointment.

"No, it's a good thing." His grin widened. "A perfect thing. And you're down to earth, which is a bonus."

"Thanks, I think," Dahlia said, gripping the door handle and feeling the moisture under her palm. She was nervous too, but how could she not be? A boy was noticing her, and she felt sixteen again.

"So tell me about you. I still don't know much besides the basics," he probed.

"Well, what do you want to know?" Dahlia tilted her head.

"Are you single?"

"Wow, getting right to it," she said. "Yes, I am. Are you?"

"Yes," he boldly declared.

"That was quick." She let out a lighthearted chuckle, looking straight ahead. She hoped the interrogation wouldn't include her age or children. Right now, she just wanted to be a girl sitting next to a boy in a truck, savoring every single second of this new situationship.

"Have you ever been married?" he asked.

She swallowed and nodded. "Yes."

"Oh." He paused while he waited for the light.

Maybe that was the wrong answer, but it was the truth. And the only truth she was willing to share. If he was scared off, then so be it.

"For how long?" Noah's forehead wrinkled.

"Too long." Her eyes widened. "You?"

"Engaged, not married. But that was . . ." He gave a hard swallow. "It's water under the bridge."

Now she really wanted to know what went down last year.

"Why did you break up?" he asked, then shook his head quickly. "Sorry, is that too personal?"

"No, it's okay." Dahlia fiddled with her purse strap. The truth was, she secretly wanted to talk about it. The more she spoke about it, the less power the memories had. "It's complicated, but short version: He never appreciated me, and I got tired of being a doormat. Sorry if that's a bit much for a first . . ." Dahlia stopped herself.

He reached for her hand and looked at her with soulful eyes. "I get it. More than you could possibly know."

Dahlia lost her ability to think straight. His hand was firm and comforting as his calluses skimmed her skin. It felt nice to be touched, and she knew in that instant that she wanted more. More of his hard-working hands, more of his expressive eyes and charismatic smile, but she quickly reminded herself that it couldn't be anything beyond friends with benefits. If he even wanted that. What did she know about what guys wanted? She was so out of practice.

"Geez, I almost forgot." He dropped her hand and did a U-turn. "Hey, do you mind if we stop at the hardware store? I have to grab a few gallons of paint for my sister."

Dahlia smiled, hoping maybe he'd gotten lost in that moment too.

Noah turned into the parking lot and up to the double doors. He turned off the truck and got out.

"You can wait here if you want. Just don't let anyone steal her." He chuckled, tapping on the door.

"Her?"

"Yeah, Bertha." Noah leaned his head back in the window. He named his cars too. Why did he have to be so likable? "She's been with me since high school."

Now Dahlia swallowed hard, repeating the words *high school* in her mind. Those two words made her feel like she was really robbing the cradle. Dahlia's high school days were so far removed from her mind that it was like it was another lifetime ago.

"Through the best and worst of it," he said with a gleam in his eye.

Then, for the briefest of moments, she wondered what it would have looked like if she had gone to high school with someone like him. Maybe she wouldn't have fallen for a guy like Spence. It was silly to think about, but Dahlia's parents' deaths lifted the roots on her life like a tree uprooted in a storm. It blocked the path to any normalcy ahead, flying past all those typical, rite-of-passage experiences.

Shaking herself from the inconceivable thought, she said, "I'll come." Dahlia pushed open her door with gusto as if she was finally ready to face the memory at the hardware store that had haunted her for years.

Crossing the threshold of the entrance, it wasn't so much that it still hurt. It was that she felt stupid for accepting the bare minimum for so long when she knew she deserved better.

"I'll just be a minute. Hopefully, the paint is ready," he said, walking left.

"Okay, I might need a few things as well." Dahlia forced her feet to move to the right.

"I'll meet you back here in five," he yelled.

Dahlia wandered down the filter aisle, which led to the plumbing section. She stalled, picking up the copper fittings that caught her eye, and willed her mind to focus on something easy, like a fun DIY project. But the flood of memories—painful memories of being in that exact store—came rushing forward anyway. Even though her mind raced, her feet were fixed. She couldn't decide whether to turn around or keep going.

It was now or never. She forced herself to face that last thing tethering her to anger. Rounding the corner, she exhaled. It felt like an avalanche all over again as she drifted to the day two years earlier when she realized nothing she did would ever be enough for Spence.

Dahlia froze, recalling Spence playfully laughing with someone on the phone while he shuffled his feet along the linoleum. He was acting like a schoolboy with a crush, the way he had when they'd first met. Coy and charming, his eyes were wide, and his smile wider.

Dahlia inched closer, pretending to inspect the assortment of contact paper. Even from afar, she could tell he wasn't on the phone with a buddy or someone from work. Within seconds, the conversation turned. His tone became louder and more defensive. "You *know* I want to see you. If I could, I would leave tonight, but I can't. My daughter's here for the weekend." His brows furrowed as he listened. "Tell me how to make it better. I'll do anything."

Dahlia tried to calm her racing heart. How could he do this? They'd never had a good marriage, but Dahlia had tried to make it work for her daughter, all while taking the scraps he gave her. How could she not have known? Was this the first time, or had there been others? Dahlia walked away. On the inside, she felt like she'd been hit by a Mack truck, but on the outside, she remained as composed as she could. He was powerful, and if she wanted out, she would have to play the game like a hand of poker.

"There you are. I just got a call from work; it's an emergency. I have to leave," Spence said with an intense look.

"What? You and Daisy are running that race tomorrow on Shelter Island." Dahlia stood there, empty and vacant. She was good at pretending; she had done it for most of her married life for Daisy. But this time was different. This time, the pretending was for self-preservation.

"What do you want me to say? Duty calls." Spence snickered.

Dahlia glared at him, trying to play it cool. This was about Daisy. It was always about Daisy. "She's going to be so disappointed. She got T-shirts made for you two."

"Oh, don't be so dramatic," Spence said in his cutting, demeaning tone. "She's eighteen, not ten." And he walked away.

"There you are," Noah said, waking Dahlia from the moment that had given her the courage to want more. "Are you okay?"

Dahlia blinked; her eyes burned despite the years that had passed. Reliving the memory still stung. No one is ever prepared for that kind of blatant deception. It forever alters your ability to trust. Yet here she was, trusting a man she'd just met. Was she crazy, or was this something that made perfect sense?

Dahlia stood there staring into the cosmos, trying to feel something—hurt, pain, discomfort, grief—but nothing. From the moment she said, "I do," Dahlia had known Spence wasn't the right person for her. But it hadn't occurred to her that he would cheat. After being blindsided that day, she vowed to always demand more for herself and rely on her instincts.

She smiled. "Yeah, never better."

* * *

The drive to the ferry was peaceful, precisely what she needed after the flashback at the hardware store, which had felt like an exorcism of sorts. Noah talked about his sister's culinary accomplishments and how she'd been a finalist on *Elite Chef.* And how, as kids, they baked, grilled, and roasted together to mute the noise of a toxic and dysfunctional household. Dahlia wanted to reciprocate and share more about her early years, but she wasn't ready. Instead, she fixed on the fact that two siblings were part of the reality TV world.

"So, reality TV, huh. You and your sister, that's interesting." She planned to wait, but this was a great segue into finding out more.

A wide, toothy grin emerged. "Have you seen the show?'

"Which one?"

"Mine." He laughed, driving onto the ferry.

"No, I haven't, but it sounds fun. A home renovation show with young, beautiful singles."

"Fun for some, I suppose." He let out a long sigh. "But yes, pretty crazy that we both ended up on reality shows. Honestly, it was a coincidence. Though, looking back, I suppose we were both in search of something."

Dahlia turned to face him. "How did you even land it?"

"There was a casting call in Denver, and a friend had convinced me to go, since I had a construction background." He glanced her way, but it lacked the typical warmth. It was obvious it was a touchy subject. "That was five years ago."

Dahlia was sure it didn't hurt that he was easy on the eyes. She also wondered about the friend and if it was her. And that was that—no mention of his ex, what happened, or if he'd go back. And Dahlia didn't push. In many ways, he was like her. She had to feel comfortable before she shared the deeper layers of herself. And that came from building trust. So, for now, she'd let it go.

Noah jumped out and watched the approaching coastline from the edge of the ferry boat. Dahlia snapped a few more pictures, feeling one with the quintessential summer day. The brief ride gave her a chance to appreciate his backside, which, no surprise, still looked mighty firm. She also noticed a tattoo on his calf, just above the line of his boots, that she hadn't seen before. It was a paw print, most likely of his dog, Nemo. She felt herself staring, her brows furrowed at this complicated yet kind and rugged man. She wondered how anyone couldn't appreciate him. He turned around and so did she, pretending to look for something in her purse.

"You ready?" Noah asked, jumping into his truck. "You're going to love Gretchen."

"I have no doubt." She meant it. Anyone who was related to Noah had to be just as kind and genuine.

"Just whatever you do, don't ask about her love life."

"Oh, I wouldn't." Dahlia pulled back. "I would never. But now you have to spill."

"Well, in a nutshell. Her ex left her after COVID when she decided she wanted to live out here permanently. Sophie returned to the city with their dog, and my sister stayed. She was crushed. She still is. A little bitter too."

Dahlia fidgeted with her dress. She knew a thing or two about being bitter. "The woes of unrequited love."

"Tell me about it. The sad thing is, they still love each other, but Sophie loves the excitement of the city more." He tsked. "They just weren't in the same place in life."

"Timing. It's everything." Dahlia paused, watching him command the wheel. She thought about all the unhappily ever afters, hers being one of them. As guarded as Dahlia was, she was hopeful for the first time in what felt like an eternity. The gate to her garden was unlatched, so to speak, and it was anyone's guess how far it could open.

"Isn't that the truth?" His glance lingered on hers, making the tiny hairs on the back of her neck stand straight up.

They drove off the ferry up the hill, passing the line of cars waiting for the next ferry. The smell of diesel eased into notes of sunblock and low tide. The tennis courts and park were both vacant. The ideal beach day had come to a close, and it was the interlude before dinner. Dahlia leaned her whole head out the window and gazed at the beautifully maintained gingerbread-style houses, each one prettier than the last.

Noah turned down a narrow street, barely wide enough for his truck, and stopped in front of the quaintest front porch she'd ever seen. It had hand-carved tulip-like railings and a bright blue ceiling.

"What's this?" Dahlia asked with eagerness.

"I want you to hear something." He turned to her. "Close your eyes."

The way he whispered it made her heart skip. "Okay."

"And listen."

Melodic sounds mingled with the sweet evening air. Dahlia didn't know where the music was coming from, but she would know that song anywhere. Her grin widened as she soaked in the full package of summer flavors. "I know this one; it's 'Je Cherche un Homme,'" Dahlia said in her very rusty French accent. "My grandparents would dance to this all the time. Especially on Sundays while Gran made her famous roast," she said with an unfocused gaze. "They were adorable."

"That's sweet. What's the translation?"

Dahlia could feel her cheeks grow ruddier by the nanosecond. She pursed her lips together and said, "I Want a Man." Hoping to change the subject, she leaned toward him and looked out his window, "Is anyone out there? On the porch, I mean?" She turned to him; his eyes were the color of the Caribbean, and tiny chestnut whiskers sparkled in his mustache. She could feel his breath, and the pulse in her neck beat wildly. Dahlia wondered at that moment what it would feel like to kiss his cowboy mouth.

He smiled, looking right into her soul. "No, no one is out there."

She pulled back, claiming her seat beside him.

"That's the best part. Around this time, every night in the summer, the owner plays jazz. It's like it's for everyone else's enjoyment."

Old houses and now this? Where had this man been hiding all this time?

"I just wanted to show you. Now, off to the restaurant," Noah said, pulling the lever into drive.

"I'm glad you did." She smiled, gazing at his perfect profile. Being with Noah was like a chance to relive her twenties. Her twenties lost to motherhood, sleepless nights, diapers, worry, and all-consuming, unconditional love for another tiny human—so much so that it was all a great big blur.

They drove two more blocks into the small town center and parked in front of an old yellow cottage with an expansive front porch.

"We're here," he said, pushing down the parking brake. "The next big farm-to-table restaurant on the North Fork."

"This is adorable," she said, her hand going to her heart. "What's it called?'

"The Hive."

"Perfect," she said.

"Let's go in. I can come back out later for the banquettes. I want you to meet Gretchen."

It felt like a big deal for him to want her to meet his sister, especially when they barely knew each other. Dahlia followed him up the staircase, feeling like she might trip. She was high on Noah and all of the beautiful things he was opening her eyes to.

"Hey, is anyone home?" he called, walking past the mismatched tables and chairs, which gave an eclectic and artsy vibe.

Dahlia grinned, running her hands over the ironwork. This place was right up Lil's alley, and she would have swooned over every last detail.

"You're here! Finally!" A tall woman with long auburn hair, overalls, and Doc Martens emerged from the back.

At first glance, Gretchen was cooler than Dahlia expected. Dahlia jammed her hands in her pockets, not feeling artsy enough. Style-wise, Dahlia was sandwiched between the creatives and academics. Never really knowing where she fit in.

"What took so long? I was about to close shop and go home." She gave Noah a long hug and looked directly at Dahlia. "And who's this?"

"Dahlia. I'm his neighbor for the summer. It's so nice to meet you."

"I know. He told me all about you." Gretchen gave a weak smile.

"Oh." Her voice peaked. She couldn't help but wonder what he'd told her, but then remembered the barbecue. "The food was amazing the other night, thank you."

"I'm glad you liked it."

They exchanged pleasantries and a few jokes at Noah's expense. Dahlia could tell they were close by their playful banter. She looked on fondly, remembering the painful nights after her parents died, staring at the shadows on the wall, wishing she had a sibling to ease the loneliness and pain.

"Have you seen what my brother can build?" Gretchen asked.

"A little." Dahlia shrunk, realizing she'd been so consumed with herself and Lil's house.

"Well, take a look at the hutch he built for my pantry." Gretchen walked through the door into a narrow alley.

"Wait, you built this?" Dahlia said, running her hands over the smooth finish. It was just one more quality to admire. After being with the least handy person alive for fifteen years, Noah was a breath of fresh air. Dahlia ogled him, feeling the air in her lungs stall, waiting for his reply.

"Guilty." He shrugged.

"He tried to match it to the period of the house with some craftsman details," Gretchen boasted.

"The carvings in the doors, very arts and crafts, and the color. This peacock blue is delicious." Dahlia giggled. "Sorry, how I think of color is probably how you think of food."

Gretchen nodded without acknowledging that Dahlia was trying to find commonality.

Gretchen was a tough customer. Dahlia didn't think she was going to score any brownie points today, but that was okay. She understood childhood trauma and how one's armor can thicken.

"I'll grab one of the guys next door and bring these pieces in. We're trying to get to the brewery before it closes," Noah said, like he was now in a rush.

His sister looked at Dahlia and then at him with folded arms, like she wasn't sure about this.

Dahlia's mouth was dry. Suddenly, she felt like she was about to be interrogated.

Once Noah had left the room, Gretchen paced around Dahlia. "You seem like a nice girl."

Dahlia wasn't a girl. She was a woman—a mother.

"But my brother is very fragile right now. I don't need anyone messing with his heart." She stopped and glared at Dahlia.

"I assure you we're just friends." Dahlia tried not to stutter.

Gretchen snickered. "Oh, honey. I know my brother, and he likes you. But there are things you need to know."

Dahlia leaned in closer, as if to say, *I'm listening.* The truth was, she wanted her to spill the tea before he came back. Deep down, she was dying to know what had happened with his ex.

"You probably know this already, but his last girlfriend broke his heart on national television. It was awful, the poor guy. Since then, he's just been out here building his heart away to distract from the pain and humiliation."

Dahlia could feel her creases deepen by the second.

"Oh, you don't know?" Gretchen's head drew back. "You must have seen *Hamptons House*. The reality show that films in Southampton? It's like *Grey Gardens* meets HGTV meets *Love Island*."

"I don't know much about it, but there has been chatter in the town." Dahlia shrugged, letting her continue.

"Well, at the end of last summer, he walked in on his best friend having, you know, having sex with Josie," Gretchen said, shaking her head.

Dahlia's heart plummeted to her feet, realizing that was why he'd been so distant at first. "What a bitch," Dahlia blurted and quickly covered her mouth.

But Gretchen just nodded. "Damn straight. Josie the Hosie is what I like to call her."

They laughed, and Dahlia let out a sigh. The moment of connection was quickly followed by "Anyway, if you break my brother's heart, I'll kill you."

A short time after Dahlia assured Gretchen she had no ill intentions with Noah, she found herself sitting on a picnic bench waiting for him to return with beers. She tapped her fingers against the splintery surface, feeling a cool waft of air glide across her face. It hung just beneath the willow branches and brought with it an earthy aroma that made her pause to soak in the goodness of Mother Nature.

"Whatcha thinking about, Dimples?" Noah placed a beer-filled glass in front of her.

Dahlia shuddered in surprise. This wasn't the first time he'd used this term of endearment, but she still wasn't used to it. It was cute, maybe not for a thirty-eight-year-old, but she'd take that over *crazy* or *bitch* any day.

Before she could answer, he said, "It's like time stands still here."

"I was just thinking that." Her eyes felt wide. How could he read her mind like that? It was like they were riding the same wavelength.

"You'll like this." He nodded at the beer and tucked his long, thick legs into the picnic table. "The guy said it's light and refreshing."

Dahlia took a long sip, feeling the froth linger on her lip. "It's citrusy; I like it."

"Good," he said, pointing to her mouth.

"Oh, thanks." She licked the foam off her lips. "What did you get?" Dahlia peeked at his glass.

"A pilsner," he said, taking a manly swig. He, too, had froth that lingered. Unlike him, she liked looking at it. At another time and place, she'd be that girl who climbed on top of him and kissed it off. But not today. Dahlia kindly pointed to his creamy 'stache.

He laughed and wiped it off. "So, what did you think of my sister's place?"

"It has a great vibe," she said eagerly. "I have no doubt from what you've shared that her culinary skills will be a hit, especially on the island."

"And my sister?" Noah asked.

"She loves you so much. That's evident." Dahlia got quiet, missing her cousin Kara. She was the closest thing she had to a sister.

"Yeah, she does. She's a protective mama bear, that's for sure." Noah let out a long breath.

"That's a good thing, Noah," Dahlia said with conviction. "You're lucky."

"Do you have any siblings?" he asked.

"Nope, just me."

"Your parents? You haven't mentioned them."

Dahlia stared into space, unsure if this was the right time to share, but there was a comfort level with Noah. It was something she hadn't felt with Spence. Even after being married to him for fifteen years, their life together had been one-dimensional. She didn't have to bend herself inside out or pretend to be someone else with Noah. She was enough just the way she was, and that made her feel connected to him in unexplainable ways.

She drew in the humid, earthy air and said, "Well, my mother was an art historian. That's why I went into gallery work, I suppose." She lifted her shoulders. "She was beautiful. My dad said she had Bo Derek's looks and Goldie Hawn's wit. She never took herself too seriously, which is a rare combination these days."

"I don't think so," he said, meeting her with a tender glance.

"And my dad was a professor at MIT. He was tall, thin, and had a great smile. He was a little tough on me at times, but definitely the fun parent growing up." Dahlia's nose began to tingle as her smile widened. "There was this one summer at Lil's. The ice cream truck came to the edge of the property late. I thought my Gran was going to call the cops the way she was yelling. We chased it all the way down the road on our bikes. We could barely see, but we laughed the whole way." Dahlia let out a lighthearted giggle. "That vanilla soft serve melted quicker than we could eat it. By the time we got home, it was everywhere, even in my hair."

"Sounds like a great memory." Noah laughed. "A man after my own heart. And your mom?"

"I just remember always trying to emulate her. She was literally good at everything," Dahlia said with a shallow sigh. "Good at her job, good at making me feel heard and valued, good at gardening, baking, and being a wife. You name it, she found a way to master it with such ease." She could feel her face turn beet red.

"What happened to them?" he asked as his brows drew together.

She inhaled. "My parents were killed by a drunk driver when I was thirteen. They didn't even make it to the hospital." A shiver ran down her spine. Not many people knew about that part of her life. To her, it needed heavy guarding because it was so layered and painful. Spence had often become dismissive when Dahlia would bring it up, almost as if he were jealous and didn't want her to get attention for having a sad story.

"Oh, I'm sorry." His tone lowered.

"No, it was eons ago. I've cried an ocean, grieved like I was the only kid to lose her parents, and then moved on. I'm not sad about it anymore, not really."

"My real dad passed away last year, but we weren't close." His voice cracked. "I never had that kind of admiration for my parents. My stepdad, though, he's the real deal."

"I'm sorry too." Dahlia wanted to sit beside him and wrap her arms around him. She wanted him to know she understood heartbreak and the searing pain that came along with it.

He lifted his shoulders. "My biological dad left when I was little."

"Still. That had to be hard." Dahlia leaned closer. "And your mom?"

"She passed away when I was young."

"Oh, Noah." Their childhoods felt parallel in many ways. "How?"

He stared down at his hands wrapped around his beer.

"Gosh, I'm sorry. Please don't feel like you have to answer that."

"It's okay." He wiped his eyes. "Ahh, it's been so long. Not sure why it still gets me."

She slid her hand over his. "Because some wounds are harder to heal than others. Maybe you can tell me another time."

Noah nodded. "Fair enough."

"Let's change the mood and make a toast." Dahlia held up her glass. "Here's to unexpected friendships and a summer of our making."

"Cheers," he said with a hopeful tone. "And to leaving the past behind us."

As they clanked glasses and linked eyes, she wondered what part of his past he was referring to.

CHAPTER ELEVEN

July 7

Dahlia woke up smiling under the bed sheet. The sun poured in, drenching the space in light. The covers were warm even though the room was still a bit cool from the brisk wind the night before. She bit her lip, thinking about the gorgeous rainbow-colored sunset they'd shared after the brewery. And how, in one look, he'd shattered her armor. She knew she needed to get up and make coffee if she had any hope of making a dent in the lengthy to-do list today. These things weren't going to fix themselves, but she couldn't peel herself from the bed and the urge to have a lazy morning. Suddenly, a claw appeared on her leg. "Harry, is that you? Or have we been invaded by zombies?" She laughed, yanking the sheet off her head. There was no denying it: Dahlia Newberry was in a good mood. A great mood!

She brushed the hair from her eyes and turned to face the wall. Harry came over and licked her face, her cue to get up and take him out. She wiped the slobber from her face. "Ugh, one more minute." The morning rays highlighted the imperfections in the pine planks. Dahlia's eyes traveled to the charcoal sketch on the nearby wall; it was a barn in the middle of a cornfield. That wasn't their barn, and it wasn't Lil's piece. It was most likely the work of one of her students. Dahlia lay there staring at it, not understanding why Lil never hung any of her own paintings on the wall.

Just as Dahlia's lids dropped again, she heard a loud knock at the front door. Noah always knocked at the back door. So, who would be showing up this early at her front door?

Immediately, Harry started barking. She threw on her cotton robe as he leaped by the door like a kangaroo. She ran down the staircase and peeked through the dusty sheers. "What?!" she squealed, not able to open the door fast enough. "Are you kidding me? What are you doing here?" Dahlia threw her arms around the dark-haired beauty standing on her porch while Harry followed suit. "I can't believe it," she said, holding her palm to her forehead.

"Are you surprised? I wanted to surprise you. Hi, boy." Kara gave Harry a scratch as he slipped between her legs.

"Yes, don't I look it?" Dahlia could feel her entire body shudder with excitement. "Come in, come in," Dahlia said, looking for Harry, who was most likely on his way to Noah's.

"What on earth are you doing here?" Dahlia asked Kara, her heart overflowing with joy.

"We have a big bash tonight in the Hamptons, but I wanted to see my favorite cousin first. Tony went ahead. I'll meet him later in Amagansett."

"I'm so glad you did." Dahlia looked past her. "Where are the boys?"

"With my mom. She says hello, by the way."

"Oh yeah, hi to her too." Dahlia's posture recoiled. Ever since she found out she was pregnant with Daisy, her Aunt Cathy wanted little to do with her. It was as if Dahlia had been abandoned all over again—this time for bringing shame to their perfect family.

"So where is he?" Kara asked, ogling the joint.

"Who?"

"McHandy," Kara declared. "I didn't interrupt anything, like a sleepover from last night, did I?"

"What? God, no!" Dahlia exclaimed with wide eyes.

"Honey, look at you. You need me."

"What? Do I look that bad?"

"No, you're naturally pretty, hon. And it always pissed me off because I work so hard to look this way." Her eyes narrowed as she pointed to her face. The truth was, Kara always turned the heads and got the guy, with or without makeup. Dahlia was the understated one who never believed a guy like Spence would be attracted to a plain Jane studyholic like herself. And apparently she was right.

Kara continued, "But you need me to remind you of how amazing you are. That's why I came to give you a little in-person pep talk," she said, walking through the tight hallway. "It still has that old smell you like." She chuckled. "I'll never, for the life of me, understand why you like that smell."

"Because it reminds me of the past, the good old days." Dahlia felt her breath hitch, missing the people in the good old days.

"If you say so," Kara smirked.

Dahlia led her into the kitchen. "Coffee?"

"I'd love a cup. Ferry coffee is gross, and I didn't have time to stop for my morning Chai."

"You poor thing. No Starbucks, huh?"

"It was too crowded, and I was anxious to see you. God, I've missed you!" Kara said, giving her a side hug. "I miss having you in the next town."

"I miss it too. So, how was your Fourth of July party?" Dahlia asked, plugging in the percolator. "It will just be a few minutes."

"Fun. Oh, Tony's work friend was asking about you."

"Oh? Who?" Dahlia's posture perked.

"Simon, the tall British guy with the unusually nice smile."

"He was?" Dahlia's mouth hung open.

"Yup, he found out about you and Spence. And as a matter of fact, he's going to that party tonight. I don't know why I didn't think of this sooner. You'll come. It will be perfect; you can make McHandy jealous."

Dahlia grew quiet. She felt her forehead wrinkle. She wondered if Kara could sense her hesitation.

"Just think about it. You can decide later."

"I don't know, Kara. I have so much to do, and I'm starting to get stressed. But it does sound fun."

"Okay, what are you stressed about? Tell Doctor Kara."

"What am I not stressed about? Getting the house in tip-top shape, finding the key before I leave . . . oh, and that job, they want me to start in less than a month. And I have to buy a whole new wardrobe."

"And you told them you needed more time, right?" Kara leaned in and stared at her with wide eyes.

Dahlia shook her head and pursed her lips. The smell of fresh ground coffee permeated through the air, giving her a good reason to get the cups ready.

"Dahlia, you do know how insane this is?"

"I know, but I thought I'd lose it if I asked for more time. And I need this job and a change of scenery." Dahlia knew she'd die a slow death if she didn't find a new sense of purpose after Lil's passing and her divorce.

"At some point, you might have to stop running and actually let people in."

Dahlia's cheeks grew warm. What did Kara know? Her life was privileged and perfect. "I'm not running. And I do let people in. Plus, Daisy is there, and Charleston is an amazing place to start over. That city has always felt like a second home."

"I just mean that there are people here who love you. Maybe give them a chance."

Like who? Essentially, there was no one left. "I know, Kara."

"Don't kill me for asking this, but do you even like gallery work? You were miserable at MoMA."

"What? Of course I do. I had a cheating husband, a dying aunt, and a monster of a boss," Dahlia declared, feeling her entire body now stiffen.

"Or is it more because it's your connection to your mom? Maybe even Lil too?" Kara asked delicately, inching closer.

"Kara, that's not fair." But could she be right? No, Dahlia loved her job. Then why was she so unhappy there? Her eyes pinched shut as she remembered she still had to tell MoMA she wasn't coming back in the fall.

"If I can't be the one to challenge you with these things, then who? This is your opportunity to figure out what *you* want. You'll never get this chance again. Don't get me wrong, I'm crazy proud of you, especially for leaving, but I don't want you to feel rushed or influenced. You deserve for this next chapter to be epic." Kara smiled, holding her hand. "Please don't be mad at me. I love you, and I'm coming from a good place. Plus, you can't be too mad at me because I'm here to help you today, whatever you need. I am your hired help until four," Kara said with unwavering eye contact, clearly trying to reassure Dahlia.

"I'm not mad. I could never be mad at you. You're like a sister in every way that matters," Dahlia said. She wasn't alone; she had Kara on her side, and that was everything. The problem was that

Kara didn't fully understand the stakes and how complicated it was for her.

"And sisters tell each other the truth. Right?" Kara asked.

"Right. But I'm not changing my plan. I don't belong here beyond the summer, Kara." Dahlia knew she didn't belong there without her family. It would be too lonely. It would be unbearable.

"We'll see," Kara shrugged. "Now, where's my coffee? I have a feeling I'm going to need it for what's ahead."

* * *

After hours of mulching and trimming in the front flower beds and catching up about Noah, Dahlia and Kara took a break. They retired from the blazing midday heat to Lil's studio with their ice-cold lemonades. Dahlia checked on her oils in the cupboard, and Kara poked around the rustic space. The wood creaked with every step, and a flowery medley was starting to overtake the scent of pine and dust.

"I never realized how talented Lil was," Kara said, pulling a painting from the bin. "There are so many gorgeous botanicals here. She could have sold them online—*you* could sell them online."

"No, I couldn't." Dahlia shook her head; she was 100 percent sure Lil wouldn't want that. She was too private.

"Okay, but Lil did ask you to find a place for these, so what will you do? You can't just let them sit in a storage unit with the rest of your stuff."

"Honestly. I don't know. This is just the tip of the iceberg of what's stressing me out." Dahlia's chest tightened.

"That's why you need to get laid," Kara said.

Dahlia shook her head and then laughed. "It's true."

"Wow, you're no longer in denial. This is legitimate progress." Kara gave a crisp nod. "But back to the art. I have an idea: Why don't you sell them as prints? I mean, look at all these lining the walls. It's like Monet and van Gogh had a baby."

Dahlia laughed. "I'm oddly impressed."

"What can I say? You're rubbing off on me." Kara smiled.

Dahlia walked closer to the pink heritage rose painting with white plumeria tucked among the stems. As she held it in her hands, the palette reminded her of spring when possibility seemed endless. The roses were a salmon hue, and the background felt like the sky on a perfect cloudless summer day. "She always loved her girls the most, though. Anne Pratt, Lady Harriet, and, of course, Georgia O'Keeffe," she mumbled as Kara looked on.

"What's that? On the back?" Kara asked. "Turn it back over. Look, there's a number." Kara pointed. "It says four."

"It's probably just markings from an art show or exhibit."

Suddenly, a loud tap came from the other side of the barn. "Dimples, you in here?"

Kara's eyes widened as she mouthed the word *dimples*.

Dahlia's heart swelled, and her hands tingled. *Dimples,* Dahlia repeated in her head. Was this her new pet name?

"Yeah, I'm in here," Dahlia yelled, feeling her voice crack. She prayed he hadn't heard any of their earlier conversation.

Noah walked through the plastic tarp with Harry and looked surprised to see Kara there. "Oh hey, sorry. I figured you were alone."

"Did you know?" Kara asked quietly with a side nod.

Dahlia glared at her with wide eyes, telling her in one look to behave herself. "Was Harry bothering you?"

"No, not at all. He's my shadow." He looked down at him, who was sitting ever so patiently next to him. It was as if Harry knew something that no one else did. Noah gave Kara a friendly smile. "Hi, I'm Noah."

"I know. I'm Kara, Dahlia's cousin. Very, very nice to meet you, Noah," Kara said, ogling him like a piece of meat, which wasn't hard because he was practically naked. Well, almost. The thin tank top, which offered a full view of his dragon tattoo over the shoulder, paired with short shorts, didn't help the drool fest.

Dahlia nudged Kara with her elbow.

"Kara is heading to the Hamptons for a party tonight, so she took the ferry over from Connecticut to keep me company for the day," Dahlia said, keeping one eye on her cousin.

"And she might be coming with. I might steal her away for the night," Kara said proudly. "Or she could stay here . . . if there's something worth staying for."

Dahlia glared at her. If looks could kill, Kara would be lifeless on the floor. "Well, I have a lot to do here. I'm really not sure." Dahlia looked at Noah, secretly wanting to stay.

"You should go. It sounds fun," Noah said, still not mentioning one thing about his old life there or how well he knew the Hamptons from the show.

"Yeah, maybe," Dahlia said, swallowing the disappointment.

Noah stared at Dahlia, as if there was something else he wanted to say. "Oh, right. I'm heading up to the chimney. I didn't want to scare you."

"Oh, I can help you," Dahlia said.

"I can help too," Kara said.

"No, that's very kind, but I'll be fine. I've done this hundreds of times," he said, running his fingers through his thick brown locks.

Dahlia just stood there trying to settle the winged creatures that took flight.

"Okay then." Noah smiled. "Nice to meet you."

"You too, Noah," Kara said, watching him stroll away.

Later that day, Dahlia said goodbye to Kara from the porch.

"He definitely has rizz. I'll give him that," Kara said.

"Rizz?" Dahlia's brows furrowed.

"Charisma, swag, glow. Geez, you need to get out more. And you better get on that before the vixen decides she wants him back," Kara said with a firm nod.

"Oh, I don't know. The more I think about it, the more I realize it's probably not the best idea to get involved. Plus, I'm so out of practice. And not to mention older than he is."

"So you're robbing the cradle." Kara shrugged.

"Don't say that. It makes it sound so illicit." Hearing it aloud had a whole other connotation. If she was robbing the cradle? Was ten years that bad? She still didn't know.

"Who cares? It's been done before. Heck, Priyanka is ten years older than Nick Jonas. Don't overthink this."

"Not overthinking got me in trouble in the first place, remember?" Dahlia leaned against the door frame.

"And look how that turned out," Kara said thoughtfully.

"Yeah, pretty great." Dahlia couldn't imagine her world without Daisy. As hard as it had been being a single mom for the first five years of Daisy's life, she wouldn't trade those memories or the gift of being her mom for anything. As Lil would say, "Some mistakes turn out to be miracles."

"Make a move. Have some fun. He didn't show up by accident, you know." Kara held Dahlia's hand, making firm eye contact. "And if you change your mind about the party, text me. I'm sure Simon would be very pleased."

"Sounds good. Today was fun. Thanks for all your help with the landscaping and some of the painting."

"It was. Any time." Kara hugged her goodbye. "Love you, girl."

"I love you too." Dahlia followed behind Kara, trying to avoid the sinkhole in the porch floor, which had magically been fixed. *When did he do this?* she wondered. Her smile grew as she waved to Kara, now climbing into her Suburban. She walked toward his property to thank Noah.

She turned onto the gravel driveway and saw him working on his motorcycle. He was wearing a backward hat and untied black work boots. God, he looked good—a bit of rogue biker sprinkled with all-American boy next door. Heat trailed through her body, moistening even her hands.

"Hi," she cheerfully said.

"Hey there." Noah briefly looked up.

"I just wanted to say thanks for all your help today." Dahlia paused, watching his sweaty body curve around the wheel. Perhaps this wasn't such a bad idea after all. She bit the inside of her lip, imagining his slick body against hers. Trying to slow her heartbeat, she asked, "What are you up to?"

"Trying to fix a leak. I'm heading out for a few days," Noah said with a slack face.

"Oh, where?" As soon as the words left her lips, she regretted it. It sounded way too needy.

"Montauk. For a boys' weekend."

Something felt off from yesterday. Had he overheard them talking this morning? Did Dahlia scare him off? Dahlia wondered if his ex would also be out there. If so, would they meet up? "Okay, well, have fun." Dahlia turned to walk away. "Oh, and thank you for fixing the porch. That was so nice of you. I'm sure there were other things to do, like fix your bike."

"Yeah, I'm running a little late, but it's okay. Any time."

"Well, I'm grateful." Dahlia covered her chest. She didn't want him to go to Montauk; she liked having him next door. It made her feel less alone.

"I'll stain it at some point, so it looks seamless," he said.

"It looks better already, and it's no longer a death trap, so . . . I can see you're busy. I'll let you go," Dahlia said. She didn't want to go, but she knew she had to. Staying meant fooling herself into thinking a summer fling could work. It was obvious that they were from two different worlds. She wanted quiet, wanted to stay home, and he wanted a party.

Dahlia walked away, feeling like the air was being sucked out of her bright balloon.

"Dahlia?" Noah asked.

"Yeah?" She turned back, holding on to the bit of air that was left.

"Want to grab dinner when I get back? I heard there's a movie on the lawn in Greenport on Sunday."

"Yeah, okay." She turned away, biting her lip. She'd forgotten how turbulent dating could be. Perhaps she'd never really known. But a little voice inside her head told her it would be worth finding out.

CHAPTER TWELVE

July 8

It had been twenty-nine hours since Dahlia last saw Noah. During that time, she went for a sunrise swim, biked to the farmers market, and repainted all the baseboards and the wainscoting in the kitchen. She also snapped a few more pictures of the garden and did something so unlike Dahlia that even Kara would be surprised—she took a selfie smelling a single white rose in Lil's European-inspired gardens, which still needed lots of work in the background.

The sun melted into the distance as her feet sank into the cold sand. She ached for Noah in a way she hadn't before. When she closed her eyes, she could feel the warmth of his hand on the nape of her neck and imagined it slowly wandering to her breasts. She could feel the inferno of his gaze as the rush of water grazed her hot skin. Dahlia walked up from the beach, trying to steady her mind. It had been so long since she felt any way about a guy, and she was still unsure how it would all work. All she knew was that she wanted him in a way she'd *never* wanted Spence. Noah was making her realize exactly what she'd been missing in her life. After this, there was no going back to a lifeless and indifferent existence.

They texted back and forth a bit, but it was all business. Noah's last text read, *When I get back . . .*

Dahlia waited with bated breath, anticipating his next message. Maybe she was fooling herself, but she was hoping he would declare his deepest desires to her and say something like, *I'm going to ravage every inch of your body.*

Instead, it read, *I'm going to power wash your house.*

Dahlia blew the hair from her eyes. She wanted desperately for McHandy to make a move.

Harry groaned from the kitchen floor.

"Don't tell me you're taking his side," she deadpanned in his direction. Hoping to distract herself further, she uncorked a bottle of wine.

Harry didn't move. All she saw were the whiskers above his eyes furrow.

"You miss him too? What kind of mind trick are you playing, Noah Sterling?" she mumbled, grabbing the wine glass and book, and strolling toward Lil's barn.

She flipped on the studio light and tried to get comfortable in the worn wingback. It was positioned right in front of the window so Lil could see the bay while she read. The high-pitched buzzing sounds of cicadas filled the twilight air. The briny breeze filtered through the screen, but it was still too hot. She yanked off her robe, revealing her trademark summer tank and navy shorts. She opened Lil's window wider and sat, finding it more tolerable.

The worn cushions scratched her humid skin, but she sat there anyway. Sitting in Lil's chair made her feel connected to her, and she didn't care how uncomfortable it was. She sipped her wine and opened a very old copy of *Wuthering Heights* that she'd pulled from the house library.

Dahlia held the yellowed pages to her nose, inhaling the must and hints of vanilla. Her smile grew as her gaze narrowed in on the bouquet of yellow roses that hung on the wall next to the cupboard door. Suddenly, her mind shifted focus to Lil's wall of art. Dahlia knew Lil to be a humble creative. So why did she have certain ones lining the walls and others in a bin? There had to be a reason. Dahlia got up and turned the painting over. It read *6*.

She carefully pulled the others off the wall and lined them along the floor and workbench in numerical order. They ranged from one through twenty-two. She was convinced it was for an art show. Then, one by one, keeping them in order, she hung them on the wood wall—that is, until she noticed Lil's signature tucked inside the right corner of one. She pried back number eleven, the bright pink rose canvas, from the edge and saw what also looked like a year: *'67*.

After over an hour of fully immersing herself in the art quandary, she stood back and looked at Lil's creative metamorphosis in numerical order. It turned out there was a rhythm to the paintings, after all. Dahlia still didn't quite understand the reasoning behind it, but she knew in her gut the paintings on the wall were more important. And she was beginning to think it wasn't for an art show. She scanned slowly from left to right, pursing her lips. They needed to be seen, Kara was right. But where?

As she was lost in contemplation, her phone dinged.

It was a sunset selfie of Noah. The Montauk horizon was a beautiful kaleidoscope of orange hues. She zoomed in; his eyelashes were wet, and there were sand particles stuck to his facial hair. She wished more than anything she was there with him, enjoying the sunset and getting lost in his presence. Dahlia could feel the swift beat of her heart through her tank top. She couldn't believe she was on his mind during a boys' trip.

Now show me yours, he wrote.

Dahlia was now visibly sweating. She knew what he meant, but it didn't stop her mind from drifting to the pages of a steamy romance novel.

Dahlia sent him back the picture she had taken earlier in the garden.

What about you? I want to see ur beautfulL face.

How much had he had to drink? He couldn't even spell.

She sent him the picture from the garden.

Cute, he wrote.

Then he sent her a crooked selfie of half of him holding a beer by a bonfire, a sure sign he had a few too many, but she didn't care. She was too excited to care.

Wish u were here.

Yup, he was definitely drunk. Dahlia hesitated. She started to write *I do too*, but then erased it. She wrote, *Have fun—* but stopped after she saw the bubble.

Where are you right now? Send me a pic. I want to see u.

Dahlia swallowed hard. *I have no makeup on, and this lighting is horrible.*

Noah wrote, *?*

"Oh, fuck it." Dahlia held her arm out as long as she could and snapped. She barely looked before sending it. She knew if she looked, she might lose her nerve. *I'm in Lil's studio.*

Wow. I cant wait to ahve u irl.

What? Dahlia wrote back. If she didn't know any better, she'd think he wrote, *have you in real life*. That made no sense. All the lingering eyes, playful banter, and skin-to-skin contact had been very PG thus far. She fanned herself and shook her head. Just to be sure she didn't have a piece of spinach stuck in her teeth or sent something that would be a deal breaker, she pulled up the picture. She gasped. All she saw were nipples, clear as day through her apparently very sheer top. Oh my gosh. She'd just *sexted* him.

She covered her face and sank deeper into Lil's chair.

* * *

The next day, in pure Noah form, it was crickets. Nothing after her last text back asking for a translation. Dahlia was slowly coming to terms with the fact that she may have accidentally come on too strong with the illicit photo. But there was nothing she could do about it, and she was not going to make the next move. She was certain of that.

Dahlia jumped into Betty and drove into town to get a few things. Noah was supposed to return tomorrow, so she decided to busy herself. The town was bustling, which was no surprise for a Saturday. The once quiet town of Southold was now overrun by city folks and foreigners, especially on a splendid July weekend. Dahlia didn't mind much, though. The North Fork was always considered the more down-to-earth part of the east end, as opposed to the Hamptons. And after fifteen years of a "keeping up with the Joneses" mindset in Greenwich, this was precisely where she needed to plant herself.

Dahlia ran into the grocery store for dog food and a few staples, like flour and milk. Then headed to the hardware store. This time, with zero flashbacks.

She received a quick text from Daisy:

Louisa is Pop's first cousin; it's official! We had dinner last night, and she brought a ton of pics from when they were little. She sent in her DNA a few months ago, so it should arrive soon. Then we can compare it to ours. We have living relatives in France! Eek! Call you tomorrow. Love you!

Dahlia leaned against the paintbrush display. There was an unexpected release of tension in her shoulders that they now knew more about her pop. For so long, his life before marrying her grandmother remained a mystery. She didn't want to admit it to herself, but part of her had wondered if her pop was a part of Lil's secret. There was substantial relief that he was exactly who she thought he was. She was also relieved she could rely on Daisy to navigate this since she was a French Studies major.

Good work, Detective Daisy! So glad your French Studies are paying off. Love you, trillions. Be safe, Dahlia wrote back.

The drive home was easy. Dahlia draped her hand out the window as the sun faded, feeling the cool tug of wind on her palm. The pebbles crunched beneath her tires as she pulled into the driveway. Her eyes couldn't help but wander to Noah's. But he still wasn't home. Even though she knew he wouldn't be, she'd hoped he'd changed his mind. It was okay, though. She had plenty to do and a book to read. At least she could cross that one off Lil's list tonight. *Wuthering Heights*, here she came.

Dahlia considered Lil's list as she pulled the bags from her trunk. And the secret that kept creeping back into her mind.

You need to know the truth. You deserve the truth.

Dahlia walked around to the back of the house and yanked open the screen door. What was the truth? She was still no closer. She squeezed her eyes shut, feeling her throat constrict. She knew time was running out, with just over three weeks to piece together this puzzle and list the house. Which reminded her that she needed to call the realtor. She flipped on the light. The lights flickered, a loud zapping sound rippled overhead, and everything went dim.

Dahlia flicked the light switch up and down, but nothing. "No, no, this can't be happening. Not now," she murmured. Harry ran in, and her body suddenly went cold. She laid the bags on the counter. She wanted to text Noah, but stopped herself. What could he do anyway? He was an hour away. Dahlia pulled on her lip, pacing the worn linoleum floor. She wanted to take care of this herself, but after the small electrical fire during the renovation of her Connecticut farmhouse, she didn't want to take any chances. Maybe he could tell her what to look for.

Hi, it's me, she texted. *I know you're busy, but my electricity just went out, and I'm freaking out.*

She waited and waited, and nothing. *Shit, shit, shit!* she yelled in her head.

"Harry, you stay here. I'm going into the dungeon." Dahlia grabbed a flashlight from the cupboard. The basement was her most feared area of the house. Dahlia swatted at the cobwebs that hung from the ceiling, wincing as she walked under them, praying a spider wouldn't crawl into her hair. It smelled musty and damp down here. Dahlia lit the way, navigating around the boxes left on the floor and bumping into a stack. She brushed the dust off the top and coughed. It read *Pressed flowers* in script. She promised herself she'd come back for the box.

Dahlia walked past the furnace and spotted the electrical box. "Thank you, God." While steepling her hands, she felt her pants vibrate. She answered quickly. "Hello?"

"Hey, you okay? I got your text." Noah seemed concerned.

"Yeah." Dahlia's breath hitched. "A little spooked out by the basement, but I'm okay." As many times as she'd been down there, it still freaked her out. It seemed like it was a place where secrets were kept.

"You're in the basement. That's good. Go to the panel and tell me if all the breakers are tripped."

"Okay, hold on, it's dark down here." Dahlia opened the door. "Yeah, they are."

"Do you smell smoke?"

"No, but should I call the fire department?" she asked, feeling her brows furrow.

"No, wait for me."

"Umm, not to sound ungrateful, but you're an hour away, if not more."

"I'm about to make a right onto our block."

Our block. She liked the sound of that. "Wait, our block?"

"Yeah, I had enough of the boys' weekend. I wanted to come home. I . . ."

"Yeah?" She felt the urge to squeal but instead waited for his response. Was he feeling what she was feeling? Is that why he came back? Did her picture drive him mad with desire? His early return was a good sign. But was it for her or some other reason altogether? The seconds felt like minutes, and she had to force herself to breathe.

"Nothing. Hang tight. I'll see you in a few. I'll grab my tool bag and be right over."

"Sounds good," she said while inside wanting to scream. She looked up at the rotting wood ceiling and cringed, not wanting to spend another minute down there.

Dahlia sat on the front porch, impatiently waiting for him. Once she heard his motorcycle pass by, she was all too eager. There was still enough light left, perfect to watch his entrance. The instant she heard the crunching of the pebbles, she knew he was on his way. Winged creatures took flight inside her stomach. Out of the darkness, he strutted over in slow motion. It was like something out of a movie. There he was, looking all *Terminator* meets *Grease* in jeans, a white tank top, and a leather jacket, holding a toolbox, like a man on a mission. Tonight's mission: to save Damsel Dahlia and fix her box. Her mind leaped to a dirty place, and she could feel her hands moisten. She snapped herself back to earth as he walked closer and met him with a great big smile.

"Hi," he said quickly as he breezed right past her with his sexy, windblown hair. No smile, no hug, no hello, nothing. "Still no smoke, right?"

"No. Hi to you too," she mumbled under her breath. That wasn't the greeting she was expecting, especially after their textathon yesterday.

"Hey, boy," he greeted Harry, giving him a sturdy pat on the head.

Okay, now she was officially annoyed that her dog got a warmer greeting than she did.

Without hesitation, he charged into the house. He took off his jacket and threw it onto the entry bench. Dahlia's eyes roamed over his thick, corded, and veiny arms until he turned the corner down to the basement. She shadowed behind. "Harry, stay." Dahlia barreled down the stairs, willing him to wait for her.

Noah opened the breaker box. "Yeah, this isn't good."

"Really? What do you see?" A mix of dread and anticipation coursed through her body.

"Well, it's corroded." He held the light up toward the exterior wall. "Probably from water getting in. You're lucky, Dahlia." He looked right at her. "This could have caused a fire. God." He shook his head and grumbled.

Dahlia stared at his profile, hoping to get a glimpse inside his head. How could he walk past her like that? She was now convinced she'd misread this entire thing between them. She was just as concerned with what he was holding back as she was with the hypothetical fire.

"I'll get someone here for you tomorrow to replace it." He closed up the box. "In the meantime, you can stay with me if you want." Noah walked to the bottom of the stairs and headed up, still not quite looking at her.

Was this a pity invite, or did he *want* her there? Dahlia held onto the banister, watching him from behind. She was getting whiplash from his wavering. She wanted to know, either way, where they stood. She knew if she went, she'd most likely be tortured, so she said, "I'll be okay here. I've got candles and maybe an LED lamp."

"Don't say I didn't offer." He laughed, reaching the top of the stairs.

That was it? She was getting frostbite from his ice-cold attitude. Dahlia hesitated, reaching the landing. What was she doing? She was too old for this.

"Can I wash my hands?" Noah put the tools and flashlight on the counter. The light giving a warm glow to the ceiling.

"Sure, help yourself." Dahlia wanted to bite her knuckle. She couldn't believe he was standing in her kitchen after she texted him that picture last night and wasn't going to make a move. Aside from showing up on his white horse in his white tank and fulfilling her acts of service dream list, he was acting like a wishy-washy teenage boy who'd forgotten he'd texted her the night before.

"What did you do today?" he asked, creating quite a lather.

"Oh, this and that. Housework mostly." She smiled through the small talk while feeling her insides tangle like vines. The truth was, she wasted way too much time thinking of him. But he would never know that. She was done.

He wiped his hands on the towel and looked her up and down. "Did you go out or something?"

"Yeah," she said, leaning back on the counter. She secretly wanted him to swirl a little. Let him think maybe she had a date.

"You look nice." He quickly looked away again, grabbing his flashlight. "Okay, so if anything happens through the night, call me. I'll keep the phone by my bed."

He was killing her softly. "Okay, sounds good. And thanks for coming so quickly." She saw him out the back door.

"Happy to help." He turned back, the light from the moon highlighting his silhouette.

She watched him fade into the dark landscape. Now it was like something out of a horror movie.

Dahlia ran her fingers through her hair in frustration. She had to remind herself that not all stories ended with happily ever after; to her knowledge, most didn't. The single life sounded really good right about now. I mean, Lil had always seemed happy.

Harry barked as if he agreed. "You are so smart; you know that?" She nuzzled her nose into his.

Dahlia walked back in and locked the door. She pulled candles from the pantry and tried to find the LED lantern Lil had bought years back when she attempted to camp under the stars with Daisy. Dahlia was on her tippy-toes when she heard a knock at the screen door. Her heart swelled. Maybe he'd come to his senses.

She ran down the steps like an eager teenager and opened it.

"I forgot my toolbox," he said, gently pushing his way in.

"Oh." Her heart sank.

"And something else."

"Your jacket?"

"Not quite, Dimples." Noah eased her against the cedar shake wall. With each step, she melted into his well-built frame. The body contact left her blood singing. But it was more than that. She was safe in his presence, in his hold. To her, that was everything. The force of his Caribbean blues captured her soul. His gaze was deep and unending, as if he saw right through her. Through to her memories, some that were heavy and painful, and yet he wanted to stay anyway. He brushed her hair off her face and smiled. Dahlia's heart felt like it was going to burst open.

The moon cast just enough light to see every beautiful curve and ridge of his face. She imprinted it in her mind and filed it under *Take My Breath Away Moments.*

"You have the most beautiful heart-shaped lips. You know that?" he whispered. His face was so close she could hear the gentle tempo of his breath.

"I do?" She looked up at him, searching his eyes.

"Can I kiss them?" he asked with a soft, unwavering tone.

Was this actually happening? Noah Sterling, reality TV star, wanted to kiss the girl next door. This was a moment she'd wanted with every fiber of her being. She felt weightless, like petals floating in the wind.

"Yes." Her entire body wilted into his touch, hoping she remembered how to do this.

He took her lips between his, and she was a swooning bubble of bliss. Noah kissed Dahlia like no man ever had. His lips were pillowy and plump, and his mustache surprisingly gentle. He teased her mouth, and then with one slip of his tongue, all bets were off. Her body flooded with warmth. He stole her air and her will. Their lips moved in sync, like a dance between old lovers. At that moment, all she wanted to do was surrender to this all-encompassing feeling and shed every piece of armor she'd ever worn.

Noah slid his hands around her lower back and brought her hips to his. Dahlia could feel the heat from his body as she drew closer. The whiff of his perspiration made every microcosm of her skin tingle and her toes curl. It was a mix of sawdust, sea salt, and musk. She'd never known explosive feelings like this existed. Maybe she wasn't so dead inside after all.

Dahlia could feel how firm he was. His hard zipper grazed her skin, but she didn't care. She was ready to tear off her clothes and give herself to him. At that moment, she craved nothing more than to make love to him under the stars on Lil's porch.

He cupped her face as his lips slowly released from hers. "I've wanted to do that for so long."

"You have?" Dahlia's pulse quickened, wanting more of his beautiful mouth and chestnut whiskers. Their eyes connected with what little light was left, and she anchored her fingers inside the top of his jeans.

"God, yes. Every time I was close to you." He leaned his forehead on hers. "But I need to take this slow. Are you okay with that?"

Dahlia reached for his hand. "Noah, I like you, and I don't need more time. But if you do, it's okay." Even though Dahlia wanted this thing between them to start yesterday, she wanted it to be right for both of them.

With that kiss came an innate urge to confess her age. He trusted her, and she felt guilty. There was a possibility that if he knew how old she was, he wouldn't want her the way he did. Her eyes darted around the room, trying to orchestrate the right words for the age announcement. But *not* the Daisy announcement. That was off the table; she wasn't ready for that. She wasn't done reliving her twenties again. The truth wasn't any match for her freedom—not yet, anyway.

"Hey, Noah, how old do you think I am?"

"I don't know. My age, I guess." His soft lips roamed the nape of her neck.

"It never crossed your mind?" She was regretting this already. What if this was a deal breaker? It was better she knew sooner than later before she became more emotionally and physically invested.

"I'm more interested in your zodiac sign than anything else," he said, continuing to explore her skin in a very PG way.

"My sign?" Dahlia was limp with pleasure but managed to laugh. He was into astrology, and that was hot too. Damn, he was full of surprises in the best way.

"I have a sister, remember? Gretchen is crazy about crystals and chakra and all that."

"You're adorable. You know that?" Dahlia liked Gretchen so much more now. She drew his face to hers. "Take a guess."

"On your sign?" he asked.

"No, my age," she playfully responded.

"Dahlia, it doesn't matter."

"Well, it might, Noah. I'm . . ."

"What are you, like, fifty?" he blurted.

"No. Thirty-eight." Dahlia pinched her eyes shut but then opened one eye.

He had zero facial expression. This was it, the end of their summer fling. Dahlia felt faint, woozy by his unresponsiveness.

Then he smiled, with one corner higher than the other. "That doesn't scare me off. In fact, I'm not sure anything would at this point." And with that, he pressed his lips to hers again and lingered.

"I'm a Pisces, by the way." She didn't ask about his age or sign; she knew he had a birthday coming up, and she looked forward to the day when she was only nine years older, not an entire decade. Dahlia also knew the zodiac, and the idea of two water signs cosmically seemed too good to be true. The energy between them was rare, explosive, peaceful, and cathartic. Every cell in her body was awake and in a state of wonder. She was at the top of the Ferris wheel and didn't want to come back down.

CHAPTER THIRTEEN

July 9

Dahlia let the tepid water run over her face and down her body. The kisses she'd shared with Noah last night were all she could think about. She pressed her fingers to her wet lips and smiled. She couldn't help but imagine Noah in the shower with her, pressing his naked body against the steamy wall and holding his cute butt cheeks in her hands. Her legs felt weak, and her lady parts ached. She immediately turned the water to cold, hoping to slow her racing heart.

After a quick dry, she hooked her bra and wiggled up her panties, wishing she didn't have to. But Noah had made his "I want to take things slow" intentions very clear the night before, and his electrician friend was downstairs waiting to be paid. Dahlia threw on a yellow ruffled short floral dress and grabbed her espadrilles from the floor.

She could hear Noah talking to Rob from the upstairs hallway. She stuck her back to the wall and, against her better judgment, listened.

"Thanks for coming on such short notice. And on a Sunday," Noah said.

"Sure thing. That box was ancient. With the two-twenty volts, you'll be able to hang Christmas lights and see them from space."

"Well, we appreciate it," Noah said.

We, huh? She liked that. Her mind went to Christmas lights. She'd be gone by then, and someone else would own the house. Dahlia was dizzy at the realization that she wouldn't be here for her favorite holiday and that someone else would be living in Lil's house.

"I'll be heading to Gretchen's this week for the inspection. Maybe I'll catch you on the other side." There was a gritty cackle, which was followed by an awkward silence. "Hey man, are you okay? I haven't seen you since . . . You know. For the record, it was shitty."

"Yeah, I'm fine. Grateful I found out when I did," Dahlia heard Noah say in a hopeful tone.

"You dodged a bullet if you ask me."

You tell him, Rob, she thought.

"Dahlia, are you coming?" Noah yelled up the stairs.

She tiptoed back to the bedroom and yelled, "Ah, yeah, be right there."

Quickly, she inspected her sun-kissed skin in the mirror and tied her hair back with a bandana. She looked closer. Her eyes sparkled like water at sunrise—void of any puffy bags or dark circles under them. A smile curled her lips. She liked this version of herself, hopeful and light. She pursed her glossy lips and inhaled. It was official. Dahlia Newberry was head over heels for a younger guy.

Dahlia flew down the stairs, causing her ruffles to flounce.

Noah turned, and with every footstep closer, his grin grew wider. Her belly flipped and tossed. It felt like prom, and she was running down to meet her handsome date. Only he wasn't in a tux. He was in gray board shorts, a white linen shirt, and Vans.

"Rob, I can't thank you enough." Dahlia handed him the check, knowing full well it was making a substantial dent in her Charleston savings. "You are a lifesaver."

"You are," said Noah, opening the door. "I'll see you on the island."

"Sure thing." Rob walked off the porch and waved.

Noah shut the door and met her eyes. "I thought he'd never leave."

Dahlia clenched the banister, hoping McHandy would make another move. Anchored to the last step, she wondered how slow he would take things. After that kiss, Dahlia wanted more, more butterflies, more goosebumps, and more floating on cloud nine. If she were being honest, though, she wanted more companionship. Dahlia had been alone for so long in her marriage, and this, whatever it was, felt good. "That was nice of him to come over on a Sunday."

"He likes me, plus he owed me one," he said, leaning against the door like he was pondering something consequential.

"What are you up to over there? What's going on in that head of yours?" Dahlia asked, raising a brow.

He glanced up with a devilish grin, closing the gap between them. Noah gave her the most passionate, steamy kiss that made her fall off the last step and into his arms. Their tongues collided, and all she could think was that he tasted like sweet peppermint.

"What was that for?" she asked, not wanting to open her eyes fully.

"For being you," he said, kissing her nose. "I could kiss you for days."

"Okay." She grinned playfully. "We don't have to go to the movie, you know. We can stay right here." Dahlia felt spellbound in his arms, and the thought of getting lost in his warm and delicious kisses for hours on Lil's couch made her giddy.

"If we stay, I won't be able to control myself." He laced his fingers with hers and kissed her hand.

"And that's a bad thing?" Dahlia bit her lip, trying to control her erupting insides.

"Dimples, you're killing me."

Dahlia wrinkled her nose.

"What, you don't like that nickname?" His brows furrowed.

"Oh, I do." She laughed, loving that he had a pet name for her. "I just feel a bit like an awkward teenager with braces when you say it." "Dimples" wasn't the sexy woman she wanted him to see her as. And if she had any chance of competing with Josie, she at least wanted that chance.

"Okay, fair enough. How about I call you D? A twofer, for Dahlia and Dimples."

Dahlia pressed her lips to his, his whiskers softly brushing her mouth. This man knew how to kiss. Whether it was sudden and lustful or tender and sweet, he knew what he was doing. "Sold," she said, not wanting to leave Lil's entryway.

"We should probably leave before I carry you up the stairs," he said with a wide grin.

Dahlia didn't want their kissfest to end. "Now who's killing who?" She smiled. "Let me say goodbye to Harry and grab my jacket. You go ahead. I'll just be a minute."

"Don't be too long." He tugged at his zipper.

Dahlia smiled, looking down, knowing full well that it was a great sign. "Oh, I won't." The front door closed, and she leaned against the wall, covering her ear-to-ear grin. It felt like there was a devil on one shoulder and an angel on the other. She couldn't get too attached. It could only be a summer fling. She was leaving in less than one month. She inhaled and blew out her concerns, telling herself it was okay to be a little reckless.

The box of pressed flowers from the basement now sat on the entry bench next to her jean jacket. She reached for the jacket and tapped the carton, setting the intention to open it tomorrow. Then she caught Harry lying on top of the couch. "Ugh, you're not supposed to be up there. Lil would not be happy you're ruining her cushions." She snickered, kissing Harry goodbye and letting him stay right where he was.

* * *

Noah laid a tartan blanket over the grass like a true gentleman. He opened up a cooler filled with wine and snacks. Dahlia couldn't believe a guy who barely knew her would go to this much trouble. In all the years she was with Spence, Dahlia had planned everything, down to her own birthday celebrations, which she had only for Daisy.

"Rosé?" he asked.

"Sure." Dahlia eagerly leaned forward. Her cheeks hurt from smiling. "When did you have time to do all this?"

"While you were showering." He popped a grape in his mouth, which made the urge to kiss him stir with feverish urgency. She wondered how she would get through the night without wanting more.

Dahlia's entire body tingled as she watched him take control of the date. Acts of service had to be the sexiest of the love languages, followed by physical touch. "So what are we seeing anyway?"

"*Casablanca*," he said, pouring wine into a tumbler.

"Are you kidding me?" A shiver ran down her back as she reached for the glass. "Thank you. I've watched that movie over a dozen times with Lil! Oh, man, did she love Ingrid—she was her favorite movie star of all time."

"Is that so?" Noah asked, meeting her eager eyes.

"Have you seen it?" Dahlia leaned closer yet.

"When I was a kid, maybe." He looked inward, pouring himself a glass. "You really like this movie, huh?'

"Here's looking at you, kid. Does that ring a bell?"

He cocked his head in confusion.

"It's from the movie." Her voice trailed off as if she were disappointed. But in what? So far, they'd been in sync with just about everything. So what if he didn't like old movies as much as she did?

"I know it." He laughed, interrupting her hopeful thought. "Everyone knows that line. It's like the most famous movie quote of all time."

"Just checking." She scoffed playfully, exhaling slowly. *Phew.* No problem here, at least not for now. Part of her wondered if she was purposefully seeking signs of capability. Perhaps that would make her feel more at ease about their age difference.

"And the song." He started whistling the tune to "As Time Goes By."

"What talent. Bravo. Bravo." Dahlia clapped as her laughter bubbled over, realizing being with him felt as easy as Sunday morning.

They sat there on the blanket as the world around them went about its natural summer rhythm. They were in their own little bubble. One she hoped would never pop. In one look, she was lost in the depths of his tender gaze. Noah held her chin between his fingers, as if he was going to kiss her with his perfectly manscaped mustache. That was until they heard, "Noah," in the distance. Suddenly, his eyes widened as if he'd been caught doing something he shouldn't, and he threw on his baseball hat and sunglasses like he wanted to be anonymous.

She wondered what the abrupt shift was all about. But it quickly dissipated when she saw how cute he looked in a baseball cap. Dahlia spotted what looked to be Gretchen in the distance. "I think it's your sister."

"Oh, phew." He relaxed his posture and took off his sunglasses.

Dahlia could feel her forehead crease. Did he not want to be seen with her? Dahlia couldn't conceive of that being the truth, but how well did she know him? Plus, he could have been rethinking the age thing. Something had felt different right off the bat with him, but could she fully trust the unexplainable pull that felt magnetic and electrifying? It had been her experience that if something felt too good to be true, it usually was. But that didn't have to be her and Noah.

"Hey, you two." Gretchen walked over in her cute maxi dress and messy bun.

Noah sprang to his feet and hugged her. "What on earth are you doing here?"

"I live here, remember?" Gretchen deadpanned.

"Right." Noah nodded.

Dahlia took a double-take. Seeing them side by side, she saw the resemblance, especially in their eyes. They both shared the most stunning blue eyes she'd ever seen. "Hi, Gretchen."

"Hey." She gave a little wave to Dahlia. "So, what are you kids up to?"

"Watching an old movie. Want to join?" Noah scanned the crowd behind her as if to see if they noticed his name being shouted across the lawn.

Selfishly, Dahlia hoped Gretchen would say no. She wanted Noah all to herself.

"Nah, I'm meeting someone for drinks."

Dahlia felt her shoulders fall in relief.

"You are, are you?" Noah said with a cheeky grin.

"Get your head out of the gutter. She and I are just friends."

"I've heard that before," Noah said, nudging her arm.

"Well, I'll let you two get to it," said Gretchen.

Dahlia and Noah looked at each other and laughed.

"Not like that. I'm a little nervous," Gretchen said, fanning herself.

"You'll be great," Dahlia said, looking up at the girl who was human after all. "You look pretty."

"Thanks." Gretchen smiled. "I'd better go." She started to walk away and turned back.

"Hey, Dahlia, maybe one day you can come by and give me some last-minute art advice. You know, before we open."

"I'd love to," Dahlia said, feeling her voice lighten. A friendly relationship with a sister was a foreign concept to her. Spence's sister Emily hated her from the very beginning for trapping him, despite it being the furthest thing from the truth. She resented Dahlia for "ruining" his college experience because he had so much "guilt." The Newberrys weren't people to own their scandals. They much preferred the blame game. Emily had said on many occasions that Dahlia only had Daisy to get their family money. The irony was that she never took a dime from them, even when she had to secure a second job to make ends meet before Spence came back.

"Later." Gretchen waved as she stepped up onto the boardwalk.

"She likes you." Noah sat back down next to Dahlia.

"You think?" Dahlia shrugged, wanting him to move closer.

"Yeah, it usually takes her months, even years, to warm up to someone." He looked up at the boat lights that flickered in the distance.

Dahlia wasn't sure what was different for Gretchen this time, but she wasn't going to waste another moment pondering it. She looked out over the water and closed her eyes, wanting to stay buried in this moment forever. In the feeling of being wanted for more than her managerial skills. Of being wanted for simply being herself. The sounds of masts echoed in her ear like a concert, breaking her from her peaceful interlude.

The putting on a hat and glasses business still bugged her a little. Although she wasn't the kind of person to get right to the point, she was running out of time and didn't want to play games. This entire situation already felt out of her comfort zone. "Do you like me, Noah?" Dahlia asked.

He was quiet. He looked around, trying to avoid the question.

"Oh, that much, huh?" She laughed, not knowing what else to do. Deep down, she knew he did. A man doesn't kiss a woman that way unless there are feelings involved. But Dahlia needed to know why he was holding back in his words. And she needed to understand why he was hiding their relationship, especially when going to a very public place had been his idea.

"D, I like you too much. That's the problem." He laced her fingers with hers.

That simple motion made her heart skip a beat. She wondered if he would always be this hard to read. "Then I don't get it."

"I don't want to get hurt." He shook his head.

"Neither do I. And I certainly don't want to hurt you." Her eyes met his.

"There's a lot you don't know," he said.

"Like what?" Dahlia asked, tilting her head with a sincere tone in her voice. Hearing what happened from him made her wonder if he did trust her. "Come on. Out with it."

He took in a lungful of sea air and blew slowly. "I got my heart broken on national television last year. There are memes about me all over social media. With my shocked face, the moment I opened the door on my ex having sex with my best friend."

Her heart sank. Hearing it in his words broke something inside her. It also made her angry—that someone could be so cruel and hurtful to someone that she cared about. "Is that why you're trying to be incognito?" She gestured to the hat and sunglasses.

"Bingo. When I heard my name earlier, I froze."

"Okay, I thought, maybe . . ." She exhaled in relief.

"Geez, I'm an idiot. I'm sorry. Come here." He wrapped his arm around her and pulled her into him.

"No, you're not," Dahlia said, settling her face into the crook of his neck. God, he smelled good.

"She made a fool out of me." He cleared his throat. "For months after it happened, the paparazzi were everywhere. I couldn't escape, which meant every day I had to relive it. I was followed, stalked, and harassed. It took a toll on my mental health."

Even after an entire year, he still seemed wrecked over it. The realization that he might not yet be over his ex crushed Dahlia. She squeezed her eyes shut and held him tighter. "I'm really sorry, Noah. You didn't deserve that."

"I swore off women after that. Then you came along and uprooted my plan with your feisty attitude and see-through tank top." He laughed.

"Oh, my God." Dahlia instinctively drew back, covering her chest. She'd honestly hoped he'd been so inebriated that he'd forgotten about it.

"I saw everything." He looked at her with lust-filled eyes. "Both times."

Her face turned as red as a cherry, and she buried her head in her hands. "I'm mortified; no wonder you couldn't take me seriously."

He tilted his head and bit his lip in the most playful yet seductive way. "Not sure I'd want it to happen any other way, D."

"Yeah?"

"Yeah."

"And for the record, I got spooked before because this"—he pointed between them—"feels like it needs to be guarded."

He went on to tell her about Josie, how they'd been together since high school, and how she changed when they landed the *Hamptons House* gig together. Dahlia sat motionless and listened intently, just as any friend would.

"What part changed?' she asked. There was a big part of her that wanted to know every last detail, and the other, smaller part of her wanted it to stay buried along with Lil's secret.

"I got the show first, and then they brought her in the following summer. She was outgoing and kind, but the fame changed her. She started caring way too much about her image, and it was clear that my past didn't serve her brand."

People shuffled by, trying to find open grass for their chairs and blankets. The sounds of a nearby microphone lent static to the twilight summer air. Dahlia didn't want Noah to feel rushed; she wanted him to feel grounded in the present with her. She leaned closer and held his hand, urging him with a warm smile to continue.

Noah talked about his best friend from college, Danny, who got the gig when he did, and how they deceived him for months. Dahlia could tell the wounds were still raw from the way he spoke down to his defeated body language. The muscles in her jaw tightened like a vice. She knew exactly how he felt. She and Spence hadn't *ever* been in a great place, but being abandoned, left, never felt good. It was like nothing you did was ever enough. Dahlia had grown to understand it was a Spence thing, and not a her thing, and she hoped eventually Noah would too.

"Looking back, there were clues. They'd always be paired together for house projects and competitions." His breath hitched.

"I often wonder if some of the producers knew and purposefully put them together. I'm a bit jaded." He snickered.

"Nah, couldn't tell." She lightheartedly brushed it off while feeling pulled to watch it for herself. The show sounded interesting. An old house, one summer to get it from fixer to fabulous, sort of like Lil's. But at the end of the day, she was remarkably protective of Noah. Seeing it would only unearth feelings that were better staying buried.

After he finished sharing, she mentioned she knew a few things from Kara, but that she'd never seen the show. Noah seemed to like that. The movie began, and it was picturesque, with the full harbor of boats clanking in the background. About halfway through, when the air had a bite to it, he wrapped her up in an extra blanket he had brought, securing her close to his chest. That was all she needed to doze off finally. After it was over, he gently woke her, never once making her feel bad. The drive home was quiet as she sank into the crook of his arm, relishing in the proximity that felt both intimate and comforting.

"Thanks for a great night." He walked her up the front porch. "I forgot how good that movie is."

"Sorry I missed most of it. It's been a long few days." She turned to face him. Plus, she'd barely slept when he was gone.

"It's okay. It was nice just to hold you. Your heartbeat is peaceful."

"It is?" Dahlia wrinkled her nose.

"It is. You make me peaceful, D," he said.

"You do the same for me, Noah," she said with a truth that felt as pure as honey. "Do you want to come in? For a nightcap?" Dahlia cringed inside. Did people still say that?

He hesitated. "I better not."

"Okay." Dahlia stared at her feet, wishing she hadn't asked.

"Can I see you tomorrow night? I have to run over to the island during the day, but we could . . . ?"

Dahlia inched closer so as not to miss a word.

"Go to dinner," he said, now leaning on the door frame.

"Sure, I'd like that," Dahlia said, looking up at him, yearning for one last kiss.

He caressed her face and pulled her up toward him. "Night," he said, pecking her nose.

"Night." Dahlia stood there, not wanting him to go. "If you change your mind, you know where to find me," she said, slipping off her jacket and throwing it onto the banister.

"I'm going *before* I change my mind," he said, walking backward.

She closed the door and dropped her aroused body onto the bench. "You're officially driving me insane, Noah Sterling." Dahlia leaned her head against the wall, for the first time feeling conflicted about her decision to move away soon.

Harry strolled over and stretched. She leaned over and canoodled him, hitting the pressed flowers box with her elbow. Maybe she should open the box tonight. It would be a good distraction, and she was certainly no longer tired. Contemplating the quandary, she felt her forehead wrinkle. If she were going to date a younger man, she needed to get on that wrinkle cream. She added it to the list in her head. The irony wasn't lost on Dahlia; in all the years Spence had asked her to put more effort into her appearance, she now wanted to, and it was because she wasn't with him. "Shall we take a peek?"

Harry barked, ogling her with his dark eyes.

Dahlia took that as a yes, pulling open the dusty flaps. She peered inside and reached for the first thick and lumpy album. She let out a cough as her fingers lingered over the top. The cover read *Rose Garden* in beautiful, romantic calligraphy.

The first page stuck, but Dahlia was able to peel it back without tearing the other pages. There was a pressed rose on every page. "This is so you, Lil," she mumbled. Most were unrecognizable but labeled, with a name and number written underneath. She turned to the last page, which was a faded pink, and read *Claire Austin*. There was a lump in her throat as she pulled back the corner and touched the dried keepsake. The surface was now hard and lifeless. Dahlia wasn't sure how she felt about it. Part of her was happy to see Lil's handwriting and evidence of her creative existence, but the other part made her sad. She didn't exactly know why. Something about this find felt different, as if she were an intruder.

Album one stopped at page seven.

The next album read *Rose Garden 2*. She carefully turned to *Fragrant Plum*, number eleven. Its once vibrant mulberry color now looked void of any depth and life. The pages were numbered eight through fifteen.

The last read *Rose Garden 3*, numbered to twenty-two. Dahlia laid them on the floor, her eyes filled with tears. "Lil, I miss you." Dahlia's voice cracked. She missed Lil but also missed having people to count on and a family to call her own. Spence had never been much of a consolation. Her dry cleaner was more like a husband than he was—he asked how her day was and took something off her plate.

Harry ran to the back door and whimpered.

She wiped her nose and got up, walking over to let him out. The screen door snapped behind her. The night air was cool as it skimmed her cheek. She paced the grass, noticing how bright and clear the sky was.

Her phone dinged. It was Noah.

Two can play, it said, along with a picture of him in bed, shirtless, chiseled and slick like he'd just exerted himself, with his finger tucked inside his white briefs.

She covered her mouth, suddenly feeling her insides ablaze. "Geez, mixed signals much?" She looked up at Noah's window.

The light was still on. Her breath quickened, and she tingled in places that had been dormant for far too long. Dahlia hadn't thought she was capable of desire like this. It made her wonder if she could have it all: a career and love. And if so, how in God's name would it work? She was moving in twenty-four days.

CHAPTER FOURTEEN

July 10

Dahlia sat motionless in the rose garden the next morning. Her legs were crossed, and her palms were open, facing the sky. The soil was damp, and it smelled like rain. It was the first overcast day since she'd arrived, and her smile curved ear to ear. Dahlia liked rainy days. When Daisy was little, she'd relished their mother-daughter time. They would go to the library, bake cookies, watch a movie, and snuggle. It always seemed like a free day and an excuse to nest and find joy in the simple things again.

Dahlia surrendered to the peace, feeling her shoulders finally relax. Lil had loved this garden, and Dahlia was starting to grasp why. She sank her fingers into the dirt. For some reason, feeling the earth, Lil's earth, made her feel connected to who she used to be and wanted so desperately to find again.

Perhaps it was the country air, the down-to-earth people, the slower pace, or maybe it was Noah, the guy torturing her with his godlike body, acts of service, and old soul ways. Suddenly, Dahlia didn't feel so calm. She felt achy, and her nerve endings were on high alert. Cold droplets hit her nose, adding to her awakened mood.

Suddenly inspired, Dahlia leaped up and twirled her dirty body in the drizzle. She danced like no one was watching. "Does this count, Lil?" she asked the sullen sky. She bounced through the Fragrant Plum, the Louise Odier, and Madame Plantier, which still needed TLC. The flowery notes of vanilla and citrus mingled through the moist air as her fingertips grazed the petals. She stopped at the pale blush bush and held a stem to her nose. Her belly tickled, and her cheeks ached. It was the feeling of belonging somewhere, and it was the same feeling she'd known every summer since she was a little girl.

She took a video scanning her entire view so that others could see it too. It was as if Monet had set up his easel in her backyard. Dahlia opened her rarely used social media account. There were six pictures and only thirty-five followers. She uploaded the video anyway and typed the caption, "Flowers are like friends. You can never have too many." Dahlia was leaning into this idea of having friends. Not the kind that whispered behind your back like in Greenwich, but shirt-off-your-back kind of friends, like Kara, who were honest, reliable, and trustworthy. Although she didn't know Noah and his sister all that well, she could tell they were the kind of friends she wanted and needed in her life.

The rain fell harder, and Dahlia scurried to find her hat and sneakers. Just as she spotted her other shoe, she noticed something blue sticking out of the dirt. "What in the world?" She knelt down and picked it up.

She rubbed off the dirt with her thumb and held it up toward the sky. It was a graduation tassel. The metal tag read 73. What was it doing in the rose garden? And whose was it? Even though it was now a steady rain, the chilled beads of water felt nice on her warm skin. Dahlia headed toward the shed. Was it possible that something else was buried with the tassel? Maybe there was more in the yard. Curiosity overcame her as she rushed through the door for a shovel.

Dahlia scanned the small rustic space for a towel or something to wipe her eyes. The only thing she could find was an old smock that hung next to the rakes. And in pure Lil style, it wasn't just any smock. It was a white button-down garnished with years of paint and dirt. She dabbed her eyes with what looked like a clean corner and sighed as she slipped her arms through the sleeves, feeling stronger and braver in her shirt. Who needed a cape when she had this? Dahlia's nose tingled, which meant tears weren't far behind.

Just as she started to sink into nostalgia, Harry ran in, soaked and filthy. Bending down to get a closer look, she realized he'd been rolling in the mud. She let out a frustrated huff and said, "It looks like we both need a shower. My excavation is going to have to wait, again." She stared at the relic still in her palm. "Seventy-three, seventy-three," Dahlia mumbled as she tilted her head like Harry often did when talked to with animation. She did the math quickly. She was convinced it had to be her mother's. Her eyes drew upward, spotting three more Hills Bros coffee cans lining the upper wood beam, which still seemed odd since Lil never drank coffee. She suddenly remembered the can that she and Noah found under the violets. It said eighteen. Then she let out a whispered gasp when she realized the connection. Eighteen was her mom's age when she graduated. The tassel made perfect sense now, especially since the can was empty. But why was a can buried in the garden with her age marked on the bottom in the first place? With a graduation tassel from high school inside it? This seemed like a logical idea, and one she clung to like the droplets of rain still on her eyelashes. It wasn't lost on her that it could have been a coincidence or something that was dropped, then accidentally buried all those years ago. But the hopeful part of her wanted to believe it was a premeditated clue from the past.

Dahlia ran through the rain back up to the house, deep in thought as Harry followed. Harry went first into the shower, and once he was clean and dry enough, it was Dahlia's turn. The warm water felt good as it cascaded over her chilled, goosebumped skin. Her mind skipped, landing on the same idea over and over: Could her mom have made a time capsule? After losing her so young, Dahlia had always clung to any piece of her. Finding something new would be a gift she hadn't known she needed. She reached for the soil-stained tassel that lay on the bench next to Harry's collar and gave them both a good cleaning as well.

The clean tassel now hung from the cold water knob. You could see the colors vividly, although the blue and white were still faded and stained. When it stopped raining, she'd go back to the garden to see what else was left behind in her mother's possible time capsule. She leaned closer, inspecting it as if it were an ancient artifact. In some twisted way, unearthing the ghosts of the past pleased her. Once upon a time, her dream had been to study archaeology, but she quickly understood it wasn't the ideal career for a single mother.

Once clean and properly groomed in all the places that mattered, Dahlia found herself back in the kitchen mopping. Her hair was still damp, and she was wearing her mother's old Boston College sweatshirt, which she had found tucked under a cedarwood sachet in Lil's drawer. It was yet another sign, telling her she was exactly where she was supposed to be: at Lil's, getting her house ready to sell, but also peeling back the layers of the past. Opening that door didn't seem so scary anymore. Plus, she was slowly coming back to life, and she knew in order to fully bloom, it was important to make peace with how her life had unfolded.

There was the entire afternoon ahead to wash Lil's slipcovers, so she decided to have a cup of tea first. Faithful Harry sat beside her, patiently waiting for a treat. "Who wants a bacon wrap?" asked Dahlia in a sweet, playful tone. Harry immediately broke into a spin, and she laughed. "Okay, okay." It was the trick that had set him apart from every other dog in the shelter, and once he looked at her with those soft brown eyes, she knew he was the one. If only finding a human mate were that easy. Or maybe it was. The jury was still out.

Dahlia held the treat above his nose. Harry didn't flinch. "Good boy, here you go."

He snatched the jerky with his teeth and exited into the hallway.

Dahlia's feet moved in the direction of the record player, the only one she'd ever known. It looked like an oddly shaped suitcase with a black top and red bottom that matched Lil's checkered wingbacks. Dahlia opened it and found a Frank Sinatra record already inside. Lil had loved him. Sinatra was before her time, but Gran and Pop were older, and possibly their musical taste had rubbed off on her. Still, Dahlia had always wondered what the draw was. She turned it on and lowered the needle right at the beginning of "I've Got You Under My Skin," which couldn't have been any more fitting.

Harry followed her back through the hallway and into the kitchen. She hummed along with the music as she pulled out the tin of tea bags from the cupboard. It was nice to be in her family's kitchen, where so much had happened over the years. Dahlia thought about Lil and Gran's annual Thanksgiving argument over how long to cook the potatoes. She imagined rolling the dough with her mother and Gran for their legendary almond Christmas cookies.

Dahlia put on the kettle and peered out the small window while she waited. The swampy puddles now engulfed the grass, and she wondered where Noah was and what he was up to. She eyeballed her phone, tempted to text him. All she could think about was their last kiss. She touched her lips in anticipation of another and smiled. Did he feel the same? All she could do was hope he shared this desire that seemed to invade her thoughts without warning.

The kettle whistled, and Dahlia flinched, waking her from her daydream. Ribbons of steam rose from the vessel as she poured the water into the cup.

On her tippy toes in the pantry, she reached past the jar of lavender, fingers just grazing the bottle of honey she was looking for. She pinched her nose and squinted as if doing so would give her more height. That's when she felt a firm hand slide around her waist and a warm body press against her. A sound escaped her lips. It was something between a moan and a yelp. She exhaled slowly, knowing it was Noah.

"What . . ." She could barely get the words out in between pants. "Are you doing here?" She wanted to turn around and see his gorgeous face, but she also didn't want to break from his hold that had her breathless and tingly all over.

He whispered in her ear, "I couldn't stay away."

Dahlia's heart raced, and her body grew feverish. It was as if he had read her mind and heart. She blinked to make sure it wasn't a dream before turning around. "Noah, I—"

Before she could utter any word, he kissed her. He tasted like cinnamon, with hints of sage, likely from one of Gretchen's test dishes.

With each glide of his tongue, her body felt more like Jell-O. Noah held her hips and lifted her onto the pantry counter. Every molecule in her body ached for him, and she couldn't bear another near miss. If he left her this time or changed his mind, she might combust. Without hesitation, she pulled back, met his eyes, and said, "Stay."

He hesitated, looking serious, then a smile curved his lips. His intense gaze screamed desire, longing, and lust. "Nothing could tear me away," he said. His thick brown hair looked windswept and messy. He smelled like damp leather and soap. "You're all I could think about today, D." He brushed the hair off her face. "I want you. I *crave* you. It's maddening."

His words stole her ability to think and speak. She'd never known this kind of penetrating, raw need for a man. To know he felt the same, and he was willing to admit it, meant something had shifted. Dahlia's body felt light and wispy, like dandelion seeds floating in the breeze.

She pressed her mouth to his and reciprocated the sentiment. Her hands slid around his thick neck, and his pulse wildly thumped beneath her fingertips. No words were needed. Their tongues danced, deepening their longing for what was to come.

But then he pulled back, searching her caramel eyes. "Do you want me? I need to hear you say it."

"It isn't obvious, Noah? I just asked you to stay." Their eyes remained firmly connected while her body trembled.

"Say it," he softly demanded, grazing her arm with his knuckles. It was a small gesture, but one that made her core ache.

"Yes, yes. I want this. I want *you*."

The old Dahlia Newberry had never been forward with a guy. But this was Dahlia 2.0, and with this kind of newfound confidence, it was anyone's guess what would happen next.

"Right here, in the pantry," she said, clenching the edge of the counter. She didn't know where this unbridled courage came from, but she wasn't about to hit the brakes. It felt too good, too right.

He leaned into her, pushing her legs open, and she yanked him closer by his jean loops. Her breath hitched as his bulge met her short shorts. Her panties were slick. There was no hiding it; she was aroused. Dahlia's heart galloped like she was seventeen again. But this time, the boy she was crazy about actually knew how to treat a woman.

"No," he whispered. "I want to make love to you, D. I don't want it to be just sex."

"Noah," she said, feeling his baby blues scan over every inch of her heated flesh. The truth was she wanted it all, to make love to him *and* have wild, earth-shattering sex.

His silky lips teased her ear, and his hips nudged her legs even wider. "But it doesn't mean we can't have a little fun before we go up."

He left her breathless, not knowing what would follow. Her head fell back against the shelves.

Without warning, he dropped to his knees and looked up at her with a wide grin that curled higher on one side. It was one that said he was about to take her to places she'd only dreamed of as he inched her shorts down.

Dahlia could see the rise and fall of her chest even through the sweatshirt. Was this really happening? *Oh, God.* Panic started to set in that Noah was about to go down on her. She wasn't well-versed in this. Spence had only done it a few times, early on, and Tristan just the one time. Noah peppered her inner thigh with tender kisses, and her fear of not being wanted in that way melted.

"Oh, baby," he whispered, nestling his face into her warm, wet entrance, only separated by a thin under layer of cloth. "You smell like powdery heaven."

Then he did something she wasn't prepared for. He nipped, licked, and sucked through the fabric. Dahlia could hear her tiny moans, but she didn't care. She white-knuckled the counter even harder. Why hadn't she insisted on this sooner?

"You taste so fuckin' good."

All she could do was succumb to this earth-shattering feeling and let him continue working his magic. And oh God, was he a magician.

"Like sun-ripened nectar and honey," he hummed. Who would have thought that Noah Sterling, with the boy-next-door charm, who wanted to wait, could do this? His tongue pressed harder into her seam, and she was going to combust if he didn't stop.

"Noah . . ."

"Unravel for me, baby."

"I don't . . . know . . ." She panted. "If I can."

She wanted more. She wanted him skin to skin. She wanted to feel his whiskers graze her swollen, sensitive flesh. Then he pushed the material to the side and sank a thick finger inside her, while he rubbed her throbbing bundle of nerves with his thumb. Breathy moans fell from her mouth, sending her tumbling into a haze of pleasure unlike anything she'd ever known.

"Oh God, Noah." She gripped his hair as her legs shuddered around his head.

"Good girl." He crooned, and it sent her soaring over the edge. Her body flooded with euphoria. Stars danced behind her eyes as she released the most incredible cosmic orgasm of her entire life. She rode out her climax with her eyes clamped shut, not caring how she looked. When she opened them, he was staring at her with the most sardonic grin. It was as if he knew she had never crested like this for anyone else.

Dahlia felt her cheeks warm because it was true. As far as she was concerned, this was her first time. Sure, she had a vibrator that had come in very handy when her sex life with Spence was as dry as a desert, which was the norm. And Tristan, he did try. But this. This was no comparison to a battery-operated machine stored in her nightstand or a man who didn't know what he was doing. Noah Sterling knew what he was doing. That much she was sure of.

Without warning, he lifted her onto him, and she let out a playful squeal. There was zero time to be self-conscious of the wet spot now pressed against his stomach. He carried her through the kitchen, passing Harry along the way. Frank played in the background, and the house was eerily peaceful and still, as if time had paused just for them. His bright blues, the color of the Caribbean, drew her in, and she knew if she wasn't careful, she could quite possibly drown in them.

She wondered if she should break their tempo to turn the music off. But she was too distracted by the gorgeous man carrying her up to bed and the threat of impending naughtiness. The only decision was to let the music play.

"You're not going to regret this," he said with a softer, serious tone.

"After what just happened. I wholeheartedly agree," she said, matching his tone. Their eyes locked in a moment she knew they both felt. A moment of intensity brought a sense of levity when he bumped them into the wall.

"Ouch." She laughed. "Watch it, McHandy."

"McHandy?"

"Yeah, that's what Kara and I call you."

"Is it now?" He started to walk them up the stairs.

"It was either that or Double H."

He looked at her with a blank stare.

"Handy Hunk."

"Sounds like a superhero gone wrong. McHandy it is. It has a nice ring to it," he said. "Umm, I think someone wants to join us."

Dahlia looked down and saw a furry black tail sail past them. "Geez, he has no idea what's about to happen. Poor guy." Suddenly, Dahlia got a pit in her stomach, realizing how long it had been since she'd actually had sex. On the bright side, she still had an appetite for it, which was a major epiphany.

They reached the top of the stairs, and Dahlia nodded down the hall. "It's the second door on the right."

He walked in slow motion through the hallway. Every step on the creaky floor only made Dahlia's heart pound faster.

They reached the door. "This is it," she said, still straddling his waist. She could feel his chest rise and fall with hers. It was a moment she knew would change things.

He bit his lip. "You good?" She nodded, realizing he was probably nervous too. It didn't seem like he slept around, and he cared enough to want to take things slow. But after what just happened in the pantry, she had a feeling they were on their way from zero to one hundred fast. Who needed brakes anyway?

"Harry, sit, boy. This is where we say goodbye."

Noah laughed. "You sound so serious."

"Do I?" She chuckled. Harry was like her child, and there was no way she was going to scare him with her newfound sexual awakening.

Harry whimpered and reclined against the wall. Noah strutted them through the doorway, and Dahlia kicked the door shut with her foot. She'd never wanted something so much in her entire life. The aftershocks from her orgasm had her craving more. Who was she?

Noah released her body from his. Her thighs grazed his damp denim jeans as she slid down. Still in a staring contest, she felt the cold floor beneath her feet. He brought his mouth closer to hers; she could feel his warm breath. His fingers eased through her hair. "Can I pick up where I left off?"

Dahlia stared inward, tugging at her lip. She didn't want to scare him off, but she wasn't sure how good she'd be at this, and well, it had been a hot minute.

"We can go at your pace, D. I don't want to rush you."

"No, no." She looked up. "It's not like that." She wanted to do everything with him. To hell with pacing. She was hooked on this man and wanted him now, but a small part of her felt that she should warn him. And so she did. "This probably isn't the sexiest thing to say, but it's been a long time for me."

"I'll go easy on you," he said with a grin.

"Please don't," Dahlia said in a soft and eager tone. If she had to sum up her sex life in one word over the last twenty years, it would be *ordinary*. And that wasn't going to cut it anymore. She'd gotten a taste of something she liked, and now her body had a will of its own.

Noah yanked off her sweatshirt and threw it onto the neatly made bed. Taking a step back, he said with a Cheshire cat smile, "This is going to be fun."

She walked closer to him in her staple white tank top. "My turn." Dahlia yanked off his dirty work shirt, revealing the chiseled upper body she'd dreamt about touching for the last seven days. Dahlia held her breath, her hands moving toward his pants, only to be met with resistance.

"It's my turn," he said confidently, tracing the outline of her breasts with his hand. Despite the layer of clothing between them, the heat from his touch scorched her insides. His gentle stroke awakened her nipples, giving him even more to look at.

He tugged the bottom of her shirt. "God, I want to rip this thing off you."

"Go for it, McHandy," she said, feeling another wave of desire bloom between her legs.

He reached for something in his work boot. "I would never, ever hurt you."

"I totally and completely trust you," she said with her shoulders back. All the years with Spence were no match for the one week with Noah. He was attentive, reliable, and caring. Spence was selfish, untrustworthy, and incapable of putting her own needs above his.

Noah flipped open a Swiss Army knife with a mischievous smile.

This is where the old Dahlia would have made a joke about *Dateline* and him being the "Army Knife Serial Killer," but she didn't. Instead, she stood a little taller, luring him with her eyes. She could feel the swift thud of her heart racing under her shirt.

"You have more of these, right?" Noah asked, reaching for her tank top.

She nodded yes, but she didn't care, even if that was her last one. All she was trying to do was not faint. The mere idea of him wanting to rip off her shirt terrified her and made her feel reborn at the same time.

His blue eyes were wide and bright. Dahlia leaned into the anticipation coursing through her body as she heard the ripping sound begin. Her whole body buzzed with a kind of frantic yearning. It was like finally breaking free from a cocoon that had kept her flightless and bound for so many years. Being free of a loveless marriage was something she'd longed for on too many days to count. Dahlia imagined the lifeline to her old life being severed by the knife so a new one could grow.

When her shirt was completely torn down the middle, Noah pushed the tattered edges off her shoulders and took a step back. This time, Dahlia didn't cover herself. She stood there in the dim rainy light, wanting to be admired and touched. She wanted nothing more than to feel his bare skin against hers.

"You are beautiful. God!" He closed the space between them and softly cupped her breasts, pinching her nipples between his thumb and finger. Then his warm mouth covered them. He flicked, sucked, and hummed until her knees thought they'd give out.

Her body felt untamed as she sank deeper into his hold. She couldn't believe this was what she'd been missing all these years. He tugged down her panties, ignoring that it was her turn. His eyes trailed down to her sex that was now slick with arousal. Again, she just stood there soaking in his admiration.

His mouth met hers in a lust-filled dance, and that only made her dizzier with desire. There was an awakening happening. One that was well earned and deserved.

"I can't wait another minute to be inside you," he whispered. With that, he dropped his jeans and briefs to the pine-planked floor. She wanted to laugh at his eagerness, but then spotted his steely length jetting out between his legs.

Dahlia needed a moment to pick her chin off the floor. She'd never seen a man that well-endowed, even when Spence and his friends skinny-dipped in her pool three summers ago. This was thick, veiny, and big.

And with that, he moved their naked bodies to the edge of the bed. He skimmed her collarbone with his lips, tickling her skin with his whiskers. "You smell good, by the way. Like lavender, mint, and honey."

"I think you already mentioned honey," she said, suddenly feeling his length against her slick entrance.

"I did, didn't I?"

Her face flushed.

"Aww. You're blushing, it's cute." He kissed her nose. Then he lowered her onto the fluffy down duvet and climbed his chiseled form on top of her.

Suddenly, she could hear everything. The sound of rain hitting the roof, the sound of sailboat masts swaying in the wet wind, her racing heart, and the sound of his throat when he swallowed. She ran her fingertips across his colorfully etched skin, down his chest, his delicious V, and then to his groin, gripping him in her hand. It's something she'd wanted to do since seeing it tent through his pants.

"What are you doing to me?" He nestled his head in the crook of her neck as she continued to stroke his hard length. "I . . . I . . . have a condom." His breath hitched. "I can't wait much longer, D."

"I've been on the pill for a while." Since Daisy was five and Dahlia got back together with Spence, to be exact, but he didn't need to know that. It was more for her cycle than anything, since Spence barely ever looked twice at her. Then with the affair, the scarcely became extinct.

"I was tested after Josie." It was the first time he'd mentioned her name. It was either a good thing or a really bad one. She hoped it was the former. "And I haven't been with anyone since."

"Okay," she said calmly, while inside, she was in disbelief that he'd been celibate all year long. That single admission made this moment feel even more extraordinary.

With that, he laced his hands with hers and raised them above her head. With one thrust, he was inside of her.

"Oh, baby, you're so freaking tight." He groaned into her ear.

Dahlia held her breath as he stretched her. With his size, it should have hurt, but she was too wet to feel pain. He filled her inch by thick inch, and she moaned like a woman who'd finally found her voice.

"Noah, oh, you feel so goddamn good." In all her life, she had never known a man inside her could leave her buzzing with this kind of joy. Nothing could compare with the release of emotion that came every time Noah returned his hips to hers. It was a feeling she wanted to bottle and hold on to forever.

"So do you, baby. So fuckin' good." He pushed the sticky hair off her face and continued his slow cadence. Dahlia wrapped her legs around his thick thighs, their eyes never leaving one another. In their hold, she knew this was more than just a summer fling.

Her hands wandered down his back and onto his bare ass. She gripped his soft skin and firmly drew him back to her. They made love on her bed overlooking the bay, taking their sweet time in an unhurried and sensual way. Then he flipped her over, so she was on top. That was another sensation altogether. His length hit her G-spot, which sent her eyes rolling to the back of her head. Although she'd never had an orgasm like this, she had a sneaking suspicion that Noah would change that. She rode him like a woman on a mission. Slow at first, taking her time leaning forward and back, up and down until he gripped her hips harder, wanting it faster. Her breasts bounced with the new rhythm, and she arched her back, feeling every atom in her body ignite.

"You're so beautiful," he said again and again. He could tell her sweet nothings all day long, and she would never tire of it.

She leaned forward, pressing her naked body against his. They were chest to chest, and she could feel his heart in rhythm with hers. The sweat and friction made her blood sing.

"That's it, D. Don't stop."

After a few clipped breaths, he let out a lengthy groan with a few expletives.

Feeling *his* release inside her was a new kind of erotic. He looked spent and satiated, and she was the reason. Beads of sweat lined his tan forehead, and his mustache glistened. The room was quiet, except for the gentle drip from the gutter that echoed through the room. Still bare and still joined, she looked into his bright eyes, which felt infinite.

"You good?" He grazed his knuckles over her thigh, sending more goosebumps across the landscape of her skin.

Dahlia nodded, with a smile that said she had never been better.

"Let's get you cleaned up," he said, tapping her leg. Even after, he was still trying to take care of her. This was so foreign to her.

"Just a few more minutes." She collapsed beside him, falling into the crook of his arm. Noah's warm lips pressed against her temple as she stared up at the shadows on the ceiling. Dahlia knew after that moment that she deserved a life of color and that nothing would ever be black-and-white again.

CHAPTER FIFTEEN

July 11

The next morning, Dahlia woke in a spooning position with Noah's arms casually draped around her waist. After christening the pantry and the bed, they had made dinner and snuggled on the couch with a movie. Then they christened that too. It was nice to have a lazy day together. It was exactly what she needed to keep going. She felt invigorated, satiated, and happy. With a wide grin, she rolled over, pressing her face against his warm chest, which still smelled of Irish Spring. The sun was already bright, shining a ray that spanned across the floor. The air was just the right temperature, not too cold and not too hot, like the morning after heavy rain. Dahlia closed her eyes and listened to the birds chirp and sing to one another outside the porch doors. It felt like a blessing from Lil.

"Good morning," Noah said with a groggy tone. With his eyes barely open, he tickled her forehead with his whiskered lips.

"Morning." She looked up and wondered what the proper protocol was for the morning after sleeping with someone for the first time. Would he stay, would he go? Would he want to continue their sexcapade and have morning sex? Should she brush her teeth? The phone buzzed on the nightstand, interrupting her wandering thoughts. It was probably Kara calling for her morning check-in to get the tea.

"Don't get it. Just stay with me." He tugged her hips closer.

Dahlia's hand stilled, unsure whether to reach behind her to get the phone or in front of her toward Noah. It could be Daisy, and she couldn't bear the thought of missing her call. *Dahlia 2.0*, she reminded herself and slipped her arm around his buff middle, wrapping her leg around his thigh. Whoever it was, they could wait.

It felt nice to wake up in his embrace. To know he'd wanted to stay and not scurry off in the night like it was all a big mistake. Nothing about this seemed like a mistake. Dahlia felt fearless; her body felt expansive. She even shocked herself by wanting more. In the past, it was one-and-done, like a chore on her to-do list, when it did happen. But with Noah, sex wasn't a chore. It was a reward.

"Hungry?" he whispered.

"Yes, famished," she said, not knowing which kind of appetite he was referring to.

"I can make us eggs," he said.

"And coffee?" she asked playfully. "Oh, and Harry—could you let him out too?"

"Of course. Five more minutes, though," he said, pulling her on top of him. "I want to feel your body on mine." His bulge pulsated against her skin. He was a good eight inches taller than she, so it met the delicate skin on her upper inner thigh. She almost laughed but didn't. She remained fixed on his eyes that felt like liquid heat. "Your heartbeat with mine."

They were chest to chest, and she rested her chin on her hand. "Can I ask you something?"

"Sure, shoot."

"What changed yesterday? You said you wanted to wait and then . . ." She felt her brows furrow.

"You changed my mind."

"How so?" She listened, circling the small scar on his right pec, wondering how he'd gotten it. She wanted to know everything about him. All of it. The good, the bad, the ugly, and everything in between.

"I don't know. It feels like we've known each other for longer than we have. Like I can trust you with anything."

"What, longer than seven days?" She gave a lighthearted chuckle while her heart constricted, knowing she still hadn't told him everything.

"Eight now, but who's counting?" He snickered, pressing his mouth to hers. It was a tender kiss, one that lasted longer than expected. "Does that make any sense? Plus, living next door to you was driving me insane. Especially at night. I barely slept."

"Me too, and it makes perfect sense. I feel the same, Noah." Dahlia smiled, feeling his morning wood. They were face-to-face, and she didn't care that they had morning breath. She was in bed with someone who was a total stranger to her as of a week ago, yet they were now something much more. What exactly, she wasn't sure. That was still to be determined.

He purred into her ear. "I'm ravenous for my cougar. Or I should call you my puma."

"You're insatiable," she crooned.

"And what are you going to do about it?" he asked, tucking her hair behind her ear, meeting her in a firm hold. And with that, she lifted her hips, and he slipped inside of her for another mind-blowing round—yielding another first for Dahlia as she orgasmed on top.

* * *

Dahlia walked into the kitchen from the laundry room in a sex-induced haze. She was a little sore from the excessive gymnastics, but mostly elated and shocked that she'd never hit that kind of bliss before. "One set of slipcovers finally in the wash," she said, walking into the kitchen where Noah was cooking in nothing but boxer briefs and an apron. She still needed to call the realtor and Daisy back, but she just wanted to stay in their bubble for now. A deep sigh of contentment escaped her lips. This cloud-nine euphoria, where all she wanted to do was kiss Noah for days, swept her away like a wave out to sea. But she also felt a tug of responsibility because there was still so much to be done. "That apron suits you."

"I found it in the pantry. Is it okay to wear it?" he asked, whisking the eggs. His broad shoulders and muscular physique taking up the tight L-shaped area.

"Sure, it was Lil's favorite. You look very domestic," she said, hooking her arm around his waist, feeling the apron strings hit her fingertips.

"Is that a bad thing?"

She scooched herself in front of him and stole a kiss. "Not at all. In fact, your rating as a handyman, and other things, just exceeded five stars."

"Note to self: cook more." His voice still sounded hoarse, which made Dahlia even dizzier with desire.

She snuck a piece of cheddar cheese from the counter. "This looks great, by the way. I didn't think there was that much in the fridge."

"There wasn't. I ran home for a few things while you were in the shower."

"So thoughtful." Dahlia slipped her hands inside the apron and caressed his bare back. "I'm starved." She pretended to nibble his bare skin. Dahlia wasn't sure what had birthed this boldness. All she knew was there was an ease with him, one she couldn't put into words.

He had a cheeky grin. "Baby, if you're not careful, you may be my breakfast."

Dahlia's face felt like a furnace at the mere hint of what was to come after breakfast. Oh, and that word—*baby*. Why did it make her knees weak and her core hum with need? "Ah, I think I already was," she said, feeling her breath hitch.

"Lunch then. But sustenance first," he said. "Plates?"

"Cabinet left of the sink."

"Thanks. I got this. You sit."

Dahlia glanced at Lil's table set for a morning feast. Her heart somersaulted. She wanted to pinch herself to see if she was dreaming. In all the years married, she and Spence never ate breakfast together, not even on vacation. He was constantly exercising, working, or as it turned out, having an affair

"Noah." Her eyes burned at the thought of what she'd missed out on. "This is amazing." She wasn't going to cry in front of him, but she couldn't help the tears of joy that threatened to rise. She was happy, and it was a feeling as foreign to her as living in a distant land. She regretted not asking for more time with her new position because now she didn't want to leave so soon.

Dahlia sat first, then Noah, draping the apron over the chair. They drank orange juice and coffee and talked like any couple would. They talked about nothing and everything as they ate their eggs and toast. She shared a bit more about her lonely marriage to Spence and how they were in the final stages of divorce. She told him more about Lil. How Gran, Pop, and Lil had been very close. Almost too close. How Dahlia often wondered if anything ever happened between Lil and her pop after her gran died. And if that might be part of the secret. Dahlia also shared more about her parents and how they expected a lot from her academically. The hidden graduation tassel came up, and he also agreed it could have come from the tin they found.

She wanted to tell him about Daisy, how ashamed she'd been at first for disappointing everyone by getting pregnant just out of high school, and how alone she would have been if it weren't for Lil. But there was a small part of her that feared that once he knew, he would change his mind. That he'd see their age difference as taboo and realize their lives were just too different. Plus, she was leaving. That was a fact that wouldn't change. So, for now, she would tuck her truth away in a drawer where it was safe until she was more ready.

Noah, too, shared things about his family. That his mom had been in and out of rehab when he was growing up, and how abusive her boyfriends were. One even burned a cigar on his chest after a drunken argument, and from that point on, he and his sister fought daily to survive. That was until his stepfather, Don, stepped in, and things got better. He touched on the football scholarship he received to play at the University of Colorado at Boulder and how he tore his ACL at the end of his third season. With moist eyes, he revealed that Don took on extra shifts at work so that he wouldn't have to drop out of school. "A shirt-off-your-back kind of guy," he said. Dahlia just smiled, realizing her feelings for Noah were growing at an express pace.

The stories he told made Dahlia swoon harder. The fact that things hadn't just been handed to him, like they had for Spence, was the biggest difference. There were also unhealed wounds from their childhood that she was pretty sure manifested into their previous unhealthy relationships. Dahlia's fear of being alone led her to agree to a marriage where she ironically was more alone. Saying yes to Spence, a man she'd never loved, had felt safe. It meant she would never feel the pain of losing that love, like she had with her parents, Gran, Pop, and later Lil. She was pretty sure Noah's fear of failure had led him to hang on longer with Josie than he should have too. But that was just speculation.

"Noah, thank you." She stared at his shirtless torso, knowing in her heart she could do this every day with him. From any logical standpoint, it was too early to have these kinds of feelings. Yet she was.

"My pleasure." He pulled her chair to him, the feet skidding across the linoleum floor. His gaze lingered.

"What? Do I have something on my face?" she asked, stroking her cheek.

"No." He shook his head. "Thanks for listening. I know some of that was heavy," he said, leaning closer yet. "I want to tell you how my mom died."

Dahlia held his trembling hand in reassurance. This felt like a big deal.

"It was a drug overdose, oxycodone. I was thirteen." His voice cracked. With his admission, Dahlia felt something shift inside her. She was the same age when her parents died at the hands of a drunk driver. "Everyone thought she was getting better. We all thought she was clean, including Don. But . . ."

"Noah." She hugged him and didn't let go. Suddenly, Dahlia's childhood didn't seem so bad. At least she'd had two loving parents for a time. "Thank you for telling me." This seemed like the perfect time to tell him about Daisy. He had just shared something close to his heart, fearing it might scare her away. It was only fair to reciprocate. But she didn't. She pulled back and gave him a reassuring kiss that said she understood.

"I've never been able to be myself with anyone this early on. And I certainly haven't shared these things about my family, especially about my mom, with many people."

She grabbed his hand. "Not with Josie?"

"She knew. But we didn't talk about it. There was an image to keep." He shrugged his shoulders.

Josie sounded awful, and Dahlia prayed she'd never have to meet her. "If it's any consolation, I could tell my ex I was on fire, and he wouldn't care." She caressed his scruffy face with an endearing smile. "And for what it's worth, I'm sorry for what you went through. No child should ever feel unsafe." She placed her palm on his scar, knowing the courage it took for him to unearth his past. If only she could do the same. "And I'm so sorry about your mom."

"It was a long time ago." He kissed the top of her head and whispered. "I can't imagine someone not appreciating you. You're an amazing person. And sexy as hell."

"Well, thanks." She hoped he'd still feel the same after he got to know her whole story. Dahlia wondered if his feelings would wear off once he realized how ordinary she was, and there was still the matter of her daughter. After all, he was still part of the mega reality television brand known as *Hamptons House*, and that brought with it its own set of standards. And she was as plain and basic as white walls. Or at least that was how she felt after being married to Spence.

"And if I ever see your ex, I'm going to kick his arse for not treating you better." He snickered, giving her a smooch, this time on her lips. "No one puts you in the corner. Not on my watch."

Dahlia's lungs felt expansive. She felt like a heroine whose lover was ready to duel to the end for her. She'd never tire of this feeling. But was she ready to give up everything for a man again? As much as she didn't want to be, Dahlia was conflicted.

He pecked her playfully one last time before getting up. "Now, let's get to work."

She laughed. "Well, okay then."

"I'll be power washing the house if you need me for anything at all." He winked, putting the dishes in the sink.

"I have one more load of laundry to do, and then I'll be out."

"Oh, and I need to run back to the restaurant later. I found this amazing old glass case on Marketplace."

"Aren't you full of surprises?" Dahlia put the mugs in the sink.

"Want to come with?"

"I'd love to, but I should probably keep going with all this." She looked around. "Plus, I have to make some phone calls. Rain check?" She wrapped her hands around his waist like they were old hat at this. "You're coming back tonight, right?" Dahlia held her breath, hoping that wasn't too presumptuous. They'd already been together for almost twenty-four hours straight.

"If that's an invite, then yes."

"Good. Now get out of here and get to work." She laughed, tapping him on his extremely firm rear.

"Yes, ma'am."

Dahlia looked around the kitchen at the mess that was left. There was a lightness in her chest. It was an odd reaction to a chore she hated. Yet this time, she was excited to clean up the counter littered with omelet ingredients because it was *their* mess. Hoping to make it to the refrigerator in one trip, she packed her arms, balancing the eggs, cheese, and orange juice. Eying the milk, inching closer, she reached for it. And missed. White liquid ran everywhere. "Shit, shit."

Dahlia dropped the food onto the counter, hearing a *thud*, and grabbed the hand towel from beside the sink. The power washer was in full force, sending a gnawing vibration through the old paneled walls. She tried to corral the flow, but the milk still dripped down the counter and into the crevice between the cabinet and floor. What a freaking mess. "Haste makes waste," echoed in her mind. It was another favorite saying of Gran's. Begrudgingly, she continued to wipe, and when the rag was saturated, she brought out another towel from the linen closet. As she walked back, she saw *Wuthering Heights* at the corner of the bar, sitting in a puddle.

There was a sharp pain in the back of her throat as she whisper-shouted, "No, no, no." Dahlia held it up by the spine and wrapped it in the kitchen towel. She leaned against the counter and let out an exaggerated, frustrated sigh.

The cover was sopping wet, and so were the first few pages. Dahlia opened it, trying her best to dry the milk-logged sheets. For the first time, she noticed smeared handwriting on the backside of the cover and looked closer.

L, I know how much you love this book. I want you to have it. With all my love. Forever, G. 1955.

L. Was this to Lil or Lizzie? If it was 1955, it had to be Lil; her Gran and Pop were already married by then, and his name was Leon. None of this made any sense unless it was written to Lil. And who was G? Was he an admirer? A boyfriend?

Lil had never spoken of anyone from her past, let alone a lover. Gran could have cheated, but she wouldn't, she couldn't, she wasn't that type of person. Dahlia's mind spun like an overloaded washing machine. It could have also been a friendly note, but friends didn't sign off with *all my love*. No, the note had to be for Lil.

Dahlia sat down in the closest chair, reckoning with the idea that Lil may have had a lover that Dahlia never knew about. Her smile grew, then wilted within seconds. What happened to him? Or her? Dahlia was going back and forth, trying to piece together this new information, when her phone vibrated. It was Daisy. This wasn't an ideal time. She pondered letting it go to voicemail again. But no, it was her daughter. She had to answer it. What if something was wrong?

"Hi, Daisy."

"Mom, where have you been? I tried calling you before."

"Ah, here. I've been home." Dahlia's voice rose to a squeaky octave. "Why, what's the emergency? You sound upset."

"I am." Daisy started crying. "I almost called Dad when you didn't answer."

Dahlia pursed her lips, so relieved she didn't. Spence didn't need to have any intel on her life. "Tell me, what's going on?"

"Mom, Pop's cousin Louisa isn't related to us. She doesn't show up as a match of yours or mine on Ancestry."

"Okay." Dahlia stood up.

"I don't understand. Louisa found Pop's original birth certificate in a safe in her parents' basement. I saw it with my own eyes," Daisy said. "He and Louisa *are* related."

Dahlia's heart began racing. "Maybe it wasn't his."

"Mom, she has pictures too; it's him. Same birthmark on his left hand. So if they were related to each other, why wouldn't *she* be related to *us*?"

"Daisy, I'm sure there's a logical explanation." Then she glanced at the inscription on the book again, and it hit her like a ton of bricks: Gran could have had an affair. Chills ran up her arms. If she had, how did that relate to Daisy's findings?

"Mom, DNA doesn't lie."

"I'm going to do some digging. Everything's going to be fine," Dahlia said, feeling her stomach churn. Deep down, she knew they had dug up something no one was prepared for.

Daisy's voice cracked. "Okay, but something's not right."

"We'll figure this out. In the meantime, go out with your friends. Forget about this."

"Not sure I can, but I'll try." Daisy let out an exhale. "Call me as soon as you find out something. "Like the minute. Promise?"

"I promise. Love you trillions, Daisy girl."

Dahlia ended the call. She didn't know what to believe or how to make sense of Daisy's findings. Her mind raced like a greyhound around a track. Her heart felt sliced open at the idea of her pop not being her biological grandfather. With her head in her hands, there was a heaviness in her chest. There was now another mission to add to her list, and she wondered if she'd ever find that key. And if she didn't, what would that mean for her and her family?

* * *

Later that night, while Noah was out, Dahlia wandered up into the attic. This new information plucked her from reality as she knew it, similar to her parents' death. Only this time, it wasn't a horrific call interrupting the best sleepover of her life. Instead, it was a shocking call disturbing the best morning-after sex of her life. Dahlia knew a thing or two about being caught off guard. For that very reason, she remained hypervigilant, never fully leaning into joy. That was, with the exception of this summer and Daisy, of course.

With Harry by her side, Dahlia rummaged through the random dust-covered boxes, looking for any clue. The air in the attic was stale and humid, so she opened the small window next to the chimney. The breeze carried with it hints of sulfur from the tide below, but it felt refreshing against her hot skin. Dahlia held the cold glass of iced tea to her cheeks, feeling the ice cubes melt upon contact. Summer rains on Long Island didn't cool the temperature off for long enough.

The open wood beams above her were marred by decades of leaks and the remnants of roofing nails. The floor was covered with boxes, containers, and random pieces of furniture. It made her woozy. And she still had everything in the basement to go through—over a hundred years of history and memories, at least. Harry anchored himself by the attic door, watching her. She felt her posture cave, knowing she had to find a new home for all of her family's belongings. The last twenty-four hours with Noah had been a vacation from the true reason for her summer visit, which was to get Lil's house ready to sell so she could take that job in Charleston.

The room felt contradictory. It was an odd medley of Lil's classic Nantucket pieces in cheerful hues, mixed with leftover seventies décor in brown, marigold, and avocado green. There were old lamps, games, an old dart board, a framed map of Long Island in its fish-like form, and too many chests to count. It was a melting pot of the home's decorating evolution, and she was along for the ride.

Dahlia meandered through the rubble, looking for the video cassettes she remembered seeing Pop carry up here years ago. Dahlia wanted to see footage of her mom, but she also wanted to see her grandparents and Lil. To see if she noticed anything off or peculiar, because if Daisy was right, not only was her pop not her biological grandfather, but he also hadn't been her mother's biological father. Dahlia didn't even want to go there, but she had no choice. She was the grown-up here, the only grown-up who could solve this mystery—whether she wanted to or not.

There was a box set on top of the distressed periwinkle blue dresser in the corner. Dahlia's unsteady hands pulled apart the top, and sure enough, there were rows of stacked VHS cassettes, all labeled with white covers. She pulled out the one that read *Rose's Communion*.

There was a television and VCR combo against the wall. In front of it sat Pop's tattered brown plaid recliner. Covered in a thick layer of dust, it didn't stop her from feeling the worn arms and imagining him in it, watching his news after dinner. No matter what was to come, she knew it couldn't compete with years, memories, or the love that bonded them to one another. Still, she couldn't escape the hollow feeling that now resided in the pit of her stomach. If Daisy was right, then the image of the family she held so dear would fall like a house of cards. And she was afraid she might too.

She lowered herself onto the arm of the recliner and pressed play on the remote. There they were, the most important people in her life, minus her dad. They were walking out of a church with elevator music playing in the background. The pace was enhanced and edited to reveal only the highlights with no real conversation or voices. It was better that way. Hearing their voices would squeeze her heart like a vice. She looked over at Harry, still in the same spot.

The next scene was of Lil, Gran, Pop, and her mother, Rose, in the garden. Her pop was twirling Rose in her white communion dress, trying to persuade a smile. She seemed upset about something. Dahlia leaned forward, trying to see their expressions through the grainy screen. Gran looked fine, but Lil wasn't smiling and seemed concerned, which was so unlike her. If there was one consistent thing everyone knew about Lil, it was that she was never without a smile.

A strong voice from below called up. "Anyone home?" By the way Harry was wagging his tail, she knew it was Noah.

Dahlia's body felt lighter as if someone had lifted an anchor that was shackled to her feet. "Up here," she called in a hoarse tone.

"Hey, whatcha doing? I was calling you for a while," he said, greeting Harry. "Hi, boy." He reached for Dahlia's waist and kissed her tenderly. It was a kiss that said he'd missed her. She wanted to lean into this moment with him, maybe even christen the attic, but she was too distracted.

"Sorry, I've been up here trying to get some answers." She quickly explained the note in the book from earlier, and her suspicions, but kept Daisy's discovery to herself.

"So, did Gretchen like the cabinet?" Dahlia asked.

"She loved it," he said, his eyes perusing the perimeter. "I think Gretchen was hoping you'd be with me. Maybe Thursday or Friday this week, you could stop by?" Noah asked, inspecting the chess set. "Wow, there's a lot of great stuff up here."

"Sure," she said, staring at the abyss of junk, feeling her eyes glaze over. "I've really got to come up with a plan for all this stuff."

"This stuff is priceless. You're not going to get rid of it, are you?" he asked.

"I have no clue." Dahlia shook her head. "Oh, by the way, the siding looks amazing. You left before it dried, but the cedar shake looks brand new. Thanks for doing that." She felt a tug at her heart, knowing he'd just increased the probability of a quick sale.

"Oh, man, is that a dartboard?" he asked, briskly walking toward it, stepping on a creaky board. He stopped and bounced on it. "I can fix this."

She wanted to say, "Your only job for the rest of the night is to distract me," but instead settled for "You're off duty."

"I'm never off duty. I have my tool bag in the car," he said, bending down to get a closer look.

At that moment, he wasn't a reality star, instead just a regular guy she was falling for who was exceptionally good with his hands—in many ways. A guy who, apparently, fancied being in an attic on a random Monday night and not back in the city with the rest of his friends.

"You're my handy hero, always there to save the day."

"Hardy-har," he said, glancing up with his bright eyes. "But it does have a nice ring to it. I think I'll get a T-shirt made."

Dahlia laughed for the first time in hours, imagining it. She was glad he was there. He was the only person besides Kara who could cheer her up—which reminded her that she needed to call her. What happened last night deserved an actual phone conversation. Maybe when Kara got back from the long weekend away.

"There's something under here," Noah said, poking at the floorboard.

She looked over his shoulder. "It's white. Maybe it's a piece of paper or something."

"Want me to lift it up?"

"Hells yeah."

"Okay, we just need something to lift the wood. I can't squeeze my fingers in there."

Fingers. The word lodged in her brain. She couldn't help but stare at his thick, magical digits that made her feel all sorts of unladylike things this morning.

"How about scissors?" she asked,

"Yeah, that might work. Otherwise, I'll run to my truck."

"I saw a pair around here somewhere." Her eyes scanned the shelves on the walls, and bingo. "Got them."

He opened the blades and used them to elevate the plank.

She slid her hand under and pulled out a yellowed envelope. "I think it's a letter." She carefully opened it. "It's typed." *Lil would never type a letter*, she thought.

June 2, 1965

Dear G,

You did it! You followed your dreams and didn't give up. And proved my father wrong in the process. I couldn't believe my eyes when I looked up and saw your beautiful smile on the big screen. That smile kept me going for the last ten years on days I didn't think I had it in me. I still miss you madly. The pain still feels as raw as the day I drove away from you, but I now know it can never be for us. My heart aches, but I am so proud of you. And our daughter would be too if she knew.

She covered her mouth, feeling a tide rise in her eyes. "I can't. You finish it." Dahlia had a feeling of where the puzzle pieces were leading her, but the words still stung like the tentacles of a Portuguese man-of-war. They were leading her to a lie six decades in the making.

Noah reached for the letter, which was firmly in her grip, and continued where she had left off.

> *It's her tenth birthday today. I took her to see* The Best Man, *not realizing you'd be in it. She looks so much like you, G, with her green eyes and thick, wavy hair. And she is as smart as a whip, a perfect combination of both of us. I named her Rose after our summer together. How could I not? There is so much more I want to tell you, but for now, I have solace in writing this.*
>
> *All My Love,*
>
> *L*

Dahlia's mind swirled like a cyclone. She paced the floor, piecing together dates. She remembered Gran's story about the anniversary vase, and how she'd just come back from a trip. That had to have been the summer of 1955, when Dahlia's mother was conceived.

"This, along with the inscription in the book,"—and the call from Daisy—"confirms it. Gran cheated on my pop, and my mother is the product of their affair. Oh God, to hear it aloud makes me sick." She plopped on a chest and held her stomach. "But why would she hide this letter where anyone could have found it? That's ballsy, even for her." Dahlia narrowed her gaze on the box of cassettes. "How could she do this to my pop? My mother died never knowing the truth."

"I wish I had an answer for you," Noah said.

"I've been lied to all my life." Her lips quivered; she felt sucker punched.

"Hey." He knelt in front of her and wiped the single tear with his thumb. "We'll figure this out."

We'll. For a brief second, that little word felt nice. "Noah, my life has just been uprooted by a category-five hurricane. The man I called Pop for thirty-eight years of my life isn't . . ." She shook her head, holding back the tidal wave of tears.

"Listen to me." Noah held her chin. "He *is* and *will always be* your grandfather, no matter what or who you find. Biology doesn't make you a parent or grandparent; love does."

Dahlia shrugged, wiping her nose. Her throat tightened as she tried to search her memory for any clues she may have missed. Had her pop said something or acted a certain way that she hadn't understood at the time? Was she too blind to see the truth? Who else in their family knew? Did Lil? The questions ran through her mind like a ticker tape of never-ending hypotheses. How could this be happening?

"He was obviously in the movie business. It can't be that hard to find him," Noah said with easy confidence. "A simple Google search will do it."

"This could lead to something I'm not sure I can handle," she said, feeling her posture cave inward.

"I think the worst part is over, D." He reached for her hand.

"Yeah, maybe so."

"Tomorrow, I can call a producer friend of mine from *Hamptons House* if we can't find him online tonight. We can track him down," he said, assuring her with a light squeeze. "Only if that's what you want."

"Noah, I don't know. I need to digest this first. I have no idea what to think or what to feel." She rubbed the back of her neck. "Lil had to have known. This has to be the secret she needed me to know about."

And the truth was, Dahlia wondered if some secrets were better off staying buried.

CHAPTER SIXTEEN

July 15

Dahlia's hand hung over the steering wheel as she hummed the lyrics of "Sparks." The escape to Shelter Island was the break she needed emotionally and physically. Organizing Lil's belongings and items collected by her family for over a century had become a daunting task with no end in sight. In some small way, the family revelation made her feel that the decision to leave was the right one. The house was now filled with heaviness, tarnishing her warm memories with soot. She looked for signs anywhere and everywhere, but nothing revealed itself—aside from Noah, that was. He was her beacon in the storm.

It had been four days since Dahlia uncovered the glaring details of her grandmother's affair. After the shock wore off, her anger bubbled to the surface. Her jaw ached from all the nighttime grinding. It was often how she'd dealt with Spence's condescending ways and affairs. It seemed there was more than one. She buried her emotions so it became actual physical pain. But this was different. On the one hand, there was this mystery that rerouted the past, and on the other, the birthing of a family connection. She could water the flowers or let the truth starve them. Every day felt like a balancing act between anguish and joy.

There was still no sign of Lil's safe deposit key, but Dahlia was sure whatever secret lay hidden in that box was about Gran, this man, and her mother. Which meant Lil had known. At this point, if she didn't find the key, it wasn't the end of the world. I mean, what more could she discover? It couldn't get worse than finding out her pop had likely been duped for five decades. Her heart felt as empty as the tin cans in Lil's barn. She was torn between being in the present, where the sun showered her with warmth, and traveling to the past, where she might get stuck.

The ferry line was slowly shrinking, and Dahlia couldn't wait to feel the breeze from the boat. It was ninety-two degrees, but it felt like one-hundred-twenty in the car, with its black leather seats and no air conditioning. The aroma of basil and sauce from the neighboring pizza shop filled her nostrils as she inched her car closer to the ferry's opening. She fanned herself as she voice-texted Spence.

"Did you email the papers? I still haven't received them."

She hit send. That man couldn't be counted on to do the right thing, ever. It was the story of her life. You would think he'd want this over with. She certainly did. She shook her head. At least she had Noah. She still didn't know exactly where it was going or what they were to one other, but whatever they were, she was content for now.

Her car puttered as she dropped it into gear. Dahlia pulled Betty, her ancient black Saab hatchback, into the very last spot just as Kara called.

"Perfect timing," Dahlia answered, feeling her tight shoulders relax a bit.

"And where are you going? You sound better," Kara said curiously.

"To the restaurant. I am a little better," Dahlia said, leaning her face into the salty air. "It's good to be out of the house, away from all the deceit. I'm sure it will hit me later when I go home."

"I still can't believe it. Your gran never crossed me as a woman who would cheat."

"Me neither. She was always so rigid and righteous."

"She did have a soft side too." Kara's voice eased.

"She did. It's just easier for me to focus on the bad things, I suppose." Dahlia felt the corners of her eyes moisten.

"Not to change the subject, but did you find anything on your movie star grandfather?" Kara asked.

"Nothing. We googled, IMDb'd him, searched the internet for any clue or nugget. It's like the man didn't exist. But then again, the cast is enormous. It could be anyone."

Kara hummed in thought. "Anyone listed in the credits with a G in their first name?"

"One, but she was a woman, Grace."

"Grace Kelly?" Kara asked with unbridled enthusiasm.

"No, it wasn't her, someone else. But Audrey was in it." Dahlia's smile widened.

Kara oooed. "Hepburn?"

"Is there any other one?" She laughed.

"So you're telling me, your biological grandfather may have starred with Ms. Holly Golightly."

"Yup. So it would seem, but again, he doesn't exist." Dahlia sighed in frustration.

"What about a name change. Plenty of people did it back then."

"Yeah, that's probably what happened. I told Noah he could ask his producer friend Penny, but I don't think he's been able to get a hold of her yet."

"Intriguing. Speaking of McHandy, how is he? How many times this week?"

"I'll never tell." Dahlia laughed.

"More than twice a day?" Kara asked with emphasized curiosity. "I bet he's giving you quite the workout."

"Oh my God." She laughed, feeling her cheeks grow red. She'd never been happier she wasn't on FaceTime. "Next topic."

"Damn, girl, you've come a long way since arriving at Lil's."

"I'll say." Dahlia felt her insides swell. Never in a million years had she thought she was capable of this kind of unhinged ownership of her desires.

"Way to own it." Kara snickered.

"Ha, yeah. Listen, we're about to pull up."

"Oh, did you take my advice about lending Gretchen a few of Lil's paintings?"

"Yeah, I have two with me, and I have a bunch of pictures for her to look at. I even posted one of Lil's paintings on Instagram." Kara was right. Lil's art needed to be seen. "Just to see what people would say. I mean, I still don't have much of a following, but that last picture of me in Lil's garden got a lot of likes."

"Wow, I never knew you were capable of being this mainstream." She laughed. "Bye, girl. Call me tomorrow."

"Okay, will do," Dahlia said, turning the ignition.

It was a Friday, just after five, so that meant cocktail hour for the residents on the small island. A time to retreat home and kick a few back before dinner at one of the upscale restaurants. Aside from the expanse of cars in front of her waiting to drive off the boat, it was quiet. Just the way she liked it. It was like stepping back in time.

Dahlia drove up the short hill; the sun pierced through the canopy of tall trees. The air was beginning to cool off, and she was no longer sticky with perspiration. She pulled into a spot across from the Hive, took a deep breath, and gave herself a once-over in her navy dress and large tote filled with Lil's art. Why was she so nervous?

When it opened, the door gave a long screech. There was music playing, but it wasn't familiar. It was bluegrass meets folk. It was very much a Shelter Island vibe, and only added to Gretchen's hipster, Williamsburg aesthetic, which Dahlia found so cool.

"Is that you, Dahlia?" a woman's voice called from the back.

"Ah, yeah. It's me." She set her tote down on a barstool and looked around. She spotted Noah's handywork everywhere she looked, from the banquettes to the batten board walls and sleek organic bar made from mahogany. Her eyes felt wide and bright as she grazed her palms across the recently shellacked bar top. He was so talented. How did he manage to do all this and help her at the house? She was still mystified. He really was something else. Maybe he had superpowers after all. She let out a light chuckle, hearing Lil's words in her head: *He's a keeper.*

"Glad you're here," Gretchen hollered from the back. "I'm testing some last-minute recipes. Let me wash up."

"Of course," Dahlia yelled back, feeling her pocket vibrate. She pulled it out; it was an email notification from the gallery. It read, *Please sign and return your onboarding documents ASAP.* Dahlia tried to swallow the boulder now wedged in her throat. Was this the sign she was looking for? She squeezed her eyes shut. As much as she'd known this day was coming, she wanted to remain in her lust bubble with Noah and didn't want anything or anyone to pop it.

"Okay, so what do you think of the place?" Gretchen walked out in a cute army green romper, her hair in a high ponytail.

Dahlia looked up with wide eyes and tucked her phone behind her back. "The wall color is perfect. I love the lighter batten board underneath." She inched closer to get a closer view. "It reminds me of shades of sea glass. Very English countryside vibe."

"Oh, that makes me happy." Gretchen clapped. She genuinely seemed happy that she was there. And that tickled something inside Dahlia that longed for friendship.

"I brought some photographs of my aunt's paintings and a few so you could see them in person." She'd left the ones on Lil's barn wall where they were. Something told her to leave them be. Dahlia opened her tote and spread the copies on the table. "The palette is bright with some moodier hues. I think the botanicals will look nice and go great with the farm-to-table vibe. And the name the Hive."

Gretchen flipped through the impressionist botanicals, still lifes, and garden landscapes. It was way too quiet. Maybe she didn't like them?

"We can mix them with any other pieces you have too," Dahlia added, feeling her tone rise. "No pressure. They may not be your cup of tea." Dahlia shifted her stance, waiting for Gretchen to respond.

"I love them. They are perfection."

Dahlia let out the breath she was holding. "Great."

"This one especially." Gretchen held up the still life of a vase of echinacea. "The colors remind me of pickled cabbage."

"I can see that." Dahlia's smile grew. She was still trying to find her footing with Gretchen. She liked the idea of having another woman in her life, even if she was leaving soon. Two weeks suddenly didn't feel long enough, and she wondered if she should tell Noah about her plans.

"It's the foodie in me." Gretchen laughed, leading the way. "Come on, I'll show the rest of the art I've collected for the space." She looked back as she walked to the back. "I was thinking of a gallery wall above the paneling."

"Love that idea," Dahlia said, following her past the swinging kitchen door.

Gretchen stopped mid-route and turned around. "Hey, listen, I appreciate you doing this. I know you have a full plate."

"It's no problem. I enjoy coming over here."

Gretchen stared at her with big eyes. They were slightly darker than Noah's but still beautiful. "Noah likes you, you know."

Dahlia drew in a breath, not sure where this was going. "Well, the feeling is mutual."

"He told me about your parents. I'm sorry. That must have been awful." Gretchen's blue orbs softened.

"It was. I had to grow up fast. Too fast." Dahlia shrugged.

"I know a thing or two about that. I practically raised Noah with the help of my stepdad. If not for him, we'd have been in foster care, split apart." There was a tick in her jaw.

Dahlia reached for her hand. "It all worked out the way it was supposed to."

"What doesn't kill you makes you stronger, right?" Gretchen's voice cracked.

"Isn't that the truth?" Dahlia replied, wanting to share more, but stopped herself. She didn't like withholding parts of herself, but she didn't have much of a choice.

"Listen, I don't want to scare you. And I know this may seem out of the blue, but I like you, and more importantly, I like you for my brother."

Dahlia leaned closer, making eye contact, feeling hope glide across her chest. Gretchen's approval was everything. And she was essentially giving it to Dahlia on a silver platter.

"But his ex, Josie, is crazy."

And then her stomach dropped off a three-hundred-foot roller coaster. "How crazy? Like, fist fight crazy?"

"As in jealous, evil crazy. She didn't want my brother, but she also doesn't want anyone else to have him either."

"How . . . ?" Dahlia tilted her head. "What? Did something happen?"

"What didn't happen? After the dust settled from the meme, people came out of the woodwork to support him. Girls were leaving comments, sliding into his DMs faster than you could blink, and Josie couldn't handle it." Her eyes narrowed with an inward gaze. "I don't know if she wanted him back or if she was just that nuts, but she threatened some of them."

Dahlia looked like a deer in headlights. She didn't know what to say, but asked the question that was now at the forefront of her mind. "Should I be worried?"

"I honestly don't know." She shook her head. "But I have to think she's over it at this point. All this happened in February when it finally aired. Plus, she was called a bully all over social media, so she toned it down a bit after that. And you're in luck, because she cares about what people think of her. Oh, and she may have roughed someone up once in a bar when she was drunk."

"How do you know all this? Noah?"

"Yeah, partly, but one of the girls she threatened was my ex." She tsked. "She was just checking in on him, leaving comments on his photos, that sort of thing."

"Wow, yeah. That's cuckoo." Dahlia smiled, while simultaneously wondering what she had gotten herself into. She was just glad he was no longer part of the show, at least for this summer. The chances she would run into this girl were virtually nonexistent. At least there was that.

"I felt it was only fair to warn you. Noah's friends are planning a big birthday bash for him in the Hamptons tomorrow night, and she'll probably be there. He wants to bring you."

Dahlia's gulp was audible. Was she even ready for this? Did she need boxing gloves? "He does?" She bit the inside of her lip, not sure how she felt about all of it. She'd never been on the other end of that kind of crazy before. Spence's sister was catty, difficult, and extremely passive-aggressive. Dahlia became skilled at handling her and knowing when to let things go, but she was never involved in an altercation with anyone. The face-to-face conflict wasn't her style.

"He asked me to go too. I'm just not sure I can make it with all this." Gretchen waved over the mess. "I still have so much to do before the opening."

"I know that feeling all too well." She had so much to do to get Lil's house ready to go on the market. And time was slipping through her fingers like sand. Dahlia's thoughts briefly drifted to the email she'd received from the gallery. Her palms suddenly felt clammy.

"I hope I didn't overstep." Gretchen winced, handing her some sage. "Burn this in the house. It will ward off negative energy."

"Oh, thanks. I need all the help I can get at this point." She laughed lightheartedly, even though her insides were clearly in turmoil. "And no, I'm glad you warned me." That's what friends did. This was what she wanted deep down. This felt like a subtle nudge to stay, even if for a little while longer.

"The art! Right." Gretchen shook her head. "It's in the office. No judging, it's mayhem back here."

"I would never. This is a judgment-free zone." Dahlia followed her lead. What was she doing? She didn't have time for any of this—yet here she was.

CHAPTER SEVENTEEN

July 16

The birds were in a playful flight as they disappeared under the eaves of Lil's bedroom porch. Dahlia slowly sipped her coffee, watching the first sailing group already out on the water. The sunfish sails formed bright clusters along the glimmering surface. The colors had a likeness to a bag of Starburst or Skittles. Her smile widened as she leaned against the door frame, letting her honey locks sway in the breeze. It was hard not to be blissfully happy with a view like that. It was the telltale sign that summer had begun. The smell of sea salt flooded the air, and she was content to be a voyeur for this Saturday morning ritual.

Dahlia ran her fingers through her knotty, humid hair, wondering if Noah would ask her to his birthday party tonight. But if he wanted her to come, wouldn't he have asked her by now? She looked out over the grass that led to the bay, realizing maybe he wasn't ready for her to meet his friends. And who were they, anyway? Friends from the city? Or "friends" as in castmates from *Hamptons*

House? She couldn't blame him; they'd only known one another for two weeks. And they'd only know each other for another two weeks after today. Going public with their relationship might change things, and Dahlia didn't want anything to change. Not even the speed of light pace at which they, as a couple, were evolving. Perhaps it was better they kept their lives separate for now.

"Morning, baby," Noah whispered, wrapping his burly arms around her waist. His toned body was on display, wearing only his tight black Calvin's. "What a way to wake up, huh?"

"I'll say." Dahlia sank into his hold, resting her head against his chest. She still felt torn. On the one hand, she had Noah. If she were honest with herself, he undid her, stitch by aching stitch. His hands, his lips, and his smell, but mostly how he made her feel when their bodies touched. And a part of her wondered if it could be more and what that would look like after the summer. But she was also torn by time, the job she had accepted, and weighted by the discovery of her grandmother's secret. "What's the plan for the day? Are you going to work me to the bone again?" He laughed, tickling her ear with his whiskered mouth.

Her body shuddered with pleasure. Even *that* sounded sexy to Dahlia. All she wanted was to be locked away with him in this bedroom all day long. She was turning into a lovemaking ninja. She didn't feel thirty-eight; she felt thirsty-eight. "I need a shower." She turned around to face him, sliding her hands up his bare back. "Then I'll start going through those boxes in the basement." Her lips tickled his neck, then his chin, then his mouth. "And get back out to the garden at some point," Dahlia said with a soft, sultry tone. "I'm going to work you really freaking hard, Mr. Sterling." Her teeth sank into her bottom lip, liking the sound of that. Just saying those words made her hungry for him. And by the feel of him pressing against her stomach, he felt the same.

He pressed his mouth to hers, and their tongues collided in the most erotic and sensual way. It was profound and far-reaching. He felt like hot silk in her mouth. She could kiss this man for hours, and it still wouldn't be enough. It was that good. Her body hummed with unbridled desire.

"I want to taste you," he said, his voice laced with bravado. "For real this time."

The sound of those four words sent zings of electricity right to her core. She couldn't believe they were going to do this here, out in the open, but something about this man begged her to be someone else. Maybe it's who she always was all along, but she'd just needed to find the right person.

He dropped to his knees and lifted her shirt like a man addicted. The idea that a man would prioritize a woman's need over his own was so foreign to her, but if he insisted.

He peppered kisses along her hip, then her pelvis. He inched down her panties, and they slipped to her ankles. She was breathless. People scurried along the beach, completely unaware of what was about to happen. His tongue gently teased her seam, and instantly her legs felt boneless. She anchored herself against the frame of the door for fear of collapsing.

"I can't get enough of you," he crooned. "You are the best thing I've ever tasted." He anchored his wide, capable hands on her hips and blew on her swollen flesh. That, along with the breeze, made her a swooning puddle of bliss.

He licked and sucked until he had to hold her up.

"Oh, God, Noah." Her head tilted back, feeling like she would shatter at any minute.

He hummed, glancing up at her, possessed.

She held onto his thick locks as he undid her will with his mouth and then fingers. The seconds eased into minutes. A heightened sense of euphoria ricocheted through her body. "Noah . . ." She breathed heavy, fast breaths. "I can't wait any longer."

"Go, baby," he demanded. "I want to taste you unravel." And that was all she needed to become undone. She saw the stars, the moon, and the whole galaxy all in one burst of pleasure that altered something inside her. Moans and groans and other unintelligible sounds escaped her lips and carried with the breeze. Part of her hoped no one heard, but the other part that just had the best orgasm of her life didn't care.

"I want you. Now." Dahlia lured him up.

He lifted off her shirt, exposing her naked body to the world. "God, you're beautiful."

Her breath mixed with his, and she whispered, "You're not too shabby yourself, McHandy."

She stood taller, ready for what was to come. Her breasts begged to be touched by his calloused hands. He took them in his palms as if he read her mind. Then he brought his mouth to one nipple and sucked and flicked while he rolled the other between his fingers. Heat pooled low in her belly.

With hungry eyes, he lifted her onto him. His neck veins bulged, only intensifying her need. He carried her aching body past the dresser. Dahlia heard her phone vibrate, but she ignored it. She wasn't concerned with who it was, even if it was Spence again. Absolutely nothing could keep her body from his.

Noah turned the shower on with one hand while she still straddled him, mesmerized by his gaze. She was jolted back to reality when the glass door whacked her head.

"Sorry!"

"This is becoming a habit." Dahlia's laugh turned into a sigh. She fell back into his eyes and wondered if he could see how hard she was falling.

He lowered her into the steam. Dahlia smiled mischievously as she watched him drop his underwear. It almost felt illegal. She felt like a horny teenager, only this time, she was smarter and more confident than she was back then. Noah made her feel like a woman in a way Spence hadn't and never could. The biggest difference was that it wasn't just about *him* having an orgasm. Noah was in tune with her wants and her needs and made them a priority. And that made their age difference insignificant, at least to her.

He lifted her naked body onto his and pressed her bare back against the cold tile wall. The stark contrast on her humid skin only made her ache more intense. One hand was propped against the wall behind her, and the other firmly held her body to his groin. With a smooth-as-silk thrust, he was inside of her.

"Is that what you wanted?" He was breathless.

"Yes." Dahlia gripped his wet back, feeling her nails pierce his skin. With every piston of his hips, she craved him more, harder, deeper. She wiped the droplets from her face, feeling like her body would implode at any moment. If she could manipulate time and feel this intoxicating rush 'til the end of time, she would. That was, until she heard a bang on the door.

Noah looked at her with a hooded gaze. Water fell from his eyelashes. "Do you want to get that?"

Still linked with him in a slippery dance, she whispered. "Don't stop, don't ever stop."

The bang became louder and now seemed angry.

"D, I think you should get it. It seems important. Maybe Harry got out; maybe something happened to him."

"Ugh, what a buzzkill." She rested her wet forehead on his. "But you're right. It could be about Harry. I'm not sure I latched the screen door."

"I'll be here waiting when you get back." He gently ripped himself from her.

"This is torture." She kissed him again, still tasting herself on his lips. "I won't be long."

Dahlia threw on her light robe and ran her wet body down the stairs. She spotted Harry, who was now bouncing by the door and barking. "You're here?" she murmured in confusion. If it wasn't about him, then why was someone at her door?

Dahlia heard the bang again, and this time, the thunder went right through her. "Open up, Dahlia. I know you're in there."

"Shit." She slapped her hand over her mouth. It was Spence. Dahlia's heart wildly beat under the cotton, like there was still something to fear from this man.

"Yeah, one minute." She wrapped her robe tighter and took a deep breath. She slowly turned the bolt and opened the door. "What on earth are you doing here?" she asked quietly, inching out of the door.

"I'm dropping off the papers you asked for," he said, looking clean-shaven and proper in his golf shirt.

Her eyes felt wider than the ocean. "I thought you were going to email them." This was so inappropriate, but it was also Spence's style.

"I'm playing golf in Greenport with some clients, so I figured I'd do you a favor," he said, with a smug tone, looking past her and into the house. "I've tried to call you several times. It's not my fault you didn't answer or call me back."

"I did call you back," she hit back, wanting to bite her knuckles. "You should have left a voicemail." She was still bitter with him for hiding Lil's deed. Who does that? Especially when you're a serial cheater who clearly doesn't want to be married. Yet another way he tried to control her. She wasn't sure what had prompted him to do it; she guessed that he didn't want to lose the comfort of having Dahlia take care of him. He was oddly dependent on her as a wife and mother to Daisy. But that was where it ended. One can only take feeling invisible for so long. Toward the end, she'd felt like she was dying a slow death in this off-kilter, one-sided relationship.

"I shouldn't have to."

What had she ever seen in this entitled, arrogant man? "Well, I surely would have called you right back if you did," she said with a blasé tone.

"What have you been doing out here the past few weeks?" He stepped back, scanning the exterior. "Doesn't look much different than it did before."

"Thanks. The papers?" Dahlia felt her eyes narrow. Although this was an inconvenience, at least it saved her a trip to town to print. She had never been more eager to sign the damn things.

"They're all signed. They just need your signature." He handed her the large manila envelope. "This has been the longest fifteen years of my life."

Dahlia rolled her eyes. He had no idea how long those years had really been. She took them from his grip, hearing footsteps from inside draw closer.

Noah stepped onto the porch—shirtless and damp—with Harry. "Everything okay out here?"

Dahlia did a double-take as Harry started to bark at Spence. Her first instinct was to make herself smaller and explain. But instead, she stood taller and said in a firm tone, "Harry, come."

"Got it. Now I know what you've been up to. Well, that didn't take long." Spence eyed Noah up and down and puffed out his chest, trying his best to claim the alpha title. "Real classy. And robbing the cradle, I see. My family was right about you all along. I did marry beneath me," he said, staring at Noah's shoulder. "Nice tat."

Dahlia shuddered at his condescending tone out of habit. She prayed he didn't mention Daisy. The last thing she wanted was for Noah to find out this way.

"Come on, man, don't belittle her. If you have something to say, say it to me," Noah said.

He was standing up for her. Dahlia's heart swelled. No one but Lil had ever done that for her. But she knew, too, that she needed to do it herself.

"That's rich coming from a serial cheater." Her hand landed on her hip as she inched closer. "What I do on my time is none of your business. And as far as your family is concerned, I may not have your status, but I sure as hell have a heart and a conscience." There—that felt good.

Noah nodded once. "I think you need to go, bro."

Spence stood there blinking. Rarely did anyone challenge him. Dahlia's insides swirled like a cotton candy machine. In all the years she was stuck with Spence, he was seldom without words.

"You can have her, man. Good luck opening that steel door. I'm done," Spence said, walking to his car as Harry chased him, nipping his golf pants. "Back off, Harry!"

Dahlia was the only person who didn't put Spence on a pedestal, which had irked him fiercely from the start. But really, he lacked confidence in himself because everything was handed to him on a silver platter. Inside, he was an insecure little boy, still under the influence of his parents—and on their bankroll too.

"That dog hates him with a passion." Dahlia laughed.

"I can see why. He's a pompous prick." Noah huffed, folding his arms.

"We should have stayed in the shower," Dahlia said, hooking her finger through the loop of his jeans.

"He would have found a way in. Plus, now you have the papers." Noah wrapped his burly arms around her. And even his armpits smelled good. "Are you all right?"

"Yeah, I'm just a little shocked he showed up unannounced. He's the last person I'd want you to meet." She pulled back wide-eyed. "Did he scare you off?"

"No. D, I told you, nothing could." He reassured her, hugging her again. At that moment, she wanted to tell him everything. About Daisy, what her life was like as a single mother, and how hard some days, weeks, and even months were. But this seemed like enough for one day.

"I do have a question, though." His eyes met hers. "How long were you together?"

"Too long." In his gaze, she knew he wanted more of an answer. "Fifteen years." It might as well have been one hundred because when you're that miserable, every day seems like an eternity.

His breath hitched. "That's a long time."

"This may sound horrible, but I never loved him."

Every muscle in her body froze, knowing what question would come next. He had to be wondering if they had kids. Then again, if she did, they'd most likely be with her. That question didn't follow, but another one did.

"I don't get it," Noah said, leaning against the porch railing. For the first time, he seemed annoyed with her, and that knocked the wind out of her sail. "Then why did you marry him?"

And there it was, a segue to tell him about Daisy. She took in a long breath and exhaled. "I mean, he wasn't always an asshole," she grumbled, chickening out again. "But even through the better years, I still didn't have the feelings a wife should have. You must think I'm horrible. And if you're wondering if I married him for his money, I didn't. That isn't who I am." She met his eyes that weren't as bright as they typically were and said, "Not loving him meant I couldn't get hurt, I suppose. After my parents died, it was the only way to keep my heart safe."

The silence was deafening. He stood motionless. She could feel her veins pulsing beneath her skin. All she could do was wait for a response and hope he believed her. "And what about now?" he asked.

"My heart is wide open." She inched closer in a sincere plea. If she got hurt again, then so be it. "I'm too happy to be worried about what might or might not happen. For the first time, I'm living in the moment. And it feels damn good." She reassured him with a smile.

"I'm happy too." He tucked a honey lock of hair behind her ear.

"You are?" she asked with a peaked voice. "Noah, you're the only one I care about." She couldn't believe she was telling him all this. It was either the craziest or bravest thing she could do.

He reached for her hand, walking them through the doorway into the hallway. Dahlia felt her chest expand and her eyes glaze over. It hit her like a tidal wave. It was over, really over.

"You okay?" he asked again, like it was his duty.

"Yeah, couldn't be better," she said, collecting her thoughts. "I'm free." She wanted to scream it from Lil's sleeping porch. "Well, almost." With that, she marched into the kitchen and came back with a pen. "It's about time this became official."

"I can leave," Noah said, rubbing his chin, now covered in a light dusting of scruff since he hadn't shaved.

"No, stay. This will only take a minute." Dahlia pulled out the stack of papers and placed them on Lil's coffee table. She eagerly flipped through, signing her name on every page with the pink sticky arrow. When she was done, she slipped the divorce papers into a large prepaid envelope and set it aside as if this were an ordinary task.

"Where were we?" She stood. "This calls for a celebration." She opened her robe and closed the space between them. She pressed her bare chest against his, feeling their heart beat in sync.

"You deserve to be cherished, D." He brushed her face with his knuckles and kissed her with a tenderness she hadn't felt before. The robe hit the floor with a gentle *swoosh*, and she smiled.

"Then show me." She unzipped his pants and dropped them to the floor with a soft *thud*.

They were naked, face to face, in the dim hallway, with nothing but a sheer curtain between them and the outside world. She didn't care if Spence came back or even saw them. She was done being tethered to a man who didn't love her. She wanted to be seen, felt, and heard. And most of all, loved.

"We need to celebrate tonight. Your independence and my birthday." He smiled. "I want you to meet my friends. Would you be up for that? I mean, I know my actual birthday isn't for a few days, but the guys planned a get-together."

Dahlia was speechless. He wanted her to be a part of his life. Even if it was messy.

"I'm sorry it's last-minute, but I was nervous to ask."

"Why?" She stared at his mouth. All she wanted to do was feel his cowboy lips on hers and finish what they started upstairs in the shower.

"They're a bunch of goons from the show. Drunken adolescents." His voice was meek. "I don't want our age difference to matter or for you to be turned off. You're important to me, and I don't want to screw this up."

"Well, I could say the same. But as long as we're okay with it, that's all that matters." She paused, making him sweat a little. "Yes, I'd love to." She let out a lighthearted giggle. "Did you think I'd say no?"

"Maybe." He shrugged.

Suddenly, her throat felt dry. Would his ex be there? Would his friends like her? She needed something really pretty to wear if she was going to do this.

Noah gripped the back of her neck and gave her a lust-laced kiss, staking his claim. Whatever had sparked his eagerness, she was just happy her official ex-husband hadn't scared him off. If anything, it fueled the opposite.

"You're all I care about. And you drive me crazy," he whispered, cupping her breasts. Dahlia felt wobbly, her legs refusing to work. His mouth slowly moved from her lips down to her stomach, making her skin quiver uncontrollably.

"Noah, come here," she hissed.

He looked up and met her intense gaze. She was falling for him. Hard and fast. She didn't have to tell him what she was thinking. The way he stared at her, he knew and felt it too.

Noah lifted her onto his bare form, and they fit as one. Her hands slid around his traps, feeling every muscle flex with each drive further inside of her. With her back against the cold wall, all she could think about was staying. Saying no to the job and seeing what would happen if she didn't leave. She bit his salty skin, feeling her atoms ignite. With every thrust of his hips, she sank deeper into the reality of what they could be. Their moans of pleasure mingled in the humid summer air. Once he hit that spot, it was all over. She shattered into a million pieces, then he did the same. Gritty, dirty grunts filled the air as he pulsed inside her. They slid down the wall, sticky and satiated. Dahlia couldn't help but wonder if their bubble was about to pop. Or was it about to get bigger?

* * *

An hour after she burned the sage from Gretchen, they arrived at Noah's bash. Dahlia's only hope for the sage was that it would keep the good energy and eliminate the bad, with an emphasis on the night she was about to walk into.

"You look really pretty. I can't wait to tear that dress off of you later. Starting with those straps first." He growled in her ear, then kissed her shoulder as they walked through the back entrance of the Social Club.

"Thanks, it's new." She'd literally bought it three hours ago. She felt her clammy hands stick to the layer of chiffon. A smile wanted to ease across her lips, but she was too nervous. Not because she was insecure, but because the Hamptons scene was a whole other world she knew nothing about. Dahlia had skipped over so many rites of passage by becoming a mother at eighteen: the going out, the one-night stands, the Hamptons share houses, and drunken nights no one remembered the next day. She missed it all. Now, at thirty-eight, she wondered if she had a shot at fitting in. And the bigger question was, did she want to?

"Did you mail off the papers?" he asked curiously.

"Yup, even sent them priority." A smile now graced her lips.

"So it's official?" He angled his face toward her.

"It is." Dahlia felt her belly flutter. This could change everything for them. But was she ready for that?

He leaned over and gave her a soft, reassuring kiss. It lasted mere seconds, but she felt more in that kiss than in some of the steamier ones.

"What was that for?" she asked playfully.

"Now, you're all mine." Noah's smile melted her heart.

"I can live with that." Dahlia wrinkled her nose, feeling the sudden urge to plant herself beside him all night and be his.

"It's going to be fun, I promise," he said, squeezing her hand. "Oh, I see my friend Ryan. You're going to love him, D." He pulled her through the hearty crowd. The music was loud, and people were already straining to hear one another. Typically, a crowd like this would make her uneasy, but not with Noah. He made all her concerns seem to vanish into thin air just by being there with her.

"Ry. Ry." Noah waved, moving closer to the bar.

"He's here," yelled the guy with the dark brown mullet. "Dude, bring it in, my man." They bro hugged, and the guy asked, "And who is this?"

"Hi, I'm Dahlia." She reached out her hand. "Nice to meet you."

"So you're the reason my friend hasn't been at the house all summer long," he said with an evil-eye squint.

Oh God, this wasn't good. She desperately wanted them to like her. And the vibe that she had stolen his time wasn't a good first impression.

"I'm just kidding. After what this guy went through last year, I'm just happy he's alive." Ryan gripped his shoulders.

Noah held her hand tighter, feeling how sweaty his palm was—or maybe it was hers. Dahlia looked up at him, wondering how bad it had gotten. It seemed like the aftermath of his breakup was messy and still a little raw. She guessed that part they had in common. She wondered if he still had feelings for Josie. They'd been together a long time. The way Noah made love to Dahlia made her think twice about that, but people tended to surprise her, so she was on alert.

"We're doing shots. You game?" Ryan asked Dahlia.

"Ah, sure," she said with an effervescent tone. She was not about to show her age.

"And a round of espresso martinis?"

"I'll just do a beer, and Dahlia will have . . ." Noah said, looking at her.

"I'll have an espresso martini. That sounds great, thanks," she interrupted him, wanting to be easy.

"Sweet, let's get this party started," Ryan said, flagging the bartender. "You'd think we'd get better service. I mean, come on, they must know we're from *Hamptons House*." He shook his head and huffed. "But really, it's so good to see you, man. We've missed you at the house this year. Filming isn't the same without you."

"How's the house this year?" Noah asked, seemingly indifferent.

"A total wreck."

"Worse than last year?"

"Oh yeah, think *Grey Gardens* meets *The Money Pit.* We're making it into a hotel," Ryan said over the steady hum of the music.

Noah's eyes widened. "That's cool, we've never done that before." Was he missing all the action, camaraderie, and purpose, or was he content? All indications pointed to the latter, but being there, the uncertainty was rising like the tide.

"Yeah, but they've got us in the barn, they made it into a bunkhouse, and the conditions are less than ideal." A sense of unease gripped Ryan's expression. Then he blurted, "Mac was let go, you know."

"I know." Noah gave him a half smile.

Dahlia felt her posture perk up. She could only assume they were referring to his former best friend and the man Josie had cheated with. Was the half smile because he was indifferent or because he hadn't known?

The song changed, and it got louder. Noah leaned in, and she lost the rest of their conversation to the noise. She wondered if the break from the house this summer was temporary and if he would return next summer. And if it was only temporary, what would that mean for them? Dahlia wasn't about to get caught up in more drama. But she was also tired of keeping people at a distance.

They chatted by the bar, waiting for their drinks to arrive. The lyrics to "Beautiful People" echoed through her mind as she people-watched. She wasn't in Connecticut anymore. She was used to beautiful people with on-trend, posh designer clothing, but this was different. This was a playground for the privileged, the elite who wanted social status and luxury. Connecticut was a bastion of old money, where privilege came with a sense of privacy. And this wasn't that. Dahlia scanned for his ex, but Josie was nowhere to be seen. That pleased Dahlia since she wasn't one for conflict—hence her overdue departure from her marriage.

"Okay, let's do the shots here," Ryan said, spilling them as he slid them down. "To my compadre and his novia. Happy fucking birthday, man!" And with that, they kicked back shots of tequila and lime.

Dahlia hid her gag reflex and leaned into him with an easy grin. "Happy birthday, Noah," she shouted over the music, finally getting comfortable. The fun was starting to flow, and she was certainly overdue for some. His castmates didn't seem so bad. This sort of good time wasn't something Dahlia knew much about since she'd skipped over it, but she was determined to keep an open mind. Perhaps it could work if he did the show next summer.

"Our group is in the far back corner. I'll ask a server to bring over the rest of the drinks. You kids go ahead." Ryan passed Dahlia the martini and Noah his beer.

Dahlia glanced at Noah, wearing a polo shirt and tight chinos. He seemed to be in another world. "Are you okay?" She hoped he wasn't second-guessing bringing her.

"Yeah. It's just that Southold has been nice. Being in the Hamptons doesn't feel as fun as it once did."

Dahlia felt her face soften with his confession. As open as she'd told herself to be tonight, she couldn't help but melt into his words. But she also wanted him to have fun tonight, and that started with her.

"The night is still young," Dahlia said, coming to life after two quick sips of espresso. "Come on, we've got some celebrating to do."

"I'm glad you're here." He pressed his lips to hers.

"Me too." She gazed into his tropical eyes, knowing full well this was a big step for him to bring her here. "Let's go."

They walked hand in hand across the pitted, uneven grass. Dahlia continued to sip her liquid courage, trying not to fall in her higher-than-usual wedge sandals.

His group of friends noticed them, and most ran over to greet them. She could tell he was adored, and that impressed her. It also told her that what you see with Noah is what you get. It affirmed exactly who she knew him to be. There were wide eyes from some of the girls, who were closer to Daisy's age than hers, but the guys were, for the most part, welcoming.

"We've missed you, man. Drunk karaoke and nude cannonballs just aren't the same without you," the guy with the ginormous teeth and pecs said.

Noah held his stomach in laughter, but Dahlia could tell it was for show. Something in her gut told her so.

"Hey, I'm going to use the ladies' room. It was a long ride," Dahlia whispered in his ear.

"Sure. Want me to walk with you?" he asked.

The group of girls on the couch just scowled at her as if they'd clearly taken his ex's side. "Nah, I'm a big girl."

"Okay, it's through those big doors and to the left. You can't miss it."

"Thanks." Dahlia smiled. "I'll be back." She glided across the grass like she was walking on air. Despite the earth-shattering news of Gran's affair and Rose's paternity earlier in the week, she was determined to make the most of the night. Burning the sage was her way of manifesting a peaceful night, and one could only hope it worked. Dahlia was crossing things off her bucket list, and a summer night in the Hamptons with a gorgeous guy on her arm was sure to be penciled in at the bottom.

A waft of cold air greeted her as she walked through the double doors. The décor was on-trend, with high-end lighting and wallpaper. The narrow hallway was filled with old black-and-white sailing images, a nice juxtaposition with the bold floral paper.

Dahlia pushed open the door and found an empty stall. She squatted over the toilet and looked at her phone. There was a message from Kara.

Girl, you got this. Call me in the am.

Dahlia smiled, feeling a light buzz settle in. Then the main door of the bathroom flung open, knocking the wall, startling her.

"Oh my gosh, did you see how she looked at him? Makes me sick," one girl said.

"Noah could do so much better than her, Josie. I mean, what a step down, girl," another said in a high-pitched voice. "And where did she get that dress, the thrift store?"

Dahlia gasped as she pulled up her thong. The thud of her heart could be heard in her throat. They were talking about *her*. She froze, not knowing what to do. She could walk out and ignore them. Hide until they left, or walk out and own it.

"No, but the worst part is she's old. Jake said she's like fifteen years older," another girl said with a condescending tone.

"How embarrassing. I'm just glad he can't humiliate me anymore with his sad family story and now this. Bye-bye, lover, this bitch has some real men to slay."

Ugh, Dahlia wanted to scream. Fifteen years older, exaggerate much? Dahlia could feel the rage travel to her cheeks. She took a lungful of bathroom air and remembered her earlier conversation with Kara. "Remember, you're Dahlia Fucking Newberry. She's a baby who needs a bottle, and you're a woman with wit, perspective, and beauty. She's got nothing on you." As much as she wanted to curl up in a ball and cry, she didn't. She couldn't. The unkind words hurt Dahlia, but she was more annoyed by the mean girl behavior. Dahlia never let the girls in Daisy's grade get away with it, and nor would she tonight. She was in protective mama bear mode, this time standing up for herself.

She opened the stall door and walked in slow motion to the sink. On the outside, she was poised, but on the inside, she was a storm churning.

It was so quiet you could hear a pin drop.

"Do you all feel better?" she said, glancing at the women. "You do know you're all going to age, right? Every single one of you. Like death and taxes, there's no way around it," Dahlia said, calmly wiping her hands. "And I may have a few more wrinkles than you do, but it's a small price to pay for humility and grace." Dahlia turned to Josie, staring right into her hollow blue eyes. "I have to say I was a little nervous that you'd be prettier in person, but honestly, mean people aren't pretty. So thanks for that." And with that, she threw her paper towel in the garbage and shoved open the door with both hands.

Who was that version of herself? She wasn't sure, but she freaking liked it. Who knew conflict could feel so damn good? First Spence, now Josie. It dawned on her that perhaps she'd projected some of her Spence anger onto Josie, but she also realized that Josie and Spence felt like one and the same. It was no wonder Dahlia and Noah had found one another. She smirked in satisfaction. It was as if she heard the song "Brave" playing in her head.

Dahlia held her shoulders back like she'd inherited a superpower and walked toward Noah.

"Hey. Everything good?"

"Yup, fine." She smiled.

Noah looked past her down the hallway. "Was Josie in there with you? Did she bother you?" His nostrils flared.

"Noah, it's okay." She reached for his forearm. "I don't care. She could say anything to me, and it would bounce right off. Her energy is that dirty." Dahlia didn't know where her nerve and confidence were coming from, but she wasn't going to question it.

"I know it is." He gripped her hand like she was being dragged to sea. "Do you want to leave?"

This was her chance to go home with him and sit by the fire pit or do other adult things. Did she?

"No, this is your night." She refused to be scared off. She was bigger than that.

He looked into her eyes. "Are you sure?"

"One hundred percent. Plus, if it gets rowdy again, I've got my boxing gloves in the car."

"Evander Holyfield, watch out." He chuckled. "Oh, Penny, my producer friend is here. You can meet her if you still want to. It's up to you."

Dahlia hesitated, feeling stronger than she had an hour ago. "Yes, I'd love to chat with her. Who knows, maybe she'll be able to track this G person down." However, she did wonder if he *wanted* to be tracked down, especially if he was famous.

CHAPTER EIGHTEEN

July 19

Three days had passed since the run-in with Noah's ex in the bathroom. Dahlia felt as if she was floating on air. Not only was it Noah's twenty-ninth birthday—closing the gap between their ages just a bit—but he also slept over every night, closing the gap between them in bed. Aside from a few trips to the island, the two of them were joined at the hip—and other places too. It was like the universe was telling her to trust in things again. Things, meaning Noah. Their relationship was moving fast, but she liked the feeling of being swept away. It meant she was still very much alive inside.

Dahlia sat motionless at the kitchen table. She scanned the paperwork for the gallery, feeling her armpits sweat. Did she want to do this? Once she did, there was no turning back. She liked Noah; that was clear. But making another life decision around a man wasn't what she'd had in mind when she left her old life behind in Greenwich. Dahlia bounced her foot under the table, feeling a tightening in her chest. She thought about all the years she had been home with Daisy and how long her career had been at a standstill. Being her mom, there were no regrets, but she'd also known standing on her own two feet was her only chance to leave Spence. She'd worked hard to move up at MoMA, placating both her male and female bosses. All for the sake of her soul and independence.

She sipped her coffee and stared at the screen. She let out a huff and leaned back in the chair. Dahlia tried to imagine what it would be like if she were in Charleston and he were in New York. Would they go back and forth on weekends? Would he even want that? They didn't even have a label. How could she decide when she didn't know what they were? Her mind played ping-pong. What if things changed after the summer? And then there was the matter of Daisy. A knot formed in her stomach. Tomorrow, she would tell him. He trusted her, and she was not going to break that trust. She just hoped he'd understand why she had waited so long to tell him. Why did she wait so long? She didn't even know anymore. It seemed so insignificant now.

The new position and Daisy could wait one more day. Dahlia closed her laptop with an easy assurance that it was the right thing. As if on cue, her phone buzzed. It was Noah. A smile graced her lips, unraveling the knot in her stomach and easing into light flutters.

I can't stop thinking about poker last night. you were 🎆

Heat engulfed her body, and she eagerly sat forward. She was glad she'd suggested playing strip poker and crossing off bucket list number nine. It was definitely the hottest night of her life.

You too 🍆. She was really doing this. Dahlia wouldn't let fear of sex emojis hold her back any longer.

Did you get a sick satisfaction watching me strip for you? Noah asked.

If I say yes, does that make me bad? she typed.

Three bubbles. *It doesn't make you bad. It makes you naughty.*

Dahlia paused, feeling a rush of desire flood her veins. She licked her lip and exhaled.

This isn't over. I'll be back for a rematch later. This time, I'll watch you peel off every single layer 🍒.

She played with the ends of her hair, thinking of what to write next. *Well, it is your birthday tomorrow. I suppose I could go easy on you.*

No free passes. We'll play fair and square.

If you insist.

He had no idea she was planning a pre-birthday celebration for just the two of them. They would hit a few vineyards, then head to the brewery for some music. Then, later, they would play poker. Her birthday suit would be his birthday present. Just thinking about what she planned made her giddy. Planning something because it was demanded was different from planning something because you couldn't imagine not celebrating such an amazing human.

Dahlia opened the window and breathed in the morning air. It smelled of dewy flowers dried by the sun. It felt familiar yet haunting. All those memories, tastes, and smells tied up in a feeling that was no longer real. Dahlia didn't know what was fact or fiction anymore. But she knew she had to follow the breadcrumb trail. The alternative was being stuck in limbo, which she knew didn't suit her well-being. As much as she didn't like the feeling that she was dishonoring her pop, she needed to dig deeper and get to the bottom of this so she could move on. The house still felt tainted, but Dahlia tried to focus on Lil and her memory. It was the only way she could compartmentalize her past.

She gazed at the cardinal at Lil's bird feeder, hearing her phone ding on the counter.

Hi, Dahlia, it's Penny. We met the other night at the club. I have some information. Are you free to chat?

Dahlia looked at the message as if it were a match about to light her life on fire. She swallowed the boulder lodged in her throat. This was the pivotal moment; she would either say yes and open that door to whatever was behind it or leave it closed forever.

She paced the checkered linoleum squares, feeling her muscles stiffen. Back and forth she went, making herself dizzy. Then she caught a glimpse of her mother's tassel that hung on the cabinet knob. Her eyes glossed over, and she knew, if nothing else, she needed to do it for her. She looked up as if heaven could hear her. "Please, please, don't be mad at me, Pop." Then, without another thought, she reached for her phone.

Sure, I'm free now. Dahlia waited with bated breath.

Within seconds, the phone rang.

"Hello."

"Hi, Dahlia, it's Penny. It was so great to meet you the other night. Your story was so intriguing that I got right to work."

"Thank you for that, Penny. Were you able to find anything?" Dahlia rubbed the back of her neck.

"Are you sitting down?"

"Umm, no, but I can." All she could think was that she was too late. That he may have passed away. Dahlia lowered herself into the kitchen chair. "Okay."

"So we cross-referenced everyone in the movie *The Best Man* with the letter G, and there was nothing."

"Oh . . ." Her heart sank, and her eyes tingled. Why was she having this kind of reaction? This was a good thing. The past would stay buried. "Well, thank you. I mean, you can only do so much, right?"

"But I found someone who had a name change in 1962. His name was Gene Obermann."

"Gene Obermann," Dahlia repeated. Goosebumps ran up her arms. In the hallows of her soul, she knew it was him. Dahlia wiped her eyes and cleared her throat. "Is he still alive?" she asked.

"Very much," Penny said with excitement.

"That's . . . wonderful," she said with tender enthusiasm. She wanted to find him more than she realized. "Where does he live? Do you know?"

"California. Dahlia, if this is all correct, then your biological grandfather is . . . are you ready for this?"

"I think so." What was he, an actor turned mass murderer?

"Charles Halston."

Dahlia's eyes widened. If she wasn't already sitting, she would have fallen over. "Wait, what? *The* Charles Halston, the mega movie star? The one who was friends with Sinatra and Eastwood all those years?"

"Yes, that's him. I have his email. It might be tough to reach him; be warned. His security isn't just going to let anyone get through the iron-clad gate, but it's worth a shot. Do you have a pen?"

"Ah, yeah." Dahlia reached over the counter, her mouth still hanging open. "Go ahead."

"Okay, it's ch@lgproductions.com."

Chills ran up Dahlia's spine as she wrote it down. LG had to stand for Lizzie and Gene. It would be too much of a coincidence otherwise. Dahlia covered her mouth in shock. She wondered if Gene had known Lizzie was married. And happily at that.

"Listen, I'm a romantic at heart. Old letters and long-lost grandfathers are my jam. If I can help with anything else, please let me know."

"I will. Thank you, Penny." She hoped she could trust her. Since Noah trusted her, that was confirmation enough.

Dahlia sat back in her chair, her body trembling excessively. Charles Halston could be her biological grandfather. Was *that* why his biography was on the bookshelf at Lil's? Did Lil know, or was it a secret Gran kept to herself?

Then suddenly, her stomach dropped. She knew nothing about this man. What if he was a horrible human? What if he didn't like dogs? What if he was mean to kids? And arrogant because he had people fawning over him all these years? What if he wanted no part of her? Uncertain of her next move, she sat in Lil's kitchen with this news, her mind racing with possibilities.

* * *

Many hours later, after a swim and a few unanswered calls to Noah, she summoned the courage. She was now at Lil's desk in the green library her pop painted, with Harry at her feet. Dahlia sat there stalling with her laptop open. The French doors were opened to the garden, and it was so quiet she could hear the bees buzzing around her lavender. The irony wasn't lost on her that the room was her pop's long before it was Lil's. She couldn't help but wonder if he'd be hurt by her curiosity. If he'd be upset by her longing to connect with a stranger who most likely shared her DNA. And would he think she was a traitor? Of all the qualities Dahlia had, her loyalty ranked above all else. The mere thought of this potential betrayal churned her stomach.

Googling him was the mature first step. Dahlia typed *Charles Halston* into the search bar. It read *American Actor (born 1936).* Below, there were images, so she clicked. They spanned decades, and some were in black-and-white. There was one of him with salt and pepper hair, holding two Oscars, and in the next, he was a young man standing by a river in a pea coat. "He was handsome, Harry," Dahlia said wistfully. She almost followed it with, *I can see why Gran fancied him*, but she stopped herself. She wasn't going to give Gran any grace for this.

Dahlia glanced around the moody room in thought and remembered his biography was on the shelves. Quickly, she scanned the bookcase filled with old books. The book's black cover was right at eye level, and she noticed now how the spine was worn on both sides as if someone's fingers had pulled it down regularly. Dahlia ran her index finger down the tattered corner with an unfocused gaze.

She pulled it down and held the worn book in her palms. The more facts she had, the better. Plus, there was still a slight chance it was just a coincidence and they had the wrong guy. She opened it and saw a heart drawn in the top right corner of the page. This act of love should have made her heart melt, but it didn't; it made her angrier that her gran left clues to where her pop could find them in his office, no less. She shook her head with a watery gaze. "She didn't deserve you, Pop."

Dahlia thumbed through the 1991 publication highlighting his career. A waft of musty vanilla filled her nostrils. She pored over the pages, hoping to discover clues in the photographs. There was a color photo from 1962 of him in a cowboy hat, his dark, wavy hair sticking out the bottom. Her mom had the same eyes and smile. The caption read, *Set of Bonanza, 1962*. Dahlia floated her fingers over the photo, feeling her tears pool in the corners of her eyes. The idea that she may have a blood relative out there who she'd never known existed and who was still alive changed things. If this was correct, then she might belong somewhere after all if she could get past the affair. But did he want to be found? That was still the question on her mind.

It was now or never. She blew out a cleansing breath, trying to ready herself for one of the boldest moments of her life. She set the book next to her computer and typed.

To: *ch@lgproductions.com*
From: *dnewberry@gmail.com*
Subject: *You May Have Known My Grandmother Lizzie*

Dear Mr. Halston,

Dahlia's pulse raced as she wondered what to write next.

My apologies for emailing you out of the blue, but I think you may have known my grandmother, Lizzie Laurent. She may also have gone by Prescott back in 1955. I've found some letters in her house on Long Island, and I have reason to believe we may be related. If you would like to chat, you can call me at 631-555-5555.

I look forward to hearing from you.

Warmly,

Dahlia Newberry

Dahlia reread it, wondering if she should be more specific. She had zero clue what to say to a Hollywood legend who may also be her grandfather. She could use a sounding board right about now. She looked at her phone—no messages. Where was Noah? It wasn't like him not to check in. Dahlia was tempted to call Kara, but they had already spoken in the morning, and she was off to the beach. It seemed it was just her and Harry for the time being.

She read it one last time and hit send, feeling like she had just descended from the top of a terrifying roller coaster. It was out of her hands now. The ball was in his court; whatever happened from here was meant to be.

CHAPTER NINETEEN

July 20

Dahlia woke up, squinting at the bright sun. Her head felt like someone split it open with a sledgehammer. She reached for the glass of water beside her bed, knocking over the wine bottle. "Shit, what time is it?" Dahlia peeked at her phone, which read 9:20, and said July 20. It was Noah's birthday. At first, she smiled, but then realized she hadn't heard from him since yesterday. She looked next to her, just to be sure, but he wasn't there. She pulled up their last text thread from the morning before. "See you soon."

Then she checked their call log. There were too many calls to him to count. The last call from her was at eleven PM. "Oh God, what did I do?" she muttered into the pillow, then screamed. She was many things, but a stalker wasn't one of them. She knew something was wrong; she could feel it in her bones. The last thing Dahlia wanted to be known as was desperate. But by the looks of her room, the truth of the previous twelve hours was slowly unfolding, and it wasn't painting her in a good light.

She lifted her head from the soft cotton pillowcase and brushed the hair off her face. Why hadn't he called her back? Why didn't he come over? She bit her nail, deliberating whether she should send a text. She started worrying that something had happened to him, but her pride got the best of her. So she called Kara instead.

She slurped the water while it rang.

"Dahlia?"

"Morning," Dahlia said with a raspy voice.

"Oh, thank God. You're alive," Kara said.

"Yeah, why wouldn't I be?" Dahlia asked. She glanced at the empties on the floor, her face suddenly feeling pale.

"I don't know—because you could hardly form a sentence last night?" Kara said sarcastically.

"When did we talk?" Dahlia sat up against the headboard and rubbed her eyes.

"You don't remember? What else don't you remember?"

"No, I don't. That's what I'm afraid of." She winced. "I know I called him a lot, but what if I went to his house? God, kill me now."

"Geez, I'm just glad I'm not you this morning." Kara laughed.

"Gee, thanks."

"Listen, with all the secrets you've uncovered, you're allowed a night to blow off steam. You missed that whole drunken college phase. Don't be too hard on yourself. Plus, it's not every day you find out your real grandfather is a leading man."

"Is that what I did? Blow off steam? It feels like I blew a gasket. Like I partied in Vegas all weekend long." She held her head. "I'm too old to drink like that. I was upset I didn't hear from Noah, especially after talking to Penny." She wondered how many more messages she'd left for him while in her inebriated stupor. She looked out the window and huffed.

"What, what is it?" Kara asked.

"His truck, it's missing," Dahlia said, blinking rapidly. "Something isn't right. I can feel it in my bones."

"I'm sure there's a logical explanation. Maybe he had a few too many and stayed with his sister. Maybe you should text Gretchen."

"Yeah, maybe," Dahlia said, feeling unfocused and hazy. "I can't believe the house will be on the market in ten days. It doesn't seem real. It feels like I just got here." There was an ache in her heart that throbbed a little harder today. She was torn between a career choice that made sense and a life she was starting to belong to.

"You can always tell the gallery no or ask for more time."

"It's crossed my mind once or twice, but I don't want to decide anything based on a guy," Dahlia said, searching for her slippers.

"You wouldn't be making this decision for a guy. It would be for you. You're happy there. Admit it."

"I am happy here, probably the happiest I've been in a long, long while. But what do I do for money if I stay?" Dahlia looked around the room at Lil's belongings.

"Maybe you could open your own gallery."

She felt a juxtaposition of emotions. Her shoulders tightened, and adrenaline coursed through her body, waking every molecule. "Kara, that's too risky. And I have zero clients, zero artists, and no name for myself here. I'm completely anonymous."

"You have one artist—Lil," Kara said.

Shivers ran up Dahlia's spine.

"You there?"

"Yeah," Dahlia's voice cracked. "It's a great idea, but I don't have the capital."

"Lil's house is going to be listed for three million. You can afford to take a loan against it."

"True. Listen, I've got to run." Dahlia held her stomach. "I have some puking to do. Then painting and boxes from the basement.

And I need caffeine, lots of it." The mere thought made her belly gurgle, but she couldn't make it through the day without it.

"Please tell me you'll think about it."

"I'll noodle on it."

"Oh, and think about the party tomorrow night. It's a fundraiser. You can bring McHandy too, if he comes to his senses."

If he ever calls me back. And I get rid of this hangover. "Sure, maybe."

"Toodle-oo," said Kara.

Dahlia's feet swiftly shuffled into the bathroom. She expelled the remnants of last night's pity party and splashed her face with cold water. "Never again," she said, looking at her puffy eyes in the mirror. She knew better than this. Plus, she had too much to do. She opened the medicine cabinet that still seemed to stick in the humidity, and grabbed the ibuprofen. Three didn't seem like enough, but she wasn't about to take any more. Harry was waiting by the door for her when she walked out. It seemed Kara wasn't the only one concerned. "Need to go out, boy?" Dahlia couldn't help but ruminate on what Kara said about opening her own gallery. It seemed risky, yet something had uprooted inside her like a tree in a storm when she mentioned it. But was that a good thing? It was yet to be determined.

They took their time descending the old, creaky staircase. She let Harry out, plugged in the percolator, and fed him. It's funny the things you do when you're drunk; apparently, making the coffee the night before was a priority. The aroma of freshly ground java floated through the air. Just smelling it made Dahlia feel more awake. But it wasn't the same without him. Where was he? She still had no idea.

She sipped her coffee and began typing to Gretchen.

Hey, have you seen your brother? Is he okay? I haven't heard from him since yesterday afternoon, and it's not like him.

Right away, Dahlia saw the bubbles, and her smile grew.

Hey, not sure what's going on with you two, but he sounded upset when we spoke last night. He said he was going to the beach for a few days.

Dahlia's heart sank. What could have happened? Something didn't feel right. It was similar to the feeling she had the night her parents died. The tiny hairs stood straight erect on the back of her neck, the way they did at the sleepover right before Lil's phone call. Obviously, Noah was fine and not hurt, but it was the same eerie sense. It was as if a tectonic shift was coming, and she needed to hold on for dear life.

K. Thx. Just wanted to make sure he was safe.

For what it's worth, I hope you 2 work it out. You better come to the opening on Sunday, regardless.

It was tough to swallow the brick lodged in her throat, but she typed back. *I'll be there.*

Dahlia's heartbeats collided, creating an uncomfortable hiccup in her body. Noah seemed happy yesterday. Did she do something to upset him? She didn't like uncertainty because with it came chaos she couldn't control. This kind of feeling always brought her back to her thirteen-year-old self, waiting for Lil to pick her up from the sleepover, not knowing what actually happened. But she wasn't thirteen; she was a middle-aged woman who'd survived the unthinkable, and because of that, Dahlia knew that whatever curveball was thrown her way, she could handle it. Or at least she hoped she could.

She instead decided to turn her focus to something she could control, like her research. She finished her coffee and got to work. Determined to find more clues, maybe even the key, she was done wallowing in the why. Whatever was left unanswered about the affair lay hidden in the deposit box. And she knew it was the only way to keep her mind off Noah. She reminded herself that this was why she'd never leap without a safety net. Charleston was her safety net. There was a reason she'd kept her options open, even after meeting the man of her dreams. Falling in love, as romantic and unraveling as it was, it was also messy and unpredictable. And certainly not something in her wheelhouse.

After dressing in layers, including a knit hat from Lil's mudroom, she was armed and ready for any low-hanging arachnids and cement crawling rodents. She inhaled the damp, moldy air as she slowly stepped down the rickety staircase to the black hole known as the basement. Meeting the last step, she looked around, feeling an emptiness in her heart. All the old boxes and containers that sprawled across the floor contained moments that had come and gone. Yet, Dahlia was the only gatekeeper to their existence and immortality after this. She squeezed her eyes shut, promising to bring them up and go through every last one of them. Even if she had to put them into storage for a bit until she got settled.

With her knit gloves on, she lifted two boxes and headed up the stairs. She placed them by the mudroom door and went back down for more. There were four trips in all, and on her fifth trip, she spotted something in the crawl space. It was hard to tell what it was at first because of all the cobwebs. All she knew was that it was green. Dahlia pushed the remaining container against the wall and used it as a step to climb up. Dahlia let out a squeal before pushing her hand through the silky threads. It was like something from *Raiders of the Lost Ark*. And she felt a little like Indiana Jones. With her hand firmly gripping the top of the object, she yanked it out.

Dahlia sat down on the stairs and blew the dust off the green rusted box. By the looks of it, it had been hidden for a long time. Decades, maybe more. Her fingers lifted the rusted clasps and raised the lid. "It's more letters," she mumbled to herself, letting out a mouse-like sneeze. There were hundreds in the box. The skin on her arms tingled as if she knew she was uncovering a mystery meant to stay buried. But the *Dateline* enthusiast inside her wondered who'd hid them and why. Her curiosity won out as it often did, and with trembling hands she reached for the last one.

It was dated September 1, 1956. A quiet gasp spilled from her lips when she spotted the sender's name and address. Gene Obermann, 6121 Sunset Boulevard, Los Angeles, California. It was addressed to Lizzie Laurent, 6 Meadow Lane, Southold, New York.

Dahlia slid her fingers under the brittle envelope flap that had never been opened. She felt like a voyeur traveling back in time. She blew out the breath trapped in her lungs and read it to herself.

Dear L,

It's been over a year since you left me, and I still haven't received a letter back. I've written you almost every day, and yet nothing. I thought I would have heard from you by now if we still had a chance. I'm not sure if your father has had a hand in keeping us apart or if you changed your mind after returning to your real life on Long Island. No matter what, I want you to know that those two months we shared in Los Angeles were the best of my life. You will always be with me in everything I do and who I become. It will always be you and me forever. I love you with all my heart and soul.

Goodbye,

G

The box was filled entirely with letters from Gene.

Dahlia sat there, letting the tears roll freely. She didn't know exactly why she was crying. She didn't know this man, yet it felt like she did. Through the years, she'd tried so incredibly hard to be strong, but now it felt like the dam was breaking. Maybe it was supposed to. Someone kept these letters from Gran. The likely assumption was that it was her great-grandfather, but it very well could have been her pop if he found out. Poor Gene. She didn't want to feel sorry for him, but she did. It wasn't his fault that her grandmother had misled him. She wiped her wet eyes with her cobweb-free cuff. What if he hadn't known she was married? What if he'd had no idea? The nostalgic young girl inside her wanted to tear each letter open and read every last word. But with her head still pounding and the speed at which the facts were unfolding, she didn't have the energy. It was as if she was in a batting cage being pelted with balls.

If Dahlia read further, she might change her mind altogether about connecting with him. She feared something inside the letters might make him a knowing accomplice. So she closed up the tackle box and left it on the stairs, where the past belonged for now.

Her phone buzzed in her pocket, and she scrambled to retrieve it. When she saw the text from Noah, everything stopped.

Why didn't u tell me you had a daughter? I heard from my ex, of all people. The only thing I asked for was honesty.

She didn't know what to say back in a text, so she called him instead from the kitchen. Her pulse quickened. What if he picked up? What was she going to say? Her throat closed, hearing it go right to voicemail.

"Hey, it's Noah. You know what to do."

She heard the beep and took a deep breath. "Hi, it's me." She paused. "I'm so sorry, Noah. I know there is no excuse for not telling you about Daisy sooner. I was going to tell you the other night. I don't know why I didn't. Being with you made me feel things I've never felt before. And I was afraid . . ." She heard a single beep, alerting her that the recording time had expired.

Panic set in, and an overwhelming sense of dread washed over her. She had more to say, but wasn't sure if she should call back and leave another message or if the last one had actually been recorded. "Ugh," she whisper-shouted. The linoleum floor was getting a workout the last few days. She paced and bit her cuticle, trying to decide if finishing her thought was more important than looking like a stalker.

It most certainly was. She dialed his number while saying a silent prayer. She wasn't a desperate person, but the fear of being misunderstood sent her into a tizzy. *Please pick up, please pick up, Noah.* It clicked, then an automated message filled her ears. "This mailbox is full and cannot accept new messages."

A stifled scream gurgled in her throat. Then she centered herself with a few deep breaths and texted him.

Noah, I'm sorry. All I can say is I was going to tell you. I guess a part of me was afraid it would scare you off. Call me back and I'll tell you why. Your voicemail is full.

What more could she say? He was either going to forgive her or walk away. It felt like a game of chess, and it was his move now.

CHAPTER TWENTY

July 21

Dahlia sat on the porch, waiting for the time to pass until she drove to meet Kara in East Hampton. Ready to go in her floral strapless maxi dress, she still questioned whether going out was the right thing to do. But another night at home would feel like a prison sentence since she still hadn't spoken to Noah or heard from Charles Halston. So here she was, in a pair of wedge sandals in hopes of a happy distraction.

Lil's wicker chair rocked her back and forth. There was a tightness in Dahlia's chest that could only come from bearing responsibility for someone else's pain. She glanced at Noah's text for the twentieth time, which still felt like a dagger to her heart.

Despite having solid reasons for withholding the details of her daughter, she still felt like an awful human. She cared about Noah in a way that was unique from every other relationship in her life. He felt like a kindred spirit tethered to her soul. Their connection was raw and organic, like it came from the earth. Or maybe it was the sky, she didn't know. All she knew was that this was unlike anything she had ever felt before. And this couldn't be how it would end.

A few gnats hovered in the stagnant air as Dahlia hung onto every detail of the bathroom incident with his ex. If she had to do it over again, she would have still stood up for herself, even if it came at a price. Josie had obviously done a little digging herself and wanted one thing: revenge. You only go to those lengths if you're ripe with envy. She watched the speck-like insects, wondering what else Josie was capable of and if Dahlia should walk away. Despite having all morning to stew about it, her jaw was still clenched. Her heart, on the other hand, was hollow. Being misunderstood was the worst feeling. In her fifteen-year marriage to Spence, she'd often thought they spoke different languages, she English and he a fictional language to suit his larger-than-life ego. After a while, she stopped trying to communicate her feelings because it never changed anything. She didn't want that fate for her and Noah, but in the back of her mind, she heard a faint whisper. And it said, *You're undeserving.*

Dahlia glanced at the new screens and couldn't help but think of Noah fixing them. How hot it had been that day, and how incredibly sexy he'd looked in his tight jeans dancing to Springsteen. She felt like a coward and, in hindsight, should have told him sooner. What was she so afraid of? He's been the best thing about this summer. All her reasons for withholding the truth suddenly seemed selfish.

Dahlia looked up at the ceiling fan, trying to dry her wet eyes. She dabbed the corners with her fingers. She'd actually put on makeup and mascara, and there was no way she would ruin that, not even for Noah Sterling.

And with that, she reached for her phone and called Kara.

It rang a few times before Kara picked up. "Kara's party hotline. Is there someone in need of a good time? If so, I'm your girl!" Kara said in a bubbly phone operator tone.

"Ha, very funny."

"I may have missed my calling. What's your ETA?"

"I was going to leave in a few," she said, letting out a long breath.

"Are you Ubering?"

"No, I'm driving Betty."

Kara groaned.

"What? Are you embarrassed or something?" Dahlia's voice flattened.

"God, no. I don't care what these rich people think of me or you. But I don't want a last-minute call saying she won't start. Ya hear me?"

"Yeah, yeah." Kara knew her so well.

"Any word from McHandy?" Kara delicately asked.

"Not since yesterday."

"I'm sorry. I'm not saying you were right in keeping Daisy from him, but I understand why you did it. You were having fun, which isn't something you've gotten to do much of. I like the guy and all, and I like him for you, but there are plenty of fish in the sea. And I don't want you to settle ever again. Do you hear me? Keep the upper hand, is all I'm saying."

"I do, and you're right." But the truth was hard to deny. She liked Noah. Maybe even more than like.

"Text me when you get here. It's going to be a blast. I'm so glad you said yes. We haven't hung out together without kids in probably over a decade. Oh, and I think Simon is coming. To give you a heads up."

"At this point, nothing would surprise me." Dahlia laughed. "I have a few things to do before I go, and then I'm off. See you soon."

Dahlia let Harry out and fed him. She spritzed her skin with a personal scent she'd mixed herself with fragrant oils and added lip gloss from her clutch. Without any additional consideration, Dahlia opened her laptop on the kitchen table and hit send on her onboarding documents email. Dahlia hovered over the screen, hoping she would feel better, only she didn't. It felt forced. Maybe Kara was right, and she was running. Regardless, there was no going back for a do-over.

* * *

Brushwood Lane was already lined with cars, one nicer than the next, when she got there. Dahlia squeezed Betty between a Toyota Land Cruiser and a Mercedes G-Wagon. The heavy hatchback door stuck with the humidity, but she forced it open with her shoe. Her espadrilles hit the hot pavement, and she was as prepared as a homebody could be walking into an exclusive, invite-only Hamptons party.

A golf cart with two college guys dressed in pink golf shirts came by. "Need a ride to the house, ma'am?" Her head drew back. *Ma'am? How about Miss?* Maybe Josie was right. Perhaps she was too old for Noah. When they were alone, she didn't give it much thought, but being among twentysomethings, she felt the age gap was as wide as a ravine.

"I'm good. I'll walk. Thank you." She gave herself a little pep talk and took a lungful of rich Hamptons air. She texted Kara with shaky hands as her steps grew closer to the estate. Deep down, part of her didn't feel likable. She knew she was aloof, but she couldn't change the circumstances that had led up to it. After losing her parents so young, trusting people didn't come easy. It came with time. And time was what most people in her life didn't seem to have. That was, until Noah.

"Eek!" Kara ran out to meet her. She wrapped her arms around her in the middle of the rural one-lane road. "I've missed you, Cuz!"

"Me too. You look pretty," Dahlia said, feeling her stomach in her throat. Kara had on a short, low-cut navy jumpsuit with flutter sleeves, paired with high nude sandals that made her legs look like they went on for days.

"Thanks, you too! Kara gave her a once-over. "Love this dress. It's sexy but also cute."

Dahlia gave a weak smile. She was already regretting this, and she hadn't even stepped onto the driveway. "Whose house is this again?"

"His name is Asher. He created a bunch of apps. He's from California but has a place here. Tony's firm does his financial planning." Kara hooked her arm around hers. "Come on; I'll introduce you. It's not that crowded yet, so it's perfect. And if you want to drink, you can crash with Tony and me. We got a two-bedroom in town."

"Not sure my body can handle more than one or two tonight, but thanks."

"Oh, right. I almost forgot you're hungover," Kara said, straining her face with a squeamish smile. "Well, if you change your mind. You know what they say, hair of the dog."

They walked in and through the back gate, and Dahlia's nerves magically eased. Being with Kara was like having the wind in her sails again. She leaned into her, feeling her insides settle, at least for the moment.

"Everyone, this is Dahlia."

Dahlia waved to the light crowd. "Nice to meet you." It looked like an episode of *On the Runway*. There were so many pretty people, one after the other, as she passed the infinity pool to the bar.

"And you know Simon. I'm going to get Tony. Keep my girl company, will you, and get her a drink. She needs one," she mouthed.

Dahlia glared at Kara with wide eyes.

"My pleasure," Simon said with a charming British accent. "What would you like?"

"I'll take a glass of rosé. Thank you," she said, her eyes darting everywhere. There was so much eye candy. It was a stark contrast to her quiet summer at Lil's. In some very small way, she was happy to be out around people tonight. Yet there was a melancholy behind each smile. If things didn't work out with Noah, she'd be okay, eventually. But knowing this was all her fault was a truth she couldn't fully grasp.

She fiddled with her clutch strap. "So, where are you from?" Dahlia asked, feeling a draft that carried with it his cologne. He smelled good.

"Leeds, it's near Manchester." He nodded to the server behind the bar. "She'll take a rosé, and I'll have a gin and tonic. Thanks, man."

She looked at him, admiring his chiseled chin, pretty profile, and eyes. At another time and place, Simon would have been her rebound. After all, he was her type, with his preppy style, thin but muscular frame, and Notting Hill vibe.

"So, when did you move here?"

"Let's see if I can do the math." He squinted, looking up at the sky. "It was 2005, I believe. No, 2004."

The server placed their drinks on the glass surface and, like a gentleman, Simon passed it to her. "Thank you. Do you like it here?" Dahlia asked about to take a sip when a man with slicked-back hair and expensive sunglasses lunged into her, spilling her wine. Dahlia felt the chilled liquid run down the front of her dress.

"Hey, watch it! You just crashed into her, buddy," Simon hollered, grabbing a few napkins for her.

"My bad," the distracted guy said, spotting someone he knew. "Darling."

"These people have an air about them, don't they?" Simon tsked, trying to avoid watching Dahlia blot her chest.

"A little." Dahlia chuckled. This wouldn't happen on the North Fork. Maybe home wasn't so bad after all. "What? People in the U.K. don't have airs? I've only been once to London for work."

"No, they do." He laughed. "But they're much more polite, at least to your face. Want to take a walk? Get out of the congestion?"

"Sure." She smiled wistfully. She missed Noah. No matter who was walking beside her, she knew she would always choose Noah. Her hand tightened its grip on her purse as she realized how royally she'd messed everything up. Not only by keeping Daisy from him but also by omitting the truth about this job she was taking. But she hadn't wanted the decision to be influenced by anyone but herself. She felt like she'd earned that since she'd given up so much in the past for others. As unfair as that was to Noah, it was the only way she knew to protect this second season of hers. Until she heard the words "I love you" from a man, she'd never fully let her shield down. But even then, could she trust it?

"I'm glad you came," Simon said, his hazel eyes bright and wide.

"Yeah, me too." That wasn't exactly the truth, but it was better than staying home eating ice cream and watching a Charles Halston movie, which she still hadn't done. She just hoped she wasn't sending mixed signals. "Look at this view. I bet they have incredible sunsets over the water," Dahlia said, changing the subject.

He continued talking with his glued-on smile and endearing accent, but all she could think about was *him*, the hunk who'd wormed his way into her barn and heart. She wondered what he was up to, if he missed her, and if he would ever return to Meadow Lane. Dahlia made a pathetic attempt to smile back at him through the ache that settled in her heart.

Simon sipped his drink, and his speckled eyes locked with hers. If it hadn't been for Noah, she would have been swept away. Maybe pushed him against a tree and kissed him boldly; he was, as Lil would describe, a "dreamboat."

They talked for a while by the water and walked back up to the party. She hung out with Tony and Kara. They insisted on shots, and Dahlia discreetly threw hers in the bushes. All she wanted was to sleep in her own bed tonight. The sunset faded over the hedge of privet as Dahlia danced with Kara. Considering everything thrown at her this week, she was actually starting to enjoy herself.

That was, until someone blew her cover. "Hey, aren't you the girl dating Noah Sterling?" the inebriated girl with long dark brown hair and blinding veneers asked. "I mean woman."

"What?" Dahlia was startled. She stared at the girl in the skin-tight pink dress.

"Wait, what?" Kara asked, pushing in front of Dahlia.

"Yeah, it was all over Page Six yesterday. Pictures of you two out in the Hamptons. They called you a divorced recluse from the North Fork," the girl said, looking Kara up and down.

Dahlia felt her shoulders drop and her ears turn red. It took her back to the day a wave crashed her to shore—without her bikini top—and her entire class saw.

"Don't sweat it, hon." Kara offered an understanding nod as she walked her away from the crowd.

"I bet Josie called the gossip rag from the club the other night." Dahlia shook her head, feeling the steam levitate above her head. She wanted to use expletives, but God knew who was hiding in the bushes, waiting for a video response.

It was just another reminder that she still didn't know where she belonged. Was it Connecticut, Southold, Charleston, or somewhere else she had yet to discover?

"I'm going to go to the bathroom," she told Kara.

"Want me to come with you?"

"No, I'm good. You stay." Dahlia's breath quickened at the thought of Daisy reading about her relationship with Noah. But she was in France. There was no way. A slight wave of relief hit her as she kept walking.

Dahlia opened the pool house door and rushed into the bathroom. The wall held her tense body. She squeezed her eyes shut, mustering the courage to look it up on her phone. After typing *Noah Sterling's new girlfriend Page Six*, she let out a long exhale and hit search. There were already too many links to count.

Dahlia gasped. She didn't like the feeling of being outed and seen, especially when it wasn't her choice and on her terms. She skimmed through the article, seeing highlights such as "much older, married with a daughter." Dahlia felt dizzy scanning the images, as if she'd willingly sipped a witches' brew. But what she was most heartbroken about was that a person would use her child as a pawn in a petty revenge scheme.

The air suddenly felt thick and heavy. It was hard to breathe. She wanted to go home. She couldn't stay another minute with these people. Dahlia slipped out the back door and bolted to her car. She stood under the lamplight. Her hand shook as she tried her best to text Kara. *I'm sorry. I need to go home.*

"Dahlia!" Kara yelled. "Were you going to pull an Irish goodbye?" Kara caught up to her. "Listen, no one cares here. Heck, their faces have probably been plastered on that page more than once."

"It's not just that." Dahlia folded her arms, feeling her eyes burn. "The write-up mentions Daisy and my marriage. It's uncalled for—I didn't sign up for this." No one messed with her kid.

"No, you didn't. It's rotten."

"And Simon seems like a great guy, but he's just a distraction. I need to make things right with Noah before I can think about anything or anyone else."

"Whatever you need him to be is fine. I just wanted you to see your options." Kara held her hand. "What I care about is us. We were having so much fun. You can make it right tomorrow. Just stay."

"Kara, you don't get it." Dahlia punctuated with her other hand. "You and I live in two different worlds."

"How could you say that?" Kara grimaced.

"I *have* to protect myself and Daisy because if I don't, no one will."

"You have me," Kara said with a hitched breath.

"Kara, did you know that your mother kicked me out when I found out I was pregnant?"

"What?" Kara's face went slack. "No, she didn't. She said you wanted to go live with Lil after the summer."

"No, she told me to never come back. She said she would pack my stuff and send it. That being unwed and pregnant would bring shame to the family and you."

Kara shook her head. "No, that's not true. My mother would never. She volunteers at the church, for God's sake." Kara's face was bright red, in defense mode.

"But it is true. She had big dreams for you. She wanted all of this for you." Dahlia pointed to the house and party. "And she didn't want me holding you back. Like I said, we come from two different worlds. I have to go." Dahlia got into Betty and sped away, leaving Kara reeling from the truth about her mother.

* * *

Later that night, with still no word from Noah, she headed to Lil's barn. It was a place that always made her feel better and less alone. The colorful walls never failed to envelop her in love, creativity, and a sense of belonging. The minute she opened the door, she was greeted by the aroma of old grass and pine. She stood motionless in the doorway, anchored in the past. The flimsy door snapped shut behind her, waking her from this moment of peace. She turned on the lamp beside Lil's chair, making everything glow. The terracotta pots lined shelves, and the garden tools hung in an orderly fashion below. Every single time she entered, she noticed something different. Yet another gift that kept on giving.

She lifted the window and soaked up the sounds of the twilight summer night. The crickets and cicadas chirped in sync, taking turns while Dahlia sank into the worn chair. She was sure Kara would never speak to her again. Dahlia regretted outing her mother for being cruel, but she was also tired of pretending. She kicked her feet up onto the nearby crate. As much as she wanted to be at peace, she still ached all over. If being with him came with this kind of cruelty and criticism, then she wanted no part of his world.

Her head said one thing, but her heart another. She had been through worse, yet grief was grief. It was still brutal, no matter the depths or circumstances. She wrapped a nearby blanket around her, feeling her lids lower.

Dahlia dozed off and woke with a vibrating phone in her hand.

"Noah?"

"Hello? Is this Dahlia Newberry?" a frail but soothing voice asked.

"Yes, it is." Her mouth was suddenly dry.

"This is Gene."

Gene, oh my gosh. It was him. *Don't be awkward*, she told herself. Dahlia couldn't get her voice to work. She wasn't one for fanfare, but she still couldn't believe she was on the phone with a man who'd won two Oscars.

"Hello, are you there?"

"Yes, I'm here." Dahlia sat up straight. "I'm just surprised you called me back. I didn't think this would reach you, or if it did, that you'd respond." She could have been a crazed fan for all he knew.

"Well." He cleared his throat. "When I received your email, I was intrigued. I have so many questions."

Dahlia pinched her lips. "As do I."

"You said you thought we were related."

"Yes, I believe you may be my biological grandfather." Hearing her say it aloud made the possibility sound absolutely insane. But she had proof. Of what she wasn't sure, but it was something. "I've been cleaning out my family's house in Southold, getting it ready to sell, and have uncovered some surprising information." She paused. "I'm sorry, this is a lot."

"It's okay." He sounded sweet. Not at all what she expected. "I do have some questions, though."

"Of course, anything."

"When was your mother or father born?"

"My mother, Rose . . ." She heard Gene's breath hitch. "She was born May eighth, 1956." There was silence, so she continued being careful not to jump to the end. The last thing she wanted to do was overwhelm him. "My grandmother raised her with my grandfather. Up until last week, that was the only truth I knew."

"I see," he said. "May I ask why you think it's me?"

"I found a letter my grandmother wrote to you in 1965 saying as much. She took my mother to see *The Best Man*, not knowing you were in it." Tiny fractures lined each word. She was still angry, yes, but her heart ached over not knowing the truth sooner. "It was a congratulatory letter that expressed her love for you."

Again, silence.

"This may seem like such a shock. And I'm happy to send you everything I have to verify this."

"That won't be necessary," he said firmly. "When I saw the name, I knew. You see, a love like ours never really leaves your heart, even though the years go on."

Tears flooded Dahlia's tired eyes, and she tucked her feet beside her. She wanted to hear him out.

"I've never loved anyone the way I loved her." His voice stuttered. "Never."

Dahlia's smile grew as she realized how real it was to him. Could a woman love two men at once? She was beginning to think it was possible. There were important questions to ask, but Gene needed to talk, so she let him go on.

"That summer, we would meet every night at the diner down the road from CBS Studios. I had my two cups of black Hills Brothers coffee, and she had her Lipton Earl Grey tea. It was at seven, after her father returned for the night shift," he said, still sounding heartbroken.

"Night shift?" Dahlia's brows furrowed. That seemed weird. Gran had been a grown woman at the time; she hadn't lived with her father. Maybe she'd been trying to hide the affair.

"He worked on the set of *Gunsmoke*, your great-grandfather."

A beep sounded on her end of the line. She glanced at the screen to see who was calling her.

Noah.

He'd finally resurfaced. But his timing couldn't be worse. Her heart skipped with indecision. *This is too important.* Now he'd have to wait. "Oh, I had no idea. All I knew was that he was a set designer on Broadway."

"He wasn't a nice man, and he was a heavy drinker, which made it worse."

"It usually does," Dahlia said, thinking of Spence and all his drunken episodes where his verbal abuse reached an all-time high.

"Her parents didn't like me. I was Jewish, came from nothing, and was older. I was just a gofer at the studio, waiting on all the big names at the time. I didn't make much money back then. They didn't see a future there."

"Yeah, I figured that much from the letters I found in the basement," Dahlia interjected.

"You found letters?" His voice rose.

"I did. Hundreds. All unopened." Dahlia took a breath, realizing how shocking and hurtful this information must have been, even after more than sixty years. "Someone went to great lengths to make sure they were hidden forever." After hearing more about her great-grandfather, he would have been the likely suspect. But after this conversation, it could have well been her pop who'd hidden them. Especially if he knew the extent of their affair.

"Oh, my." His voice cracked. "So she never got them?"

"No, she didn't, Gene." Dahlia's heart sank. It was possible that she did get them and never opened them, fearing she might make another choice. But the letter she wrote in 1965 told a different story. She would have at least opened them and read them.

He was quiet. Too quiet.

"Gene?"

"Yes, I'm here," he said.

"So, you never married?" Dahlia asked.

"Oh, I did. Many times. Too many times. But they just weren't her."

"I apologize if this sounds too forward, but did you have any children?" Dahlia rubbed the back of her neck.

"One with my second wife, a daughter named Ingrid, after the actress."

From Casablanca, Lil's favorite movie, she thought.

"She passed away a few years back, from cancer."

"I'm so sorry." There was a weight in her lungs. He knew loss too. She couldn't imagine losing a child, no matter what the age. And now it seemed he'd lost two.

"That became the greatest heartbreak of my life after your grandmother." His voice weakened.

"I know a thing or two about that." Dahlia didn't have the heart to tell him about her mother being gone just yet. But she did need to get something else off her chest. "Did you know she was married when you were together?" Dahlia blurted.

"Who?" he asked.

"My grandmother."

"Dahlia, Lil was sixteen that summer. I was nineteen. Neither of us were married."

"No, she wasn't. She was . . ." Dahlia looked up and did the math in her head. "Twenty-six. Wait, did you say *Lil*?"

"Yes, that's who I figured we were talking about."

"But the letters, they were addressed to Lizzie," she said.

"Her sister Lizzie covered for us, but that was all."

Tears filled her eyes like a rising tide during a storm, and it became hard to find air. L was *Lil*, not Lizzie. "Are you saying you had a relationship with Lil?"

"Yes, and the age difference didn't bother me. She was wise beyond her years. She saw life through a bright and beautiful lens. I never knew anything like it."

Her heart pounded through her shirt. Dahlia couldn't think straight. Her eyes darted around the room.

"When did she die? And how?" he asked softly.

"A few months ago, of cancer," Dahlia said, barely able to think. It was like a tornado in her head and a cyclone in her heart.

She heard him start to whimper on the other end.

"Gene, I'm sorry." This time, she felt sucker punched and left for dead. She couldn't breathe. Her skin boiled, and the barn walls spun. "May I call you back tomorrow? I need to process this."

"Sure." His voice fissured as if he was going to break the moment they hung up. "Dahlia, I'm so glad you reached out."

"I am too," she said, feeling the heat rise higher in her body. "Night, Gene."

"Night, Dahlia."

Dahlia stood up and paced the rickety wood floor. She tried to steady her erratic breaths by inhaling over and over again, but that just seemed to make them worse.

Her grandmother hadn't written that letter; it was *Lil*. Had Lil actually been her grandmother? So, she had a boyfriend when she was a teenager that she never spoke about. But why? Was it because of her mother? And Daisy had recently discovered that Pop didn't share the same DNA. It was all adding up, but there was no real proof.

Dahlia was drowning with no lifeboat in sight, and now she had even more unanswered questions. If she was right, and Lil was actually her biological grandmother, why would she have let Gran and Pop raise Rose as their own and never tell anyone the truth? There would have had to be a really good reason for it.

"I have to find that key if it's the last thing I do." She wiped her eyes, making eye contact with the row of coffee cans on the top shelf. She grabbed the stool and lifted them off the shelves one by one in a fury of blind fury. Finding that key and maybe even proof had never felt so urgent. Catching them as they fell, she peeked inside each one and tossed them to the ground. There was one left.

"Please, please be in here." Dahlia inhaled the stale air one last time and reached for it slowly. She peeked inside the worn old tin and started to weep. Slowly, she reached in and pulled out a gold key, pressing the cold metal between her fingers. She leaned her shoulder against the nearby wood beam, hoping it would hold her emotionally taxed body upright.

Whatever was in the box had better be an explanation—and a good one at that.

CHAPTER TWENTY-ONE

July 22

The next morning, Dahlia settled into her worn bucket seat, waiting for the bank to open so she could finally retrieve the contents of the box. She nursed a latte, her eyes glued to the gold key on her dashboard, while she counted the minutes until she could go in.

Dahlia couldn't wrap her head around the fact that Lil could have been her grandmother, and all these years said *nothing*. Not even on her deathbed. Dahlia wanted to feel something besides betrayal—she wanted an explanation.

She rolled the window down while she waited. The town was quiet for a weekday, but it was also a summer Friday on the North Fork. The air was crisp and fresh, inviting Dahlia to find the silver lining. She could hear the landscapers already at work, gearing up the mowers for a full day ahead.

She pondered what Kara had said about feeling like *herself* here. This town and its people made her feel whole and, more importantly, healed. But she couldn't let herself go there until she knew what was in that box. She rested her head on the doorframe, closed her eyes, and wondered if Noah would respond to her call and text from this morning asking if they could talk. It was her second attempt, and most likely her last.

How could she stay if he didn't want her there? She was now doubting everything they had shared, starting with that first day in the barn. Although she never claimed to be an expert in relationships, she knew one simple thing: If he wanted to work it out, he would.

She wanted to call Kara too. But after last night, she couldn't. She should never have told Kara the truth about Aunt Cathy trying to keep Dahlia and Kara apart.

The truth was, there was a small part of Dahlia that was so used to grieving alone, and in some sick and twisted way, she felt like she deserved it.

The clock read 8:46. Fourteen minutes until she could finally piece together the remains of her complex family tree.

A ringing sound came from her seat cushion. She quickly glanced at the number, and her stomach dropped. It was a FaceTime from Daisy. She couldn't see her like this. There were too many questions Dahlia still couldn't answer. She rubbed her forehead and debated letting it go, but instead threw on her sunglasses and ran her fingers through her unkempt hair.

"Hi, Daisy girl," Dahlia said, moving her face toward the light.

"Mom." Daisy looked serious.

"Yes." Dahlia felt the blood drain from her face.

"Are you dating Noah Sterling from *Hamptons House*?"

"What?" Dahlia stuttered. "Where did you . . . ?"

"From Page Six." Daisy's eyes widened.

"How? You're in France?"

"My friends sent me the link. The internet is everywhere, Mom." Daisy sighed with exaggeration. "How could you think I wouldn't see it?'

"I don't know. I didn't think about it, Daisy. I'm just trying to live my life and be happy for a change."

"Does Dad know?" Daisy's voice lowered to a slow, incriminating tone.

"He does." Dahlia cleared her already raw throat. "But the papers are signed, and it's officially none of his business," she said calmly. "I'm sorry. I should have told you about Noah myself."

Daisy huffed and looked off.

"Say something," Dahlia said, wishing deeply that she could reach through the phone and hug her daughter. "Please."

"I'm happy for you. You deserve to find someone who treats you with the respect you deserve. Dad was a horrible husband. But for the love of God, could you find someone your own age?" She shook her head, causing her bun to fall over. "I've been in panic mode all morning."

"Daisy, we've just been spending time together. Last I checked, that was okay."

"Well, if I'm being honest, it's kind of embarrassing," Daisy grumbled. "Plus, he's a reality star. I mean, Mom, you don't even watch that stuff. What could you possibly see in him or have in common?"

Everything, absolutely everything, she thought. There was a dagger now piercing her heart. Being misunderstood was her Achilles heel. "He lives next door, and he's been helping me with the house. Listen, I'm not going to argue with you. You have every right to feel the way you do. But I'm a grown woman, Daisy. And I've taken care of everyone else through the years but myself. This is my time. And if he makes me happy, then so be it." Dahlia pursed her lips, owning her words for the first time. She didn't want to drag Daisy into the mess, which ironically was about her. "I wasn't looking. Trust me, finding a boyfriend was the last thing on my mind. I mean, heck, I took the job in Charleston."

"Boyfriend? Job? What?" Daisy's eyes widened.

Dahlia inhaled before answering. "I told you I was looking for a job."

"Yeah."

"Well, I found one at an upscale gallery off King Street. Are you okay with that?"

"I don't know. I mean, what, is he going to move with you?"

"God, no. I don't know." Dahlia's posture shifted. "I haven't thought that far ahead."

"Then you're just going to leave him?" Daisy flailed her hands.

"I don't know." Dahlia shook her head. "It's complicated. I don't even know what he wants past the summer. I'm just having fun. And all I know is I deserve to have a little."

Dahlia was now past empty; there was no more energy for show and tell. Not about the secrets shared between two sisters, not about Gene, not about the key she'd finally found. And certainly not that she'd fallen hard and fast for a younger man.

"I've gotta go anyway," Daisy said with a pinched expression. "Love you."

"You too. Bye."

If it wasn't one thing, it was another. Dahlia felt like she was dodging bullets from every angle.

She knew she should feel more guilt over upsetting Daisy. But she didn't. And for that reason alone, she sighed and looked out the window. It was as if someone opened the door to possibility the minute she arrived at Lil's, and she willingly walked right through it. She was proud of herself for that, at least. No matter what happened with Noah, she had no regrets.

Finally, the bank employee was outside putting the bank sign on the curb. She took a swig of summer air and opened her car door. It was now or never.

"Good morning," she said, feeling her insides toss like an overloaded washing machine. This was it. So much was riding on this moment.

"Beautiful day." He held the door for her. "What can I help you with today?"

"I have a safe deposit key. I would like to open my aunt's box."

"Do you have the paperwork?"

"No, I don't. Just a number. Is that a problem?" Dahlia asked the gray-haired, stocky man named Jim.

"I'll have to see your license to ensure you're a co-owner."

Co-owner? Her posture caved as she slid him her license. Of course, it was another setback. *Please, please*, she prayed. *If I don't see what's in that box, I'll . . .*

"Let's see here. Lily Prescott. And you're . . ." He looked at the license. "Dahlia Newberry." He looked up. "Someone liked flowers, didn't they?"

Chills ran up her spine. "Yeah, and my mother's name is Rose." *We were named after the flowers in Lil's garden.*

Suddenly, she wasn't mad or powerless. She was heartbroken. Heartbroken for a life Lil had felt she needed to hide.

"Hold on." He typed away. "Almost there."

Dahlia held her breath.

"Yup, you're on here."

Dahlia exhaled. "Wonderful." Inside, she was a bundle of tightly wound nerves. This was it, just a few more minutes until the truth would set her free.

He passed her a card. "Just sign and we're all set."

She signed her name and slapped the pen against the hard surface.

"You can follow me." He waved her down a bright and narrow hallway. "I'll need to open it with you, with my key."

Dahlia followed him, squinting as her mind ran wild. What if Lil's reason wasn't good enough? What did she want to hear? That Lil lied because she had no other choice? Yes, that was what she wanted to hear.

They scanned the wall of metal for the number 222 and spotted it right in the middle. They entered their keys simultaneously, and it opened. She breathed a sigh of relief. If that wasn't the key, she may have gone a lifetime without knowing what was inside.

She followed Jim down the hall into a private room. He set the box on the counter-height table, and Dahlia thanked him. Once he left, she unlatched the clasp and lifted up the top.

There was a stack of black-and-white composition books with a letter addressed to Dahlia on top. *Her journals.* Her eyes widened, remembering Lil writing in these books when she was a kid. She presumed it was just daily reminders, recipes, or garden notes. An image popped into her mind of Lil in the pantry, with her lilac handkerchief wrapped around her head, sitting on the sill, writing in one of these books. The pulse in her neck quickened as she pulled the contents from the box.

Dahlia walked down the hospital-like hallway, hearing the squeak of her soles against the vinyl tile. Her sweaty palms gripped the cardboard covers, and her chest pounded as she walked to her car. This was the moment she'd anticipated from the instant she found Lil's first communication from beyond the grave. The veil was about to be lifted, and all the pretexts revealed.

Dahlia opened her car door, pushed back her seat, and slid her fingers under the envelope flap. There were two folded sheets of paper inside. With unsteady hands, she opened the official-looking one with the embossed seal first. She gasped. It was her mother's original birth certificate from 1956. It read mother: Lily Ann Prescott, and father: Gene Frank Obermann. Under the child's name, it read Rose Ingrid Obermann.

There was a dull ache that felt like it made a permanent home inside Dahlia's heart. It was true. Lil was her biological grandmother, and Gene was her biological grandfather. A medley of emotions collided inside her as she stared out her window. She felt relief, regret, grief, and joy too. It didn't change what Gran and Pop were to her; it only made her feel more loved. But she still needed to know why Lil did what she did. Dahlia folded the certificate back up and rested it on top of the journals, making a mental note to show Gene. The other looked to be a handwritten letter from Lil. Dahlia slowly pulled it open and read it to herself.

Dear Dahlia,

Enclosed are my journals. They hold the key to a secret that has been buried for far too long. I didn't have the guts to share it while I was alive, and I am deeply sorry for that.

I met an amazing man in 1955. He was what Daisy would call my twin flame. It was the summer my father took a job at CBS Studios in California. I was just sixteen but wise beyond my years. He was nineteen, and oh, was he a looker. He swept me off my feet, and we fell madly in love within weeks. It was the kind of love that moved mountains and parted the seas. It was the stuff movies were made of and books written about. At the time, he was just an errand boy, but I knew he would make it big in film someday. He had so much drive and determination.

Dahlia swallowed, fighting her looming tears. "Our stories are so parallel," she whispered and kept reading.

My father found out the week we left and cursed our union because Gene was poor and of a different faith. He beat him and left him to die on the sidewalk. He threatened to have him arrested for statutory rape if I stayed. I would have left everyone behind for him, I loved him that much, but I knew my father would deliver on his promise. I couldn't bear the thought of Gene in jail. So I went home and, shortly after, found out I was pregnant. My father gave me two choices: to give the baby, your mother, up for adoption or let my sister raise her. She and your pop couldn't have children of their own, so we agreed. We made a pact between sisters that we'd never speak the truth until after my father died. It was the only way I could be in her life. It was the only way I reckoned I would survive. After my father died, we couldn't bring ourselves to tell Rose and uproot her life. So the secret stayed buried out of love for her. There were many times I wanted to tell you, but I was afraid you would hate me forever. And I couldn't leave this earth like that.

Lizzie let me name your mother Rose. In my mind, she was always Rose Ingrid, but to everyone else, she was Rose Kathleen. I built a garden to heal myself, and on every birthday, I planted and painted a rose. I couldn't be her mother in real life, but in that garden, I was. I wrote her letters and birthday cards and buried important things in tin cans that only a mother would keep.

Tears rolled steadily down her cheeks, wetting her lips. She realized it wasn't her mother who'd buried a time capsule; it was Lil. She grabbed a tissue from her glove compartment and kept going.

This must be shocking, but I need you to know where you came from. Your biological grandfather's name is Gene Obermann, but he changed his name to Charles Halston when he hit it big in the movies. I am hoping he is still alive. Please get in touch with him, tell him what happened, and that I died loving him. It would be my last wish fulfilled.

Dahlia felt gutted for ever doubting Lil. She pressed her fist against her chest and continued.

With this letter, I hope to set decades of shame and guilt free. Please know I love you with all that I am. You're a gift I didn't deserve. I know you felt like you didn't belong anywhere after your parents died, but you did. You belonged with me. You are meant for a life of color, like the hues of a sunset and the palette in my garden. Own and chase what brings you joy, my sweet Dahlia, and don't ever let it go. Whatever you decide to do with my house, you belong somewhere, everywhere, but mostly to yourself. I hope you can find it in your heart to forgive me.

Love, your grandmother,

Lil

"Oh, Lil." Her body shook as she sobbed. "I would have understood and forgiven you," she whispered, feeling like a blubbering mess.

All Dahlia could think about was all the years, if she had known, it could have been different. But would it have changed anything? To her, Lil was as close as you could get to a mother and grandmother, if not closer.

Dahlia's hands trembled as she drove back to the house. She had to call Kara. She dialed her number, and it just rang. The sound was hollow. Her voicemail came on, and Dahlia quickly hung up. There were no words for what happened in the last twelve hours.

Her chest physically hurt, and her lips quivered. She was grief-stricken. It was yet another death and rebirth all at once. This time, the end of a life unlived and the birth of the truth. She hoped being back at Lil's would give her the time to process this information without feeling pulled in any other direction. And she hoped Kara would call her back.

* * *

A few hours later, her new reality was slowly rooting itself. With still no word from Noah, she admired the midday view of her gardens from the bench. The sun glowed over the bright blooms, making it seem almost heavenly. Harry sat at her feet, knowing all too well that something was wrong. It was hard to find even the slightest bit of air in the sweltering heat, but she fought for every molecule.

Dahlia's mind floated back to the day she told Lil she was pregnant after her Aunt Cathy kicked her out. It was a spring day, and her cherry blossoms in the front yard were in full bloom.

Dahlia walked up to the front door, and before she could open it, Lil was standing there with her arms wide open. "Come here, my girl."

Dahlia rushed into her arms and sobbed on her shoulder.

"There, there. Everything's going to be okay. I'm here. We're going to get through this together." Lil squeezed her tight.

"But I've just thrown away my scholarship to RISD." Dahlia couldn't get the words out. "And I've disappointed everyone, including my parents."

Lil pulled her back and held her cheeks. "You listen to me. What you are doing takes more courage than getting a degree, and while your parents might have been shocked at first, they would have eventually come around. A baby has a way of bringing people together. You'll see."

Harry barked at the squirrels in a playful chase up the willow tree, waking Dahlia from the memory. Dahlia had always wondered how Lil could say that with such certainty. And now she knew. Daisy had brought everyone together, just as her mother, Rose, had. She leaned forward, feeling her heart sink to the bottom of the ocean. Being unable to be a mother to your own child, and watch her grow up right before your eyes, must have been the worst pain imaginable.

Dahlia looked up through her wet lashes at the rainbow of colors that surrounded her. It dawned on her that this was Lil's lighthouse, serving as her beacon of hope. Lil's journals sat beside her, waiting to be opened, but Dahlia was unsure how much more pain she could endure for one day. Her eyelids were gummy, and her nose swollen. The flowery aromas from the garden were lost on her as she was too stuffy to smell anything. Maybe it could wait until tomorrow, after the restaurant opening.

The nearby willow branches bent in the breeze, easing her angst. She closed her eyes. She thought about the courage it took for Lil to choose happiness every day when she could have been bitter. The stack of marbled notebooks glared at her. Dahlia sucked in a lungful of sweet, flowery air as the breeze opened to a random page. What was Lil trying to tell her?

August 12, 1955

Dear G,

Tonight, we drove along the Pacific Coast Highway with the top down in your borrowed Capri. The sun melted into the horizon, painting the sky with a kaleidoscope of colors that had only lived in my imagination. It was truly the most beautiful thing I'd ever seen until I glanced over at you. Your slicked-back, wavy dark hair waffled in the California wind, and you smiled at me with such confidence. You reached for my hand and laced your long fingers with mine. My stomach took flight, and I knew I could no longer control my heart.

The smell of you lingers on your sports jacket as I sit on my bed, too tired to take it off. My skin tingles from your touch, and my lips still feel joined to yours. No matter where I go or who I become, it will always be you and me from this point on. I twirl the single rose you gave me in my fingers. The silky petals tickle my nose, and I inhale their sweet fragrance. I smile, knowing a rose will never again be just another rose.

Forever Yours,

L

Dahlia gasped in astonishment. That was why she named her mother Rose. With a heaviness that felt endless, she kept going. She flipped through the pages and read words from beyond the grave.

I felt her kick today.

I miss you more than words.

I wish you were here.

My heart aches for you.

I don't know how I'm going to do this without you.

I cried myself to sleep last night, imagining you holding my belly beside me.

I'm scared, Gene.

The neighbor saw me today. I hope she doesn't tell anyone.

My father says I bring shame to his family.

She'll be here any day, Gene.

How can I give her to my sister? How can I let someone else raise our daughter?

We had a daughter today. I named her Rose. She's perfect.

Today, someone stopped Lizzie at the grocery store and told her how pretty Rose was. My heart broke. It's so hard not being her mother. It's a pain that breaks me into pieces.

It's her birthday. Rose is one. I planted a rose bush in her honor. She ate cake and got it all over her face.

She's a ham. She has your wit, Gene.

I'm painting again, just flowers from her garden.

My heart aches for you. It's as raw as the day I left.

Dahlia's eyes and throat were as dry as the desert, but she continued. This time, skipping ahead.

June 18, 1983

G,

Our girl graduated high school today. Rose looked regal in her green cap and gown. She's independent, fierce, charming, and kind. You'd be so proud. She got a full scholarship to Boston College and will head there this fall.

All My Love,

L

Dahlia rubbed her temples. On the one hand, she felt like someone had sliced her open and held her heart in their hand. On the other hand, she felt chosen for this and that it was a privilege to be a voyeur in this timeless love affair.

With that, she peeked at the last page—January 20, 1997—and closed it up. Dahlia was trying to hold it together. She considered calling Kara again but didn't. If she wanted to talk, she would call her back. She thought about Daisy but didn't want to burden her. And Noah, well, that was obviously not happening. As hard as it was to accept, she was on her own.

The rest would have to wait. She couldn't bear any more tonight. Her soul felt like it needed CPR. She still had to call Gene back but maybe tomorrow. It wasn't even four yet, but after what she'd been through, she could sleep for days.

* * *

After a long afternoon nap that faded into the night, Dahlia lay there staring at the ceiling. The moon was bright, lending just enough light to the room. She tossed and turned, feeling the sheets stick to her tacky skin. The clock read 12:38. Her eyes moved to the tassel that hung on her lamp. She rolled onto her back again and thought about the last entry she read. She heard Harry moan on the floor. "You're having a tough time too, bud?"

Suddenly, her feet hit the floor. She threw on her sweatshirt and ran to the backyard. She needed to see what else was buried.

She hit the spotlights inside the barn door, illuminating Lil's raised garden beds.

Dahlia funneled her way under Lil's roses as carefully as possible but came up empty-handed. Her hands and legs were marred in dirt. None of this made sense, so why should digging in the dark be any less crazy? Her eyes burned, but she kept going. One tin can was all she needed to find, and then she could call it a night. She was so close, yet so far.

The more she dug, the more she ruminated about Lil and Gene and how bad she felt about accusing Gran. It was all coming to a head. She couldn't get rid of the heaviness and the ache that felt like death, no matter how hard she tried.

As she dug her way to the back of her grandmother's rose garden, Dahlia finally hit metal. "Hallelujah!" she let out a whisper-yell as her eyes wandered to Noah's place. It was still dark. She was glad he wasn't home to see this. He might think she'd lost her marbles. But he would also think it was pretty freaking cool.

With her hands, she scooped out the soil. It began to rain, but she couldn't stop; she was too close. The tin can was lodged between the roots. She jabbed it with the shovel and pulled it with all her might. The large droplets cooled her sweaty body. It was cathartic, as if the rain were washing away the secrets. It felt poignant. Dahlia yanked it one last time and fell on her butt. She sat there in the rain, feeling Lil with her. With the can pressed to her swift-beating chest, she whispered at the dark sky. "No more secrets, Lil. It's time to set them free."

CHAPTER TWENTY-TWO

July 23

Dahlia's cheek stuck to the worn gingham fabric as she pried her eyes open. Her head was still wedged in the nook of the wingback, and Lil's barn was a mess. Shovels lay scattered across the floor, and dirt was caked on her beautiful diamond-painted floor. That reminded Dahlia that she still needed to fix that chipped board. The details were still fuzzy, but slowly coming back into view like binoculars that required adjusting. She held her head, feeling like she'd just weathered the worst emotional hurricane of her life.

She didn't want to get up, but she knew she couldn't hide inside their shared structure forever. At some point, Noah would come back, and she'd have to face him sooner or later. Heck, they were bound to run into each other, if nothing else, in the very spot where she hid.

Twenty-four hours earlier, she was angry and gutted, looking for answers, but now, just a day later, she felt peace. Like the calm after the storm. The sun illuminated the tiny dust particles in the air, lending a sense of magic. It was like a rebirth of sorts. She sat up, noticing the cozy cover draped over most of her body. She didn't recall having a blanket the night before. In fact, she remembered being cold before she dozed off here. So then, where did it come from?

She lifted the chunky knit blanket off her legs and scanned the paintings that hung in numerical order. "I will find a way to honor you, Lil. If it's the last thing I do," she whispered to the walls as if they could hear her. Dahlia wanted to shout from the rooftops that Lil was her grandmother. If she could drive through town with a megaphone, she would. Her smile grew as she pulled out the hand-drawn birthday card from the tin that sat beside her. There was a single red rose painted on watercolor paper. It was something you would see in a vintage botanical book that you stumbled upon at a flea market. In beautiful calligraphy, it read *six*. Her fingers grazed the surface, feeling the bumpy texture under her skin.

Dahlia looked out the window, feeling puffy all over. Despite going through the tin the night before, it still seemed new, like a toy at Christmas. She had to keep playing with it to make sure it was real. She didn't want to fall apart again. If there was any hope of making it to Gretchen's opening, she would have to keep it together—at least until after it was over.

She glanced over at Lil's art one last time, rubbing her lips. A mix of emotions had hijacked her since the day in the attic, and she was still navigating her way through the complicated and layered maze of shock and grief. Her gaze landed on a vase of red roses. She looked at the card, then back at the painting, doing a double take. They were the same. Removing herself from her cozy sheath. Dahlia pulled the canvas from the wall and peeked inside the frame. Sure enough, it read *six* below Lil's signature. "They're the same." Her voice lightened.

Dahlia lowered herself to the ottoman, feeling as if she'd just solved the biggest riddle of her life. Rose's birthdays! So *that* was why they were all numbered. She recalled Lil's mention in her journals to Gene that she'd started painting again. She eyed the kaleidoscope of color, feeling a little woozy. She knew she needed coffee and a carb, but she couldn't peel herself away just yet. "That's how you stayed so positive through your art. This was your life of color, the way to see past the black-and-white circumstances of your life," Dahlia mumbled to the walls.

She heard tiny footsteps and opened her eyes. "And where have you been?" she asked, feeling Harry's shiny black coat. "And you're wet. Great."

Harry barked like he was trying to tell her something, but she kept going with her visit to the past. Dahlia pulled out the rest of the objects from the time capsule, feeling a little stronger and taller than she had the day before. In a plastic bag was her mother's fragile report card from 1961. A smeared note from the music teacher saying how well she sang at the talent show and that she was a born entertainer. There was also her class picture, which featured a missing front tooth, a few spare marbles, a hair ribbon, and an actual tooth, which was a little creepy, despite Dahlia's infatuation with detective shows. Harry sniffed the pieces like a sleuth and then went to lie down. She read the card one last time.

Dear Rose,

You turned six today. I planted another rose bush this year, Rosa McComb, to honor you. You are my pride and joy. I love watching you grow and learn. Your mind is like a sponge, and you continue to amaze me every day. The things you say blow my mind and make me laugh. You are a conscientious student, love people, and, best of all, you are happy. And that's all a mother could hope for. Right now, you are into space and science. You are reading on a third-grade level; I think you get that from your dad. You recently found an old copy of The Secret Garden *in the attic, and that's all you talk about.*

Which is very apropos considering you have your own. I know every parent thinks their child is exceptional, but you truly are my Rose Bud. The sky is the limit for you. I can't wait to see what life has in store for you.

All my love,

Mom

No matter how many times she read it, she couldn't believe the irony of the secret garden and how her heart still ached for her mother and Lil. That part of being an orphan never really goes away. When good things, bad things, funny things, or just mediocre things happen, you have no one to share them with. She wiped her eyes and stared down at the card still in her palm.

Dahlia got up, feeling the wrath of the late-night shoveling in her ribs. Every muscle in the fingers, arms, and back hurt. Ten more days of this and then . . . Dahlia stared into space and exhaled. How on earth could she leave now? But could she stay? With every passing day, it became clearer that she wanted to. Not for Noah but for herself. For the first time, she was putting her wants above everyone else. And it felt pretty good.

Her eyes wandered to the curtain dividing her area from Noah's. She hadn't been able to bring herself to look since his birthday. Her mind ping-ponged with *Should I look? No, it will make me miss him even more. But I already do. It can't get any worse.* Dahlia's feet decided for her, slowly shuffling in that direction. The dusty curtain hung like it always did, separating the spaces. Bravely, she pulled it back and let out a mouse-sized sneeze.

The area was neat, considering he had been building in there for the last few months. His tools were tidy, and there was a picture of him and Gretchen thumbtacked to the wall next to the workbench. Underneath that was a torn-out magazine page. It said,

Your Only Limit Is You. It was a reminder of the kind of guy he was. He was one of the good ones. His plaid flannel hung on the hook next to his scuffed goggles. She reached for the shirt, feeling the soft cotton graze her palm. Dahlia brought it to her cheek and held it there. There was a lingering scent from his musk. She inhaled it, wanting nothing more than to feel him sneak up behind her and tell her it was all a big mistake. Only it wasn't. She'd been wrong, and he had every right to never want to speak to her again. A single tear tracked down her cheek.

"What am I doing? I'm a grown woman," she mumbled, hanging the shirt back on the hook. She had things to do and a day to get on with. Gretchen's opening being one of them. Sure, she hadn't anticipated losing an aunt and gaining a grandmother, and losing a grandmother and gaining an aunt, in a matter of twenty-four hours when she said she'd go, but a commitment was a commitment.

Dahlia meandered toward the house with Harry by her side. Her pulse slowed as she stood motionless in front of the rose garden, which now looked like an excavation site. It was yet another thing she had to fix, regardless of her fate. Out of the corner of her eye, she caught the carving tucked at the bottom of the wood rail behind the bench. "RIO," she whispered. Dahlia bent down closer with wide eyes. The last piece of the puzzle had been solved. *Rose Ingrid Obermann.* She looked up at the sky and let out a sigh of relief. "Of course."

It all made sense now. All Dahlia could do was smile. She was fresh out of tears. In her heart, she knew it was time to set the secret and Lil free. It was the only way forward.

Harry whimpered by the steps, so she continued back up to the house. The back door was open, and the smell of freshly brewed java flooded the air. The percolator was plugged in, and there was a note. Winged creatures took flight in her belly. There weren't many people who would do this. In fact, there was only one.

She opened the folder paper. It simply said,

D-

I miss you so God damn much. Please come today, we can talk.

-N

He did care. She was a swooning bubble of bliss. But there were still a lot of unknowns and bridges to cross, including telling him about the job.

* * *

Dahlia walked up onto the curb, feeling her insides toss and tumble. She took a swig of Shelter Island air, and blew out her worst fears. What would she say to him? "Noah, I was wrong," and pray for his forgiveness? The steps going up to the Hive suddenly seemed too steep. Dahlia's hand gripped the wrought iron banister, hoping it would hold her anxious body up.

Just as she hit the top stair, she glanced up and saw Gretchen through the large window, waving eagerly. Now, let's hope her brother was that happy to see her. The door was slightly ajar, but her push still felt labored. A medley of excitement and nerves ensued. A waft of sweet and savory greeted her, and suddenly, her shoulders dropped every so slightly. Who could be anxious in a place like this, yet she was. Muted jazz played in the background, bringing ease to her tight face. As she closed the door, she heard "Dahlia, you came" among the chatter. And with that, a warm embrace wrapped her like a cozy blanket. Of all the times she'd walked into a party in Greenwich, she'd never been greeted like this.

"Of course. I wouldn't miss this," Dahlia said with a smile that felt forced. There was no way to know what would happen. Sure, his note was a good sign, but there were still so many things to say and share. She glanced around the room, scanning the faces for that special one with eyes the color of oceanic bliss. It was a hearty crowd, but it appeared low-key, not like the Hamptons, thank God. She glanced at the unfamiliar but welcoming faces, and her jitters slowly melted like ice cream on a summer day.

"Gretchen, I feel like I'm in a little French café off a cobblestone street." Dahlia spotted the botanicals stacked on the wall behind the bar. "Lil's paintings." She hesitated, knowing the storm she'd just survived had left debris in its wake. Dahlia's nose tingled, and water pooled in her eyes. This time, they were happy tears. Tears that came from pride. "They look perfect."

"Oh, don't cry. She'd be happy. Wouldn't she?" Gretchen asked.

"She would be tickled pink." Dahlia blotted the corner of her eye with her finger.

"Come, I have someone I want to introduce you to. He took a liking to Lil's paintings. He owns a gallery in Southampton." Gretchen hooked her arm around hers and led the way. "He could be a good connection for you. I told him that you worked at MoMA."

"Okay, sure," Dahlia said, looking up, praying her makeup hid her swollen eyes. She gulped so hard she thought the entire room full of people could hear.

And then Noah's bright gaze met hers from across the room, and a bolt of lightning shuddered straight through her body. God, he was a sight, so much so that her cheeks instantly grew warm and most likely red. She wanted to swim in those eyes and never leave. He nodded toward the back door, and that was all Dahlia needed to end her torment. "Gretchen, I'll be there in a minute."

Gretchen looked at Noah and snickered. "Go. This guy will be here for a while. And I know that guy"—she pointed to Noah—"can't wait."

"Thanks. Be back in a few."

Even though Gretchen was five years younger than her, Dahlia knew she was wise beyond her years too. Childhood pain and trauma did that to a person, and that was part of their connection. They were warrior sisters, and maybe for that reason, Gretchen liked them together.

She rubbed the folds of her floral dress as she walked over to his beautiful, chiseled face, tucking her curl behind her ear. Why did she feel so awkward suddenly? "Hi."

"Hey," Noah said with a crooked smile, pulling his body off the wall. He was wearing a chambray button-up, and all she wanted to do was yank it closer. "Can we talk outside?"

"Sure." Dahlia could feel her veins pulse in her throat. She followed him down the back door steps to the landing overlooking the vegetable and herb gardens. The air was stagnant, with a hint of warm dill and basil that clung to the air. Her chest thumped wildly, and her eyes landed on his Adam's apple, bobbing most likely in anticipation of what was next.

"I'm sorry," they both said at the same time.

"Oh, gosh." Dahlia shook her head. "You have nothing to be sorry about."

"But I do."

"You don't. I assure you." Dahlia tried to find the right place to start. "I kept something from you that I shouldn't have. I was wrong, but I want to explain why I didn't tell you I have a daughter." She took a breath, and he nodded, giving her the floor to continue. "You and I and what we've shared these last few weeks have been beyond anything I could have ever planned or hoped for. I wasn't looking for anyone when I arrived at Lil's. All I wanted was to heal and find me again while I packed up the last of my family's memories."

He stepped closer; she could feel the heat emanating from his body. All she wanted to do was get lost in his arms, his eyes, and his presence, but she needed him to understand.

She collected herself and resumed. "But then I saw you in the barn, and everything I thought I wanted vanished into thin air."

"I assumed you hated me that day." He laughed, raising one brow.

"No, that was me flirting. And doing a very bad job at it." She grimaced playfully. "I wanted you so bad I could taste it. In the days that followed, I've never felt so seen, protected, and helped in all my life. I felt like I had a do-over of my twenties." She gazed at him with sincerity. "And I didn't want to let that feeling go."

"I wouldn't have been upset if you told me, D." He reached for her hand. "I was just angry you didn't trust me enough to tell me."

"I should have." She wanted to say more, but let him talk.

"I was so damaged when we met. I could never really trust anyone after the childhood I had, and then Josie used it all as a weapon. But you made it easy. I felt safe with you too. It blindsided me, and I was triggered. It brought me back to the lies my mother, the addict, told us daily. And the messed-up part is she believed them, every single one."

"Noah, I'm so sorry. My heart breaks that I brought you back to that place. And I do trust you." She laced her fingers with his, telling him in her touch what she felt. "Me omitting this vital detail was about me leaning into a time in my life I skipped altogether." She exhaled. "I found out I was pregnant with Daisy at eighteen, right before college. I'd accepted a full ride to RISD, and I was eager to start a new chapter in Rhode Island. When I found out, it was like I was pushed off a cliff and left to fly without wings."

Dahlia's eyes burned, and her throat closed. Talking about it brought her right back to the day. "I grieved; there was so much shame and guilt. I told Spence right away, and he didn't want a baby. So I had her on my own."

"That son of a bitch," Noah said with a pinched face.

"No, I wouldn't trade that time with her for anything. He came back later when she was five and offered us a chance to be a family. It didn't feel right, even then, but I was so tired. Tired of working two jobs making ends meet, going to school at night, and feeling the weight of the world solely on my shoulders." She shrugged. "I was just a kid, and in the blink of an eye, I was a mom, responsible for another tiny human. There were no more teenage years, college days, travel with friends abroad, or drunken fun twenties. I let it all go. And I don't regret it for a second."

"Baby, you don't have to explain." He slid his hand around her neck and under her hair and kissed her like the world was ending and starting at the same time. It was like a promise of what was to come. He cupped her face with his strong, capable hands. "You're an amazing person. What you gave up to be a mom . . . your daughter is very lucky to have you."

"Thank you." She wrapped her hand around his, still tucked in hair. She knew he saw motherhood through a unique lens. One that made him more than qualified to give her such a compliment.

"I mean it, D. Everyone should be that lucky," he said adamantly.

"Noah." She rested her head on his. "I never meant to hurt you. I just wanted to be me for a change. You made me forget all the heaviness. And selfishly, I liked it. And a small part of me thought if I told you about her, you'd see me differently," she said, closing her eyes.

"God, never, ever." He caressed her cheek with his thumb. It was tender but also laced with yearning. "Look at me. I want you to hear and see me say this. If anything, I care *more* about you because of this. Whatever you went through, it led you here to me. Don't you see?" he asked, his eyes locked with hers in a plea that said more without words.

"I do," Dahlia said, feeling like all the bumps and detours brought her here to him. She glanced toward the garden in thought and sank her teeth into her bottom lip. "Noah, I'm falling hard and fast for you. It scares me."

"Me too, D." He pressed his mouth to hers again, and their tongues collided. This time deeper, with a longing she'd thirsted for over the last few days. Her body flooded with warmth. Every morsel of skin craved him, and her core pulsed with need.

"God, I want you so bad." He kissed every inch of her face. "I've never wanted to skip out on a party more in my life."

"Me . . . too," she said breathlessly while imagining Gretchen's wrath, knowing they couldn't.

"I missed you like crazy. And I should have come home sooner," he said, slipping his hand around her waist. "I almost woke you up this morning on my way through the barn, but you looked so peaceful."

"Home. I like the sound of that." She smiled.

"Listen, I wasn't there for you, and I am sorry." He looked away. "I talked to Penny yesterday, and then Kara reached out to me on Instagram last night."

Ride or die, no matter what. Kara always had her back. "She did?" Dahlia couldn't wait to talk to her and tell her everything. And to apologize.

"She knocked some sense into me. Told me how lucky I was to have you. And I am a total arse."

"No, you're not." She laughed. "But maybe it was good that I went through the last few days alone, to break through the noise of everything. It was a lot."

Noah gave a light head shake. "I don't know much, just that what you found was shocking and that you needed me."

Thank God for these girls. Between Kara, Gretchen, and now even Penny, she was starting to feel like she belonged to a tribe. It was something she envied other girls for but never thought she'd have.

"You don't know the half of it. Are you ready for this?" Dahlia asked quietly as a server walked past.

"Let's go over here." He pulled her into the section of woods in the back, as if what she was about to share was top secret. In a way, it was.

"I can't believe I'm actually going to say this out loud. Aside from Harry, you're the only person I've told."

"Okay," he leaned closer. She could smell his musk, with hints of the sea and sandalwood, and her knees weakened. If she was going to make it through this tell-all, she had to lean against the tree.

She inhaled a whiff of him and blurted. "My grandmother didn't have an affair. It was Lil. She had the baby with a man named Gene."

Noah yanked back in shock. "So wait, what are you saying exactly?"

"That Lil was my grandmother." Dahlia felt the tide rise in her eyes. "I found the key. The safe-deposit box held a letter to me and her journals. Noah, she was sixteen when she got pregnant, and madly in love. Her father was a monster. She didn't have a choice but to let my gran and pop raise my mother. Otherwise, she would have lost her to the system forever."

"That's incredible." He took a long pause, most likely because it hit close to home. "Sounds like your stories were similar. You and Lil."

"You have no idea. Lil was the only one who stepped up to help me in the beginning. I was so alone when I found out I was pregnant, and she gave me hope." She smiled through the tears that threatened to spill.

"Now you know why."

Dahlia nodded. "I owe her so much."

"So who's Gene? Penny said she gave you a solid lead but didn't say who it was."

"If there were a nearby stump, I'd tell you to sit down."

"Spit it out. The suspense is killing me." He laughed.

"It's Charles Halston."

Noah was speechless. He just stood there blinking. "What? The guy from *Shotgun* and all those old westerns." Noah's eyes widened, and he cocked his head like something had just occurred to him. "Yeah, now that I think of it, he was in the movie *The Best Man*."

"And friends with Ol' Blue Eyes," Dahlia said eagerly. There was a substantial age difference. She had to remember to ask Gene about it at another time, and how it came to be.

"Is that right?" Noah's mouth still hung open.

"Want to know the best part? He's a kind and sweet man, and boy, did he love Lil something fierce."

"You spoke? Damn, you've been busy, girl." His voice elevated.

Dahlia gave a light chuckle. "You know it all feels very serendipitous, like a plan from above."

"It does." He gently tugged her from the tree and into his strong hold. "Thank you, Lil."

Dahlia was settling into her new set of circumstances. And with that, she went on to tell him about the job in Charleston and how she had some decisions to make. He took it well and said he had faith it would all work out. They kissed for what seemed like days under the sycamore until they heard Gretchen calling them.

After Dahlia spoke with Tomas, the gallery owner, they snuck out. They drove back to Meadow Lane in Noah's truck, enamored with one another the entire way. They camped on Lil's sleeping porch and made love like it was their very first time. Dahlia didn't know if this was love, but she knew this was the closest she'd ever come. But she was still on a tightrope, walking the line between having the strength to move on and finding the courage to stay. Regardless, it was progress.

CHAPTER TWENTY-THREE

July 24

Dahlia's cheeks hurt from smiling. The morning sun made everything seem brighter. The cicadas chirped outside the open window, and the candy-colored phlox blooms brought a sweet smell that eased through the kitchen window. Her laptop was open to a crisp new email addressed to the Whitmore Gallery. All it said so far was *Dear Christine*, with *Date Extension* in the subject line. Dahlia was unsure what she wanted to do about this job, but asking for a delay was the first step. She needed more time to figure out if this thing between her and Noah was the real deal. But she also needed more time to figure out what she wanted.

Dahlia heard the staircase creak, along with whistling. She closed her computer, not to hide the email but to put it out of her mind for a bit longer, hoping the answer would come to her by tomorrow. There were more pressing matters to tend to, like kissing Noah for the gazillionth time. And she wanted to see what his plans were after their summer romance and if the *Hamptons House* franchise was something he still needed to be a part of.

He walked into the kitchen bare-chested, with damp hair. His muscles were thick and corded, and his tats were on display. He looked like a bad boy. And he was all hers. The fantastic fact wasn't lost on her, and neither was his forgiveness. Her insides pulsated, and she wondered if that deep, rooted sensation would ever fade. She hoped it never would. As foreign as it was, she belonged when she was with him. Although Dahlia didn't know where he'd been the past few days, it no longer mattered. What mattered was they'd weathered a storm and found a compass that led them back home.

"Hi," he said, wrapping her in a ginormous hulky embrace. "How's my favorite girl?"

"Favorite, huh? I like the sound of that." It was certainly a departure from last night's "good girl." But she'd take any pet name he'd give her. Dahlia leaned her head against his. There was a peace about him, one she hadn't noticed before. It was like he finally knew how he felt and what he wanted. Only it was still a secret to her, and she didn't want to ask. Not yet, anyway. Knowing would make it harder to make an unbiased decision about Charleston.

He kissed her forehead. "Please, let's never fight like that again."

"Never," she said softly. "Although the makeup sex may have been worth the torturous three days." Dahlia wrinkled her nose.

"Last night was . . ." He made a mind-blown gesture with his hands.

Dahlia smiled coyishly, feeling her face flush.

He held her chin between her fingers. She watched as his brows furrowed, like he wanted to get something off his chest. "You make me happy. You make me want to be the best version of myself."

"I do?" she asked, feeling the weight of that statement in the best possible way.

"I'm just Noah with you. And that seems to be enough for you. I've never had that with anyone I've dated."

"You are more than enough," Dahlia said, loosely wrapping her arms around his shoulders.

He kissed her with a soft sincerity that held depth and certainty, and when he released his lips from hers, she met his glance and point-blank asked him, "What will you do after the summer?"

"I don't know. Uncle Bruce and Garrett will be back by then." He looked off toward their house. "I do know I want to be with you, though."

"And I do you."

"I have the city apartment that I share with another guy, but I haven't been there in months. And he's been asking if I'm ever coming back."

Dahlia could feel her armpits sweating from dancing around the real issue, which was the show. She wanted her anonymity. "Will you go back to the show next summer?"

Noah stared blankly into the hallway. "My agent has been hounding me, but I haven't signed the contract yet. They assured me Josie wouldn't be returning."

The air in her lungs felt suspended in time while she waited for him to answer the question.

"Honestly, I don't care what road I'm on as long as I'm with you," he said, trying to reassure her without answering the question.

Dahlia sighed, trying her best to hide her disappointment. He didn't owe her anything. She needed to make this decision on her own. It was the only way. She nuzzled herself into his burly chest. His body felt warm, and the ground beneath her feet felt solid and firm. She could have spent hours or even days there in his arms. She looked up at him, and in one look, he hijacked her soul. The answers would come for both of them, she was sure of it.

"Oh, did you talk to Kara yet?"

"Yes, she couldn't believe it. This secret had more twists than a country road." As for what Dahlia said about Aunt Cathy, all Kara said was, "I'm sorry she wasn't there for you." Dahlia knew what she meant, and there was no need to talk about it again.

"So, what else is on the agenda for today?" He kissed her nose. She didn't want to move, let alone think.

"Oh, geez. I still have to call Gene back and Daisy." It felt good to say that out loud and not hide her like she was a dirty secret. They were making progress. "It's been a few days, and I have so much to tell them." She shook her head. "I don't even know where to start."

"Just be yourself, and the rest will follow."

"My mother used to say that." These coincidences were starting to add up. The messages from the universe were received loud and clear.

"Smart woman, your mom."

"Yes, she was." Dahlia's eyes felt bright and full of hope. She wondered at that moment if Rose would approve or what advice she would have. *Follow your heart, my sweet Dahlia*, echoed in her head.

"I have a piece I'm working on for a client. Then we can hit a vineyard later," he said, giving her one last smooch.

"Perfect."

This all seemed like one giant jump across a vast canyon, but was she ready to do it without a net? What she learned from Lil and Gene was that there was no certainty in love, no matter how strongly a person's feelings were, and that was the scariest part of the equation.

* * *

Dahlia sat on the bedroom floor, surrounded by Lil's love story, both with Gene and her mother, Rose. Black-and-white marbled notebooks, yellowed letters, time-worn paintings, and relics from another time lay in a U-shape around her bare legs. The jute rug was starting to make dents in her butt, but there was one more phone call to make. The call to Daisy had gone as well as could be expected, and Noah barely came up. Daisy was struggling with their new set of circumstances and the idea that Pop was never really biologically theirs. She, too, felt tricked and blindsided, but Dahlia reassured her that DNA was no match for love or memories, as Noah said.

It would all take time, and right now, Dahlia's hourglass of sand was starting to run thin. She had some big, life-altering choices to make, and she just prayed she could make them with a clear head.

Harry strolled in and lay beside her, resting his head on her thigh. Dahlia blew out a cleansing breath, running her hand through his soft black fur. She picked up her cell and scanned for Gene's last call. There was a golf ball–sized lump in her throat that she couldn't swallow, no matter how hard she tried. All she had to do was tell him what Lil wanted him to know. It didn't mean that anything had to change.

Her pulse grew faster as she scrolled through her calls. Without hesitation, she pressed the Burbank, California, number.

"Hello?" the man answered right away.

"Ah." Dahlia didn't know what to call him.

"Is this Dahlia?"

"Yes, sorry, it's me. I wasn't sure what to call you." She shook her head.

"How about Gene, or G for short."

G for grandfather, she thought. Maybe she did want this connection after all. "That works."

"How have you been? Has the news settled in?" his frail but eager voice asked.

"I guess you could say I'm slowly coming to terms with my new reality. It's all been quite shocking to unearth. But I found something important after our call. Lil's safe deposit key, in a random coffee can."

"Well, I'll be damned."

"It was like finding a teardrop in the ocean. I didn't think I'd ever find it until you mentioned your coffee dates. See, she was collecting these coffee cans for as long as I could remember, but I didn't know why. She didn't drink coffee, you know," she said with an unfocused gaze.

"I'm glad I could help you solve the puzzle."

"You unlocked everything, literally." Dahlia took a breath, feeling a smile curl her lips. "Lil kept a journal. It was filled with messages to you. There were pages from when you were together to when she was pregnant with my mother, Rose. Your daughter. Lil gave her the middle name Ingrid, just like you named your other daughter."

She could hear his small gasp.

"There's so much you need to read for yourself. There was a letter in the box, along with my mother's birth certificate, naming you as the father."

"Dahlia, I don't need a paper to confirm what I know in my heart."

"Well, it's here if you need it. I don't want anyone thinking I'm a swindler."

"Never, darling."

"Gene, I need to tell you something before I go any further. I don't want to give you false hope."

"Go on."

"My mother, Rose, your daughter, died twenty-five years ago."

There was a long pause. "I suspected as much when you didn't mention her. And the fact that you reached out instead of her."

Dahlia wanted to tell him everything: how smart, kind, and funny she was and how at peace she was before she died, but instead, she told him about his great-granddaughter. She wasn't sure how Daisy would react if they ever met, but he deserved to know.

"Would you like me to read the letter to you?"

"Very much," he said softly.

Dahlia reached for the letter tucked under Harry's foot and read Lil's proof of love.

Dear Dahlia,

Enclosed are my journals. They hold the key to a secret that has been buried for far too long. I didn't have the guts to share it while I was alive, and I am deeply sorry for that.

I met an amazing man in 1955. He was what Daisy would call my twin flame. It was the summer my father took a job at CBS Studios in California. I was just sixteen but wise beyond my years. He was nineteen, and oh, was he a looker. He swept me off my feet, and we fell madly in love within weeks. It was the kind of love that moved mountains and parted the seas. It was the stuff movies were made of and books written about. At the time, he was just an errand boy, but I knew he would make it big in film someday. He had so much drive and determination.

Dahlia read on about Lil's monstrous father, what he'd threatened to do to Gene if she didn't obey his wishes, and how there was no choice but to have her sister raise Rose. There was no doubt in her mind that he was the one who hid those letters.

Reading Lil's words to Gene stirred an emotional tsunami inside her. Her shaky voice barely made it to the end. "Are you still there?" Dahlia asked, feeling tears slip from her eyes at a quiet pace.

"Yes. Please continue," he mumbled.

> *This must be shocking, but I need you to know where you came from. Your biological grandfather's name is Gene Obermann, but he changed his name to Charles Halston when he hit it big in the movies. I am hoping he is still alive. Please get in touch with him, tell him what happened, and that I died loving him. It would be my last wish fulfilled.*

There was silence on the other end. She was praying his heart didn't give out.

"Gene, she died loving you. Every day, it was you, her, and my mother Rose. You can read about it in her journals too, if you'd like." She peeled herself from the floor, returning the blood flow to her legs.

His voice faded as he asked, "I wonder why she didn't reach out to me ever?"

"Maybe she was scared that you moved on. I'm sure she saw your big life back then. Knowing Lil, she probably didn't think she'd fit into it. You know, square peg, round hole." She knew that feeling all too well. But it was more than that. As a mother herself, she knew Lil's reason was Rose. Just like she'd stayed in a hollow place for too long for Daisy but kept that part to herself. "And don't forget she never got your letters, so she didn't know what you felt after she left that summer."

"I never stopped loving her. We would have always fit together no matter the time or space."

All she heard was quiet sobbing on the other end, which made her weep with him. "Oh, Gene, what are we going to do without her?" Dahlia asked, picking up a small, framed picture of the two of them on her dresser. It was from Dahlia's sixteenth birthday when Lil made a big fuss with balloons and homemade pastries.

"I don't know." He blew his nose, and she imagined him using a crisp white hanky from his pocket. "We're going to be in each other's lives. That's for certain," he said firmly. "I want to meet my granddaughters."

"You do?" Her fingers touched her lips. In the back of her mind, she'd hoped out of protection for her own heart that he wouldn't want to meet. Loving someone, anyone, meant eventually losing them.

"Either you could come here, or if you have a service for Lil, I'd love to come there."

"Oh, sure, yeah." Service for Lil. Dahlia hadn't even thought about it. They'd had something small in Connecticut as per her wishes, but now that didn't nearly seem enough to honor such a remarkable person.

"Listen, I have an appointment that I've got to get to. Can we chat tomorrow? I want to know more about you," he said.

"Of course. Tomorrow." She nodded.

"Dahlia, thank you."

"Of course, Gene," she said tenderly as her mind whirled with ideas. She hung up and rested the phone on the dresser. A smile tugged at her mouth. That was it. They would have a celebration of life party to honor her. But if she was going to do this, she was going to have to brighten up the place. It needed to match her colorful barn and life. And with that, she grabbed the keys from the dresser and headed to the hardware store.

* * *

Dahlia dipped her roller into Tranquility and rolled the pale blue onto the living room walls. With each motion, the cream all but disappeared. It was like a fresh start. Dahlia didn't care if it was good for resale. All she cared about was honoring Lil the best way she knew how: by highlighting her optimism and her ability to rise from the ashes and create something beautiful from the pain. Dahlia knew from her past that painting was the best way to do that. Dahlia had painted every room in her old house, even though they'd had a contractor.

Looking at the contrast with the red buffalo-checked chairs, she knew this color would be the perfect backdrop for Lil's paintings. Feeling a vibration in her pocket, she rested the roller on the tray and answered.

"Hey," she said.

"Where are you?" Noah asked.

"At home, painting. Why?"

"Wait, didn't you just repaint everything cream for resale?"

"Well, I changed my mind. I decided something. I'm going to have a celebration of life for Lil here, in the house, and I want the house to reflect her love of color. Right now, it doesn't."

"Your house, your rules," he said, grinning.

"Smart man." She laughed, lifting her chin in the air.

"Want to meet me at the vineyard a little early?" His voice sounded perky.

Dahlia looked down at her paint-splattered shorts and legs. "How early?"

"Now early? The house crew is at Croteaux. Come on, it will be fun to catch up."

"Is Josie there?" Dahlia stared at the crack in the floor.

"She's away at a wedding this weekend. It might be nice for you to get to know them without her."

"Are they filming?" This show and these friends were still important to him. And he wanted her to meet them. She should go.

"Yeah, I think they are," he said.

Her neck muscles tightened, and she hesitated. "Noah, I'm sorry, but I think I'll sit this one out." There was no way she was walking into that lion's den as the cameras rolled. "But you go." Could this really work? They were obviously in two different seasons of their lives.

"Are you sure?"

"Yes, I've got plenty to do here." She blew the hair out of her eyes. "Have fun." No matter what season Noah was in, she wanted him to embrace it. She knew what it felt like to miss out and didn't want that for him. And whatever was meant to be would be. Dahlia was starting to grasp the idea of faith. But how much she'd lean into it was anyone's guess.

"Okay, I'll come by later then," Noah said.

"I'll be here."

She ended the call, realizing she'd missed a text from Tomas, the gallery owner from Archive in Southampton.

Great meeting you yesterday. Come by the gallery tomorrow at 11?

It was presumptuous that he'd assume she'd be free. She tossed the phone on the bench, uncertain if she'd go or even answer. "Looks like it's just you and me, boy, and maybe Sinatra." She couldn't forget to ask Gene about him.

Harry lifted his head off the floor for a brief moment, snorted, acknowledged the comment, and went back to sleep.

Dahlia put her humid hair up in a bun and tied the oversized off-the-shoulder T-shirt at her waist. The navy short shorts she found in a drawer were old and essentially falling apart, so paint splatters weren't a concern. She filled her water bottle and turned on the record player. This was good. Although she was alone, she didn't feel lonely. A peaceful painting night was exactly what she needed, even though she still had heaps of stuff to get through. She stretched her hands over her head, watching the bold hue erase the ordinary color of the walls. Memories of how many times she had painted Daisy's room through all her phases infiltrated her thoughts. There was lilac, bubblegum pink, sunshine yellow, and who could forget gunmetal gray. She didn't mind, though. Painting was always a way for her to center herself, think, and find answers. She swayed to the hits of the fifties and belted the lyrics into the wet paintbrush while trimming the room in blue.

There was a knock at the door, waking Harry from his slumber. He barked, which quickly turned into a whimper. It was a clear sign that the person at her front door was a friend. Dahlia set the blue brush on top of the can, turned the music down, and stepped up into the hallway. She peeked from behind the sheers and beamed. It was Noah, holding up a bottle of wine and a brown bag.

"What are you doing here?" She opened the door as giddy as a schoolgirl.

"What can I say, I'm addicted," he said, giving her a playful smooch. "I brought the vineyard to you."

She felt her heart flutter under her paint-stained hand. "You're supposed to be hanging out with your friends." Her eyes trailed an easy line up and down his body. Fitted black jeans clung to his thighs and other parts too, and a gray T-shirt hugged every curve of his corded arms.

"Do you want me to go back?" He pointed to the door with a goofy grin.

"Hell, no." Her smile reached the heavens. He had to be the most thoughtful and incredibly sexy man alive.

"I need to tell you something," he said after kissing her thoroughly.

Her stomach sank.

"I didn't sign on for another season of *Hamptons House*. You mean way too much to me, and that chapter of my life, well, it's closed. And if I'm being honest with myself, I didn't really belong there in the first place." He held her hand, which most likely meant his hands were now covered in paint too. But he didn't seem to care. He didn't pull away or say a word. "This, what we have, is real, not that. But . . ." He hesitated with a smile she couldn't quite place.

"But what, Noah?" Her heart hammered against her rib cage.

"Can you handle me just being me without the celebrity status?"

"Noah." She held his whiskered face with an unwavering glance that said everything and more. "That never meant a damn thing to me. You know that."

He claimed her mouth again, this time with a hunger like no other. It was as if her reassurance unlocked something inside him. Her legs felt boneless, and her blood hummed with need. It took all of her willpower not to yank off his shirt right there. This is what she'd been waiting for, and she wanted to lean into this moment with all she had. But she also had a job to finish, and now he was there to help her, whether he wanted to or not. But she'd make it worth his while.

When they finally broke free, he gave her a closer look. "D, you've got paint all over your clothes." Then his eyes wandered down to his hands, and they too were covered in pale blue paint.

"Oops." She shrugged with a devilish grin. "I have a proposition for you. How about you help me, so we can finish and go upstairs?"

He raised an eyebrow. "I'm listening."

"Every time I get paint on something, I have to strip."

He smiled and moved closer, reaching around her slim waist.

"But you have to do the same." She reached for a paintbrush dipped in paint and handed it to him. His warm hands left her hips, and she silently groaned from the loss.

"That's easy, you'll be naked within ten minutes. That doesn't seem like a fair trade."

"Oh yeah," she said, painting his cheek. He stared at her in shock, but then dipped his fingers inside the can with a look that both terrified and tickled something low in her belly.

"That's it," he said, chasing her into the kitchen as she squealed.

Within ten minutes, they were both naked, which led to a much-needed premature paint break. So much for willpower.

CHAPTER TWENTY-FOUR

July 25

Dahlia and Noah painted into the early morning hours and managed to finish the living room and hallway. They retired to bed just before three AM, after Dahlia brought most of Lil's paintings from the barn inside the house. When she held them against the wall, they both knew it was the right choice. The bold palette felt like opening a brand-new crayon box. Dahlia stared unapologetically, slowly releasing her breath, knowing in her gut it was time well spent.

It was now just after nine. Noah was still sleeping, but Dahlia was already up and on the back porch, slurping her coffee. There was only a week to get the house ready for Lil's party, and there was still so much to do. Her first mission of the day, though, was to finally ask for an extension from the gallery.

With palms firmly planted to her face, she sat there thoroughly proofing the revised "extension" email. Not because she was scared they would say no. Heck, that would be much easier, then the decision would be made for her. Dahlia was nervous because she always kept her promises. She wasn't the type to call in sick unless she or Daisy were. She wasn't the type to pawn off less-than-desirable duties at work or goof off while on the clock. She was steadfast and reliable. Harry rested his head on her lap, giving her that reassurance she needed. With her lips molded into a straight line, she bravely hit send.

Dahlia ran inside the house to get more coffee and realized she missed Kara's call. With her beverage and phone in hand, she grabbed a dog treat and went back down to the porch.

The air was already muggy, and the sun was strong. The smell of low tide drifted through the screens, and the seagulls' squawks offering an annoying but oddly comforting sound. Living miles from the beach in Greenwich, she relished being this close to the water. It made her feel alive and awake, something Connecticut couldn't offer her, no matter how hard she tried.

Harry snapped the treat from her hold, wetting her fingers. "Geez, you almost bit my finger off."

After wiping her Harrified hands, she dialed the phone and waited while it rang.

"Hi, hold on a second," Kara mumbled.

"Want me to call you back?" Dahlia asked.

"Nah, just getting my latte. Yes, double shot, please."

Dahlia heard an echo of a commotion in the background.

"Are you at Brew?" Dahlia asked. Brew was a favorite local spot in Greenwich. She missed how easy it was to meet up with Kara for an impromptu cup of coffee.

"Yeah, it's packed. I don't know where everyone came from," Kara shouted.

"It's summer, Kara."

"True. Okay, spill the tea. Give me an update. Is loverboy still behaving?"

"Ha, no more McHandy?"

"I feel like we've moved past that. Loverboy is more fitting, don't you think?"

"Whatever you say." Dahlia laughed. "So he came by last night and skipped a night out with his television fam."

"Aww, he chose you. How sweet. That's big."

"Yeah, I know," Dahlia said with a wide, toothy grin. "And… he's not signing on for another season."

"What? Wait, this is good news, right?"

"The best news."

"And what did you do about your job?"

Dahlia wrinkled her nose. "I asked for more time."

"How much?"

"I left it open. I told them something came up with my Aunt Lil's estate." Dahlia cleared her throat. Part of her felt deceitful, but she didn't have a choice. She was backed up into a corner with no real way out other than to twist the truth a little.

"Which isn't a lie. Plus, it gives you more time with Noah," Kara said.

"Yeah." Dahlia sat a little taller. "The real reason is I've decided to have a celebration of life for Lil."

"Oh, honey, that's a great idea."

"But it has to be this weekend," Dahlia firmly stated.

"Yikes, that's not much time."

"I know, that's why I need your help. You can come, right? Sunday?" Dahlia squinted, clutching her hands in prayer.

"Ah, let me look in my phone." It was quiet. "The boys have a doubleheader, but I can ask Tony to take care of it."

"Phew." And that's why she was her ride-or-die. She always came through. There was a release of tension in her shoulders, knowing she wouldn't have to do this alone. Asking for help suddenly didn't seem so bad. "I need you here. I can't do this without you." Dahlia knew she probably could do it without her, but she didn't want to.

"Who are you inviting?" Kara curiously asked, as if she knew Dahlia didn't know anyone.

"Well, that's the thing. I'd like her students to come, so I'll need to locate them, maybe on Facebook somehow, and then some neighbors, the garden club, and town people. All I want is to celebrate her." Dahlia's mouth curved upward. Honoring Lil would be like honoring the truth.

"That sounds like a good plan. I'm proud of you," Kara said, emphasizing each word.

"Thanks. I'm kind of proud of me too." Dahlia had an all-knowing grin, one that wasn't going to leave any time soon. "Listen, I've got to run. I have a meeting with that guy, Tomas, from Elevate in Southampton."

"Fancy, why?" Kara asked.

"It's just a backup in case the Whitmore Gallery says no to the extension, which they might," Dahlia said, taking the last sip of her coffee.

"Okay, toodle-oo. Call me later."

* * *

Betty's muffler was growing louder by the day—not an ideal first impression for this well-known, swanky Hamptons town. She turned off the car and flipped down the dusty visor, then reapplied her lip gloss and calmed her flyaways in the mirror. She blew out a long breath, wondering why she was even there. It was apparent the Hamptons hated her, and if she was being honest with herself, she wasn't a big fan either. But that didn't matter as much as having choices and a job did.

There was a message from Kara. *Check your Gram.*

Why? Dahlia typed.

Look, she replied.

Dahlia opened the app. Her notifications exploded at the top in red, and all she saw was *12K followers* next to her picture. Dahlia gasped; her eyes felt like they were going to pop out of the sockets. She wasn't one to value stats, but this was unexpected.

When she opened the notifications, she saw a bunch of tagged images of her and Noah, way too many to count. Her jaw clenched as she scrolled through private photos that they had no right to use. There were images from that night in the Hamptons, not too far from where she was parked. They were holding hands, kissing in the corner, dancing with Penny, then ones from the Gretchen's restaurant opening, and even one from the day at the Brewery.

Ugh, I don't want followers like that, Dahlia typed.

The three dots appeared. *Regardless, they're followers. And if you ever have a business someday, this is good.*

She was probably right, but Dahlia wasn't about to read the comments. That would blow her day up into a million pieces. When things were finally looking up, she didn't need that. Some small part of her hoped all of this fanfare would ease now that Noah was officially no longer part of the show.

If you say so, Dahlia replied.

Dahlia's pulse raced as she reached for her purse. The new Instagram intel didn't help her nerves, which had suddenly gone haywire. Why exactly was she so anxious? She was a curator in the city and ran some of the rarest exhibits, for goodness sake. As much as she could reason her qualifications, this would be a completely different position, if it were offered, than the one she'd endured for the past few years. Once she was out of the car and on her feet, she pressed the wrinkles from her skirt and walked toward town. As she turned the corner, she spotted the sleek signage from across the road: ELEVATE in big block letters. Unease tensed her shoulders, but she held her chin high and kept walking.

Dahlia weaved through the Monday Main Street lunch crowd, catching a glimpse of herself in the glass reflection. Her head jerked in surprise, followed by a smile at how professional and cool she looked in Lil's linen blazer, floral pleated skirt, tank top, and heels. It was a *Gossip Girl* vibe, one she hadn't quite settled into. She opened the stainless-steel door to the gallery and walked in. A low-volume instrumental faded into the background, and she was met with Tomas's firm finger in the air, which right away seemed awfully rude. There was a sinking feeling in her abdomen, telling her ever so subtly that this was a bad idea. It was the same patronizing feeling she got with Spence, like she wasn't as important as he was. She walked around the cold space, waiting for him to finish his call. The art was avant-garde, mainly abstract and mixed media, with a Warhol flavor.

"Sorry about that." Tomas walked over in a pale pink collared shirt and fitted white pants. His wavy hair was neatly slicked back. "Can I get you water, a glass of wine?"

"No, I'm good, thank you." She just wanted to get this over with so she could retreat back to Lil's.

"Well, thanks for making the trip over to the South Fork," he said curtly.

Dahlia nodded and smiled. "Of course."

"Well, tell me. What do you think of the place?" He pivoted toward the art.

"It's beautifully curated." She wanted to say that it lacked warmth and intimacy but didn't.

"Walk with me. What do you think about, say, this one?" He pointed to the large-scale, unlabeled square canvas with bold, shaded circles.

It looked like a game of Twister. "It reminds me of summer: ice cream, sunsets, the ocean, the color of petals in a garden when the sun pierces through them," she said with an easy breath.

"How would you sell it?" He raised an eyebrow.

Dahlia smiled; this was her jam, after all. Suddenly, she wasn't nervous. She was excited.

"I would say it encapsulates summer and marks the best memories of two months spent in paradise. I would ask them what they see. I would appeal to their sentimental nature and make a connection. Art should feel personal and tickle your insides when it catches your eye from across the room."

"And what about this one?" he asked, pointing to a Picasso-inspired oil painting with two forms interlaced and a tear coming from the male's eye.

She tilted her head. "I see vulnerability, I see pain and healing. I see belonging and loss. I see the life cycle of a relationship." It was poignant and beautiful, laced with contradictions. She saw the relationships of everyone she loved in that painting. Yes, they were all different, but love anchored and tethered each one.

"Why do you think he's crying?"

"Because he feels seen." She smiled.

"Not because he's heartbroken?" he firmly asked.

"We see what we want to see, I suppose. The way her arm is laced inside his, I see kinship."

"Interesting." He folded his arms.

"Who are your artists typically?" Dahlia asked, needing to be sure her instincts were right.

"Well-known artists that have shown in some of the best Soho and Chelsea galleries, mostly," he said.

"Do you ever give a newcomer a break?" she asked.

"Not typically."

"That's a shame." She flinched, shocked that she'd said that aloud.

"Well, they don't draw a crowd the way the more established artists do. And crowd means revenue."

Dahlia's eyes darted. In other words, Lil would never have had a chance to be shown here. Did she want to work at a place like this, a place that valued money over authenticity? The answer was that it was a job, one that could enable her to stay at Lil's.

"Listen, I'll get right to it." He cleared his throat. "I'm looking for a gallery manager. It would be part-time at this gallery in the summers and winters in Palm Beach and/or the Aspen Gallery. Wherever you are needed most."

"Oh." Her arms went still. That was quick.

"This is what I'll pay you." Tomas grabbed a yellow sticky note from behind the desk and scribbled, then folded it before she could see what he'd written.

Without looking into my references? She wanted to ask but didn't. It was better to act unaffected.

He gave her the folded-up paper. "Think about it. I have another appointment to get to." He looked at his Rolex. "But please stay and look around. My assistant is here if you have any questions about the artists. I think you'll find them . . ."

Sterile. Lacking emotionality, she thought.

"Awakening."

Dahlia nodded. "Well, thank you." She held up the folded paper.

"I'll be in touch," he said, strutting out the front door and into the thick crowd of patrons.

Dahlia stuck the paper in her purse. She had heard and seen enough.

Making sure the pink shirt was nowhere in sight, she walked to her car. As soon as she got in her hatchback, she opened the small piece of paper. She slapped her hand over her mouth and gasped. "Holy shit." It was double her salary at MoMA and then some.

But would it make her happy?

CHAPTER TWENTY-FIVE

July 28

In only a few short days, a solid plan for the gathering was in place. It was a miracle, but Dahlia couldn't take all the credit. It was turning out to be a joint effort, one Lil would appreciate. Dahlia created a colorful botanical graphic invitation with lilies, dahlias, daisies, and roses, which only seemed appropriate. It was decided that Gretchen would provide the food, and Noah would pick it up early that morning. An invite was also extended to Penny since she was instrumental in the timely unveiling. If it hadn't been for her, she would never have had the conversation with Gene and known about their dates at the diner, which led her to find the coffee can and the key.

Daisy was stuck in France, but Kara and Noah would be there to support Dahlia through the bittersweet day, and that was enough. They'd become the dream team. If they couldn't pull this off, then no one could.

She leaned her body against her hot car as the sun faded behind the brick building across from the grocery store. When Noah pulled up to the curb, Dahlia climbed over the flimsy, rotting fence and jumped into his arms. Her hair flung forward as she wrapped her entire body around his. Her grip was tight and unwavering, hearing the cars whizz by on Main Street. His wide hands supported her ass as her legs anchored to his waist.

"What's this for?" he asked, meeting her eyes.

"For being you. And for finding me." She pressed her mouth to his. His whiskered lips tickled her skin, but she didn't care. She wanted more. More of his sweet and savory taste, more of his silky lips, and more of his hold that made her feel like she'd never feel alone again. "What took you so long? I was worried," Dahlia asked, locked in his gaze that felt brighter than the Caribbean sea today, if that was possible.

With the evening glow highlighting his face, she stilled. The realization that she couldn't imagine her life without him hit her like multiple arrows to the heart. She climbed down from his frame, holding his feverish stare, and smiled. Her legs were weak, but her heart was wide open.

"There's no need to worry about me." He gently cupped her face. She could smell the furniture oil still on his hands. It was an aphrodisiac. "I was just taking care of a few things."

"That sounds mysterious. Should I be concerned?"

"Nah." He shook his head, reaching for her hand. "Liquor store or grocery store first? We're right in the middle."

She tugged his crisp cotton shirt toward the sliding doors of the grocery store, making her decision clear. A wave of cold hit her chest upon entering. It was refreshing, but she could feel her nipples harden. He looked down and then back up like he wanted to devour her right then and there. He whispered in her ear, "I can't wait to get you home."

His velvety promise tickled her skin. "I bet you can't." She slid her hand into his back pocket and squeezed. If she could snap her fingers and instantly return to the house with him, she would, but she was on a mission. And that mission was to put a copy of the invitation on the famed grocery store wall so that anyone who knew Lil could come.

"Here, this way." She pointed to the front. They passed the cashiers with only a few long stares and stood in front of it.

"You sure you want to do this? Some crazies might come," he asked.

She rubbed her lips in thought and stared inward for a few beats. "Yes, this was Lil's wall, and it deserves to be up here. It's what she'd want," she finally said confidently. "The older people in town don't have social media, so if I don't, they won't know."

Feeling her posture straighten, she pulled the pretty floral cardstock from her bag and thumbtacked it to the holey corked wall in between the hutch for sale and free kittens.

Dahlia couldn't help but feel grounded despite the Whitmore Gallery only giving her another week, and even though she still hadn't gotten back to Tomas with an answer. His offer was a good one, but she was uncertain about all the travel required, and she was hesitant about working for a gallery that didn't give up-and-comers a chance. She had choices, which was a juxtaposition to her life just a year ago. She just had to make the right one, and it was anyone's guess what that would be.

The gravel crunched beneath his large tires as they pulled up to the house. The sun had all but disappeared, and the crickets were already in their nighttime rhythm. The honeyed smell of night-blooming jasmine floated through the open windows of the truck. It was something she recently found growing wild near the base of Lil's cherry blossom. It was apropos, as if the universe had known and brought her mom and Lil together, even after death.

Noah parked the truck under it, leaned over with a devilish look in his eyes, and whispered, "You're all mine now."

"Only if you can catch me," she laughed, opening the door. She leaped from his truck to her feet. He strolled around the front, and she slipped around the back. She bolted left, and he bolted right.

Noah grabbed her waist and hoisted her into the air. "I got you, gorgeous."

Dahlia couldn't stop laughing; her belly ached. She considered relinquishing herself to his seductive ways right then and there in his flatbed, but instead, she slipped under his arm once her feet hit the ground again. "Not quite."

She sprinted to the front door, kicking off her shoes. That's when he hooked her from behind and held her. Noah pressed his body into hers and grazed her ear with his scruffy lips. "You're mine," he growled.

Those two simple words made her heart race and heat bloom between her legs. She lost any will she had in their cat-and-mouse game. Spellbound, Dahlia turned around and held his sweaty cheek with her palm. His hair was messy, his mustache groomed, and his eyes wide and eager. "I surrender."

"That's a good girl." Noah gently pushed her limp body against the porch pillar. He still smelled of sawdust and oil. Of all his scents, that was the most weakening. She could feel his breath; they were that close. Their eyes locked in a lustful dance. Her neck pulsed, and his Adam's apple bobbed, the clarity sounding like a stethoscope. He reached up her skirt, slid down her panties, and slipped one thick finger inside her.

"Noah." She let out a breathy moan. She didn't want him ever to stop touching her. She didn't want the cadence between them ever to end. As much as she wanted to feel him inside her, she wanted to savor every last morsel of this sensual feast where her body was the meal. There wasn't a moment in her thirty-eight years of life that could compare or compete with this raw and honest moment. But she still hadn't pleased *him*, and she desperately wanted to show him what her mouth could do.

"I want to see you," Noah whispered.

She looked around; there was no one in sight. Plus, they were on a private road at the end of the street. But it was still risky, considering the photos she was tagged in on Instagram. What if someone was hiding in the bushes and this private moment was shared for everyone to see? With the pulse between her legs growing more needy by the second, she threw caution to the wind. The light tap of her bra hitting the porch step brought a devilish grin to his perfectly chiseled face. She stood there in just a flouncy summer skirt. He studied her naked body as dusk faded into night.

Noah cupped her breasts with his coarse woodworking hands, then rolled her nipples between his fingers. She leaned into his touch, letting out a hungry exhale. He swallowed her moans as their tongues collided as if they were two atoms finally becoming one.

A shiver of pleasure rippled through her when his mouth found the tiny, swollen bud. He nipped, sucked, and licked until her chest felt like it would explode. She could do this forever, but what's fair is fair. "My turn," she said.

He ripped off his T-shirt and threw it onto the blue hydrangeas. She arched her brow and wondered if they were Gram-worthy now. His strong, capable body led her onto the porch. There, he removed his shoes with an intensity in his eyes that felt like laser beams straight to the soul. He pushed the hair from her cheek, igniting something powerful between them.

The moonlight illuminated his muscles, and she ogled every curve. She still couldn't understand why he chose her. Dahlia felt like the luckiest girl alive. There was a never-ending tingle low in her belly and a compulsive need to be his. Closing the space between them, she ran her hands down his washboard abs, feeling every divot beneath her palms.

Noah brought her hand to his chest. It felt like a plea. "I want it to always feel like this."

"Like what?" Her gaze was unyielding.

"Like if I took my last breath tomorrow, this is what I'd remember. A cosmic collision of madness, desire, and lust and . . ." He stopped himself, leaving Dahlia to fill in the blanks in her head. Joy, happiness, or maybe love?

Noah was opening Dahlia's eyes to a whole other world. One where she was the leading lady in her own story and could own her sexuality. But it was also so much more than sex, and Dahlia no longer wanted to be twentysomething again. She wanted to be the age she was because it meant freedom. And she wanted to own it with every fiber of her being. She was all in for a nighttime romp on the porch and whatever it was that tethered them by an invisible but strong string.

Dahlia's fingers slipped inside his pants, feeling his hard length partially fill her small palm. It was thick, veiny, and apparently ready. "I want to taste you," she whispered in his ear as she squeezed.

"D." He shuddered against her, then quickly released the bulge that pressed against his zipper. His shorts dropped to the floor, and to her surprise, he was commando. She raised her eyebrow, then dropped to her knees.

"Wait," he said, pushing his shorts under her knees. "I don't want you to get splinters."

If he didn't deserve this before, he certainly did now. She should have been nervous; this wasn't something she typically did. But anticipation and desire overthrew every other feeling. There it was, standing at attention right before her eyes.

"You don't have to," he said.

No response was needed. She wanted this; there was no stopping her. She opened her mouth and ran her hot tongue against his silky skin. He tasted like soap, leather, and a touch of salt. She hollowed her cheeks, determined to make Noah see stars.

"Oh, baby," he grunted, gripping her hair. "Your mouth . . . it's fucking amazing."

She sucked and licked, running her hand up and down his thick shaft in tandem until she felt his legs quiver. A cool breeze from the bay blew, making her tight, sensitive nipples ache, and the bundle of nerves between her legs throb recklessly. Once he hit the back of her throat, an ungodly sound spilled from his lips, filling the twilight air with moans of his pleasure.

"Baby, I'm going to . . ."

And with that, she swallowed his release. It was briny, sweet, and a little bitter. It was also his. This was her first time swallowing, and she knew it wouldn't be her last. She may have found her new favorite pastime. Not only was he addicted, but she was too. Dahlia 2.0 was here to stay.

"Let's go inside." He pulled her from the hard surface and to her feet.

Her hands shook with anticipation as she flung open the front door, meeting Harry in the hallway. "Hi, boy," she said as he eagerly greeted them, wagging his tail.

Noah gave him a long scratch before he retired to the kitchen. "Now, where were we?" He pinned her against the wall, and as inconceivable as it was, he was still hard. The benefits of dating a younger guy. His velvety lips roamed her skin, trailing a line from her breasts to the crook of her neck. "I want you," he whispered.

"Me too Noah. More than anything."

He led her into the living room, where she shed her last piece of clothing. He gently lowered her onto the sofa and just stared in awe. "God, you're beautiful."

Dahlia's smile widened as she tried to cover her face.

"Don't do that. Look at me. I want you to see me."

She looked up, meeting his bright eyes.

"I want you to feel what I feel when I look at you," he said, pressing her palm to his swift beating heart. "Your honey-flecked hair feels like sunshine on a cloudy day. The tiny freckles that arch over your nose when you smile make me smile, even when I don't want to." He traced his finger over the bridge of her nose, tickling her already sensitive skin. Her smile grew somehow bigger. "Your hazel eyes with flecks of gold in the center warm me like cognac on a wintry night. And those adorable dimples make me want to open my eyes first thing in the morning just to see them. I am so drunk on you, D. And it scares me."

His words altered her body chemistry, and she suddenly felt like the most beautiful woman in the world. "Noah . . ." She tugged him closer, and in one smooth, slick thrust, they were one. Dahlia was weightless, like a balloon lifting off into the cloudless sky. A tingling surge spread to every molecule in her body as he made love to her. Their unyielding rhythm felt expansive and free. Time stood still, and she branded the unhurried, euphoric feeling on her heart and her soul.

Their bodies tangled in a slow, building tempo that quickened after she said, "Harder, Noah." With one deep, torturous thrust, he hit that spot and she soared over the edge, giving her a toe-curling orgasm of historic magnitude. And he followed right behind her with a long, breathy groan, shuddering into her neck.

"Noah. That was . . ." She was breathless, not being able to put into words what exactly had just happened to her body.

He lifted his head with a look of yearning, as if he wanted to say something important. "What we have may not make sense to the rest of the world, but I don't care," he said softly. "When I'm with you, my life feels right, and the world is as it should be." He rested his forehead on hers. "You're like a tool I didn't know I was missing that magically fixed me and put me back together again."

A tear fell from her eye, and he wiped it with his thumb. She felt the same way: found, fixed, and whole. It felt like magic and a miracle all in one.

"I love you more than I thought I could ever love anyone," he said, finally finishing the sentence from earlier on the porch. It was love.

Her pulse felt steady, yet her heart galloped like a wild mustang. It was a feeling unlike any other—unconditional love and belonging. It was something she'd dreamed about for so long and never thought she would find with a man. She hesitated, willing herself to let go. "I love you too." Her eyes flooded like a breached dam. "I wasn't looking for anyone, you know that. But then you invaded my barn. And my heart in the process."

He laughed. "I did do that, didn't I?"

"Yes, you did." She giggled tearfully and felt it fade into something more serious. "I was lost before, wandering the forest without a compass. And you found me and brought me home." She gently pressed her lips to his.

"Home, I like that," he said.

Harry howled from the linoleum floor, and they laughed.

"I think he's happy," Noah said, kissing her nose this time.

"He is, and so am I, Noah. So freaking happy." Tiny winged creatures took flight inside her. She tugged his body closer to hers, never wanting to let him go.

So *this* was what earth-shattering love was supposed to feel like.

CHAPTER TWENTY-SIX

July 31

Kara walked into the kitchen from the back screened-in porch with a basket full of blooms. "I think this should do it. The tables and chairs are set on the porch with linens, votives, and flowers in case anyone wants to sit outside." She set the basket on the counter. "I just have to find a few more jars or vases for these, and we should be set."

"Check the hutch and the pantry," Dahlia said.

"Great." She opened the weathered green door. "How about this one?" Kara held up her gran's blue and white vase.

"Perfect," she said with a quiet voice. A piece of Gran and Pop would be with them today.

"I still can't believe Daisy surprised you with that portrait of Lil and that it came in time," Kara said, filling the vase with water.

"I know, it's pretty great. She's pretty great. I wish she were here," Dahlia said, feeling her heart shrink like a raisin.

"We'll take lots of video for her," Kara said, looking over her shoulder.

"I don't know what I would have done if you hadn't come last night. It was so nice to have an extra set of hands this morning."

"Happy to, but are you sure loverboy didn't mind?"

"Gosh, no. He did his own thing. Plus, I needed some girl time. It was fun to have a sleepover, just like the old days when we took turns sleeping in each other's rooms. By the way, thanks for the advice on the job situation." She grabbed her hand. "I desperately needed a sounding board."

"Did you decide anything?" Kara asked, putting her hair in a ponytail.

"No. What if I let go of this job in Charleston and things fall apart?" Dahlia leaned over the counter, her palms holding up her head.

"Well, no one can tell the future. But you two are solid. You'll kick yourself if you don't at least give this a fair shot."

"Anyone home?" A sexy echo came from the hallway.

Dahlia looked wide-eyed at Kara and mouthed. "Do you think he heard?"

Kara shrugged.

"Hot food coming through," he said, balancing three big trays. "Where do you want it?"

"The bar is good," Dahlia said, moving the basket of flowers to the sink.

"I can help," Kara said.

"Cool, I just have a few more trays and sternos. They're in my back seat."

"Right-o," Kara said.

Dahlia leaned up and gave Noah a well-earned kiss. "Thanks for picking all of this up. The lemon chicken smells incredible," she said, eyeballing the food. "Will Gretchen come by later?"

"She's hoping. Sundays are unpredictable, though," he said, walking backward toward the front door again.

"These aromas are making my mouth water," Kara said, carrying a tray and an insulated bag of goodies. "I think Tony and I are going to have to make a special trip to Shelter Island."

"You'll love it. The Hive has a great vibe. And you haven't met Gretchen yet, but I think you'll hit it off." Dahlia smiled, pulling out the plates. She could see them all being good friends. She was in awe of how far she'd come since arriving in Southold just four weeks prior. "Hopefully she'll come by later."

"This is the last of it," Noah said, setting the food down. "The place looks great. You two have really worked your magic in the last twenty-four hours."

"Girl power." Kara cackled.

"Lil's painting makes this place come alive. It's like the place was sleeping before, and now it's awake."

Dahlia leaned into him, and they both gazed at the wall in awe. "I love that."

"Yeah, me too," Kara said, her eyes wet. "Geez, Noah Sterling, who knew you were so poetic."

* * *

Kara was in the shower, Noah had gone home to get changed, and Dahlia was washing the last of the dishes. The cooler morning temperatures gave way to a stickiness comparable to a hot summer day in the south. The breeze from the bay gave just enough relief, but Dahlia was now questioning whether everyone would melt without air conditioning.

Dahlia was scrubbing the pan with vigor when she heard the front door creak and footsteps in the hallway. "Ugh," she said under her breath. She wasn't ready for guests. With the sink water running, she yelled, "You're early!"

"I should hope so," a youthful voice said.

Dahlia's nose tingled, and tears flooded her eyes. She knew exactly who it was. She threw the sponge into the sink and turned around. Heat radiated through her chest, and her heart skipped more than a few beats. Her cup runneth over, as Lil would say. She hugged Daisy with all her might and then pulled back, holding her arms. "What on earth are you doing here?" Dahlia asked with a permanent wide grin. One that could only come from a surprise visit from your only child. One you hadn't seen in months. "Are you eating? You look thin."

"Noah booked me a flight. And yes, I'm eating very well. None of that processed crap anymore." She looked around. "Wow, this place looks so . . . colorful."

"It's wonderful, isn't it?"

"Yeah, Mom, it is. Aunt Lil would love it." Daisy's eyes widened in shock at her own words. "Gosh, I don't even know what to call her now."

"Yeah, it's going to take some getting used to. Baby steps are good." She hugged her again. "I still can't believe you're here. But wait—*Noah* flew you out?" Dahlia's voice rose to a bright and perky level.

"Kara gave him my number," Daisy said, pulling off her backpack.

"She knew you were coming?"

"No, it was a secret. If she knew, she'd surely tell you." Daisy raised her brows playfully. "I couldn't take that chance. I think he made something up about following up about the portrait."

Dahlia stood there with an inward gaze. She couldn't believe he would do that for her. For them.

"Mom, I'm so sorry." Daisy pursed her lips together with a watery gaze. "I want you to be happy, and he's clearly crazy about you."

She cupped Daisy's freckled, round face. "Oh, Daisy girl, don't worry about any of that. I'm just so happy you're here. Let me look at you." Dahlia twirled her like when she was little. "This is the best gift ever."

* * *

"I've held off from making this speech long enough," Dahlia said nearly two hours later, leaning against the hallway wall.

"Who's Gretchen talking to?" Kara asked.

"Penny, the producer who told me about Gene."

"Ah, could there be a love connection happening over there? They look pretty cozy." Kara playfully nudged her arm. "Maybe this house has special 'love' powers to bring people together."

"You know what? Now that I think about it, I bet Lil is up there playing matchmaker." Dahlia's smile grew as she glanced over at her picture and the wall behind it. It all sounded crazy, but was it? Lil being up there being a champion for love made perfect sense. She felt a soft tickle of a breeze on her neck. Goosebumps ran along her legs, and she could only come to one conclusion. Lil was there.

"It's time." Dahlia looked at Kara, then at Daisy sitting on the arm of the sofa.

"You got this, girl." Kara squeezed her hand.

Dahlia blew out a long breath, watching Harry settle beside her. "Can I have your attention?" The conversation began to lighten, and the room full of strangers suddenly felt familiar. She saw Hank and his wife Jean, Lil's friends from the garden club, and her students, ranging in age from twenty-two to almost fifty. She saw the man she loved, leaning against the door frame, gazing at her. The tension left her body as she scanned the room. It was a stark contrast to when she first arrived, and the house was cold, stale, and lonely.

"Shh, everyone, let Dahlia speak." Hank, Lil's former handyman, hollered, which was followed by a whistle from Daisy.

All eyes were on her as she stood in the hallway. Dahlia's heart raced as she pulled the crinkled piece of paper from her pocket. "I want to thank you all for coming. As I look out at your faces, I can't help but feel tickled that the reason we all came together was for Lil. As friends and students, you all knew how special she was, but there was so much more to Lil than met the eye." Dahlia heard the front door creak open.

She glanced to her left and saw a tall, dapper, white-haired man dressed in a beige linen suit with a cane shuffle in. It was Gene. Dahlia's heart swelled; at that moment, she felt complete. She hadn't realized how lonely she'd been for never letting anyone in.

Gene smiled, nodding graciously for her to continue. Dahlia wiped her eyes and smiled back at her grandfather. She couldn't believe he came. Yes, part of her initially feared his arrival, knowing she would eventually come to need him in her life. And loving family meant losing them. But she was no longer scared.

She cleared her throat and carried on. "As I was saying. Lil was a fiercely optimistic person, never without a smile, but no one knew the will it took for her to see life through a colorful lens. She had an enormous amount of strength when the seas became stormy. And she had an incredible amount of resolve when her journey seemed unnavigable." She hoped Lil would forgive her for sharing her story. "Her creative catalog behind me is a testament to how, when life gives you lemons, you make lemonade. These paintings hold a story." Dahlia pointed to the botanicals covering the hallway wall. "One of hope when all seemed lost. You see, Lil wasn't just my aunt; I recently learned she was my biological grandmother." There were gasps from the crowd of friendly faces. "She fell in love with an amazing man in 1955, whom she loved dearly.

Unfortunately, they were forced apart by a world that only saw their differences. But their love story was far from over. From their unbreakable bond, my mother, Rose, was conceived. My grandparents, whom many know as Lizzie and Leon, raised her with Lil in devotion. I'm sharing this with you because I don't want any more secrets to stay buried. I want her story to take root and bloom. If anyone deserves that, it's Lil," Dahlia said tearfully as she glanced over at Gene, standing next to Noah. "I want you all to meet someone very important to me. My grandfather, Gene."

Gene walked over with the help of Noah, and Dahlia gave him the warmest embrace. Daisy leaped from the arm of the chair to join in. Whatever changed her mind, she was grateful for it. Dahlia waved to Kara, and it became a cuddle puddle. There were enough tears to drown the Sahara. All Dahlia could hear was clapping and curious chatter from their audience about the Hollywood legend gracing their small town.

They stood there together like a real family, smiling in awe at how fate brought them back to one another. All the while, Dahlia acknowledged in her heart that it was Lil's doing.

"Let's raise our glasses to Lil," Dahlia said as she held tight to Gene's well-worn hand.

"To Lil." Everyone raised their plastic cups.

"And to love conquering all!" Daisy shouted.

* * *

After the day's festivities were over, Dahlia strolled along the grass, watching the lightning bugs light the way to Noah's. She pulled her cardigan tight, feeling a slight nip in the air. Her heart was full.

She passed his truck, rounded the corner of the porch, and spotted him sitting on the steps. "Hey," she said tenderly. "What are you doing out here?"

"Just enjoying the peace and quiet. What a night, huh?" He paused with a watery gaze. "Lil would be proud, D."

"Thanks, babe," she said, soaking in the nighttime sounds. "You're right. It is peaceful out here. The smell of this air never gets old." She felt mated to this place in her bones. If a place could also be a twin flame, this would be hers. And now, after all that had happened, she couldn't picture being anywhere else.

"Here, come sit." He patted the spot next to him. "Did everyone get settled? You've got a full house over there."

"I do, and I'm loving it," Dahlia said, lowering her body next to him. "Daisy and Gene are looking through old photo albums of Lil. I have a feeling no one is going to get much sleep tonight."

Noah twirled a piece of grass in thought. "I'm glad he came. I knew you were holding back because you were scared."

"I was scared. I thought if I kept my heart guarded by a wide and deep moat, then I'd be protected and never get hurt. But I was wrong." She laced her fingers with his, in a hold that said *not going anywhere*. "I would rather love and lose than never have it at all. If there's anything Lil and Gene's story has taught me, it's that."

She turned to face him. "I'm not taking the job—either of them. And I don't know what I'm going to do for work yet, but I know I belong here in that house." She nodded toward Lil's. This decision wasn't for Noah; it was hers. She needed the extra time to make sure it was for her. But it didn't hurt that with that came Noah. "And I belong with you."

"You mean it?" he said with furrowed brows and a relieved smile. His vulnerability was sweet and tender, just another reason to love this man. Maybe he'd been more concerned about her leaving than she thought.

She nodded. "The answer was right here all along. I just needed to clean my spectacles."

Noah gave her the most affectionate kiss. His lips tasted like sweet peppermint fresh from the garden. The kiss lingered and lingered. She didn't want it to end. Eventually, she settled into the crook of his arm. She sat there peacefully, silently marveling at the miracle of their circumstances.

Dahlia finally knew where she belonged and with whom. But she'd also realized that she could only come to that conclusion by understanding she belonged to herself first and foremost. The armor that had served her for over two decades was no longer needed. There were no guarantees, and she knew that, but she owed it to Lil to be brave enough to try. She had a life to live and now a place to plant roots and bloom.

CHAPTER TWENTY-SEVEN

October 20

The wind swirled against the house as Dahlia sipped the remnants of her late-morning coffee. The French doors were open, and there was a chill that seeped through her knit sweater. She wrapped her arms around her body, walking closer to the water and the railing on Lil's upstairs porch. She wrapped it tighter, walking closer to the water and the railing on Lil's upstairs porch. The trees were decorated in ochre and spice. The air was void of summer scents like sunscreen and salt, but replaced by a sweet-earthy aroma courtesy of the blanket of leaves covering the ground below. A cool breeze drifted across her face, bathing her in the most delicious fall flavors. This was precisely where she was supposed to be. After three months, it felt good to be finally settled.

Her phone buzzed in her back pocket. She lifted it to eye view, feeling her face beam. She swiped swiftly, answering the FaceTime. "G, what are you doing up this early?" Dahlia smiled, looking at her handsome grandfather on the screen. From what she could see, he was wearing a thick white robe that matched his hair and was sitting poolside on his California patio. "Look at you all fancy, FaceTiming me."

"Well, thank heavens for my tech-savvy great-granddaughter. I think I'm finally getting the hang of it," he said, his voice laced with tiny fissures. She'd gotten used to the tone of his voice, and she found it quite comforting since he was the one elder she had left.

"Well, you're better than me. It took me years." She laughed, walking into her bedroom. It had taken some time not to call it Lil's, but day by day, the house was feeling more like hers.

"Dahlia, I couldn't sleep. Please tell me you'll come to California for Thanksgiving. I have so many people I want you to meet."

He was the sweetest man alive, and she still had so much to do before the gallery opened, but how on earth could she say no? "I will under one circumstance." She slipped on her suede booties.

"What is it?" he asked.

"That you'll think about coming here for Christmas and Hanukkah and stay longer this time." Her breath was caught in her chest, waiting for his response. It would be so nice to host a holiday there again. And she'd never celebrated Hanukkah. Dahlia couldn't think of anything better than to honor his faith in Lil's house, which was now hers.

"Yes, of course, I'd love to come and celebrate with my girls."

"Okay, good, then it's settled. Daisy will be here too." All Dahlia could think about were the Christmas lights. The ones she hadn't thought she'd be here to see and enjoy.

"You can fly into Burbank and stay at my place when you come in November," Gene said. "And bring Noah. We've gotten pretty close these last few months."

"I know you have, but I'm not sure I want to share you, G." She laughed. She didn't care that he was one of the most beloved actors of all time. To her, he was just G, short for Gene, and now Grandpa.

She felt like the luckiest girl in the world. "Listen, I've got to run. I have lots to still do before the big day," she said, closing the bedroom door.

"Okay. Good luck, honey."

"Wait, G?" Dahlia stood still in the hallway.

"Yes?" His voice cracked.

"I love you," Dahlia said, feeling her heart expand into the ethers.

"Oh, sweetheart. I love you too."

"Bye, for now." With that, she ended the call.

She held the phone against her chest and beamed. The feeling of *having people* never seemed to get old.

Dahlia walked down the creaky, wooden stairs, admiring her gallery wall of framed botanicals. She ran her fingers across the climbing yellow roses, feeling taller and wiser. Harry was sitting by the door with the leash in his mouth, ready to go.

Dahlia chuckled. "Aww, Harry. You coming today, boy?" Dahlia walked into the crisp, bright kitchen and stopped to admire the changes. *I did this*, she thought. She gazed at all the updates that transformed this outdated space and brought it into the current century. "I think you would approve, Lil. I'm finally living a life of color." Dahlia scanned the white marble countertop and freshly painted green cabinets with a satisfied smile. Willow Leaf had turned out to be a solid paint choice, Noah was right.

Dahlia grabbed her jacket from the chair and stuffed her tote with a few manila folders and the lunch Noah had made for her in the morning before he left. She poured coffee into a to-go and reached for a lavender scone off the counter. "The last thing on your bucket list, Lil."

On the way out, she passed her mother's watercolor birthday cards framed on the wall. In all the twenty-two containers, they found eight still in good condition, untouched by the elements.

Dahlia felt goosebumps and a tingling in her nose. Her only regret was that her mother wasn't there to witness this evolution and that she'd never know the truth of her parents' love story. The one that, after all these years, had a conclusion and a happy ending after all.

Her phone buzzed. *Have I told you lately how proud I am of you?* Kara texted.

Dahlia exhaled a happy sigh. She was proud of herself. *Thanks, Cuz!* she wrote back.

She opened the heavy wood door and heard it shut behind her. It was the sound of home; no matter how many times she'd heard it since arriving, it always made her smile. She walked onto her freshly painted porch, which had a Portico Blue ceiling and stacked pumpkins. The ladder shuddered from above, prompting Harry to run, bark, and play detective.

Dahlia stepped onto the grass and looked up at the exterior. "You think you'll finish today?" she asked, covering her eyes from the blinding sun.

"That's the plan. We have just the trim left. The weather is going to get cold after this week. So I want to get it done," shouted the painter from the second story.

Dahlia stood back while Harry sniffed.

"Do you still like the color?" the painter hollered.

She lifted her chin, feeling her chest swell with pride. "Oh, yes. Buttercup yellow was the perfect choice." She couldn't wait to see it in the summer against the flowers in bloom.

* * *

Dahlia pulled faithful Betty right in front of the old brick building on Main Street. Her head leaned to the side to get a good look at the sign above the two large windows. Seeing *The Prescott Gallery* in sleek, classic letters still made her cheeks ache. And to know it was a place for new and underrepresented artists was the cherry on top. She wasn't Monica anymore, nor was she Rachel. She was just Dahlia, bravely chasing her dreams without a backup plan or safety net.

Noah opened the gallery door and stood there. He was wearing dirty jeans, a torn plaid shirt, and a T-shirt that clung to his contours. It was like something out of *The Notebook*. She wanted to pinch herself that this was her life. He walked over to her side of the car as she rolled down the window.

"Hey, handsome." She smiled. "How's it going in there?"

"Good. Are you coming in?" he asked, tapping on the window frame.

"Yeah, I was just admiring the sign. I still can't believe this is all real, Noah."

"Well, it is, D. And it's going to be a huge success. I'm going to make sure of it," Noah said, flinching from the blistery gust of wind that blew down Main Street. "Between my contacts and social media accounts and now yours, which have exploded since you shared Lil's story." He shook his head. "I still can't believe how connected people feel to her."

"Yeah, I guess when you're honest and put yourself out there, people can relate on a whole other level. And to think I almost didn't share it." The old her would have shrunk herself, but not the new Dahlia. She owned her story and wore it like a badge of honor.

"They surely can. It's getting cold out here. Come in. I finished the cypress counter, and the walls have a fresh coat of white, ready for the first show." He opened her car door.

"That was quick," she said, grabbing her tote from the back seat.

"Well, I had to. I'm getting so many furniture orders that I can't keep up."

"You might need a bigger barn." Her eyes lit up.

"One day at a time." He chuckled. "Let's get your gallery up and running first, huh? Need help?"

"Yeah, I have some of Lil's paintings in the back."

"Did you sell any downloads on the site today?"

"Too many to count." She shook her head in disbelief. Kara was right. Who would have thought selling an image could be so profitable? This was a whole other side to the art business she was learning, and it was beyond exciting.

With a crate in one arm, he hung the other arm around her shoulder. "Takeout and a movie later?"

"Sounds perfect," Dahlia said, leaning up to kiss him.

"Oh, and my sister asked if we wanted to grab dinner tomorrow night with her and Penny. Up for it?"

"I'd love to." She smiled so hard her cheeks hurt. It was like she had been living under a cloud for most of her life, and now that the skies parted, she could finally feel the warm sun on her face. "Now show me your masterpiece."

As Dahlia walked up to the front door of her new professional endeavor, there was an all-encompassing tickle of exhilaration in her belly, as if *this* was what she was meant for all along. She stood there, holding her middle. She couldn't help but think about her pop and his ability to always see the silver lining in any situation. Dahlia wondered what he would think of all this. Gran too. Dahlia's family was anything but conventional, yet as she looked back, she wouldn't change a thing. After all, she had been blessed with more love than people ever got in a lifetime.

EPILOGUE

May 15

Noah

As Noah packed the rest of his truck, his eyes wandered past the row of lilac bushes in bloom and out to the bay. There was a good amount of foot action on the beach for a Friday. The sun was bright and warm on his skin, and the quiet hum of a boat's motor faded into the background. He stared out at Shelter Island in the distance.

Was he making the right decision? Only time would tell, but he had to follow his gut on this. It had been nine months since he'd moved in with Dahlia, and although the winter was long and quiet, it was precisely what they'd needed. They had been snowed in, isolated, and left with only each other and their imaginations for a good portion of that time. They'd cooked, danced, played lots of strip poker, finished the house, and christened every nook and cranny and surface. The days were short and the nights long, and they made the most out of every minute they had together. If they hadn't been inseparable before, they certainly were now. That's why this decision was so hard. But deep down, he knew the choice that had to be made. It was the only choice.

The fresh, heady rose-like smell drifted with the breeze, anchoring him. He pulled his phone from his back pocket, checking it for the tenth time this morning. Still no text back from his agent. For all the pieces to line up today, he needed to hear back. With a pinched expression, he texted Baz.

Tell me you have good news.

To Noah's surprise, the three bubbles were oscillating.

Not yet.

Make it happen, Baz, and today. Please. Text me as soon as you hear.

I'll do my best.

Noah knew Baz was good at playing hardball. But he also knew what he was asking was not only out of the ordinary but improbable. In late February, he had been offered the job of a lifetime—the lead in his own renovation series. Apparently, the two things people love most are hating on a cheater and a good love story. The only catch was that it would be filmed every summer in Nantucket. They'd pitched it as a modern *This Old House* meets *Fixer to Fabulous*, minus the female sidekick. The only partner in crime he was interested in was the woman walking toward him with a bounce in her step and a smile that could brighten a room full of serial killers. Oh, and they watched a lot of *Dateline* too.

Noah had no interest in spending his summers in Nantucket. He'd told his agent: North Fork or no show. He wanted it to emulate *Home Town*—with his own twist, of course. His insistence on staying local wasn't because he didn't have faith in his and Dahlia's relationship; it was that this was his home now too, and after the childhood he'd had and the upheaval of the show, he needed to finally plant roots.

"Hey, loverboy," Dahlia said, casually hanging her arms around his neck and planting a tender but firm kiss on his mouth. It was yet another nickname that stuck. Only Kara was sworn off from using it. It was now for Dahlia's lips only. And he didn't mind a bit.

Noah slipped his warm tongue inside her mouth, giving her a teasing taste of what was to come—then tapped her on the butt. "Get in before I take you back inside and have my way with you again."

"Is that a threat?" She laughed.

"Yup," he said with a pop of his lips. His eyes roamed over her like a predator about to pounce on his prey. She had on a short army green romper with thick straps, a red handkerchief tied like a headband in her sun-kissed blonde hair, and large gold hoops that, for some reason, strained his zipper. "Now get in."

They both climbed in, and the doors closed with a clunky metal *thud*. Her smile never wavered, not once, and that tickled something deep inside him. To know *he* brought that smile to her face and that she was all his still felt like a dream. It was his time to smile, and his was bigger and brighter with a side of mischief. All she knew was that they were headed to the island for a weekend getaway before the crazy season began. One last hurrah before the summer people arrived and the mayhem ensued.

Noah turned the key in the ignition, only to be met with a whining sound and a burning smell coming from the hood. Usually, an incident like this wouldn't rattle Noah—he could fix anything—but this wasn't a typical day or normal circumstances. He was also in a bit of a rush.

"Shit," he muttered under his breath, hearing the seagulls' untimely cries overhead. It sounded like a warning, yet he was determined to ignore it. Nothing was going to get in the way of his plans today. Not even a broken truck.

"We can take my car." She reached for his arm. "Noah, it's fine."

"No," he said, opening his door and lifting the hood, banging his head in the process. There was an anxious cloud following him. He just prayed she wouldn't feel his heightened nerves, which felt like they were leading their own rebellion right about now. Today needed to be perfect or as close as possible. He was determined to give her the love story she deserved. His body was hunched over the engine bay. "It's the alternator, I'm sure of it."

"Can we jump it?" she said with a gleam in her happy hazel eyes, now standing next to him. It was one of hope and one of longing too. If he had to guess, she couldn't wait to feel his strong, capable hands on her as soon as they got to the hotel, and that made him want to solve this conundrum as quickly as possible.

"Nay. Stay here." With that, he closed the hood, ran inside, and grabbed his motorcycle keys.

"Harry okay?" she asked.

"Yup, he's just sitting on the couch waiting for my uncle to come by and get him." Which reminded him he had to figure out how to get their bags for the weekend. He grabbed his phone from inside the truck and started typing to Bruce.

Hey, I have a huge favor to ask. After you get Harry, can you run our bags over to the Airbnb? My truck won't start. Taking the motorcycle.

Bruce answered right away, most likely because he knew how important all of this was.

No problem. When?

Maybe two to three hours? Noah wasn't sure what would happen after, or for how long, so he had to keep it flexible.

A thumbs-up followed. With that, he opened the truck's cargo bed, felt for the small box inside his bag, and tucked it into his pants pocket. If Dahlia wondered, he'd hope she'd think he was just really eager to make good on his promise.

"We're taking the bike," he said, whooshing past her like a man on a mission. "Are you okay with that, baby?" He knew before she answered what her response would be.

"Yes, of course. You know I love koalaing you from behind. And feeling my hair blow in the breeze." She wrapped her hands around his corded waist, emulating the action.

"Oh, but what about our bags?"

"Bruce. He's going over to the Hive anyways."

"Well, that's convenient."

Noah smiled weakly, hoping she didn't know something she wasn't supposed to.

She'd said being on the back of his bike made her feel exhilarated and terrified, yet safe all at the same time. Noah had opened her eyes to all sorts of things that contradicted her old and stale Greenwich life, and now she seemed to be addicted to the adventure, which was all fine by him.

He grabbed their helmets from the nearby storage box and helped her fasten the strap. "You're too cute, you know that?" His heart swelled like the ocean during a storm. He couldn't wait to get there. It felt like Christmas mornings after Don adopted him and Gretchen. His insides buzzed with unbridled excitement. Today was the day he'd ask her to be his forever. But he still had one thing to tie up, and that was the show. Dahlia had made it clear she didn't want to hold him back. But this wasn't about her; it was about him. He knew exactly what he wanted and wasn't going to settle for anything less.

Once they were on his bike, they cruised down the one-lane road that led to the ferry. Her delicate arms wrapped around his waist, her core pressed against his ass. It was the best feeling in the world. She trusted him, and in turn, he treasured it as the gift it was. Her hair whipped against his bare cheek, smelling both sweet and savory, like mint and honey. *What could be better?* he thought.

With that, he drove just a little faster, hearing the gritty drum of the engine kick into gear.

The ferry was a midday medley of pedestrians, cars, and work trucks getting the houses and estates ready for the season. Noah and Dahlia didn't get off the bike. They didn't need to. It was a short ride, plus they had all the open air they could need.

She whispered, "I love you, I love you, I love you" in his ear from behind, sending shivers down his spine. He was convinced that she had no idea what was to come. Not the house he'd rented, not the ring that now rested in the console, and not the fireworks—both literal and figurative—after. But there was always a chance he could be wrong, especially after that comment she made back at the house.

They drove off, inhaling the promise of spring and notes of diesel fuel. It was her understanding that they were staying at a fancy hotel called the Rosemont. To confuse her a bit more, he took a few-minutes detour and finally pulled up to the house they'd be spending the weekend at. It was the gingerbread house with a wrap-around front porch and ornately carved balusters that they'd pulled up to on their very first date. Only "Je Cherche Un Homme" wasn't playing; it was "Secret Garden" by Springsteen on a loop, courtesy of Gretchen's handiwork.

"Noah." Her breath hitched. "What are we doing here?" Following his lead, she took off her helmet and placed it on the handlebars.

His eyes burned as their feet crunched on the tiny pebbles. Why was he so emotional? It probably had something to do with this being a once-in-a-lifetime moment with her. One he needed to draw out just a little bit longer.

"I saw this place on Airbnb and thought it would be a fun surprise. Plus, this is where I first wanted to kiss you desperately, you know." His eyes widened with a playful grin, while inside, he was a hot mess of jitters and angst. With still no call from Baz, he realized he may have to improvise.

"Babe, me too. That mustache of yours was way too sexy." She laughed, leaning up to press her mouth to hers. "Wait, is this song from *Jerry McGuire*?" she said, turning toward the portico. Her face was dappled in the sunlight, which made his heart skip a beat or two. She was the most beautiful woman Noah had ever dated, by far. It was her natural looks and her slender but sporty body, but it was also her ability to rise above with grace and humility. And there was also the matter of her kindness, which was vast and endless, even for strangers.

"D, wait." He rushed in front of her as her feet began to move.

"What?" Her laugh bubbled over. Either she was just excited about their getaway, or she knew.

"Listen, baby. Just listen to the song."

And she did. She closed her eyes and opened her ears, and hopefully her heart too. He tugged her hand to his chest, feeling his heart thud wildly under her delicate touch. It was his love letter in this song. It spoke of a path, a secret garden, a house, a hammer, and parts of ourselves we keep hidden, even in love. The only difference was that Noah knew he didn't know everything about Dahlia, but he knew enough. And if she said yes, they'd have all the time in the world to bridge that gap.

Her eyes released and met his glassy gaze. Growing up, Noah had often heard "men don't cry" from the men his mother brought home. But this one did. It was only a matter of time before the waterworks began; he could feel it. It was the perfect storm; he had the girl, the home, the secure life he'd always dreamed of, and a love he'd never believed he deserved after feeling abandoned by his mom.

"Come, baby," he said in a quiet tenor she wasn't used to. Her smile matched his tender warmth. Hand in hand, they walked up the steps, hearing the soft tap of their shoes on aged wood.

Dahlia gasped before she hit the last step. Feeling her hand slip away, Noah turned to face her. Both hands were covering her mouth, and she was visibly shaking as she glanced over the gorgeous porch picnic before her eyes. It had a low table in the center surrounded by pillows, poufs, and blankets. Lanterns of all shapes and sizes, as if they'd been collected over time, flanked the refined but bohemian vignette. And flowers as far as the eye could see. There was food too, courtesy of his sister. It was indeed Instagrammable, thanks to Gretchen and Uncle Bruce. He had to remember to go overboard with his thanks when seeing them later.

"Noah, you did all this?" Delight and surprise danced across her face.

"I may have had a little help," he said, pulling her up the rest of the way.

"It's . . ." She shook her head as an ocean welled in her pretty caramel eyes. "Gorgeous, beautiful, stunning, spectacular." She took a breath. "And I love it to pieces."

Before she could say or do anything else, he planted her in front of the window, behind the canopy of climbing white roses. The smell of musk and citrus floated through the quiet country air. There wasn't a car or person in sight. It was like the rest of the world was muted to this one moment. His hands were trembling and his heart pounding as he took her hands in his.

"D, it's crazy to think how much my life has changed in a year. Last May, I was lost, drifting anchorless in the cold, bottomless ocean. I was broken and unfixable, but something told me if I could fix a few pieces of old furniture, then maybe, just maybe, it would fix me. Then I came to Meadow Lane, thanks to Lil." He winked. "And you barged into my barn."

She laughed through her tears. "*Your* barn, huh?"

He nodded. "And into my heart. You found me, and in your kindness and our fucking extraordinary connection, I felt whole." He lowered to one knee, with the song still playing on a loop in the background. Their eyes met as little whimpers fell from her lips. "I wasn't looking for you, and yet somehow you found me. I know this has been a whirlwind romance, but if there's anything we've learned from Lil and Gene, it's that when you know, you know. And baby, I know."

She stood there silently, shaking.

"Dahlia, you complete me in every possible way." He pulled the box from his pocket and, with trembling fingers, opened it. It was a simple princess-cut emerald set in platinum. It wasn't a conventional ring by any means, but it had a story. And once she knew it, it would mean that much more. "Will you marry me and walk through this life with me?"

"Oh, Noah," she cried. "Yes, yes! There's no one else I'd want to walk this life with."

She'd said yes, even with the knowledge that they'd probably be spending the summers apart for the next few years at least. Noah chalked it up to blind faith, something he'd known nothing about before last summer.

He slid the ring onto her finger and kissed her hungrily, like the rest of the world was still on pause. It was a kiss that awakened the beast inside him and tented his faded blue jeans. There was plenty of time before the small gathering at the Hive for him to make a mess of her. But for now, he would take his time and savor each moment.

"The ring. I love it, babe." She held it out—the vibrant green looked pretty with her short pink nails.

"There's a story." He went on to tell her how it was Gene's mother's. On the day Gene was supposed to meet Lil to say goodbye, he was going to give it to her as a promise for their future. But her father showed up instead, leaving him for dead. Noah had had a two-carat oval diamond on hold in the city, but Gene insisted. He knew Dahlia would want the heirloom; that was the kind of woman she was.

Dahlia cried and laughed at the full circle moment. To think a chance encounter seven decades ago between two people who weren't supposed to fall in love could lead them here, to one another.

They cuddled, talked, ate, kissed, christened the kitchen and bed. Their bags arrived courtesy of Bruce, and they finally got dressed.

Dahlia was surprised by the celebration that followed at the Hive. Being the center of attention suited her, and she beamed as she mingled, chatted, and showed off her ring. Noah couldn't help but want more of that for her. The crowd was intimate. His stepdad, Don, had flown in from Colorado and settled in at his uncle's after they left. Bruce and Garrett brought him to the party, but Harry stayed home. There was Daisy, who'd arrived with Kara, Tony, and the boys. And there were Penny, Gretchen, and, of course, Gene. This day was turning out to be a plethora of surprises, including the offer Gene made on the first cedar shake house on the property, which was built in the late 1800s and faced the bay. It was the grandest and Dahlia's favorite architecturally. With a cash offer, they were all but sure he'd get it. Little by little, their family was growing, and that tickled something inside him that no longer felt like a lost boy.

Later that evening, after the sun faded, they all walked to the bay for the small fireworks show, including Gene. For ninety. he was a rockstar and didn't miss a beat. He even talked about setting up a garden at the new house on Meadow Lane. Dahlia begged him to tell everyone about his friendship with Sinatra that began the year after Lil left. He said he, too, felt adrift, and Frank took him under his wing. "The rest was showbiz history," he said with a lighthearted chuckle. He seemed happy, and after all he had been through, it was a miracle.

There were lawn chairs set up on the beach, something Bruce, Garrett, and Don did on their way through. It was touching to see everyone come together for them in this way. They all oohed and ahhed over the display as light chatter ensued.

Just as it was ending, Noah felt his pocket vibrate. He stepped away behind the beach grass. With a quick glance, he saw it was from Baz. The words on the screen would ultimately decide what kind of life he, Dahlia, and the kids they may someday have would have. He blew out a breath in both anticipation and fear. And opened the text.

You got it, kid, your hometown wish. They said yes.

Noah wanted to scream; he was so overjoyed and relieved. He couldn't help but go into a full karate chop as he came back into view.

"What's going on over there, brother?" Gretchen asked from her comfortable spot next to Penny as Dahlia rushed to his side. No one but his now fiancée knew about the show.

"You're not going to believe this, but I got my own renovation show. D knew, but I know this is a surprise to the rest of you." He planted a kiss on her forehead as she squeezed harder around his waist.

There were offers of congratulations from everyone, and now he was the one at the center of attention, beaming with pride as Dahlia looked on with a knowing grin. It was one that said she couldn't be happier for him. But there was also a sprinkle of confusion written on her face—one he needed to extinguish right away.

"But there's something else. It's going to be filmed here on the North Fork."

Dahlia looked up with wide eyes. "Noah? But how?"

"I told Baz it was out here or nothing."

"But why?" Her eyebrows furrowed in concern. "This is a dream job offer! I told you we would get through anything."

"Because this is home." He smiled at her with a certainty he could have never claimed last year at this time and tugged her tighter. His eyes wandered over the faces lit now by only the moon and a few beach lamps. Home. It was a simple word, yet it encompassed everything he loved. He wasn't about to give that up for a TV show. Not now, not ever.

If there were a choice, he'd always choose his family.

ACKNOWLEDGMENTS

They say the hardest things are the biggest teachers, and I'll go a step further and say they can lead to the brightest moments. That's if you've got the gumption, as my grandmother would say, to stick with it. Through all the peaks and valleys of this entire writing journey to publication, I have seen and felt it all, from humiliation to elation, from doubt to swelling pride, and all the ugly and beautiful parts in between. As I look back, I can say with certainty that I wouldn't change a thing about this crazy ride.

When I sat down to write this book, I was at a low point in my writing journey. I had written book one, and my agent at the time couldn't sell it. Any other person may have walked away. But not me. I couldn't. There were still stories to be told and books to write. Plus, that stubborn six-year-old inside me, who never felt heard or seen, knew it would be worth it someday. All I had to do was not give up. It sounds so simple, yet it is the *only* reason I'm sitting here writing this.

On the days when my drive and determination were depleted (which, as I look back, were many), I had my very own band of fireflies lighting my way. Without them I'd be lost, wandering the forest without this big, bright dream of mine taking flight. My husband and two boys, you are my why. Thank you for not complaining on all those mornings and evenings I was anchored to my chair, striving to become a writer I could be proud of. Thank you to my parents and sister, Jackie, whose passings were my biggest teacher. Grief was a quiet awakening that taught me so much about myself, but, most of all, about the true legacy of love we leave behind.

Thank you to my fantastic agent, Rachelle Gardner, for taking a chance on me. Your yes made this all possible. For years, I heard authors talk about their editors as if they hung the moon. I am happy to say I am now one of them. Jess Verdi, thank you for your incredible insight in making this book everything it is. To my family and friends, my biggest cheerleaders, you have been filling my bucket for many decades, and I am a rich woman because of it. To my book besties and "research" partners, I'd be lost without you! Thank you to my childhood friends for showing me what unconditional female support looked like at such an early age. To Nancy Meyers, you have inspired me over the years with your real, complex, and lovable characters and stories centered around family, love, and friendship. Oh, and swoon-worthy interiors to boot! And last but not least, to my Denver, the best writing companion a girl could ask for. You kept my feet warm and my heart full on many days.

This book is a love letter to family, whether it's found, conventional, unconventional, biological, or chosen. Motherhood is the most selfless and courageous experience involving the purest kind of love. While this book is fiction, it pulls from a personal experience close to my heart.

Last but not least, to you, my reader. Thank you for taking a chance on me and this book. Stories have a way of healing, entertaining, and making us think and feel more deeply. If my book did at least one of these things, I am brimming with pride.

DISCUSSION QUESTIONS

1. Dahlia heads to her Aunt Lil's house to get it from fixer to fabulous in just one month, still uncertain how she'll pull it off. Have you ever owned a fixer-upper? If so, what was the most challenging part? Would you ever buy a house that needed TLC again? For those of you who land in the dream zone, what stopped you?
2. The minute Dahlia gets to Aunt Lil's, everything seems to go wrong. Specifically, three things within twenty-four hours. Have you ever had an instance in your adult life where everything that could go wrong did? When you look back on it now, can you at least laugh about it, or does it still feel unsettling?
3. Dahlia stumbles, literally, upon a family secret buried for generations. Have you ever unearthed a family secret? Is it something that brought your family closer or further apart?
4. Dahlia & Noah fall hard and fast. Have you ever fallen in love quickly? Were there any tropes involved? How did the story end?
5. Did the beach setting enhance the romance between Dahlia & Noah? Could you picture this setting? Can you see how the setting and forced proximity added to a whirlwind romance?

6. If you could spend a week in the summer at Aunt Lil's (now Dahlia's) house in Southold on the bay, after all the fixing, who would you invite and why?
7. In this story, Dahlia keeps something rather important from Noah. Would you forgive someone who kept an important part of their life a secret at the beginning of a relationship?
8. In this story, we see the idea of family change through Dahlia's lens. What was the most unexpected part of her found family journey? Do you have people in your life who feel like family but aren't?
9. We see the years of loss and unhealed grief culminate in an awakening for Dahlia this summer. Whether with people she once loved, the youth she never got to experience, or with herself in a loveless marriage. What aspect did you connect with the most and why?
10. Reflecting on the title, *The Summer I Found You*, what do you think Dahlia "found?" And what aspect resonates with you the most?
11. We get to experience Dahlia's juxtaposition of emotions packing up the only house that felt like a home after her parents' death. Have you ever had to say goodbye to a house and all the memories? If so, what was it like?
12. Themes of the book are second chances, second seasons, found family, and reinvention. Which theme do you connect with most at this time in your life and why?
13. If there's one quote that could sum up this book, it would be, "Sometimes the hardest things lead us to the brightest moments." Have you ever been through something hard that led to a happy outcome that would have never materialized otherwise?
14. Who was your favorite character and why? Can be a primary or secondary character. It can even be Harry.
15. If *The Summer I Found You* was made into a movie, who could you imagine playing each character?